REBECCA & THE SPIRAL STAIRCASE

I'VE BEEN HERE BEFORE

VOLUME I

A NOVEL BY STEPHEN M DAVIS

Stephen M Davis was born in East London in 1957. He was educated at Woodbridge High School,

Woodford, Essex, and St John Cass Royal School of Art, East London. He started writing in 2009 once

retired from Royal Mail.

Favourite quotes:

Trust your reader. Kill your darlings. Twenty years to be an overnight success.

*This book is dedicated to my beloved wife, Jacqui Davis, and our
cherished son Ryan Scott Davis.*

SETTING - MODERN DAY

Free-spirited, fearless, and independent, Rebecca is far from your average twenty-first-century 15-year-old girl.

She'd rather leave her mobile phone indoors and being a dreamer, sit in the woods, sketching imaginary worlds.

When her parents move to a Gothic mansion in the north of England, she sets off exploring their 26-acres.

On one of these jaunts, she finds a Victorian key that opens the door to a ramshackle summerhouse.

Inside, she finds an old spiral staircase, which is the start of her adventures through time.

Each door leading from the staircase takes her back to a different point in the history of the old house.

Join Rebecca as she uncovers the secrets beyond the staircase.

She may help change the way you see the world around you.

REBECCA & THE SPIRAL STAIRCASE

Chapter 1 - The Whispering Pond

Chapter 2 - The New Old House

Chapter 3 - Message on a Chair

Chapter 4 - The Key

Chapter 5 - The Locked Door

Chapter 6 - The Sepia Photos

Chapter 7 - The Spiral Staircase

Chapter 8 - The Hospital

Chapter 9 - The Newspaper

Chapter 10 - Final Exam, then Florida

Chapter 11 - Bear Forest

Chapter 12 - The Door Back

Chapter 13 - Supper

Chapter 14 - The Next Article

Chapter 15 - Amanda's Birthday

Chapter 16 - Which Way Now?

Chapter 17 - Where am I

Chapter 18 - How Did that Happen

Chapter 19 - Realisation

Chapter 20 - Return from Uni

Chapter 21 - Meredith's Box

Chapter 1 - The Whispering Pond

As Rebecca arrived home from school, she was greeted by her mother, Elizabeth, leaning against the gate at the front of their house.

'Is that your brother Tommy, I can see climbing over a garden fence?' her mum asked, putting her glasses on.

Spotting a familiar look of suspicion, and guilty, Rebecca beamed a smile. 'Hello, Mother. Kiss, kiss. I am famished.'

'That is your brother, what was he doing in the Howe sister's garden?'

Rebecca smiled again. 'I chucked Tommy's football in their garden. Silly child, so deserved it. He's been annoying me all day with that ball of his.'

As they made their way into the kitchen, her mum put her hand on Rebecca's shoulder. 'You shouldn't do things like that, 11-years-old or not; he is still your brother. You're fifteen and should know better. Besides, it's just not worth annoying the men in our life,' she said and raised her eyes. 'So, why did you throw his ball in their garden, especially as you know how cantankerous the sisters can be?'

Sighing, Rebecca sat down and leant her elbows on the kitchen table.

'Take your elbows off the table please, Sweetie,' her mum said as she started cutting at a loaf of bread. 'Would you like ham, cheese, or both in your sandwich?'

'Both please, Mum, and none of that horrid pickle again. I was hoping one of the sisters would be in the garden, and then he'd get it, ha.' She then waved her bloody knuckles in her mum's face. 'See what he made me do.'

'Oh, Rebecca, how on earth did you do that?'

'Well, there I was walking home from school, minding my own business, again, when suddenly his ball flies towards me for the umpteenth time today. So, I had to duck, and wallop, raw knuckles. Anyway, when he said that I was just a girl and pointed his finger in my face, I wasn't going to let him get away with that. We need to stand up to these men, even if they are bigger, Mum.' She grabbed her sandwich, smiled, and hurried off to her bedroom before her mum offered up any more passive advice.

While changing out from her uniform, she decided she would visit the whispering pond and with a bit of luck avoid her silly brother. However, when she returned to the kitchen, he was standing by the window scoffing a sandwich, acting as if she wasn't there. Knowing he was trying to bait her, she ignored him. As she started making another sandwich, he came over, a little too near for her liking, and grinned annoyingly. Before she had a chance to respond, he scurried out of the kitchen, banging the door on the way.

'Blinking stupid twit of a child,' she mumbled.

'Don't talk like that about your brother or I'll wash your mouth out with carbolic soap, Missy.'

Seeing the expression on her mum's face, Rebecca almost laughed even though she knew she was serious. She nodded politely. 'Well, you don't have to put up with his antics all day.' She stuffed the last

6

bite of sandwich in her mouth and before her mum could answer, she garbled, 'Right I'm going down to the pond.'

'Rebecca, please don't talk with your mouth full. Anyways, why are you so hungry? Did you miss lunch again?'

'Err yeah. I was too busy.'

'Honey, there is nothing of you as it is; you can't afford to keep missing your meals.'

'I know, Mum, just so busy drawing, and well... I'm off down the garden now, kiss-kiss.'

'Supper is in an hour and a half when your father is home. So, Rebecca, please make sure you are in and ready, you know he gets huffy if he has to wait.'

Rebecca paused on the patio, raised her eyes to the heavens, and muttered, 'Dad's always huffy.'

The kitchen door opened and her mum's face appeared around the corner. 'Does Madam need some carbolic soap?'

Rebecca chuckled. 'No soap, Mum, unless you need to wash your ears out.' She grinned, turned, and headed down the garden, waving as she went.

By the time she entered the woods at the end of their two-acre garden, she was back in Rebecca's world. Heading towards the pond, she paused briefly to pick a couple of ripe blackberries. She then continued along the path, greeting the odd tree as she went. She knew most people would laugh if they could hear her, but didn't care.

As she arrived by the whispering pond, the late evening sun was sparkling through the trees. All year round, this was her favourite place, but she especially loved its autumn mood. To her, this was

Mother Nature at her best. Turning to the old wooden shed door, she opened it to a creaking sound, and she just knew it was saying hello. 'Hello door, hello shed.'

Inside, she kept a small oak art box that her Grandfather had made for her twelfth birthday. This was still one of her favourite presents, and she'd since stocked it with a maze of paints, pencils, and a good supply of paper. As always, she gathered her bits and pieces together, and in the same particular sequence, took each piece outside, placing them in a particular position on a rickety wooden bench. Then she took a small red clock, even though she didn't want to, set the alarm for five-thirty and hung it on an old fishing rest. Sitting down, she picked up her pad and pencil and looked around.

Squinting into the sunlight, she could just make out the fish splashing and wondered if they'd seen the fairies today. Through the hazy glare, she focused on the swaying heather at the far side of the pond. Narrowing her eyes, she blinked a couple of times, convinced she'd caught sight of fairy wings dancing among the heather. She sat back and whispered, 'have you come to say hello?'

She didn't expect an answer because there never was, but she was sure they listened. She sighed, looked back down at her pad, and started doodling. Now and then, she glanced across the pond, hoping to get another glimpse. Before she knew it, the alarm was ringing in her ears. She groaned, knowing it was time for tea. She sat for a second staring aimlessly and then started putting everything away. As she ambled back to the house, the nearer she got, the slower she walked, wondering if her father would be in one of his, *awkward moods*.

She looked through the kitchen window, and seeing Tommy hovering, decided to wait for a moment. Once he disappeared into the hallway, she went inside. 'Hi, Mum, I'm just going to wash my hands.'

'Quickly please, Rebecca, dinner is nearly ready, and your father does not like waiting.'

Rebecca hurried upstairs to the bathroom and started frantically washing her face and hands. Having splashed water everywhere, she dropped the flannel in the sink. Annoyed with herself, she looked in the mirror and asked why she was rushing. Taking a deep breath, she dabbed her pink freckled cheeks with a soft towel, and then combed her long blonde hair several times. Lastly, she tied a pale blue ribbon loosely at the back of her hair. Still angry with herself, she paused at the top of the stairs.

It was a little after six-thirty as she entered the dining room. The atmosphere was broken only by the sound of her father James tapping his pen against his neatly folded Financial Times. Rebecca took a deep breath and sat down.

He pointed at his watch, glanced at Rebecca, and then huffed in an annoyingly familiar way.

For some bizarre reason, today this tickled Rebecca. Trying not to grin, knowing it would get her in more trouble, she stared down at her plate. She then looked up and opened her mouth to speak.

Before she had a chance to say anything, he put his finger over his lips. 'I don't want to hear your feeble excuses. We eat at the same time every day, six-thirty. This you know.'

It wasn't the words her father used that made Rebecca's facial muscles tighten, but more the delivery. She took a deep breath and held it for a few seconds. From the corner of her eye, she could see Tommy grinning like a *Cheshire Cat.* That wasn't helping, but she knew his game and had no intention of biting. She wanted to say something to her father, but noticing her mother's bottom lip quivering, Rebecca stopped herself. Staring at her mum, she wondered how her father managed to create such an atmosphere with so few words. Frustrated and on the verge of saying something to her

9

mother, Rebecca decided this perhaps wasn't the right time. After a few seconds, she thought *enough*. She could feel herself trembling and knew she was asking for trouble but had to say something. She glanced again at her mother, then turned to her father, and said, 'I wasn't that late.'

His eyes widened as he pointed his finger in her direction – something she detested, especially since Tommy had started copying him. 'Be it one minute or thirty; you were late.'

Rebecca knew she was in the wrong but was tired of supper being like some kind of military manoeuvre. Just as she was about to answer, she felt her mum gently squeeze her knee under the table.

Rebecca smiled but inside felt irritated by this continued charade. After supper, she helped her mum clear up in the kitchen. While she was loading the dishwasher, she kept glancing at her mum, wanting to say something.

As if her mum had sensed Rebecca watching her, she turned, and quietly said, 'Stop staring, Rebecca, I know what you are thinking. It is easier to keep quiet sometimes. Your father seemed so cross, and when he is in that sort of mood, well, it's just not worth debating anything. He has probably had a stressful day. We need to allow him some space, and if that means him being grumpy, so be it.' She then stared through the window almost as if she was contemplating her own words. After a few seconds, she turned back and smiled. 'Tell me, Rebecca, what did you do at school today, and what do you find so interesting in the garden?'

Rebecca was used to her mother avoiding the real issues in this way, even so, couldn't resist saying, 'Oh change the subject, Mum, why not?' She then grinned but inside knew her mum wasn't happy. She glanced down for a second, and looking up, smiled again. 'Normal stuff at school, you know I always do well, although...' She grinned and mumbled, 'actually a new boy started today. He's cute.'

10

Rebecca paused and clenched her lips tight, then said, 'very nice indeed. His name is Ryan; I think.'

Her mum sat down, put her elbow on the table, her chin in her hand, grinned, and said, 'Oh, I see, well you know...'

Before her mum could finish, Rebecca held her hand up. 'Yeah, yeah, Mum, I know, and you know I know. Anyway, I didn't talk to him. All the other girls were like bees around a honey pot. He's bound to get a big enough head without me helping. Oh, and by the way, Mother, take your elbows off the table, there's a Sweetie.'

She folded her arms and grinned. 'So, what were you doing in the garden and how did you end up with all those red marks on your new white jeans, the ones you got for your birthday, yesterday?'

'Oh, I was doing the usual stuff, Mum, sitting by the pond, drawing, watching the fish, that kind of thing. I love it there. It's so peaceful there, and it gives me time to think. The sunlight through the trees was especially lovely today.' Glancing down at her jeans, she looked back at her mum and raised her eyebrows. 'I'm sorry about my jeans. I guess blackberries, and white jeans don't mix.'

'Well, you best get them off, they'll need a good soaking. Tell me, what were you doodling today, another imaginary world, I suspect? Your English teacher suggested you could use your imagination to write a good book, and I reckon she's right.'

'I have thought about that, Mum, but with drawing it is easy, I start, and it just flows. With a book, I wouldn't know where to begin.'

'Perhaps you should do the same as you do with your painting, just start writing about one of your amazing worlds. I have always had a nagging little voice telling me to write. I suppose it's too late for me to start now. Besides, I have the housework to do.'

'It is never too late to start anything, Mum. Maybe we should do something together. I will have a think and come up with some ideas. Right, I am going back in the garden for a while.'

Just as Rebecca closed the kitchen door, she heard her father start speaking. She knew she shouldn't eavesdrop but couldn't resist listening in. Her father, in his usual concise tone, told her mother he had bought an old derelict mansion up by the lakes at a bargain price, and she should be ready to move sometime in the next few weeks.

On her way down to the woods, she struggled to get her head around the idea of moving. She sat on the bench, staring into space, and then just as she started thinking about something else, she spotted her mum walking towards her. Her mum rarely ventured down the garden and certainly not this far, so she couldn't help wonder why.

Without speaking, she sat down beside Rebecca. After a moment or two, she looked up and spoke quietly. 'It is wonderful here, Bex. I can see why you love it so much.'

Even though her mum's tone was relaxed, Rebecca could feel the tension. 'Is everything alright, Mum?' She asked, knowing it wasn't.

Her mother raised her eyebrows, and although she smiled, it didn't hide her anxiety. 'Yep. Just fine. Thanks, Rebecca.'

Rebecca touched her mum on the arm. 'You can say when something is bothering you, Mum.' She knew she was probably wasting her breath, and there would be the usual subject change, but wanted to try to get her to open up. She was sure that if her mother shared her feelings, it might make her feel better. 'It's good to talk sometimes.'

'This is a lovely drawing, honey. Did you make it up?'

Rebecca shrugged her shoulders and said, 'You don't have to answer me, Mum. But you've always told me it's good to talk.' The

12

way her mum glanced up from the drawing, Rebecca knew that she wasn't in any sort of mood to talk. 'Well, I did make it up, and I didn't if that makes sense. Perhaps I should explain a little. It's where the fairies live,' she said and pointed. 'Look just over there on the other side of the pond. Can you see that little dark area at the foot of the tall oak tree?'

Her mum glanced back and forth between the tree and the drawing. Nodding, she said, 'You know, Sweetie, I do believe that I can.' She then stared across the pond. 'When the time is right, Rebecca, I promise I will talk to you.'

'I know, Mum. Anyway, that is where the fairies hang out. If you watch as the sun goes down, the rays' shimmer through the leaves, flickering on their wings as they *dance the heather*. You will see, just watch with an open mind.'

Her mum squinted, and appearing a little puzzled, asked, 'Sweetie, "Dance the heather." Tell me more.'

'Mum, that's what I call their dance. To most people, especially adults, it just looks like the heather swaying.'

'I do so love you, Rebecca, and the way you see the world. I suspect you have a wonderful life in front of you. I know I mentioned it just now, but your English teacher was right, you should write a story, perhaps about the fairies.'

'Maybe, Mum, maybe.'

'I know, Bex. How about I occasionally sit here with you after supper, you tell me your stories, and I will type them up on your laptop? I might need some practice, but I used to type well.'

'That's a nice idea, Mum, but you said you have the housework to do.'

'I can do the housework while you're at school,' she said with an unusually energetic tone.

A little surprised, Rebecca was thinking about her mum's idea, when she noticed something from the corner of her eye. She whispered, 'look, look carefully over there.'

Her mum peered across the pond. After a few seconds, she sighed and whispered, 'Do you know, Rebecca, I believed for a moment there. Fairies or not, this is an amazing place.'

Without making a sound, the two sat staring across the pond for a few moments. Her mum broke the silence, and in a forthright tone, said, 'Rebecca, if we are going to do these stories, we need to start soon.'

'Why so, Mum?'

Raising her eyes, she said, 'Well, your father has just informed me we are moving soon. That's the first I knew about it, huh.'

'Soon, how soon?'

'A month or two at most. Just before Christmas, perfect, not.'

Although Rebecca had overheard them earlier, she never guessed it would be so soon. At a loss what to say, she sat quietly. After a few minutes, her mum broke the silence.

'Well, he did show me some photos and to be honest it looks lovely. Big old house up by the lakes, in fact, it has a lake of its own. You will love it there, all twenty-six acres, woods, fields, all sorts. It has a very intriguing French name too, "chère à Votre Maison", how cool is that, not that I know what it means, huh.'

'But, Mum, I have all my memories here.'

'Well, that's all the more reason for us to start writing and saving your memories.' She then seemed to think for a moment. 'Maybe, I can get my dear old friends Amanda and Ruth to help with the move. I know you love having them around, and so we could make this work for us. Right, best we are getting indoors as it's nearly dark.'

The next few weeks flew by, what with packing, especially as Elizabeth wanted everything in its own particular box and labelled carefully. Rebecca did become a little frustrated with her mum's fastidiousness, but it was great having the help of Amanda and Ruth. Rebecca and her mother did find time to sit by the pond where Rebecca told her stories, while Elizabeth typed them up. They enjoyed this so much that they swore to continue it in the new house.

While making a final visit to the pond a couple of days before the move, Rebecca found a pen her Grandparents had bought for her. It had vanished the summer before last, but there it was sitting at the entrance to the shed. A cold shiver went down her spine, guessing the fairies had probably pinched it in the first place and aware she was moving, had brought it back. To confuse her feelings further, the pen was like new, with not a mark on it anywhere.

The next couple of days passed in the blink of the eye, and it was the morning of the move. Fortunately, Ruth and Amanda had stayed over the night before to help. Rebecca loved having the girls around because they treated her like an adult, and to add to that, her mum was so happy when they were around.

After a brief chat, they decided that Rebecca and Tommy would travel with their mum. James would go with the removal men, and Amanda and Ruth would make their way separately.

Chapter 2 - The New Old House

Rebecca was miles away when the car came to a juddering halt in front of a large arched, gated entrance. Her mum had given her one job, navigating, but she had lost track of where they were ages ago. Glancing at the map, she grimaced. 'Are we there, Mum?'

'Well, you should know, Rebecca. You're the one with the map,' she grumbled. 'Yes, we are here, finally.'

Rebecca hadn't heard her mum this irritated for a long time and wasn't sure what to say. She glanced back at the map and thought *ooops*. She'd never been one for long journeys, and utterly bored, had found a couple of pencils in the glove box and then doodled over every available blank space on the map.

Her mum glanced at the map, raised her eyes brows, and grumbled her words again, loudly this time. 'Yes, we are here.'

Deciding not to respond, she turned her attention to the archway. As her eyes probed this once fine structure, it oddly reminded her of something. Scratching her head, she vaguely remembered an old gothic mansion she'd visited on a school trip. She was now so deep in thought, she hadn't heard her mum speaking. 'Did you say something, Mum?'

'Rebecca, be a love, jump out and open the stupid gate. Ideally, before it gets dark.'

After Rebecca had opened the gate, she got back in the car and smiled at her mum.

'Sorry, I got touchy, Honey. I am exhausted after the long drive, what with Tommy jumping around like a possessed child, and well...

And, just to add to it the car radio is broken, even though I've mentioned it to your father thirty-eight times. Well, I tell you, I could do with a nice G & T, or three.'

As the car rumbled down the long drive, Rebecca soon became engrossed by an area dominated by huge, twisting bare oaks. Just as she was considering it had a witch-like feel, she spotted a smattering of tall, youthful willows. The way the sun sparkled through their skinny branches, changed her mood a little. That was until they passed through an area dominated by a dense thicket of elms. 'Brrrr, elves,' she muttered.

'Did you say something, Honey?'

Rebecca leaned back in her chair. 'Hmmm, lots of elm trees, so there are bound to be elves here about, I suspect.'

'How so?'

'Mum, don't you ever listen to anything I say. I did tell you before. Where you find elm trees, you will find elves.' She then turned to Tommy who was tickling her neck. 'Leave me alone or else.'

She turned back just as the car was pulling into a clearing. Right in front of her, she could see an imposing church-like arch, standing proudly to the front of a vast grey house. Gobsmacked, she was unsure where to look first. Her eyes flitted between the arch, with its odd-shaped roof, having an elevated pinnacle affair in each corner and the magnificent main house. She couldn't recall seeing anything like this before, not even in a book.

Just then, she heard her mum mumble something, and as she turned, caught sight of a vast lake off to her right. It took her a few seconds to see properly due to the diluted winter sun reflecting from the calm, almost glass-like water. As she focused, she could see a white building sneaking its head out from behind some short conifers close to the water's edge. She was totally invigorated and engrossed

17

by her surroundings, when the car grated on some gravel, breaking her attention. As she turned back towards the house, she spotted a tall turret protruding from the second-floor roof. She narrowed her eyes and peered up at a handful of small single arched windows that sat just beneath a spiral grey slate roof. Sometime back, she'd briefly studied old buildings at school, and this one seemed to be a complete mishmash of styles, and eras. As she peered up at the turret again, she muttered. 'So, that has got to be where they kept the princess.'

'And which princess would that be, Rebecca?'

'The one they locked up here, Mum,' she responded in an ironic tone to match that of her mother. Just then, the back of her seat bulged. She turned, waved her fist, and elongating each of her words, grumbled, 'Stop kicking my damn seat, twit.'

Squeezing Rebecca's knee, her mum glared in the rear-view mirror and growled, 'Thomas, sit. It is difficult enough driving without you bouncing off the ceiling. Rebecca, stop bickering with your brother.' She then pulled the car up on a large horseshoe drive directly in front of the main entrance, stopping abruptly. 'Out, the pair of you, and behave.'

Ruth and Amanda came over to the car just in time to save Rebecca and Tommy from any further trouble. Ruth opened the car door and exclaimed. 'Liz, this house is monstrous. It is more like a castle, nothing like the photos.' Pointing, she turned halfway towards the house. 'What's the deal with the spooky turret, are there any witches here?' She then chuckled and glanced at Rebecca. 'I must say it does have a certain charm though, rather imposing, but somehow inviting.'

Elizabeth got out of the car, stretched, and then kissed Ruth and Amanda on the cheek. Stretching again, she said, 'Yeah, I know what you mean, I wasn't expecting this. Bex suggested earlier that it looked like the kind of place to lock up a princess. She also muttered something about elms, elves, or both, hah.' She glanced around. 'I must agree, Ruth. It certainly has a unique charm.'

18

Rebecca grabbed hold of her mum's hand. 'It is just the sort of place to lock up a princess.' She chuckled and continued, 'I can see what Ruth means about its charm.' She paused for a moment and raising her eyebrows, added, 'strangely though, there is something a bit odd too. I can't put my finger on it.' Rebecca tightened her lips a little, looked around and nodded. 'Hmm, some mysteries here, I suspect.'

Elizabeth put her hand on Rebecca's shoulder, 'Yes, dear, and I am sure you will have fun nosing around, unravelling the odd, as you put it.'

Seeing Amanda standing on her own, Rebecca went over and linked arms. 'What do you think, A? It is rather cool, in a spooky kind of way. You wait until you see the interesting looking summerhouse. I caught a glimpse of it poking its head around the Christmas trees down by the lake. Hmm, that definitely looks like my sort of place.'

'I love the way you call me A. I'm sorry if I seem distant, Rebecca. To be honest, I am a bit gobsmacked by this place. It is huge, and the size of the garden, well it's more like a farm. It all looks ancient too. Do you have any ideas about its age?'

'Not sure really, the research I've been doing is all a bit unclear, the little bit I have found is at best sketchy. I would guess it has many tales to tell, one way or the other. Perhaps it is hiding its history.'

Amanda shook her head and squinted as if she needed glasses. 'Really, hiding its history, can a house do that, Bex? You'll have to fill me in while we take a box or two up to your room.'

With a box each, Rebecca pushed at the heavy front door. At first, it didn't move and then leaning against it with her shoulder, it grumbled and opened with a tomblike creak. 'I love it the way some doors have their own character. Although, I suspect this one is a bit moody, ha. Hello moody door, hello lovely house.'

Just inside the front door on either wall were two large female portraits, which instantly grabbed Rebecca's attention. She stared at them for a few seconds and then turned to Amanda. 'These paintings are a bit odd. It's as if they're watching us, but I like them very much. Both ladies are beautiful.' She nodded to the left one. 'I love this white lacy dress, gorgeous, and the woman has a divine natural beauty.' Then, she indicated to the one on the right. 'I like this one too, a sexy black number she's wearing. Odd though, I'm not sure about her, she looks, hmm... I don't really know. There is just something peculiar about her, something I can't put my finger on. She's pretty for sure, but there's something in her eyes. Actually, I am not even sure it is in her eyes. There's just something that radiates from her, odd...'

'She looks distant for sure, and there's a strange insincerity about her.'

Eager to see her room, Rebecca led Amanda along a wide hallway to a broad sweeping staircase. The staircase climbed a few steps opening onto a large landing with stairs leading off either side. Above the landing, in a prominent position, was a large male portrait. A dark-haired, stern-looking man, dressed in a heavy black cloak, looking down with an air of authority. Just as with the other paintings, he had those eyes that somehow follow you around. His long dark beard added to his steadfast persona. Pausing, Rebecca pointed up and said, 'He has to go. He is far too surly-looking, sneering at everyone like that. I bet he planted the elm trees and locked up the poor princess.' She then shivered. 'Brrrr, he gives me the spooks. You wouldn't wanna be walking around at night with him looking down at you like that, would you?'

'I know what you mean.' Amanda said, 'it's as if the women of the house greet you, and he, well, makes you feel like you have to tiptoe around.'

'Going by the name plaques and the dates, it would seem these are paintings of the people who lived here in the eighteen-fifties. I think one woman may have been his wife and the other his mistress.'

Amanda shook her head. 'What are you like, Rebecca? That sounds like a wild guess. So, where did that idea come from?'

'Well, one plaque says beloved Mrs, whatever her name was. Meredith, I think. The other plaque reads, for the exquisite Miss Millicent Black. Not rocket science, is it? And, I just have this feeling, call it intuition if you like, but I can sense something.'

Amanda stopped and leant her box against the rail. She turned to Rebecca, who was still standing on the second step. 'You are funny, Bex, the way your imagination seems to grab at any straw. Come on, this box was light, but it's getting heavier by the minute,' she said and chuckled.

'Sorry, A, I'm dithering a bit.'

'I'm rather intrigued by your idea about the ladies, Rebecca. If that is indeed the tale, which I guess it could be. If it's true, it's an odd way to live. Although, the way I understand it, back in those days, the women didn't have much choice. From what I've read, you married into money, or married because you had money, and then had to put up with your lot, even if you were unhappy. Not as if a woman in those days could just leave, then go, and get a job as a legal secretary or something. Adding to that, divorce, or separation was frowned upon, hmmm...'

Rebecca remembered one of her teachers referring to this period as the *Female Dark Ages*. The whole concept had irritated her, and this reminded her how she'd felt. She grumbled, 'I cannot believe what women have had to put up with over the years. It strikes me it is not a lot different now.' She pouted her lips and let out an elongated sigh. 'I would love to go back somehow, see how they managed their situations, get inside their heads, and see how they felt. I am sure a better understanding would help me avoid ending up...' She stopped, and glanced at the floor, knowing this was neither the time nor the place to talk about how she felt about her parent's relationship. 'Right, my room is on the second floor,' she said and led Amanda up a narrow staircase that opened onto a large landing with an enormous church-like window giving it a bright, airy feel.

Rebecca and Amanda simultaneously placed their boxes on the wide concrete windowsill and peered through the window. Rebecca stood for a moment, watched everyone coming-and-going in the forecourt, and then turned her attention to a smaller gothic style window to the rear of the landing. 'This view is amazing, Amanda. Can you see that white building? I spotted that earlier. I think it looks like some sort of summerhouse. If it's not a summerhouse, it should be. I will investigate that later for sure,' she said and nodded. 'Right, let's go see my room.'

'I must say this house is divine, although I am a little unsure about the odd dark corridor here and there.'

Rebecca followed the hallway toward another large arched window. 'I think this is my room,' she said, gripped a bulky brass handle and pushed at a dark wooden door. As with the front door, it creaked at first and then opened onto a large, bright room.

'Bex, this room is enormous.'

Dropping her box on the floor, Rebecca headed for a window that ran the entire width of the room. Peering through the grey nets, she turned and waved Amanda to join her.

'Is that a balcony out there?' She then moved a heavy net drape, which instantly filled the room with dust. Between coughs of laughter, she uttered, 'Whoops. We might need one of those industrial vacuum cleaner jobbies.'

Excited by the prospect of a balcony, Rebecca yanked at the curtain, which collapsed on the floor, and filled the air with more dust. She then peered out, and said, 'it is a balcony, but I can't work out how to get outside.' She made her way along the window pulling at what was left of the curtains until she found a door. She tried the handle a few times, and moaned, 'stuck. I reckon we need to find the key.' In her eagerness to get outside, she scurried her eyes around the room, not knowing where to look first.

Amanda tapped her on the shoulder, and smiling, pointed to an old metal key attached to a silk thread right next to the door. 'Is this what you're looking for my dear?'

Rebecca grinned, unhooked the key, and fumbled it into the lock. The key made a horrid grating sound at first and then stopped halfway. She turned it back and forth a few more times and growled, 'stuck.'

'Here, let me have a go, Rebecca.' Amanda took hold of the key with both hands and turned it several times. 'I suspect it's a while since this door was opened. Hey, maybe there will be some oil or something downstairs. I am sure one of those hunky removal guys will have something.' She pouted her lips and flicked her eyebrows a couple of times.

The two went downstairs, and after Amanda had flirted with one of the removal guys briefly, the two returned upstairs with some oil. A few squirts later and the door opened with what Rebecca described as an icy groan. The two then stood outside on the balcony, staring towards the lake.

'I love a winter sunset, especially after a clear day, Amanda. It's captivating the way the setting sun weaves all those oranges, reds, and yellows.'

'It is stunning, Bex. You make me see things I wouldn't notice as a rule. I guess us oldies take things for granted. From now on, I'll always try to see more than just a sunset. I guess it is part of the

23

spiritual path we are supposedly on, which you are clearly a long way further down than most of us.'

'For some reason, I keep imagining the woman in the painting standing here, just as we are. I feel like there is something I need to find out.'

'What do you think that is all about?'

'Oh, I don't know, really; just getting this peculiar sensation while standing here. I keep thinking there's something I should know, which I guess sounds a bit daft.'

Amanda nodded, and said, 'I am guessing you are talking about the woman you believe is the wife. What was her name, Meredith? So, can you expand on that?'

'No, not really, it's just this peculiar feeling I have had since I saw the painting. To be honest, I've had a strange feeling ever since I knew we were moving.' Rebecca could sense Amanda's uncertainty and decided to change tack. 'Come on, let's go and help the others. Dad will wonder where I am.'

It was dark by the time the furniture had been unloaded into the house. Having taken the last box inside, Rebecca stood outside talking with Amanda and Ruth. While they were chatting, the removal lorry started to head out of the drive, and then stopped sharply on the gravel. As the girls looked up, the cab door opened, one of the guys jumped out and hurried over to Amanda. He smiled, nodded to Ruth and Rebecca, then handed Amanda a piece of paper, grinned and returned to his cab.

Rebecca stood with her mouth open and then noticed Ruth was doing the same.

Amanda raised her eyebrows and put the piece of paper in her pocket. She then nodded to Rebecca and said, 'Close your mouth, sweetie; there's a good girl.'

Ruth pointed back and forth between Amanda and the lorry. 'So, what was that all about, Amanda?'

'Nothing, Ruth,' Amanda said, grinned, and then turned to Rebecca. 'Come on, Bex, I think your mother has some food and coffee ready. Shall we?'

While having a coffee, Elizabeth suggested Ruth and Amanda stayed over for the night. Later, that evening, Rebecca overheard her father giving her mum grief about asking the girls to stop over, often referring to them as, *hangers-on*. This made Rebecca so angry, leaving her adamant she'd speak to her mum the following day, especially as her mother didn't say anything, other than sorry about twenty times.

The next day, Rebecca tried to talk to her mum a couple of times, but as always, she didn't want to talk about it and quickly changed the subject.

Chapter 3 - Message on a Chair

It had been raining for five days solid and completely bored, Rebecca decided to go and explore the house. Heading down one of the dark corridors, she couldn't resist sneaking a look inside a room, even though her father had told her all these rooms were out of bounds. This just served to tempt her even more. Inside the first room, she came across a pair of old wrought-iron chairs. Reckoning they would look nice on her balcony, she dragged them back to her room. While cleaning one of the chairs, she noticed a small red mark on the underside. Running her fingers over it, she could feel a series of grooves under the paint and thought it was worth further investigation. She rubbed it briefly with a tissue but quickly realised something more substantial was required, so decided to head downstairs and see if her mum had any ideas.

'Mum, have you got anything to clean some paint from an old white chair?'

With a look of concern, she asked, 'Which chair and what paint, Rebecca?'

'Oh, nothing to worry about, Mum, I've not spilt anything.'

Narrowing her eyes, she handed Rebecca a cloth and some household liquid. 'Try this, if that doesn't work, I think there is some stronger stuff in one of the garages. Tell me more about this chair.'

'Oh, it's just an old pair of white metal chairs I found.'

'Found where?'

'Upstairs, in one of the rooms. Look, Mum, can I explain later, there really is nothing to worry yourself about.'

'In one of the rooms indeed,' she said and narrowed her eyes, 'well best you explain later, madam.'

Rebecca hurried back upstairs and set about continuing her investigation. She rubbed for ages, and just as she was considering going down for something stronger, the paint started to fade, revealing a word scratched into the metal. Turning the chair on one side and seeing the letter *M*, she rubbed the paint some more, sadly to no avail. Just as she was again considering getting something stronger, an idea came to her. Grabbing a sheet of paper, she laid it over the mark, and with a thick lead pencil, rubbed gently. Eventually, it revealed the name Millicent with an arrow scratched through the middle. With her thoughts now going in circles, she peered at the paper for ages. She was miles away when she suddenly heard her mum calling her for supper. She headed downstairs, still staring at the piece of paper. Pausing by the paintings, she mumbled loudly, 'how very intriguing.' Then from the corner of her eye, she noticed her mum standing by the kitchen door watching her.

'Talking to yourself again, Rebecca? And do tell, what is so intriguing?'

'Nothing, Mum, just the same name on this painting is scratched on the bottom of one of those chairs.' She glanced again at the painting before following her mother into the kitchen.

'Yeah, well you'll have to tell me all about it later, and where you actually found those chairs. For now, though, supper is ready, so quickly wash your hands.'

During supper, Rebecca was miles away thinking about the chair.

Her mum gently squeezed her arm, and asked, 'Why are you so quiet, Rebecca?'

'Just thinking about the paintings, Mum,' she said and glanced towards her dad. Once supper had finished, she helped her mum tidy away and explained where she'd found the chairs. After a lecture from her mum about not going in those rooms, Rebecca decided on an early night.

She lay in bed, but the harder she tried to sleep, the more the chairs rumbled around in her thoughts. She nearly got up to have another look, feeling confident these chairs held the key to something that had happened a long time ago. However, it had gone midnight and reluctantly, she forced herself to think about something else until she eventually dropped off.

The following morning, Rebecca sat on the balcony watching as the sunlight eased across the lawn and dissolved the early morning mist. Although she found this captivating, the chairs continued to dominate her thoughts. She kept wondering if Millicent had scratched her name on the chair and then sometime later, Meredith scribed an arrow through the middle and painted over the top. The more she thought about it, the more convinced she was that there had been some kind of conflict between the two women. All day, Rebecca pottered about, between searching the Internet for any history on the house, looking at the paintings, then back to her room and the chairs. By now, she was convinced it was a message. The following day was a cold but beautifully sunny day, and in an attempt to take her mind off the chairs, she decided to sit on her balcony sketching. Although focussed on her drawings, the two women kept nagging at her thoughts, almost as if something or someone was sending her a message. She found herself imagining what it would have been like living here all those years ago. These women had preoccupied her thoughts all day, and she was now getting a headache. She thought, *enough's enough,* and decided to distract herself by wrapping her Christmas presents.

She spent the next couple of days with her mum preparing for Christmas, which helped take her mind off the chairs. Then all Christmas morning, the two of them were in the kitchen, which again helped. She kept wondering why the girls did all the work. As tempted as she was to say something to her mother, decided not to mention it just now.

For Christmas, her parents had given her some watercolours, and she received a beautiful antique wooden easel from her Grandparents. It was now late in the afternoon on Boxing Day, and Rebecca was sitting on the balcony, using her new easel, and paints. Just as she'd finished a drawing, her mum came out and sat next to her.

Pulling her collar up, she said, 'It is odd what with the sun being so bright and the sky such an intense blue, it's surprisingly cold.'

'I love it when it is like this, Mum. The colours you get in the sky this time of the year are wonderful. Mother Nature at her best and the colours will explode when the sun sets, which will be soon.'

While they chatted, her mum surprised Rebecca by saying she'd suggested a New Year party to dad, one that could double as a house warming. She went on to proclaim how startled she was that he'd agreed, with not so much as a blink of an eye.

Taken aback, Rebecca wondered if her dad had some ulterior motive. She asked her mum why he'd agreed, but as usual, her mum just shrugged her shoulders and then suggested they shouldn't knock it. After an amazingly colourful sunset, they went inside and set about writing an invitation list. While compiling the list, they speculated how many would come what with them now living so far off the beaten track. In the end, they just wrote down everyone they could think of, including a couple of aunts and uncles Rebecca had never heard of, let alone seen.

Later that evening after supper, Rebecca was once again helping her mum in the kitchen.

'So, Bex, I was wondering, how do you feel about a theme for this party? I'm just thinking aloud; what about a sixties fancy dress affair?'

Rebecca grinned, surprised by her mum's not so middle-of-the-road idea. 'That sounds cool, Mum, though people may not have enough time to organise their costumes. And, actually, how do you think Dad will handle that?'

'Hmm, he agreed to the party without any debate, so we can only ask him and see what he says. You know, most of the people we are inviting grew up in the sixties, and may still have something knocking around. What do you think then, do you have any ideas?'

'That's true; I reckon sixties will be fun. I don't think you need to run it past Dad, especially as he agreed to the party. I am sure you can sort something out in his wardrobe, most of the stuff he wears is the sixties anyway, isn't it?'

'Yeah, let's go for it.'

Rebecca was a little taken aback by her mum's response and wasn't sure what to say. 'Umm, yeah, let's do just that.'

The next couple of days passed at a hectic pace for Rebecca and her mother as they sorted the final additions. The party proved a big hit with everyone, culminating, much to the delight of Rebecca, in a wonderful firework display. Something her mother had organised in complete secrecy.

Rebecca was disappointed that her dad had chosen not to dress-up, but was over the moon when she heard him compliment Elizabeth on a fantastically well-organised event. As she lay in bed that evening, she thought about the way her mum had taken control of the party without having to ask her dad for anything. *That was a job well done.*

Chapter 4 - The Key

Stirring from a deep sleep, Rebecca had the remains of something odd rumbling around in her head. She guessed she'd been dreaming, and as she lay there, trying to recollect the details, her bedroom door opened, and her mother walked in.

'Morning, Rebecca.'

Before she had a chance to answer, her mum had banged the breakfast tray down, yanked the curtains open, and then slammed the door on the way out. Now wide-awake, she eased her legs out of bed and after a few seconds, stretched and sat up. Heading towards the balcony, she pondered her mum's bad-tempered display and wondered what could have put her in such a bad mood. She opened the door, and the warmth of the early spring sun soon helped her forget about her mother's outburst. Being such a lovely morning, she decided to have her breakfast outside. While sipping her orange juice, she again tried to recall the remnants of her dream. As she sat there, she had this overpowering urge to explore the woods, which were continually nagging at the back of her thoughts, as they had for a few days now. She again considered her dream, but that had faded completely, and all she could focus on was this need to visit the woods. With spring finally here, she reckoned it was time to get out and explore. She was contemplating the day ahead when the sound of her mum's slightly smoother voice broke her attention.

'Bex, come on, time for school.'

'Okay, Mum, I'll be with you in two tics.' She puffed out her cheeks, having forgotten it was a school day.

All morning, the woods pulled at her thoughts. Again, she was miles away, when her teacher asked if she was okay. Before she had a chance to answer, he reminded everyone that the school was closing at lunchtime for a health and safety inspection. She was so excited at the prospect of an early day, having forgotten all about the inspection. She then proceeded to watch the clock hand move slowly towards noon. At one minute to twelve, she put away what little work she'd done and with the sound of the bell still ringing in her ears, headed for the door.

She arrived home and went straight to the kitchen. 'Hi, Mum, forgot to tell you, there was an inspection at school today, so I'm home early, Tom is playing football at school and will get a lift home later. I'll get changed, and then I am going for a stroll through the woods.'

'You're in a hurry, so does your mother get a kiss?'

Rebecca shook her head, remembering her mum's mood this morning and thought she at least deserved a proper hello. 'Sorry, Mum. Hello, I've just been thinking about the woods all morning.' She then beamed a smile. 'By the way, I made a new friend at school. Her name is Roxy, and I would like to ask her over to stay for the weekend if you're okay with that.' She then kissed her mum on the cheek. 'She has just moved from London and doesn't know anyone, and I thought she might be feeling lonely, so I made friends with her. I think you will like her, especially the way she talks. She said something like, "na, leave me out, ain't playing 'ockey." Or something like that, either way, it made me laugh. When the teacher said we were going home early, she said, "shur-rup', ya' kiddin' me". She is such fun.'

'Oh, how lovely, well that will be nice.' She frowned and then grinned. 'So, what's this inspection at school? Is it something I should know about? Actually thinking about it, I do recall getting a letter about it some time back.'

She recognised her mum's pitch and knew she was in the mood for a chat. 'Yeah, that's right; it was some standard health and safety thing-e-ma-jig. Roxy taught me that word. Mum, can we chat when I get back? I really need to go to the woods on a hunch.'

'Oh, one of your hunches,' she said, shaking her head, 'that's ok then, sweetie.'

Rebecca realised the way her mum picked up the newspaper she was a little putout. She kissed her mum on the cheek. 'Mum, sorry I must dash; you know what I am like with my hunches.' Her mum smiled in a way that made Rebecca feel better. 'I promise you'll get my undivided later.'

She tugged her trainer's on, dashed out the front door and hurried down the slope towards the old summerhouse. As soon as she arrived by the lake, she slowed a little and wandered around for a while. In her head, she was trying to work out why she needed to be here. After a few minutes, and following an impulse, she headed into the woods from a direction she hadn't taken before. She ambled for an hour or so and eventually arrived in an area covered with crocuses. Having decided that this was where the young pixies play, she trod carefully around the outer edge, trying not to disturb them. She paused for a moment, enchanted by the array of colour. In the back of her thoughts, she was sure there was something stronger pulling her to these woods. She pouted her lips and continued. After a while, she came across some silver birch trees lined up like a group of soldiers. Following the trees, she soon arrived in a glade. On the far side, she could see two huge oaks just showing the first signs of spring. Rebecca made her way over and looked up at the broad twisting branches. She loved oaks, both spooked and exhilarated by the odd mystical feel created by their long limb-like branches. The thick spongy moss that lay in the shade of these old trees just intensified her mood further. She stood there for ages and watched as their shadows eased across the clearing. As the light began to fade, she knew it was time to head indoors. On her way home something strange was still tugging at Rebecca's inner thoughts. It was something so strong, she knew she had to come back here soon.

Throughout the remainder of the school week, her mind often returned to the woods, but it had always been too dark by the time she got home. When Saturday finally came, Rebecca sat up in bed to the sound of the dawn chorus. Moments later, her mum walked in with breakfast. 'You're up early, Mum.'

'I heard you stirring a while ago and guessed your *hunch* may still be calling you, so decided I'd get up and sort you some breakfast.'

'Thanks Mum,' she said and blew a kiss.

Rebecca thought about having breakfast on the balcony but was now so fidgety thinking about the woods, decided to eat while she got ready. She slipped on her coat and hurried downstairs into the kitchen.

'Mum, I am nipping down to the woods. Maybe do some drawing. Okay?'

'I guessed you would, honey. Take your phone with you. What time is Roxy coming over?'

'Got my phone, Mum and Roxy won't be here until around four this afternoon, is that okay?'

'Yeah, I am looking forward to meeting her.'

'Should be cool. Right, I'm off; see you lata'.'

'Later, not lata'.'

'Yeah, yeah, see you later, Mother,' she said, grinning.

On her way towards the edge of the woods, Rebecca decided to avoid the crocuses, not wanting to disturb the baby pixies again. As she walked under the first of the trees, something seemed unusual today, and it wasn't just because she'd chosen a different route.

Whatever this sensation was, it was making her feel quite peculiar, having not felt like this before.

Making her way down the ancient path, she scrutinised every tree and shrub. She didn't know what she was looking for, just something that may point her in a particular direction. Without intention, she'd found her way back to the big old oak trees. She surveyed the area and for the first time, noticed a cluster of youthful willows thriving in the early spring sun. Rebecca watched for a moment as they swayed in the gentle breeze, their twisted branches dancing back and forth, full of bronze pussy willow buds. She grinned, thinking they would make great pillows for the pixies.

She felt at ease here and looked around for somewhere to sit down and enjoy this lovely setting. Her eyes again examined the area, searching for something that would suit her needs. Off to the far side, she noticed the early morning sun streaming through the trees and resting invitingly on the trunk of a huge fallen oak. She made her way over, perched herself on a wide section and eased her back against a stout branch. Although it served perfectly as a backrest, it left her feet dangling uncomfortably. *A small price to pay*, she thought, as the warmth of the sun gently kissed her face. She knew this was the best spot, but for some reason, felt a little puzzled. On the one hand, it seemed bright and cheerful here, strangely though it also had an almost mystical, slightly spooky feel.

She lifted her left leg and balanced her foot in a small recess in the tree. Leaning her elbow on her knee, she again considered what had drawn her to this place. After a few minutes, she settled back and started drawing. As she leaned towards her eraser, her foot slipped, and although she managed to hold onto her pad, her pencil fell to the ground. She climbed down, but there was no sign of it and guessing it may have bounced under the tree, knelt on the soft damp moss. She peered under the tree into a dark, dank area and wondered if this could be a pixie hideout. To her, it seemed so perfect, complete with the tiny white mushrooms, odd coloured lichens, and new stems of this year's fern. She then remembered she was looking for her pencil and with no sign of it anywhere, pushed her hand gently under the tree. She fished around to no avail, removed some damp decaying leaves, and briefly wondered if the pixies had pinched her pencil. She then chuckled and thought, *don't be daft.* Her chuckle turned to a frown as her hand engaged a cold heavy object. Running her palm over it, she knew it wasn't her pencil. She wriggled her outstretched fingers, this way, and that, mumbling, 'Oh, come along now.' After she'd twisted and pulled several times, an elaborate key the size of her palm, surrendered to her call.

Feeling excited by finding such an unusual key, she sat wondering how it had ended up here. Her mind raced with ideas, reckoning it had to be a key to a door, if so, which door, how long had it been hanging around, and whom did it belong to originally? With the key clasped firmly in her hand, she stood up. 'What,' she muttered, as she spotted her pencil perched right in the middle of her pad. A cold shudder went down her spine. She knew she'd definitely dropped it, and couldn't work out what was going on. Then her thoughts raced back to the whispering pond and her pen that had turned up just before she'd moved from their old house. At the time, she was certain the fairies had returned it because they knew she was moving home. Thinking about it, she was confident the pixies were playing a similar game, just this was less of a game.

She sat, gazing at the key wondering what secrets it had in store. After mulling over so many ideas, she decided the least she could do was to give it a good clean. After all, she reckoned, the poor thing had been sitting here, clearly stuck, and quite obviously waiting for her. She wondered where this key might lead her, but knew she was unlikely to know until she found its rightful home. Then perhaps, just maybe, she might understand why the pixies had hidden her pencil if they actually did. Thinking about it, she knew they'd done it so she would find the key. Considering this, she reckoned it wasn't a game after all, and it might actually be leading somewhere. She'd always had half an idea that pixies were a tad more serious than the playful fairies, and perhaps this was proof. *So where is this going to take me,* she thought.

Stimulated by her ideas, and with the key held firmly, she made her way beyond the young willows, wondering what was leading her this way. She was now following her instinct, and after scrambling through some old fallen branches, and avoiding a mass of tangled, dense brambles, she arrived by a sparkling stream. *How did I end up here*, she thought, *oh well, perfect?*

She knelt down, peering into the crystal-clear water and spotted a shoal of tiny fish as they flicked back and forth between the pebbles and weed. She wondered if these minnows were playing here waiting to grow big, and one day soon venture out into the vast lake. She then remembered why she was there and holding onto a branch for steadiness, eased forward and lowered the key to the water. The water was so cold it made Rebecca snatch her hand away and almost drop the key. She braced herself and lowered the key again, wriggling her outstretched fingers, removing as much dirt as possible. Shivering, she pulled herself back up the bank, perched on a small rock, and rubbed the last few spots of dirt away. Inspecting the heart-shaped handle, she searched for a clue of sorts. She sat and stared at the key for a while, knowing it had been here a long time, but how long, she wondered and again asked where it would take her.

She knew the time was getting on, and Roxy was coming over, so with the key clenched in her hand, headed back. Arriving at the front door, she tried the key, but it wasn't even close to fitting. She then tried every door she passed on her way to the kitchen. Seeing her mother, and unable to contain her excitement, she blurted, 'Mum, Mum, look what I have found.'

Taking hold of the key, her mum said, 'crumbs, honey, this looks old, where did you get this?'

'Oh, I found it down in the spry wood, under an old fallen tree where the pixies live.'

Her mum raised her eyebrows and shook her head gently. 'Rebecca... So where is this spry wood?' Shaking her head again, she smiled, and continued, 'and pixies, hmmm, have you seen any?'

'Mum, you know about the fairies, well the pixies are the same. You just get an idea they are there. Don't expect them to jump out and say, hello, here we are. Honestly, you adults know nothing. Anyway, the spry wood - as I've named it - is behind the summerhouse, between the old oaks and the brook, where all the young willows grow. Back to the pixies, well here's the thing, they hid my pencil so I would find the key.'

Her mum narrowed her eyes, and said softly, 'Okay. I'm intrigued now, so tell me more. Should I think about writing this down? And please, explain what you meant when you said, "they hid your pencil to make you find the key"?' Appearing perplexed, but nonetheless fascinated, she sat at the kitchen table and picked up her coffee. 'Okay, I am all ears.'

'Well, there I was sitting on the old fallen oak, drawing. I lost my footing, grabbed my pad, dropped my pencil, bent to look for it, found the mushrooms, then the key, and when I stood up, there was my pencil, placed carefully on my pad.' She took a deep breath. 'What's that all about, if that wasn't a setup, what was it?'

The kitchen back door thudded, and Tom burst in shouting, 'what key?'

'Tom, have you been listening outside the door?' She glanced at Rebecca, shaking her head. 'It's just a key that your sister found somewhere in the woods.'

Tom was jigging from one foot to the other, beckoning with his hand. 'Let me see the key, and what you on about, pixies?'

Rebecca turned to Tom. 'No pixies, Tom, it was just a joke.'

'Well, it didn't sound like a joke to me. I might follow you tomorrow.'

Rebecca screwed her face up. 'You won't, or I will kick your football in the lake and then kick you in the lake too. Mother, will you talk to this, this twit.'

'Rebecca, he is not a twit. Both of you behave yourself. Tom, you will not follow Rebecca, and Rebecca, say sorry to Tom.'

'Mum, why do I have to apologise?' Noticing her mum's expression, she mumbled, 'Err sorry, Tom.' and then muttered, 'not,' under her breath. She paused for a second, and then said in her nicest tone, well as nice as she could manage for her stupid, not so little brother. 'Tom, please don't follow me. I will take you down soon enough so you can see there are no pixies, just some big trees, and a brook.'

'Can I look at the key now?'

'Please, Tom, say please.'

'Sorry, Mum. Please let me look at the key, Bexie.'

Rebecca glared at him for a few seconds and then handed him the key. 'Be careful with it, Tom, it is very old. And, don't give me that, Bexie, just because you're trying to be nice for once in your life.'

Tom grumbled, 'just a key,' handed it back, picked up his football, and swaggered back into the garden, muttering some football song.

'Pick your feet up, Tom.'

'So, Mum, where were we before he rudely interrupted us? Oh, I remember. You asked if I thought you needed to write down my story about the key. I guess so, that might actually be a good idea.'

'Well, honey, Roxy will be here soon. Her mother called a while back just to confirm a time. We can go and visit the woods tomorrow afternoon if the weather is good. Then you can tell me all about the key, maybe take Roxy, and have a picnic. On the subject of Roxy, I must say, I struggled to understand Roxy's mother at first, very strong accent. She seemed ever so friendly though.'

'I am sure if she is anything like Roxy, she is friendly. Going to the woods tomorrow is a cool idea, Mum. How long do I have until Roxy arrives? I want to go and *Google* this key, see if I can find anything, like its age and so on.' She then looked around the kitchen for the clock. 'Mum, where's the clock?'

'Oops, it fell off the wall when I was cleaning.' She glanced at her watch, and said, 'You have about thirty minutes before Roxy is here. Why don't you ever wear your watch, honey?'

'My watch is where it always is, in my bedroom. I have to live by the clock at school. That's enough time watching for anyone.' She raised her eyebrows and headed upstairs. Placing the key on a hanky, she powered up her computer and typed in *old keys*. Within seconds, hundreds of key images appeared on her screen. She flicked through, and just as she was beginning to think the key was going to remain a mystery, something very similar appeared on her screen. She started reading, and realised the key was possibly from the mid-1800s'. After reading up on the key for a few minutes, her thoughts oddly turned to the paintings in the hallway. She picked up the key and headed downstairs unsure what she was looking for, but something was nagging at her inner thoughts.

Rebecca briefly glanced at the woman in the black dress and knew she had nothing to show her. Turning towards the other painting, she started admiring the detail on the white lace dress, when something on the table in the painting drew her attention. All of a fluster, she called out, 'Mum, Mum, come and look, quickly.' She shivered, turned to her mum, held the key up to the painting, and panted, 'Look, Mum, look.'

Her mum put her glasses on and asked, 'What am I looking at, Bex?' She then stood back and gasped, 'it can't be, can it? The key on the table is the same as... Oooh, I have gone all goosey.'

'Brrrr, did you feel that chilly draft, it was as if someone had opened the front door.' Rebecca was unable to stop her voice trembling, 'We have so got to find out where this key belongs, Mum.' With the words still hanging on her lips, she turned to the door on the right and tried the key again, even though she'd tried all the doors in the hallway. 'Na, it is not even close, Mum.' She then turned her attention towards the next door.

'Bex, Roxy will be here in ten minutes, and supper is a little while after. As fascinating as your discovery is, you need to put the key down and go and get ready, quickly.'

'Okay, Mum, I won't be long. I'll just try a couple of doors.' She nodded, but was now on a mission and turned to the drawing room.

Her father looked up from his paper and asked, 'where are you going in such a hurry, young lady? It is polite to knock before entering a room.'

'Sorry, Dad, I didn't realise you were in here. I found this old key and am trying to find its rightful home.' Rebecca said, glancing around the room eyeing up every keyhole.

'Where exactly did you find this key, Rebecca?'

She smiled and handed her father the key, but in the back of her mind was sure he wouldn't be at all interested. 'Oh, it is just a key I found in the woods, rather old, and I was hoping that it may fit a door somewhere in the house, or come to that, a cupboard.'

'It looks like an old key, Rebecca.' He handed the key back, and although he was looking at his paper, Rebecca could see him thinking and wondered what exactly was coming next.

Having tried the three doors in the drawing room, Rebecca noticed two old cabinets, also with keyholes, but soon realised the key was far too big. Forgetting her dad was in the same room, she muttered, 'Oh dear, where do you belong? Come with me, key.' Heading for the hall, she turned to her father. 'Sorry to disturb you, Dad.'

He glanced up from his paper and appeared distantly interested. 'I am guessing you had no luck. One of my colleagues at work collects keys, and he might know something. By the way, I had an expert look at those cabinets. They can't open them without a key, and even then, they may have to break them open, so keep your eyes peeled,' he said and grinned.

'Excellent, Dad thanks. As for the cabinets, I would be interested to see what's inside. I bet they hold some secrets, and answers, hmmm.'

Her father shook his head and returned to his normal condescending tone. 'Incidentally, young lady, you really must refrain from talking to yourself so often and so loud too.' He nodded her out the door and turned back to his paper. 'And talking to a key isn't any better,' he said in an unusually witty tone.

Rebecca was a little taken aback and wasn't sure how to respond, 'does talking to Tommy also count the same?'

'Rebecca, not funny.'

Rebecca grinned to herself, headed upstairs to her room, and on the way, tried a big door on the first floor. She was convinced this was the door and paused for a second before trying it, but once again, it wasn't even close. If she'd had any doubts before, she now knew her search was going to be a lengthy business. Once again, getting sidetracked and heading down one of the dark corridors, she heard the doorbell ring. Seconds later, her mother was calling her.

'Bex, Roxy is here.'

As Rebecca made her way downstairs, she could see her mum frowning.

'Rebecca, I told you to get yourself cleaned up; you look like you've been playing football.'

Rebecca grinned. 'Sorry, Mum, I was carried away with the key. I'll take Roxy to my room and get changed.' She led Roxy upstairs, and on the way showed her the key, briefly explaining where she'd found it.

Rebecca had just turned the corner on the stairs when her mum called out. 'Rebecca, supper is in ten minutes, so get out of that football kit!'

'See what ya' Mum means about footie kit. Ya' gonna struggle to get those green marks off ya' knees, Bex.'

'Yeah, my Mum's gonna give me grief. Best we get downstairs for dinner.'

During the evening meal, Rebecca chatted but her mind was on the key, and without realising, she ate far too quickly. She then sat on the edge of her seat holding her tummy.

Her father tapped his knife on his plate and said, 'Rebecca, will you sit straight, please. You will give me indigestion, and your friend is still eating, nicely, I might add. I know you are in a hurry to try the key on a few more doors. However, I assure you that the doors will still be there in ten minutes.'

Appreciative of her father's thoughtful words, Rebecca nodded several times. 'I'm sorry, Father, sorry Roxy.' Rebecca sat chatting to Roxy but still sat twiddling the key under the table. It seemed to take an eternity for everyone to finish eating. However, as desperate as Rebecca was to get going, she knew better. Much to her dismay, her

Dad then started chatting to Roxy about school. After about ten minutes, which felt like an hour, her dad eventually rose.

'Okay, I am going to the drawing room where I would appreciate some peace and quiet. That means no bursting in with your key, Rebecca.' He smiled at Roxy and Rebecca, and then on his way out, turned to Elizabeth. 'Elizabeth, I would like beef tomorrow for our evening meal.'

Tom jumped up and headed off in the opposite direction towards the garden, grabbing his football on the way. 'If we have beef, does a burger count, Mum?'

'Tom, it is too dark to play football. And you shouldn't be playing football until your dinner goes down. And no, it doesn't mean burger.'

'No rule about playing football in the dark, and a beef burger is beef, Mum.'

'Tom, I said no. Go to your room to play, and that doesn't mean playing football in your room either. And you can drop the attitude while you're at it, young man.'

He skulked off into the hallway, huffing and puffing as he went. He then turned and grinning like a Cheshire cat, said, 'I will play football on my computer instead.'

'Enough of your lip, young man, or you won't be doing anything.' She waved her hand at him and said, 'due to a serious throttling injury, Tommy won't be fit for football anytime soon, said a spokesman at the club.'

'Sorry Mum. And very funny, ha-ha. I see where Rebecca gets her wit; the apple doesn't fall far from the tree.'

Roxy laughed so loud it made Rebecca jump. 'Jeez, your Ma's a blast, and you're right about Tommy.'

'What,' Tommy blurted, 'what's she been saying about me?'

'I said you's actually quite amusing for a,' she paused, 'err, a younger bro.' Roxy then excused herself to go to the bathroom.

Sneering at Tommy, Rebecca noticed her mum standing by the kitchen window. She was waving her arms about, muttering under her breath, clearly oblivious to anyone else. She could sense her mum was annoyed. Curious, she moved a little closer.

Obliviously, her mum continued muttering quietly, 'no please or thank you, just I want beef, well I want fish, and so he can pee-off.'

Rebecca laughed aloud, hearing her mother use such language for the first time, 'what did you just say?'

With wide eyes, she turned. 'Oops, you didn't hear that, did you? Obviously, you did.' Smirking, she stumbled, 'err... I thought you'd, umm, gone with Roxy.'

Unable to hide her amusement, Rebecca held both hands up. 'You wait until I see Roofy and Amanda. Ha-ha, Mum told Dad to pee-off.'

With her hand over her mouth, clearly stifling her laughter, she blasted, 'right missy; it is carbolic soap time for you. And don't even think about saying anything to my friends. If you do, I will lock you inside whichever room that key fits. And leave you there. Actually, it might not be a room at all; it might be a cupboard, even better.' She turned away laughing.

'On that subject, guess what... Dad reckons someone at work is into keys, kind of suggesting he'd show it to him.' she said, raising her eyes, and shaking her head a little. 'Oh yeah, and in all seriousness, you should tell Dad you want fish, at least now and then. You don't

45

have to swear, but it would be a laugh, well for us it would be. Love to see Tommy's face.'

'I used to say no to him, and mean it, all the time.' Her mum turned away, swigged her drink, and nodded. 'I actually wouldn't mind swearing at him, just to see his reaction. A long time ago when he was late for a date, I swore at him good and proper.'

'Well, maybe that is what he needs, a smack in the mouth, metaphorically speaking.' Rebecca laughed aloud and continued, 'You wait until I see your mates.' She laughed again and said, 'Hello Ruth, hello, Amanda. Get this; mum told dad to..., and then she smacked him in the mouth,' she stumbled through her words, giggling. 'What have you got to say about that girlies?'

The two joked for ages about what they'd like to say to James. Her mum glanced at her watch, straightened her face. 'Rebecca, stop it now. Go and find your metaphorical door and metaphorically lock yourself inside.' She touched Rebecca gently on the cheek and said softly, 'Bless you, honey; I do so love you.' She sniggered and muttered, 'James, if you want beef, maybe try a MacDonald's burger, keep Tommy happy too, for five minutes, maybe.'

Giggling, Rebecca cuddled her mum. 'You are funny; I love you so much it hurts, and I loved that bit about a spokesman from the football club, brilliant. Right, I am going to find my cupboard, maybe it will fit two people, and we know who that would be.' With the key waving in her hand, she went through the kitchen door. 'Come on key; let's go find Roxy.' As she was closing the kitchen door, she heard her mum mumble, 'One day, I will tell him to do more than pee-off.'

'I heard that, Mum.'

'Leave me alone and go and find your cupboard.'

That evening, Rebecca and Roxy tried every door they could find, many more than once, with no joy. Sunday morning was a dreary affair and inspired by Roxy the girls turned their attention to various makeup and clothing combinations. Her mum popped her head in to see how they were getting on and clearly surprised to see Rebecca with make-up, hung around for a while making a few suggestions.

'Hey, Rebecca, what about that pink dress, the one you got for your birthday? I don't think you've ever worn it, have you? Right, I am off downstairs, have fun.'

Following her mum's suggestion, with a full face of makeup, and wearing the pink dress, Rebecca went down to the kitchen to show her mum. Seconds later, the kitchen door opened, and Tommy came in as if he was still playing football. Then he seemingly noticed Roxy - who was wearing what Rebecca had described as a ludicrously short dress – and subsequently bumped into the kitchen table so hard that he nearly knocked himself over. Tempted to give him both barrels, Rebecca could see how embarrassed he was and decided to give him a break. Tommy's sheepish reaction made Rebecca think a little differently about how she could deal with his boyish behaviour. In fact, it opened an entirely new concept of how the male species react to certain situations. *Hmm, learn something new every day,* she thought.

After lunch on Sunday, Roxy's mum came to collect her. As soon as she'd gone, Rebecca set about trying a few more doors, again, many of which she'd had a go at the evening previous. Although the key fitted two of the bigger oak doors on the first floor, their locks wouldn't turn. On the verge of giving up, she spotted a door right at the end of a dark, narrow corridor. The key fitted perfectly and even turned halfway around. However, after spending ages and using half a tin of oil, she gave up.

The following morning Rebecca woke early and was first at the breakfast table. While sitting waiting for the others to join her, she twiddled the key repeatedly, wondering where she could look next. Moments later, her dad sat beside her.

'So, young lady, did you find a suitable keyhole?'

'Well it fitted one door perfectly, the small one on the second floor; you know the little brown door? It even turned halfway around, but it wouldn't open. That was it, very frustrating. You mentioned a friend at work. Do you think he'd have a look at the key, Dad?'

'He is not my friend, Rebecca, no friends at work, just colleagues. You never know when you may have to dismiss one of them, so best keep your distance. That said I am happy to take your key, and I will see what I can find out. The brown door you mentioned leads to the attic. Do not even attempt to go up there until we have had it checked.'

Rebecca wrapped the key in her pink hanky and handed it to her father. 'Thanks for doing this, Dad. Changing the subject, I fancy fish for supper tonight, would you mind?' In the back of her mind, she was thinking, *attic, interesting*.

Her father raised his eyes in a questioning manner. 'I am not sure about the hanky.' He then flicked his eyebrows and continued, 'Why do you want fish, Rebecca?'

'Well, at school, we've been doing a project on declining British industries, and I thought it would be nice to support the local fishing families, many of which go back for several generations. Some are now suffering badly through a combination of fishing quotas, declining fish stocks and large conglomerate supermarket chains demanding unsustainable prices. It is becoming almost impossible for a small family business to survive. It is people like that who made our country great, giving individuals the chance to succeed. It is solely up to us, the buyer, to support them and thereby sustain what makes our nation a proud one.'

'Your argument is sound, compassionate, and I value your moral ideals. Therefore, Rebecca, I concur.' He then turned to Elizabeth, who had just joined them, and said, 'Elizabeth, fish tonight, please.'

A few moments later, he left for work, and Rebecca knew that meant time for school. She glanced at her mum who was grinning and shaking her head. She smiled, 'I stepped in there a bit, Mum, sorry,' and raised her eyebrows.

While waiting for her mum to get the car from the garage, Tom was playing kick-ups and making so much noise he was starting to annoy Rebecca. Just as she was about to say something, her mum appeared in the car. Not a moment too soon either as Tommy had just turned to her, gesturing his football towards her legs. Rebecca waved her fist, and as she climbed in the front seat, mumbled loud enough for Tommy to hear, 'hmm, I think I will tell Roxy to watch out for Tommy's football.' She then turned to him and grinned. As they drove down the lane, Rebecca sat staring out of the window then turned to speak at the same time her mum started speaking.

'Bex.'

'Mum.'

'You go first, honey.'

Rebecca spoke quietly, hoping twit-face wouldn't hear. 'I am so pleased we are having a fish supper.' She then said loudly, 'can't wait to tell my friends about Tom and the table.'

Tom looked up and pushed Rebecca's seat. 'Mummm, tell her.'

'Rebecca, zip it.' Moments later, she pulled the car up outside the school gates and pointed to the clock. 'Have a nice day, Tom. Rebecca, be as good as you can be. No bitching, the pair of you.'

Rebecca kissed her mum on the cheek, and said, 'Mum, I hope you have a nice day.' She then banged on the car window and waved Tom - whose head was buried in his games console - out of the car. 'Come on, we need to hurry, or we will be late.'

Tom glanced up and looked surprised. 'Well, let's hit the road, 'coz I don't wanna be late, I got footy first lesson. See ya, Mumsy.'

'Bye, Mother, I love you.'

'Bye, be good guys and don't argue. I love you two,' her mum said, holding her hand out for Tommy's console.

'But, Mum.'

'Tommy, just hand it over.'

That evening at supper, Elizabeth hesitated for a moment before placing the serving dishes down. 'James, I got some lovely fresh line-caught bass, and it is local too. I thought it would go nicely with some green beans and potatoes.'

James shook his head. 'Line caught, is that right, Elizabeth.'

Rebecca could see signs of pressure in her mum's eyes and decided to change the subject. 'Dad, did you have any luck with the key?'

He handed the key to Rebecca. 'Yes, actually my colleague was rather enthusiastic about it. He asked if he could add it to his collection. He suggested that the design on the key handle dates from around eighteen-fifty, and was specific to this area. He also said that it was very rare, and it could be worth a considerable amount of money, to the right collector, adding that it was made by just one local locksmith. He added that because of its robust nature, it would be reasonable to assume it was for a large cattle barn or perhaps a substantial outbuilding.'

Rebecca took the key and said, 'thanks, Dad. I would truly like to keep it for myself. Hey, if it is for an outbuilding, maybe it fits the summerhouse. I never considered that,' she mumbled, grinning like the cat with the cream. She twiddled the key back and forth, inwardly smiling knowing it was half-term next week. Now deep in thought, the sound of her father's voice startled her.

In his usual straightforward manner, although with a surprisingly gentle tone, he said, 'Rebecca, I am surmising by summerhouse, you are referring to the old outbuilding down by the lake. No one has been near that for many a year and it is in an awful state of repair. I appreciate how intrigued you are, but please wait until we have had a survey before trying to enter. It is mostly wood and therefore, may have rotted and become extremely dangerous.'

'Dad, thanks for finding out about the key for me. I did mean the old building by the lake, but you're right about getting it checked over first.' Rebecca said, nodding in agreement, thinking something completely different.

Her mum nodded. 'I can see you thinking, Rebecca. Your father is right about the summerhouse. It is far too dangerous to go anywhere near it, as eager as you may well be.'

Rebecca smiled and then let slip, 'maybe I will try the key; no harm in that is there?' Instantly regretting what she'd just said.

Her father shook his head and stated, 'Rebecca, don't test my patience.'

She nodded to her father and then glanced at her mum, who had the same look on her face. She smiled and nodded agreeably, 'I know you are both right, and I will just have to wait. Any ideas when we might get a survey, Dad?'

'There are significantly more important issues to deal with inside the house. I will ask the surveyor to give it a once over. However, that won't be for a month, at the earliest.'

Rebecca nodded the way she does to her math's teacher but was thinking *I am not waiting a month.* After supper, she went to help her mum in the kitchen.

Her mum smiled, handed her the tea towel, and said, 'I know what you are thinking, Rebecca. Your father is right though; it is very dangerous. Wait until tomorrow when he is at work and just try the door, but do not go inside. In fact, I will come with you, is that a deal?'

'That's cool, Mum; I thought you were adamant the way you looked at me during supper.'

'Well, I gave it some thought, and...'

'Being on school holidays and not being able to try the key would have driven me mad.' She narrowed her eyes. 'Tell me, Mum, what happens if I try the door, and it opens, and then what? If I can't go inside and have a look around, what am I going to do with myself for the rest of the time?'

'Bex, don't push your luck. I am sure you will find something to do, as you always do. Why don't you invite Roxy over one day? No, honey, I am sorry. As I said, I will come with you to try the door, and I mean only the door. Anyways, your father is having a rowing boat delivered tomorrow so we can go for a row on the lake. I am sure that will be fun.'

'Oh okay, Mum, I'm not sure rowing is my idea of fun, though. Incidentally, I asked Roxy, but they are going back to London to visit their family.' Rebecca smiled and continued to help clear away the dishes. 'I am still telling Ruth and Amanda about you know what.' She said and grinned.

'Bex, you dare, and I really will wash your mouth out with soap.'

Rebecca couldn't believe her bad luck when her mum twisted her ankle the following morning. After soaking it, Elizabeth decided she'd best put off both the boat delivery and with it went any hopes Rebecca had of trying the key. The day dragged for Rebecca as she pottered around in her room, sat on the balcony, and wandered around the garden. No matter what she tried, the summerhouse kept nagging at her thoughts. For some reason, she knew she had to try the key and get inside for a look. She had a strange sensation, and it wasn't just to find out if the key fitted. No, it felt like this was something more.

It was now Thursday, and Rebecca was once again sitting down near the summerhouse. She glanced across the water as a gentle breeze caressed her cheeks and carried that familiar sweet smell of pine from the forest on the far side of the lake. Breathing deep, she turned back to the summerhouse, and whispered, 'I will open your doors soon enough.'

By Friday, her mum seemed to be over the worst of her twisted ankle and was moving around much easier. Noticing this, Rebecca asked if they could try the key today or at the least on Monday, knowing her dad would be at home all weekend. After her mum had agreed to Monday, Rebecca headed off for a walk down to the lake. She meandered around for ages wondering how she was going to wait until Monday. A couple of times, she glanced back up to the main house and thought about trying the key in secret, but she'd promised her mum and knew she had to wait for Monday.

Chapter 5 - The Locked Door

The weekend dragged by and to compound Rebecca's frustration further, her mum started limping again on Sunday. When Monday did decide to turn up, it was to the sound of a particularly loud dawn chorus. She leaned over in bed, and bleary-eyed peered at her clock. Yawning, she mumbled, 'three hours 'til dad leaves for work. She laid there for a couple of minutes with her legs dangling over the side of the bed and then decided to get up. Making her way to the balcony window, she peered out, and it was just light enough to see a heavy frost, which she found odd, as it had been so warm the day before. It had taken her ages to get off to sleep the previous night and feeling heavy-eyed, she got back in bed and pulled the covers over her head. Although, she laid there with her eyes shut her mind was now going in circles. She yanked the covers back and stared at the ceiling for a few minutes. This time, she decided to get up and stay up. After a shower, she put on some warm clothes and peered at the clock again. 'Still only seven,' she mumbled, grabbing her pencil and pad on her way out onto the balcony.

The spring sun was now up behind the house, casting long dusty shadows down towards the lake and watching them creep towards her, energised her with thoughts of warmer days ahead. She sat there for ages with her pencil in hand but felt uninspired to draw anything. Deciding to sketch the key, she went inside to fetch it, and as she did, her mum walked in.

'Good Morning, Rebecca, did I make you jump?' She said, gently squeezing her shoulder. 'You were up early; I heard you opening and closing the balcony door a couple of times. Maybe we should try some oil on the lock. Come and have some breakfast, your father has already gone to work, and he took Tom with him.' She then offered half a grin and raised her eyebrows. 'Evidently, he is getting Tommy into the work environment. I reminded him that Tom's eleven. Still, the good news, we have the day to ourselves. By the way, they delivered the boat this morning before your father went to work, hence why he was up at silly o'clock and that's probably what woke you up. Anyways, Amanda and Ruth are coming over tomorrow, and I thought it might be fun if we all had a go on the boat.' Her mum then paused for a second and started grinning. 'You dare tell them about our chat.'

Rebecca winked. 'As if I would, Mother.' She followed her mum downstairs but couldn't resist mocking her on the way. 'Hey, Amanda, Ruth, guess what Mum said, she said...'

Turning, her mum waved her fist. 'Brat.'

'Mum, honestly, I am a lot of things... Anyway, if I am a brat, who is to blame?'

'Shush, child.' She paused on the stairs. 'It's funny; I kind of want to tell them myself.'

'Tell them, if you don't, I know someone who might. By the way, Mum, your ankle seems better.' Rebecca followed her mum into the kitchen, but her mind had once again become consumed by the key. Mulling over the significance between the key in the painting and the one in her hand, she jumped, feeling her mum squeeze her arm.

'Rebecca, am I talking to myself?'

'Sorry, Mum, I was miles away.'

'I said that before we try the key, we could have a look at the boat and maybe give it a go. I know you said it is not your idea of fun, but I would like to have a practice. Then maybe I won't look stupid tomorrow.'

Not feeling hungry and pushing her favourite scrambled eggs and salmon around her plate, she noticed her mum staring. 'Please, can we try the key, Mum, and have a go in the boat after? Pretty please. Incidentally, you never look stupid.'

Her mum shook her head slightly. 'Oh okay, if we must. Now stop pushing your food around your plate, sit back, and eat your breakfast; we will go soon enough.' She shook her head again. 'I so knew when I mentioned the key, I would lose your attention.'

'Sorry, Mother, I just feel like I have a piece of the puzzle that, well, you know.'

Her mum kind of nodded, but at the same time shook her head, then smiled, and sipped her coffee.

Rebecca sniffed the air. 'Mum, why can I smell alcohol?'

Averting her eyes, she glanced at her coffee. 'Put a nip of scotch in my coffee to keep *Jack Frost* at bay. Have you seen how cold it is out there?' She shook her head. 'You're not buying that, are you? Well, how about medicinal purposes then, for my ankle and all?'

Deciding to say nothing, she finished her breakfast and started tidying up. She put away the last piece of cutlery and glanced at the clock. 'Mum, soon enough is here, in fact, it's ten past going by the new clock.'

'Okay, Miss Excited, come on, let's go see if we can find out where this key belongs. I wonder, sometimes you act as if you are twenty, the next minute you're like a little girl at Christmas.' Her mum nodded and smiled. 'It is lovely though, I adore the way you've held onto your youthful innocence, and I hope you never lose that. You will always be happy if you stay the way you are. I remember my dear old Nan saying to me, "If you want to stay happy, first you need to become a woman, and then somehow find your way back to being a little girl again." Back in those days, I thought, hey, why not just stay as a girl. Then I got married and...'

Rebecca decided this might be an opportunity to mention her mums increased drinking. 'Yeah, and the little girl hides behind a drink sometimes. Sorry, Mum, but it's true.'

'Rebecca, now is not the right time; I know how you feel.' Her mum looked away briefly. 'I have cut down, and that's a promise. Now come on; get your coat on.'

She could see her mum wasn't at all happy and knew it was best left alone. *Besides*, she thought, *I made my point.* She grabbed her coat and was outside before her mum had even put her boots on. Trying to lighten the mood, she stood, swinging the front door, tapping her fingers.

'I know you're in a hurry, Rebecca, but swinging the door won't make me go any faster.'

As they arrived at the water's edge the sweet smell of pine filled her nostrils. 'I do sometimes miss the old house, Mum, but that smell from the forest certainly makes up for it.'

'Yeah, Honey, I miss it too, but there are so many nice aspects to living here, the fab house, the view, the smell, and of course, the secret key, ha. On the subject of the smell, I thought if you are up for it, maybe we could row over to the pine forest. I rather like pine trees as they remind me of Christmas.' Her mum then lifted her nose and took a deep breath.

'I must say, Mum, I think rowing all that way might be a bit too far for our first trip. And to be honest, although I love the smell, the forest looks so dark, well it does from here, and there's something a little ominous about it too. It looks like the sort of place you would expect bears to live.'

'Honey, don't be silly; there are no bears over there.'

Rebecca shook her head. 'None that we know about, Mum, none that we know about, there're no fairies, or a Loch Ness Monster either.' She then raised her eyebrows and grinned. 'And I suppose a police box can't travel through time?'

'Is that right, none that we know about?' She smiled and appeared rather intrigued. 'Well, maybe you can tell me about the bears, hey, and more about the fairies while we're at it, and the pixies that hid your pencil. We have got some catching up to do; that's for sure. As for the woods being too far, I might be an Olympic standard rower for all you know. I'm not though. Oh, and don't tell me that there might be a monster lurking in the depths of the lake. By the way, I thought you disliked the *Doctor Who* shows?'

Rebecca squeezed her mum's hand while thinking, *Monsters in the lake. I wonder.*

Standing in front of the wooden jetty, Rebecca paused. To her right, the path was gravel and headed along the lake's edge before disappearing behind some tall Silver Birch. To the left, the path was made of stone slabs edged by the remnants of a wooden fence and headed in the direction of the summerhouse. Although curiosity often beckoned her to the right, trying the key was far too important, and as always, she decided to save that adventure for another day. Holding her hand out to her mum, she called, 'Careful, Mum, it's a bit overgrown, and one or two of these slabs are a little loose. Are you staying there?'

'I'm coming.'

Rebecca smiled and with her hand on her hip, chuckled, 'Today would be nice.' As her mother joined her, Rebecca took her by the hand, trying to avoid the remains of last year's brambles, and they soon arrived by the summerhouse. With her eyes focused on a large keyhole, Rebecca stepped straight onto a wooden veranda. She pulled the key from her pocket and was just about to try it when her mum called out.

'Hold on; I'm not too sure about this, Bex, it looks a bit the worse for wear. As for this wooden porch floor, well, Amanda would probably get her heels stuck.' She glanced around, clearly undecided, and then let out a gentle sigh. 'Okay, as you've already tested the floor, I guess we might as well try the key. But that's all.'

Feeling a little hesitant, Rebecca paused by the front door. 'Hang on a mo, Mum; I'm feeling an odd vibe. Not sure that's the right word, can't really explain it, hmm.'

'Vibe, Bex?'

'Yeah, Mum, you know what I mean, the mood of the place, it's a little amiss. I can't find the right word.'

'Well, it looks lovely, old and rundown, but still lovely.'

'Yeah, very lovely, but I am picking up something very peculiar here, something I can't quite put my finger on.' Rebecca stood there for a moment longer staring at the door unsure what she was waiting for. 'Hey, key, is this where you belong?' In the back of her thoughts was a nagging idea that something had happened in the past. 'Key, what secrets are you hiding?'

'Rebecca, what are you like, talking to a key? You don't even know if it fits yet.'

She glanced towards her mum and grinned. 'I am going to try the key in a minute, and it will fit; I just know it will. Even so, I first need to get my head around the strange sensation I keep getting. Oddly, it's a mixture of good and bad. Hmmm.'

'Oh, you know it will fit, do you?' her mum said and raised her eyebrows. 'Would you like me to try the key, Rebecca?'

Rebecca clenched the key tight, aware her mum was eager to get on with it. 'No, honest, Mum, it is fine.' She took a deep breath, pushed the key into the slot, and just as she'd reckoned, it fitted perfectly. She turned to her mother. 'See, I told you.' She then took another deep breath and wriggled it back and forth. After a few attempts, she stepped back and groaned, 'it fits okay, but it's not turning all the way even though I know it is right.'

Her mum took hold of the key and twisted it back and forth, grimacing as it made a horrid rusty sound in the process. She banged her hand a couple of times just below the keyhole, reinserted the key, and twisted it again. After a few seconds, there was a clunking sound. Turning, she stared at Rebecca for a moment, and then said, 'How odd, I've come over all shivery, and I'm not entirely sure why. It is either what you said that spooked me, or I'm getting the same vibe as you.'

'Mum, I've always known I get my sensitive insight from you.' Rebecca then stepped up to the door, twisted the brass handle, and pulled. After a few seconds, it creaked and moved a little. She glanced at her mum, and although a little apprehensive, her eagerness took over. Putting her foot against the side rail, she grasped the handle with both hands, pulling with all her strength. This time the door groaned, and then opened fully, making her step back as a whoosh of warm, odd smelling air, billowed out. She shuddered, 'Bloody hell, Mum, that was a bit unexpected. Oddly, it's not at all creepy, although it should've been. In fact, it was the complete opposite.'

'Don't swear, Rebecca, although, I must say it was bloody, err something or other. I mean that whoosh of air and the smell too.' She shivered, 'I know what you mean, not in any way menacing. It seemed to come from inside, well it definitely came from inside, but it was so warm, how can that be?'

'Strange, Mum, strange,' Rebecca said, turning back and peering into the darkness. As her eyes adjusted, she could see a door either side of the hallway, and could just make out a small door at the end of the corridor. She hesitated for a moment, took a deep breath, and stepped inside.

Her mum grabbed her arm. 'No, Rebecca, it is too dangerous. We must wait, at least until your father has had it surveyed.'

'Yeah, Mum, but what about all the secrets it's holding on to. If we don't find them now, we may lose them forever, especially if some big burly surveyor goes waltzing in. Then who knows, they may be gone for good. Anyway, why are there no stairs?'

Clearly puzzled, her mum shook her head, and asked, 'what secrets, Rebecca, and what stairs?'

'Well, Mum, you said you felt something too, an odd feeling, well that's the secrets it's holding onto, waiting for the right person to come along and uncover them. That isn't going to be a surveyor, is it? As for the staircase, Mum, there is an upstairs, so how do you think we get up there? Don't suppose there's a lift, do you?'

'Just because you can't see the stairs doesn't mean there isn't any, Rebecca?'

'Well, you normally expect to find stairs in the hallway, and as you can see,' she said, inviting her mum to have a look, 'there are no stairs.'

'Hmmm,' her mum said, standing back and looking up to the windows on the first floor. 'Bit dark and gloomy up there, especially the way those old grey nets just hang there. I am not so sure I would want to go up anyways.'

'I am sure it's safe, moreover, with no stairs, we won't be going up anyway. Besides, in the old days, they used much stronger materials than they do now. We did something at school on this.' She thumped her hand on the door and continued. 'Look at this door; this is oak. In fact, all the wood, including the floors are oak and oak lasts forever.' Rebecca produced a small red penknife from her pocket, the one normally used for sharpening her pencils. She opened it up and dropped it point down on the floor. It bounced. She picked it up and did the same again. After a couple of goes, she bent down and tried to dig it into the wood. 'See, Mum, rock solid. So as funny as Amanda becoming stuck might be, it just won't happen. Shame though, that might have been fun. In all seriousness, it is fine, Mum, let's have a quick look inside, hey?'

'Well it may appear safe, Rebecca, but I don't think it is safe enough. Come on; let's have a go on the boat.' Her mum hesitated for a moment, and then added, 'I must admit...' She narrowed her eyes a little. 'So, remind me where you found this key again.'

Rebecca pointed. 'Just up there in the woods, I will take you for a look later, if you wish. It was by an old fallen tree, an oak tree, I might add, which hasn't rotted, unlike the fallen pines.'

'Yeah, that will be nice. I was wondering why the summerhouse has stayed empty for all these years unless this was the only key. Still, that does not make any sense because they could have broken in, or got a locksmith, or something. Oh, I am even more curious now, and we know what happened to the cat. And stop going on about the oak, I get it.'

'Dad said that the last time this was used was during the Second World War. Maybe the locksmiths were busy elsewhere. And without a key, you would struggle to break through that front door. It's made of oak.' Rebecca said and banged her hand again on the wood.

'Yes, yes, I get the oak thing. But surely they could have gone through one of the windows?'

'I don't know, Mum, you would think they had more than one key. It needs some investigation.'

'It's like a big puzzle, with lots of bits missing.'

'Yeah exactly, Mum. Also, no one has lived in the main house for years. Then Dad's pal saying they only made this key in the eighteen-fifties. I mean, what's that all about? Come on, let us have a quick look; maybe we will find some answers inside; it won't do any harm, will it? Anyway, you can look after me.'

'Oh, Bex, I am not sure that's a good idea. I understand your need to get in and have a look, and I must say I'd like to have a look too, but...' She shook her head and gave Rebecca one of those looks.

Rebecca clenched her lips together. She was sure her mum wouldn't move on this but wasn't going to give up easily. 'Oh, Mum...'

'Let's see if we can establish what happened first. There must be some records, somewhere, maybe on the Internet. You're a bit of a whiz on there.' She shook her head and continued, 'Look, let us go and have a play with the boat, and that will allow me some time to think about everything.'

'Mum, I'm serious about what I said; we don't want any old starchy surveyor charging around in here. We might never find out what happened.'

'Yes, Honey, I know.' Her mum stood there with her hand on her hip, as if she was waiting for Rebecca. She then turned and started heading for the jetty. 'When your father says a month, it will probably end up being six, so there is no rush. Now for once, do as I ask, please.'

Rebecca batted her eyes and deliberately walked a few steps behind. As she was making her way back to the jetty, she was somewhat surprised to see mist hovering by a huge willow just along the shore, especially with the sun high in the sky. She was about to mention this to her mum when she saw something moving close to the tree. Stopping in her tracks, and pointing towards the tree, she called out. 'Mum, did you see something moving out there?'

'What do you mean, Rebecca, something, and where exactly?'

'I am sure I saw something moving over by the willow,' she said, pointing. 'I don't know, err, it looked like a...'

'Looked like what, Honey?'

'I don't know, Mum, just thought I spotted something moving.' Rebecca was as certain as she could be about what she'd seen, but it sounded absurd to her, so heaven knows how her mum would react. She hesitated for a moment. 'Well as daft as it sounds, I thought a woman was standing up in a boat, right next to the willow, but it was hard to see because of the mist.' She shook her head, doubting her own words.

Her mum frowned, peered across the water, and said, 'I can't see anything other than mist, and that's drifting away.'

'No, I can't see anything now, but for a second, I am sure I saw something.' She then shivered and took a deep breath. 'What I want to know is why there is a mist at this time of day. Whatever I thought I spotted, one thing I do know, you never see any mist at this time of the day.'

'Maybe it was just the mist swirling up,' her mum said, sounding a little unsure. 'I have learnt never to doubt you, Rebecca, but...' Still peering across the lake, she asked, 'so why don't you see mist at this time of the day?'

'Well, mist forms after a cool night, the water temperature drops, boring. In essence, it's how clouds form, cold air on the warm water.'

'Oh right, hmm.'

Feeling perplexed, Rebecca stared across the water. She then heard her mum calling and noticed she was standing halfway along the jetty. 'Wait for me, Mum.'

'Actually, Bex, just thinking about it, the guys who delivered the boat commented on this jetty. One of them said something about it being made from oak and lasting forever, so perhaps.' She shook her head and ushered Rebecca towards the boat.

Before Rebecca had a chance to help, her mum was halfway down the steps 'Mum, let me help you.'

Her mum turned placed one foot on the boat and screamed as it rocked from side to side and started easing away from the jetty.

Reacting to this, Rebecca held out her hand to her mum. 'Here, Mum, hold my hand.'

'I am okay, just finding my sea legs.' Easing the boat back towards her with her leg, she bellowed, 'This is going to be madness tomorrow with Amanda and Ruth.'

'I was just thinking that we're going to have a laugh, although, I'm not too sure how far we'll get without sinking.' She then glanced again towards the willow, 'see, Mum, the mist has gone completely. What is that all about?'

With both of them settled into their seats, Rebecca untied the boat, allowing it to drift a little. She then lowered her oar and started to paddle. 'Okay, Mum, we are just going in circles, unless of course, you decide to use that thing in your hand, it's called an oar, by the way.'

'Ha-ha, very funny,' she said and giggled again. 'Well, I still fancy the pine forest, or should I say the *bear wood*, but on reflection, it may be a little too far right now. Let's have a splash about and see how we get on. Then perhaps we can decide if we are up for rowing any sort of distance tomorrow.'

'Yeah, I think you're right, Mum, considering how difficult it was just climbing into the boat.' Rebecca flicked her head towards the jetty and said, 'Hmm. We've got to get back to the jetty at some point, and then try to get out.'

'Bex, perhaps we should definitely save the forest for tomorrow when the girls arrive. That way, we could take a picnic and make a day of it. Of course, that's if we can go more than a few yards without capsizing,' she said and laughed.

'That's a great idea, Mum; a picnic will be fun. Hope it is nice tomorrow. Do you know what the forecast is?'

'Well, how accurate it is, heaven only knows, but the guy on the TV said that it would be sunny with a light wind, which is kind of what your father's barometer indicated.'

As they continued to row around, Rebecca pointed out that although they were doing a lot of splashing, they weren't going anywhere, other than in ever-increasing circles. She kept suggesting they should at least try to row at the same time, but in spite of her mum agreeing, she never really got the hang of it. If she had any doubts, Rebecca knew for sure that the forest was out of the question for some time yet. Her mum was now spending more time holding her stomach with laughter, and when she did try rowing seriously, it always resulted in an almighty splash. With water dripping from her hair, Rebecca suggested it was probably time to head back.

After they'd climbed out, Rebecca asked if they could go back to the summerhouse. She grinned hopefully, but recognised that look and knew what answer was coming.

'Not today, Honey, I don't think it is safe enough. Besides, I am not ready to go inside yet. Hey, at least you know where the key belongs and that will have to do for now. Although, I have to admit that it does hold a certain intrigue, and I buy into what you're saying, but... Look, let me think about it, Bex. We can chat with the girls tomorrow, see what they think.' Her mum then glanced at the floor. 'I know I keep fobbing you off, and I am not sure what I am so worried about, but I am, and there you have it. Sorry, I must follow my mother's intuition.'

Rebecca accepted her mum's point, as frustrating as it was and reluctantly followed her up to the house. Although they were laughing about their feeble attempts at rowing, Rebecca's mind kept returning to the mist, and she was certain it was some kind of sign. As they entered the house, Rebecca turned to her mother and raised her eyes. 'Dad is home early,' she said, as she greeted the two girls in the paintings, 'Afternoon ladies.' She then heard her dad's voice.

'Who are you talking to, Rebecca?' he said in that tone, now standing by the kitchen door.

Rebecca couldn't stop herself responding with an element of contempt. 'Actually, I was saying hello to the ladies in the paintings, Dad.'

'Silly girl,' he said, and then turned to Elizabeth. 'So, where have you two been?'

With water still dripping from her hair, Elizabeth glanced at Rebecca from the corner of her eye. 'Oh, just down to try the key and have a go in the boat.'

He huffed only the way he can. 'I told you not to go near the summerhouse.' Without waiting for a response, he stated, 'I hope you wore life jackets.'

'We only tried the key in the door, and err, we didn't go inside. Hmm, I didn't know we had any life jackets, James,' she said, her tone edgy.

'What would happen if you capsized? Although by the look of you both it would seem you may have.' He then shook his head, and half grinned, which surprised Rebecca. 'Leave the summerhouse well alone until we have had a survey. As things stand, it is a long way down the priority list.'

'But James...' Her mum said, with an unusual amount of conviction.

'Elizabeth, I suggest you leave it now and go dry off and then prepare the evening meal. Thomas and I are hungry. Remember we have been at work all day, unlike some people.'

With her eyes wide, she said, 'James, you were the one who suggested I gave up work, so you can hardly level that one at me.' She then brushed past him and headed for the kitchen, huffing as she went.

Without a word, James watched her walk away. For the first time, Rebecca could see her dad was lost for words. She followed her mother along the hallway, shocked by her response and bemused by the look on her father's face.

As they entered the kitchen, her mum slumped down at the table. 'He can be so condescending sometimes. The way he said no, well it just makes me want to go inside the summerhouse more. And the way he spoke to me about the life jackets, what life jackets...' She turned her lip up and sneered, clearly spoiling for a fight. 'Work, huh... Well, I tell you...' she then got up and opened the cupboard so forcefully it's a wonder she didn't pull the door off its hinges.

Sitting with her mouth slightly open, Rebecca watched her mother slam the pots down so hard she half expected her dad to come in to investigate all the commotion. She'd never seen her mum like this, ever, and just had to say something. 'Mum, I am so glad you had that reaction. I get tired of biting my lip all the time. One day I know I will say something to him, and he won't like it. His tone and the way he bangs his eyelids, infuriates me. I know he grinned, but even so, he's still...'

'Rebecca, shush, that is your father you are talking about. It's okay for me to have a moan, even though I shouldn't, but...' She shook her head, and continued, 'and I really shouldn't challenge him in front of you. That makes me as bad as him, not that he is...'

Aware of her mum's tension and unsure of what to say, Rebecca decided to change tack. 'Mum, after supper, let's have a look on the computer, and see if we can find anything about this house.'

'Oh, okay,' she said and nodded with a willing look on her face.

After they'd cleared away from supper, they headed up to Rebecca's room.

Sitting with her fingers hovering over the keyboard, Rebecca asked, 'How do you spell the name of this house again?'

'I can't remember. Hang on a mo; I've it written down somewhere.' She then fumbled through her bag and handed Rebecca a small piece of paper.

Rebecca typed the name into the search engine. After a few minutes trawling through the results, the only thing she found was a very basic translation from chère à Votre Maison to deer to your home. She peered at the screen mulling ideas over in her head. After a few seconds, she tried a couple of variations, but still nothing of consequence. 'Strange, there's nothing other than this translation, and I am not sure if it's referring to a sweetheart dear, or an actual deer with antlers and such, huh. Perhaps we should go to the local council offices or something like that. Hey, at least we sort of know what it means in English, well...'

Appearing somewhat embarrassed, her mum frowned before speaking. 'Whoops, I forgot to tell you, Ruth told me the translation some time back, but it is only seeing it now, well... Thinking about it now, I am sure she said she found out from some guy who is a bit of a history geek. Hey, perhaps he can help a little more, although I am sure she would have asked. Look, to be honest, we'd only just moved in, and I didn't take much notice. I will speak to her tomorrow.'

The following morning James had left for work early and again taken Tom with him. As it was a surprisingly warm morning, Rebecca and her mum decided to have breakfast outside. It was a little before nine when they heard a car pull up in the drive.

Elizabeth jumped up, appearing a little surprised. 'Who's that, it's a bit early for Ruth and Amanda?'

'What time did they say they were coming over, Mum?'

'Didn't, just said they would be early, but I never thought this early.'

The way the doorbell started chiming several times, they knew this could only be Ruth and Amanda. Heading for the door, Elizabeth shouted, 'Amanda, take your bloody finger off the bell.'

Bright and breezy Ruth walked straight in and said, 'Oh take your time, Liz, and coffee would be nice.'

'You're early, girls.'

'Yep, thought we would join you for breakfast,' Amanda said, still pressing the doorbell.

Elizabeth pointed at the doorbell, glared at Amanda with a half grin. She shook her head and then greeted each with a kiss on the cheek. 'Join us out the back; we've just started.'

'It looks like we are in for another lovely day, girls. By the way, one sugar please.'

'Ruth, give me a chance. I think you've got a caffeine addiction,' she said and turned to Amanda, 'would you also like a coffee, Amanda?'

Ruth grinned. 'Well, Amanda wanted to stop at some coffee place on the way, but I said you're cheaper.' She then giggled in her lady-like way.

'So, like that is it, cheap, am I?' Elizabeth sniggered.

Rebecca chipped in, 'anywhere is cheaper than that coffee shop, if you're talking about the one just off the main road.'

Nodding, Amanda said, 'Yeah you're right, Bex. Hey, on that subject, look at me, now this is cheap, forty-ish, maybe, high heels, full face of makeup, just for breakfast at silly o'clock.'

'Yeah, but you look fab, Amanda,' Liz said, 'I wish I could be asked to get dolled up at this time of the day.'

Having discussed yesterday's poor attempt at rowing, they still agreed that a picnic over by the pine forest would be a great idea. Rebecca suggested it might be a tad too far at this stage, but that was partly because her mind was on the summerhouse.

The girls sat around drinking coffee and nattering for the next couple of hours. As the sun rose a little higher, Ruth suggested they headed down to the jetty.

As they made their way down the path, Amanda linked arms with Rebecca and chatted about makeup.

Some way back from Rebecca and Amanda, Ruth was chatting to Elizabeth, 'I admire your daughter, Liz. She has a natural inner strength, blessed with enough wisdom for all of us. Life will be a breeze for her. I know she is only fifteen, but you could do a lot worse than take note of her feisty nature. I know she is away with the fairies

71

sometimes, literally.' She then paused. 'You trust me right; we are old friends, right? To be straight with you, Liz, if you do not get James to back-off a little, you are in danger of losing her for good. I could see her upping and going to Australia or something like that. As she gets older, she won't put up with his behaviour. You can see she gets angry now, right? What do you think she'll be like in a couple of years? Besides, James hasn't always been like this, so there is a way back.'

Elizabeth nodded. 'I know you're right, Ruth. The problem is that I don't know where to start with James.'

'I know it's none of my business, but if I can't tell you, who can? You need to make him aware of how his behaviour affects you, Rebecca and Tom.'

Elizabeth glanced at the floor. 'I know you're right. It is difficult though, and the biggest problem is that he frightens me. I feel silly saying that because he has never raised his voice, let alone lose his temper.'

'For Christ's sake, Liz, why are you frightened then?'

'I just don't know; I just am. Well, it's a bit like the Elephants in captivity. I saw a documentary on them, they are kept in place by a small stick and rope, one they could rip out easily, but they don't, and I guess...'

'Well, I mentioned Tom, he will end up a mirror image of his father, and the girlies nowadays don't put up with that, they will just kick him into touch.'

Elizabeth shook her head. 'I know you're right, Ruth.' She glanced at the floor as if she was mulling over what Ruth had said. She then looked up, wide-eyed, and growled. 'Yesterday, James told us not to go in the summerhouse, well, he's at work, so...'

'Liz, I can remember when you two were deeply in love. So, what happened, other than you losing your voice?'

Elizabeth slowed a little, looked up, and nodded at Ruth. 'I do know, Ruth, I really do, and I often think back to those days. Where did I lose my voice?' She then called out to Rebecca, pointed towards the summerhouse, and held her thumb up.

Rebecca turned to Amanda. 'Wonder what's gotten into her, she said she would think about going in the summerhouse, and by that, I thought she really meant no. You know how she can be.' Rebecca glanced back towards her mum and then led Amanda up to the summerhouse. Hearing her mother just behind her, she turned and pointed to the key still in the lock. 'Mum, I don't remember leaving the key in the lock, do you?'

Elizabeth looked at the key and put her hand to her chin. 'Err, umm, maybe.'

Rebecca shook her head and hesitated briefly before opening the door. Again, the same sweet-smelling air billowed out. Then from the corner of her eye, she noticed Amanda appearing a little startled. 'Are you okay, Amanda?' she asked.

'I'm not altogether sure, what was that rush of air?' She then lifted her nose and asked, 'and what's with the Christmas cake smell?'

Elizabeth answered, 'If I am honest, I find it all a little prickly if that's the right word. The same thing happened yesterday when we opened the door, just a whoosh of warm, odd smelling air.'

'It is not a rush or whoosh of air,' Rebecca said with verve, 'it's a whisper as if it is saying something. By the way, Amanda, you're right about it smelling like a Christmas cake. I think it truly smells of almonds, which is very... I remember reading that the smell of almonds in an old building is associated with...' In a flash, her thoughts returned to what she'd seen the day before and feeling a little uneasy, she glanced back towards the lake.

Ruth touched Rebecca on the arm. 'Honestly, Bex, you see everything in a different way from the rest of us, whisper indeed. Incidentally, it does smell of almonds. You said it's very, then stopped, and said it is associated with, and again stopped. Do we get a full sentence?' she asked and smiled.

'It's just fascinating, and err,' she hesitated unsure if she should mention the connection between the smell of almonds and spirits, what with Amanda already appearing uneasy. 'Not seeing it differently, just as it is, you grown-up people lose sight of what's really there.' She then sniffed the air. 'I think something's happened here, back in the past, maybe the summerhouse wants to show us something. Hey, perhaps it happened at Christmas. Interesting,' she said and chuckled, hiding her feelings of uneasiness. 'I know that might sound silly to you guys, but, well, you all felt that whisper of air when we opened the door, true?' With her thoughts now on the day before, she turned to her mum. 'Mum, maybe that woman in the boat yesterday, the whisper of air, and the smell from the summerhouse are all entwined.'

Amanda and Ruth both turned to Liz and said simultaneously, 'what woman, what boat?'

Elizabeth nodded. 'I am beginning to understand Rebecca's stories. Over the last few months, she has been telling me her tales, and I have been writing them down, and I've now started to see things her way, to some degree at least.' She then turned to Rebecca. 'But honestly, Rebecca, it was just the mist on the lake. Even you said you weren't sure you'd seen anything, let alone a woman.'

Ruth appearing a little uneasy, asked again, 'What woman, what boat?'

'Well, it was when Mum and I walked towards the jetty yesterday. I was sure I saw something on the lake over by the willow tree.

Although it was only a glimpse, it looked like a woman standing up in a boat. However, when I looked again, there was nothing.' Rebecca knew by Ruth's reaction that it might be a good time to change tack. She turned and peered inside the summerhouse. 'As Mum said, it was probably just mist. Come on let's go inside and have a nose.'

'And you tell me I change the subject, hmm.' Her mum then held her hand out. 'Be careful; it is a bit dark, Rebecca.'

'It is okay, Mum. I brought my torch, just in case we needed it.'

'What are you like, that certain I'd agree to go in, were you?'

'No, yeah, Mum, just hoping.' Flicking her torch on, she widened the beam, put one foot inside and pressed hard on the floor. 'The floor seems solid enough to me,' she said and banged her heel down. 'See, it is fine.' And in she marched.

After a couple of seconds, Elizabeth and Ruth followed Rebecca inside.

Amanda stepped back onto the grass, and said, 'you guys go in first, and I'll come in presently.'

'Amanda, are you okay there?'

'Yeah, Ruth, I am fine. I'd rather wait here for a while.'

Rebecca smiled to Amanda, turned, and headed straight for the small door at the end of the hallway. 'Come on guys, I'm guessing this door might just answer some of our questions, probably hiding the stairs, and all the secrets.'

Elizabeth glanced at Ruth and shook her head. 'Bex seems to think the house is holding a secret of some description. I know she fleetingly mentioned it outside, but she seems so adamant. It's hard to ignore her.'

Rebecca brushed away the cobwebs and muttered, 'Hello door, what are you hiding?'

Elizabeth turned to Ruth and shook her head. 'Rebecca likes talking to doors, anything that will listen really, including herself, a little too often if you ask me. In fact, she was talking to herself so loud in the hallway the other day I could hear her in the kitchen. She does make me smile.'

Rebecca gripped the doorknob and turned it a little. 'Nothing.' Then using all her strength, she tried again and still nothing, not even a creek. It seemed no matter how much force she used it wouldn't budge. She shrugged her shoulders and stood back. 'There is no lock, no movement, and look,' she said pointing at the door frame, 'even this is painted over, how very odd.'

'Let me try, Bex.' Her mum twisted and pulled the handle then pushed her foot against the door-rail, and pulled at the handle. She puffed loudly and banged it with her hand. Frowning, she turned to the others, 'stupid door.'

Ruth then tried and after a bit of huffing and puffing suggested it might just be for show and not a door at all.

Amanda, who had now joined them, frowned, and said, 'I'm not sure what you mean, Ruth, it looks like a door to me. She then made a tentative effort and shook her head, 'probably locked for a reason.'

With her hands on her hips and peering at the doorframe, Rebecca said, 'you can't even tell which way the thing opens. And, it can't be locked, because there's nowhere to put a key, which is very peculiar.' She turned and glanced up the hallway. 'Let's try the other doors,' she said, heading back towards the front door. 'I suspect this may have been Meredith's room, and the other room was probably for the bitch.'

Ruth held her hands up in a questioning motion.

Elizabeth took hold of Ruth's hand. 'Now that's another story. In the main house, you know those two large female portraits. Rebecca suspects one is a painting of the wife, Meredith, and the other one is the bit on the side. She has some crazy idea they all lived in the house together.' She shook her head. 'Interestingly, there's a table in the Meredith painting and on it is this key,' she uttered pointing towards the front door.

Amanda added, 'she suggested that the day you moved in.' She turned towards Rebecca, who was now pulling at the door handle to the left-hand room. 'But I didn't know about the key in the painting. No wonder Rebecca's imagination is running away with her and I can feel mine following suit,' she said and chuckled.

After a few turns, the door opened, and without any hesitation, Rebecca stepped into a large square room. To her left was a square bay window, shrouded with cobweb riddled net curtains, which muted the light. Peering, she could see a large tallboy standing in the far corner. 'It must be years since anyone's been in here.' As she spoke, her voice echoed a little. Wide-eyed, she glanced towards the others. 'What's with the spooky echo, this room is big, but not big enough to cause an echo, how very odd?'

Amanda moved to the window, and before anyone had a chance to stop her, she'd yanked at one of the curtains. It collapsed on the floor and masked the room in thick dust. Coughing, Amanda uttered, 'Well, at least we can see. Once the dust settles, that is.'

'Oh, don't worry about it, A, I am sure the dust will settle, eventually.' Grinning, Rebecca coughed once in the direction of Amanda and moved up close to the tallboy. She pulled at one of the cupboard doors, which opened easily, knelt, and peered in. Inside, right at the back, she could just make out something. Leaning forward, she stretched in and removed a hardback book covered in thick dust.

Ruth held her hand out. 'Oooh let me have a look. I am into old books, big time. Crumbs, this feels very fragile.' She then gently blew some dust away. 'Gosh, how wonderful.'

'What is it, Ruth?' Rebecca asked as she carefully removed three more books.

'Wow, it's a classic love story, Sense and Sensibility.' She carefully peered inside the front cover. 'And it's a first edition as well, wow.' She looked through the other books, and stated, 'Hang on a minute, this one's also Jane Austen. They all are; there's, Persuasion, Mansfield Park, and Emma.' She glanced up at the ceiling, as if she was thinking, and then continued. 'This is very interesting, especially after Rebecca suggesting this was the wife's room. Maybe she stole herself away in here and found solace in these stories.' She then shook her head and laughed. 'Listen to me, getting carried along, although it pieces together well, and is oh so intriguing.'

'That is exactly what I was thinking, Ruth. I would love to know how she felt, what she thought, and how she dealt with her situation.' She then returned her attention to the bureau and four small flat drawers. 'Oh, not going to let us see inside today.' She said, pulling at a tiny handle. After making a few more attempts, she shrugged her shoulders and headed for the other room. It was similar in size with the light also muted by dust-rotten curtains. Although the two rooms were mostly alike, Rebecca was sensing something different here. She couldn't put her finger on it, but something was making her feel uncomfortable. She was deep in thought when she heard an almighty crash. Amanda had not only pulled the curtains down, but the whole rail had come with it shrouding the room with thick rotten smelling dust. 'While I am waiting for the dust to settle,' she said, coughing and laughing simultaneously. 'I'm going to try the little door again.' After a few unsuccessful attempts, she went back to the second room only to find it empty. She then noticed everyone standing outside. Joining them, she reiterated, 'no staircase, Mum, anywhere.'

'Hey, that's a point; there must be some stairs, somewhere,' Ruth said pointing to the upstairs windows.

Rebecca nodded. 'Exactly my point Ruth, this building becomes stranger by the minute. I've gotta find out what's behind that door, even if it's just the inexplicably hidden stairs.'

Elizabeth shook her head once and waved her hand. 'Not on your own you won't, young lady. It may be that we have to get a specialist to fix the door first if it is indeed a door.'

'But Mum, if we do, well you know what I said about them spoiling it. You must admit it is very fascinating, what with the books, and then you have the key in the painting, the door that won't open, and the other room smelling so horrid. Do I need to go on? I agree with Ruth; the pieces are all adding together.'

'Well, that may be so. Nevertheless, I do not want you going in on your own. Now, let that be an end to the subject.'

The girls made their way back to the boat, with Rebecca walking behind muttering under her breath.

'Rebecca, hush now. Come and join us in the boat.'

'Sorry, Mum,' she said, climbing onto the boat.

With the boat rocking from side to side, Ruth giggled, 'And that's before we start rowing,'

No sooner they'd managed to get a few yards from the jetty the wind changed direction, creating a chop on the water. Although the waves added to the fun, after they'd spent half an hour going in circles, they all agreed they needed a lot more practice. After a few attempts, they docked the boat and clambered ashore. Before they made their way back to the main house, Ruth went and fetched the books, which she'd left on the veranda. Now back at the house, Ruth and Amanda had another coffee while discussing the books, agreeing that Ruth would take them and get an expert opinion.

When they'd gone, Rebecca turned to her mother. 'See, Mum, I told you no one would judge your rowing, any way you were easily the best. We did have fun, but I can't stop thinking about the summerhouse and that locked door. I am going to have another go on the computer, see if I can find anything out. There must be some history somewhere. Call me if you need some help with supper.'

'While you were getting changed this morning, Ruth said she'd checked on a historical database at the local council, and found no history, no records, nothing. It was suggested to her by some guy at one of the offices that the house might have had its name changed, or something along those lines. I guess if we are searching with the wrong name, then that would answer a lot. Evidently, someone else offered up that something might have happened, which resulted in a name change. He went on to say that the people who lived here could have been in a prominent position and may have intentionally lost the records.'

With her mouth opened, Rebecca asked, 'Something happened, did they say any more?'

'Now this is where it gets interesting. Some other person at the council said there was a lot of confusion caused by the whole affair on a couple of aspects. Firstly, they did not know that the council owned this house until your father entered into negotiations with them to buy it. By all accounts, a private legal firm was holding the deeds, which is perhaps why the council didn't know.'

'Crumbs, that makes it all the more strange, so what was the other thing, you said a couple of aspects?'

'So okay, secondly, the person said that it was all very curious as to why no records of the property existed anywhere, other than the title deed, which gave the ownership to the council. Although, they did go on to say that there was a fire at the old council offices just after the Second World War when most local records were lost.'

Rebecca nodded several times. 'It all just adds to it, Mum. Oh well, I am going to have a look at my computer, anyway. So, did anyone come up with a different name?'

'No, just the name we have. All a bit odd if you ask me.'

'Yeah, Mum, my point exactly,' she said and grinned. 'Right, I am going to have another search on the Internet, Mum.' She went to her room and tried every variation she could come up with to no avail. After a couple of fruitless hours, she gave up and returned downstairs to help her mother with supper.

Chapter 6 - The Sepia Photos

Rebecca couldn't get the summerhouse from her thoughts and not having the chance to get back for a couple of days was just making it worse. Every time she'd mentioned the summerhouse to her mum, it was met with an indifferent response. She had known for a while that her mum was a little uneasy about going back, especially after their last visit. So, with a new tack, she headed down for breakfast.

'Morning, Mum. I was thinking, as it's so nice out, shall we take a stroll down the lake?'

'Okay, Bex, it's a lovely day, so why not, and while we are there, you can show me where you found the key.'

A little surprised by her mum's upbeat tone, Rebecca hurried through her breakfast. 'Come on Mum,' she called standing by the front door.

'Hmmm, I wonder why you're so eager, as if I don't know, Missy. Of course, it has nothing to do with that building does it?' she said and chuckled.

Rebecca was feeling a little confused. For some reason, her mum's tone had changed today, and she seemed open to the idea of revisiting the summerhouse. Not sure what stance to take, she decided to talk about where she'd found the key and their rowing attempts, anything but that summerhouse. 'There's that smell of the pine again, Mum. It so reminds me of Christmas,' Rebecca said, as they got close to the lake.

'It makes me think we must get over to the *bear-wood* someday soon. I guess we could always take the easy option and drive over there.'

'With our current rowing skills, we risk capsizing, crashing into the islands and anything else along the way.' Rebecca giggled. 'But driving, Mum, that's a bit lightweight if you ask me. Anyway, the nearest road is some distance from the lake. It is quite a big forest, certainly appears so on the map that Ruth gave me. I would rather we took our chances rowing.' Rebecca took her mum's hand and said, 'Right, Mum, let me show you where I found the key.' On the way past the summerhouse, she couldn't help herself and stepped onto the veranda.

'Where do you think you're going, young lady?'

'I'm just having a little nose, Mum.'

Standing back a little, her mum said, 'Rebecca, hang on, I'm not sure I am ready for this. This place leaves me feeling uncomfortable. And besides, I thought we were going for a walk through the woods.' She narrowed her eyes, 'I don't understand it, but this place gives me the collywobbles. It was all I could do just to come down in this direction today, and I only agreed to that because I kept putting you off. I have tried to go through it in my head, but it leaves me feeling prickly, so you are going to have to bear with me and give me plenty of thinking time.'

Rebecca could see how uncomfortable her mum appeared. 'Mum, I think what you're feeling is the same as me. It makes me feel a little uneasy, to be honest, but I think it is just intrigue and excitement. I know this sounds silly, but do you remember how sick I used to get at Christmas, and you would say it was just excitement. Well, I think this is a similar emotion.' She took hold of her mum's hand, 'it is all the mystery of what happened here. When we open the door, something, or more likely, someone, whispers to us.'

'You keep saying that, Rebecca, what exactly does that mean?' Her mum said, still hovering half on the veranda. 'And like that's going to make me feel better, I think not!'

The second she'd mentioned whispers, she could see by her mum's eyes she shouldn't have said that. 'Mum, if I knew the answer, we wouldn't have to investigate it, would we? It is like the fairies and the pixies. You must keep your mind open as well as your eyes. I've told you all this before, and this is no different. Something happened here, maybe years ago, and it just needs unravelling. You need to look at it as an adventure.'

'Hmmm, well maybe,' she said, stepping onto the veranda.

That was all the encouragement Rebecca needed and not waiting for her mum to change her mind, she opened the door, and headed down the hallway. Sensing her mum wasn't with her, she turned, 'Come on, Mum,' she said, waving her in. Turning back to the little door, she tried everything she could think of, including thumping it a couple of times, not that she expected that to work. She looked at her mum and shrugged her shoulders. 'No keyhole, so it's not as if we need to find another key; it's just a door.'

'Come on, Bex, clearly it isn't going to open. If indeed it is a door, because it might just be for show,' she said and shrugged. 'Let's have another look at that old tallboy. There might be something we missed, a clue to the secrets perhaps.' Her mum smiled, raised her eyebrows, and laughed. 'Listen to me, the secrets, ha-ha.'

Rebecca nodded. 'That is it, Mum, a clue to the secrets, now you're thinking with an open mind.' She rather suspected her mum was playing along but was pleased she was, at last, giving the idea some thought, and importantly hadn't ushered her out, yet.

'Hey, Bex how about we try the two tiny square doors right at the bottom. They looked like the kind of place you would put a key,' she said and giggled.

84

Standing with one hand on her hip, she looked across the room and shook her head. 'How on earth did I miss those?' Without any hesitation, she went over, opened the left door, and probed her fingers around in the dust. 'Empty, apart from this dust,' she said brushing her hand. She turned her attention to the right-hand door. 'What's the deal with all the flipping locked doors in this place? Interesting this one has a keyhole, but no key. We might need something to force it open, maybe my penknife.'

'Or perhaps a key,' her mum said pointing to the top of the cupboard. Stretching on tiptoes, she scurried her hand around and produced a tiny silver key. 'I noticed the light catch it when we came in.' Before Rebecca could react; her mum had placed the key into the slot, turned it, and opened the door. 'Rebecca, look here.' She then took out a photo, shook some of the dust away, and examined it closely. 'Gosh, it looks like the lady in the painting.'

Leaning on her mum's shoulder, Rebecca said, 'You're right, it is Meredith.' She then took the photo and peered at the woman's face.

'Be careful; it looks very old and is probably delicate.'

Nodding, she wiped it carefully with her hanky. 'Look, she has those same sad eyes,' she said and felt a shudder of anticipation come over her.

'How weird, although she's smiling, she looks troubled.'

Carefully Rebecca probed inside the cupboard and produced another photo. 'This one's Meredith with a young girl, and a very small boy,' she said handing her mum the photo. While her mum looked, she took out the last one. 'Mum, this one is a man in a military uniform.'

'Look, Honey, there is some writing on the back, although it's very faded.'

'Let me have a look. When you're not wearing your glasses, everything looks faded to you.' She laughed and took the photo. After peering at the writing for a few seconds, she read, "*My one and only true love.*" She squinted. 'Then it says, *dear,* something, and right at the bottom, there's the word, *lost,* which is followed by what looks like a year, *eighteen-fifty something.* Flip, this is exciting,' she said, turning the photo, 'he is not the man in the painting on the stairs.' With her mind racing with ideas, she said, 'hey, maybe this was Meredith's first husband, and she lost him in the war or something. Perhaps he was the father of the two children. Then she may have married the man in the painting.' Rebecca could see her mum frowning. 'I know it's a wild guess, Mum. To be honest, I'm not altogether sure if they went in for second marriages in those days. Hey, maybe it was a marriage of convenience, just thinking aloud here.'

Looking somewhat bemused, her mum shook her head and asked, 'what did you mean by convenience?'

She placed her hand on her hip, thinking. 'Well, perhaps the man in the hallway took her as his wife and agreed to look after her and the children. Obviously, this would have happened after her first husband died at war, if...' She paused, realising how this must sound. 'Perhaps it was for money or the estate, or just convenient for him and her. And, then Millicent - the mistress - followed later, hmmm.'

'Honey, I don't know how your brain works. I have to say, your idea is, hmm, shall we say, fascinating, even though it sounds like you're making it up as you go.' Her mum shook her head. 'As remote as your idea is, I am now a little intrigued and would love to know more. It is a shame we can't find out anything about their history. Your theory would add weight to it all being hushed up.' She shook her head. 'See what you have done now, I am beginning to sound like you, next thing I'll be seeing fairies and such-like.'

'Blast, I want to know more.' Animated, Rebecca ran her eyes around the room hoping to see something they'd missed. 'Maybe we should try to get hold of some old newspapers; they may tell us something.'

'I forgot to mention that when Ruth rang this morning, she said that she had been to the council office again, looking for exactly that. Only you suggesting it reminded me,' she said and flicked her eyebrows. 'Here's the thing, she found nothing relating to the period we want. Although someone suggested, there may not have been a local paper in this area as our house was the only building for miles. The earliest paper she could find was from around the Second World War. Interestingly, the house was an evacuation home during that time, but that was pretty much it. Oh, she did add that it said, "The house, which is now known as; *chère à Votre Maison.*" Now that was dated nineteen forty-three, so presumably, it was something different before. The only way she could find anything was to use the name of the road running by our house. I don't know why we didn't think of that before. Hey, that's why Ruth is a lawyer, smart.'

'This is all very bizarre.' Rebecca stared at the photos for a few seconds and then turned to her mum. 'I feel like I need to speak to her somehow, Mum. I know it's not going to happen, but...' The way her mum shook her head slightly and raised her eyebrows, Rebecca knew it was time to move on, and so suggested a walk in the forest. Inwardly, she was hoping to unearth something near where she found the key.

As they were leaving the summerhouse, her mum glanced up at the sky. 'Rebecca, it looks and feels like it might rain; that's a shame.'

'Yeah, earlier on I noticed that the crocuses had closed their eyes.'

'Closed their eyes?'

'Yeah, Mum, when it becomes cloudy, their petals close. They are the flowers of the pixies, where their babies' play when they are growing up. Although, you'll rarely see them because they use the crocus leaves as camouflage.'

'Rarely see them, does that mean you have seen them?'

'Well, sort of for a split second, you can sense them hiding, maybe watching you. However, when you turn, they freeze, hidden behind the nearest crocus. You can definitely sense they are there though. It's as if they are playing with you, quite amusing really, but nonetheless, exasperating. Do you know when you are sitting in a traffic jam and can feel someone looking at you? Then the second you turn, they look away. Well, it's the same thing; you just feel them looking.'

'Oh, Bex honey, you do make me proud to be your mother. You will be a wonderful mother one day. We need to start writing again, and as it is a little cloudy, perhaps we could go do some now and leave our walk in the forest for a better day? Incidentally, I get what you're saying about sitting in your car.'

'Yeah okay, let's go. We're unlikely to see any pixies; especially now it's turned a little cooler. They will be hiding underground in case it rains. As for showing you where I found the key, well that is definitely at its best when the sun shines, so...'

'Oh, they'll be hiding, okay. I am looking forward to seeing where you found the key, but as we said, another day.' Elizabeth smiled and took Rebecca's hand as the two made their way back to the main house.

When they arrived back, Rebecca suggested they sat in the kitchen and catch up on their stories. In her usual way, Rebecca walked around, arms waving while telling her tales. Now and then, she sketched the odd drawing of pixie's and their homes, always adding that she hadn't seen enough to be sure. Occasionally, she noticed her mum had stopped typing and was staring out of the window. For once though, she was smiling instead of the usual empty gaze. A while later, while she was going through one of her ideas, she realised her mum hadn't heard a word she'd said. She tapped her on the shoulder and smiling, held her palm up in a questioning way.

'Sorry, Bex, I was miles away. I was just thinking about Meredith and the things you suggested. Perhaps she sat here like this, reading her books, occasionally staring through this very window thinking about her plight. It makes you wonder, especially if your ideas are right. This might sound daft, but do you think this house is somehow fated to be a male domain.'

'Crumbs, Mother, can a house be that? I must say, it is very masculine, hmm. And daft it is not.'

'Well, it's a very manly house, big, and bold, just how men see themselves, macho. Oh, I don't know.' Glancing away, she shook her head faintly and then smiled. 'So, let's get back to our story.'

She raised her eyes at her mother's all too familiar change of stance. She smiled and continued with her story until it was time to get supper ready.

Over the next couple of days, it rained almost non-stop, so Rebecca and her mum carried on with the tales, occasionally mentioning Meredith. Three days had now passed, and again they were sitting in the kitchen, eating breakfast, and chatting.

Elizabeth jumped up and started rummaging around in her handbag, pulled out her diary, and grinned. 'Oh goodie, Amanda and Ruth are coming over today.'

'Yes, Mum, you did tell me yesterday. I'm not sure about rowing today. It may be a tad too wet and windy. Looking in your diary has reminded me, back to school next week, yippee.' Rebecca raised her eyebrows and then smiled at her mum. 'I have really enjoyed the last few days.'

Elizabeth touched Rebecca on the cheek. 'It has been lovely. Do you know it looks like it may brighten up, so maybe some retail therapy today? See what the girls say when they get here.'

'That might be fun, but I have a fair bit of homework to catch up on, and so I might give it a miss. If you're okay with...' she was interrupted by the doorbell chiming several times.

'Talk of the devil,' her mum said and headed to the door. 'That'll be Amanda's finger stuck...'

'Hi, Liz, it's just me today. Amanda had something she needed to sort out. She said she would give you a call later.'

'Oh, okay that's fine, Ruth, come through to the kitchen. I just mentioned to Bex about going shopping, but she said she has too much homework to do. I was convinced that was Amanda ringing the flipping doorbell,' she said and laughed.

'Well, we can just sit around and catch up.'

Rebecca looked up, 'why don't you two go out. I'll be just fine here.'

'Hmm, I'm not sure about that.'

'Mum, really, I will be fine. You two go out and enjoy yourself. I have lots to do, and you'll be back before I'm finished. I won't even notice you've gone.'

'What do you think Ruth?'

'Well, Rebecca's a big girl now. I have an idea; do you remember the health spa near the village? I popped in and checked it out last time we were here, and it looks divine. So, how about we go down there today and get booked in for the full works.'

'Ruth, that's a great idea, and maybe Bex will change her mind and come with us after all,' she said turning to Rebecca.

'Mum, I'd love to come, but I can't, really. I must get on with my homework. You two go and enjoy yourself. It will do you good to have a nice relaxing day. Don't worry about me; I will be just fine.'

'How is this for role reversal, me saying to Bex to leave her homework, and her saying no?'

'Well, just shows you how grown up she is, Liz.'

'Are you sure you don't fancy, Honey?'

'Mum, I am fine, and you're wasting time, go.'

'Well as long as you're okay, Rebecca, phone me if you need anything. There is some lunch in the fridge, so make sure you eat.'

'I will. I promise, Mum. Go, have fun; I will be fine. I am more than capable of looking after myself. I am almost old enough to have my own family.'

'Oooh, get you. Nothing planned, I hope.'

'Mum, go...'

As soon as they'd left, Rebecca went upstairs to her room. She spent the next couple of hours engrossed in her homework. Just as she finished, her phone rang, again. She glanced and noticing it was her mum once more, answered with a frivolous tone. 'What now, Mother, you only rang about a half-hour ago? And, before you ask, I am still okay; I've nearly finished my work too.'

'Oh, have you, Rebecca, do you want us to come back and get you?'

'No, it's fine, Mum, I am going to try to find out some more about this house on my computer. In fact, that is precisely what I was starting when you called, again. And before you ask, I will have lunch, at lunchtime. Thanks for the offer anyway.'

'Oh well, as long as you are okay, just making sure.'

'Yeah, but you don't need to check every ten minutes. Ruth, she probably has me on loudspeaker, as per normal, so tell her to go have a massage and chill-out. Mum, I am fine. Go and enjoy yourself.' She then heard the pair giggling in the background. 'Go.'

Rebecca turned back to her computer and tried everything she could think of but to no avail. She knew there must be some information about this house somewhere. *If only I had the original name,* she thought. She sat back, stared out of the window, wondering if there might be an old nameplate knocking around, perhaps outside. Heading downstairs, she rustled up a sandwich and headed towards the front door.

Chapter 7 - The Spiral Staircase

Grabbing her cardigan, Rebecca crammed in the last bite of sandwich and pulled the front door closed. She then stood, twiddling the key in her hand for a few seconds, unsure where to look. Feeling positive, she was sure there'd be something somewhere. She ambled down the path towards the lake hoping something would grab her attention. Just as she thought she'd end up back at the summerhouse, the old stables popped into her head. Although she'd always intended to have a close look, something else invariably cropped up. *No time like the present,* she thought. As she drew close, her positivity started to fade. The place was in total disrepair, complete with a couple of willows growing through the rafters. Although it didn't look like it would offer her any answers, she wasn't put off.

The twisted brambles covering the first stable door were at least three feet deep and just as high, so she decided that was out of the question. She didn't mind the odd scratch for a handful of berries but wasn't prepared to tackle this much just on a hunch. She took a step back and was able to see that all four doors were equally inaccessible. Undaunted, she balanced a few bricks against the wall and stepped up to peer through a small gap where she guessed a window had once been. On her tiptoes, she spotted a possible way in at the rear via a broken-down wall. With renewed optimism, she headed around the back.

Clambering over the remains of the dilapidated wall, she heard a horrid crunching sound and felt an odd sensation under her feet. She pushed back the knee-high grass, uncovering a mass of broken roof tiles, and knew searching this wreck wasn't going to be easy. Focused on an old nameplate or something that might give her a clue, she scanned the remnants. Spotting a perfect sized piece of wood against some fallen bricks, she waded through the straw-like grass.

Optimistically, she scraped at the rotting wood but quickly realised it was just a piece of old timber that had probably fallen from the roof.

She continued searching, finding umpteen bits of decaying wood, and some odd-shaped pieces of slate, but nothing of any significance. Just as she was about to leave, something caught her eye in the far corner. With her dampened mood again invigorated, she clambered towards the object. Not watching her step, she tripped and stuck her hand straight in some nettles. Dusting herself off, she spat on the back of her hand – her Nan had said to do this for nettle stings – and continued. As she came closer, the curved corners and a splattering of green paint stimulated her senses. Grabbing it with both hands, she turned it over, to reveal the name, *Nadine. Sounds like a horse-name,* she thought. Using her hanky again, she rubbed away most of the dirt and shook her head, realising it probably wasn't the house name. She looked around for a little while longer but felt there was nothing else here, so decided to head back. On her way up to the house, she examined the nameplate a little closer and decided it was definitely worth a google.

She placed the nameplate just inside the front door and headed to her computer. On the way upstairs, she had an odd sensation nagging her to go to the summerhouse. Strangely, this time it was stronger than normal. It was as if something was calling her. Without hesitating, Rebecca decided to leave the nameplate for later. She paused for a split second, knowing her mum would be cross if she went alone, but curiosity had taken a firm grip, and she was now on a new mission.

When she arrived at the summerhouse, her nagging sensation had all mostly gone, but as she was here, decided to have a look in Millicent's room, anyway. She opened the door and glanced inside having already made her mind up it had nothing to offer. As always, this room felt devoid of any emotions and or clues. *Only checking,* she thought. Turning to Meredith's room, as always, she felt something calling her to this place, but like the other room, today it felt empty and soulless. As she stood there, an odd shivery sensation

94

passed through her body, the likes of which she hadn't felt before. Somehow, she just knew she'd find the answers she so desperately sought on the other side of the locked door.

Heading down the corridor, she took a deep breath and tried the handle. As usual, there was nothing to encourage her, not even a tiny creak from the door. For some reason, she'd had an odd feeling it would open today. Not put off, she took another deep breath and tried again, but still nothing. She stood back, held the handle, and muttered, 'come on, Meredith, let me in.' No sooner the last word had left her lips the handle moved. She blinked a few times. Although she knew it was a ridiculous thought, it had almost felt as if someone had opened the door from the other side. She stood back and pulled the door towards her, not really expecting it to move. It did budge a tiny amount but still felt locked. Looking at the doorframe, for the first time, she grinned, noticing it opened inwards. With one heavy push, the door creaked, opened, and the handle pulled from her grip, seemingly on its own.

Feeling excited, but nonetheless, uneasy, she stared into a dingy room, trying to adjust her eyes to the darkness. Gradually, she focussed on what appeared to be a spiral staircase on the far side. Tentatively, she made her way over and with barely enough space, eased her way between the wall and a metal bannister. As she brushed past the rail, a cloud of thick dust filled the air, making it almost impossible to see let alone breathe. She stood at the bottom of the stairs for a few seconds, regaining her composure. Peering up into the darkness, she reckoned if nothing else, she might find some more clues upstairs. With her senses now tingling, she edged up the narrow stairs until she arrived by a small door set off to the right. 'Aha,' she muttered, remembering her trusty torch attached to the inside of her jacket. She flicked the switch, and with barely enough room to move, shone it through a tiny window.

Even with her torch on wide-beam, she could see next to nothing. *Well, I've come this far* she thought and turned the door handle. Feeling it click once, she gasped as again it pulled from her grip and opened inwards. Wondering what was going on with the doors, she tried to regain her bearings. Then to compound her senses further, the torch flickered, and went off, leaving her in total darkness. As a thousand thoughts raced through her mind, she held the inside of the doorframe, and widened her eyes, trying to focus. Fumbling in the dark, she shook her torch and flicked the switch several times. Briefly, it came on shining in her eyes, and then just as quickly it went off again. Unable to see her hand in front of her face, she stuffed the torch in her pocket and tried to re-adjust to the darkness. As her eyes came back into focus, she could just make out on the far side of the room what looked like a window frame with a tiny speck of light to one side.

She took a step and felt an odd spongy sensation under her foot. Probing with her foot, she reckoned like everything else in this building the floor was covered in a thick layer of dust. With her eyes firmly fixed on the glimmer of light coming from the window, and mindful of the dust-covered floor, she gingerly crept forward.

Standing by the window, still unable to see much, she explored the edge of the frame with her hand. Coming across what seemed to be heavy velvety material, and guessing it might be a curtain, she reached out to move it. As she did, an icy chill brushed her left cheek, instantly followed by the door slamming behind her. Even if she wanted to, she couldn't move, the cold silence interrupted only by the sound of her pulse pounding in her chest. With her hands by her side, she closed her eyes and tried to steady her nerves. Suddenly, she could see light through her closed eyelids. Frozen to the spot, and with her eyes firmly shut, she heard a female voice that was oddly familiar.

'Rebecca.'

Panting, she shook her head.

'Rebecca.'

Who is calling me? she thought.

'Rebecca.' The call came again.

It was as if her mum or someone similar sounding was calling from downstairs. *But how can that be, mums at the spa?* Barely able to get the words out, Rebecca called back, 'M Mum, is that you?'

Suddenly, the voice seemed to be coming from her left. 'Did you address me as Mum?' the woman said. 'That is a divergent term,' the voice said, with an inquisitive, yet smooth and well-mannered tone. 'Did I hear you coughing, dear Rebecca?'

She knew this wasn't her mum, *but this person referred to me by name, so who is it,* she thought. Releasing a nervous breath, she opened her eyes. Squinting both from nerves and the light, she was astonished to see the curtains were open allowing the sun to stream through. 'What is going on,' she muttered, looking around an immaculate room, complete with a neatly made bed. It had a white lace edged cover, a frilly pillow, and a small, worn-out teddy propped up at the side. On a small wooden desk next to the bed, she spotted a newspaper of sorts, and muttered, 'maybe a clue.' Breathing deeply, she was about to pick up the paper, when the voice came again, much closer this time.

'Rebecca, with whom do you speak?'

This woman's voice was oddly familiar, but it wasn't anyone she knew. Completely at a loss what to think, she called out, 'This room looks new,' thinking *this is obviously someone who knows me.*

'Rebecca, your room is decorated newly. The Blacksmiths son, young Timothy helped complete it only two days since.'

What is going on? Rebecca muttered, 'Timothy, Blacksmith's son, which Blacksmith?' Then she heard the door open and could sense someone stood behind her. She took a sharp intake of breath and

97

turned slowly. There was a petite, dark-haired woman, wearing an oddly familiar white dress standing with her back to her. The woman was looking inside a small cupboard just inside the door.

As the woman turned, Rebecca could barely breathe. So confused, she couldn't hear what the woman was saying. She pinched the back of her hand sure she was dreaming or something. *This is not happening* she thought.

'Be hurried, Rebecca, luncheon is ready. Then after, we must change to work clothes and then tend the stables in preparation for tomorrow's hunt. Now, put back on your dandy green dress, and be suitably attired to eat. Haste please.'

Rebecca couldn't stop staring at this woman. *It looks like Meredith,* she thought, *but that's ridiculous.* Knowing there had to be a rational explanation, she regained her composure a little and then realised the woman was staring at her. 'Ummm, green dress, sure.'

'Are you in order, Rebecca? You sound uneasy and appear all at sea. Look here; you have goosebumps. Perhaps you should have worn suitable clothes for this time of the year, instead of...' the woman looked Rebecca up and down. 'Where did my daughter acquire those absurd clothes?'

As if Rebecca's rationale wasn't already all over the place, this woman now referring to her as her daughter had compounded her thoughts even further. All of a fluster, she hesitated for a moment, aware the woman was frowning. Trying to sound routine, Rebecca said, 'No, I am fine, thank you. I just felt a strange shiver.' She looked down at her drills and inwardly smiled, which composed her a little. 'Ummm, I found these under my bed, umm, Meredith.' She knew she was taking a chance, but it looked like her, so.

The woman shook her head. 'Why do you refer to me as Meredith? You are acting most odd, dear Rebecca. As for your apparel, we shall have words about that presently.' She then pointed to the green dress.

How can this be? It is Meredith. 'Err, sorry, Mum, I was going to wear the green dress, but I thought as we are going to the stables perhaps it wasn't a good idea.'

'Mum, indeed, well I prefer Mother. Nevertheless, as you wish, Meredith or Mum either would be fine. Clearly, you are still convalescing from that ghastly infirmity. Now, let us make haste and eat our luncheon.' She then pointed again at the dress. 'After luncheon, your father's horse, Nadine, needs checking. Remember, he has brought forward the hunt for tomorrow. We must make sure we have everything shipshape just as George, your father expects it to be.' The woman then glanced at the floor before continuing. 'It is a misfortune we are not invited. I do so adore those proceedings.'

Rebecca had so many questions she wanted to ask, and the list was growing with every moment. Her thoughts were now so befuddled that she was finding it impossible to focus. She realised the woman was again staring, waiting. She took a deep breath and shook herself. 'Yes, Mother,' she muttered while changing into the dress. 'Umm, I am sure you have told me, but why does father exclude us from this event?' As the words left her lips, she knew she had to be a little more tactful with her questions.

The woman narrowed her eyes a little. 'When George was previously referred to as your father, you stressed that you only had one father and that you lost him to that horrid disease. Can I surmise from your present reference to George as father that you are somewhat accepting of him? Moreover, Rebecca, please refrain from posing such questions. We have discussed this before, and you know events of this stature are not for us. Our job is to make sure everything is just dandy, and then we can enjoy the occasion from afar.'

'Warming to George, I dunno,' she said, thinking *this George sounds like an arrogant so-and-so.* 'Please tell me, I know we may have discussed it before, but why are we not invited?'

'What word did you just expel, Missy, dun what?'

'Err, sorry, Meredith,' she said, unsure what to say, and then muttered, 'It is slang for do not know, dunno.'

'Well it is most unlike you, and I would urge you to discontinue such language. Besides, your persistence with muttering is irksome. Also, one moment it is Mum, then Meredith and then Mother, what has gotten into you today?"

Rebecca shook her head considering this woman's words and gentle tone. Although they were forthright, they were also tender and compassionate. Previously, she'd initially dismissed the idea that this was a time-travel thing, though it seemed to be the only answer. As she was putting the dress on, which fitted perfectly, she thought about the woman calling her Rebecca and treating her like a daughter. She had so many questions but knew she had to be patient and go with it. Fastening the buttons on the dress, she stood up and mumbled, 'Hmm, whatever, let's see what happens.'

'Rebecca, you seem again in the sticks and quite indefinite, mumbling and such. Moreover, where has all this slang speech come from? Have you again been chatting with the gardener's son? Now, where is that carbolic soap?'

Standing there with her mouth open, she thought, *carbolic soap, you are kidding me.* At a loss what to think, or say, she tried to focus her thoughts. 'Mother, please tell me why the invitation does not extend to us?' she said, carefully picking her words.

The woman, as if responding to her tone, said, 'Oh, my lovely. It would seem I must explain. George agreed with my father – for considerable monies, and conditioned ownership of the estate, I might add – to espouse us as his family. There was an exacting schedule put in place by the men. To which, he lives in the Manor House. Our position is to look after all the effects away from the main house. In return, he took me as his wife, by which the family name and reputation are unexposed. I do not know why you bother yourself with such things, so often you enquire of these issues. I have informed you before that in this modern society this is an acceptable practice.'

Looking down at her green dress, she thought, *modern society.* 'But, Mother, how do you live like this,' she said, glanced at her green dress, and half grinned. 'Have you ever discussed the situation with George?' A little disturbed, Rebecca shook her head. 'I take it you are allowed to talk to George,' she said and flicked her eyelids.

'I find your questions and manor unusually churlish, Rebecca. However, I do indeed talk with George, although much of his time is with his associate Millicent. Therefore, I am discreet and select my time to speak with prudence.' She frowned, 'Rebecca, please make your mind up, one minute you call me Mother, then the next it's Meredith. Now, I really have no concern, either way, conversely, even by your frolicsome nature this disposition is, well...'

'He lives in the Manor House, you speak with prudence, seriously, arranged marriage, or not, it just isn't right. Mother, you said, Millicent. She's the woman in the other painting, in the hallway, correct?'

Meredith raised her eyebrows and asked, 'Of which hallway do you speak?' She then shook her head. 'Your sentence construction and language are unpardonable. I am finding it difficult to understand you today, Missy. Turning two words into one is unacceptably indolent.'

Grimacing, Rebecca answered, 'the hallway in the main house,' again realising she should think about what she says. 'The paintings in the...'

Before Rebecca had a chance to finish, the woman held her hand up. 'Rebecca, you know you are forbidden from entering the main house. More importantly, I know of no paintings in the hallway. Now be done with you, Young Woman. We have spoken too long, come, have luncheon. Then we must go and ready the stables.' Beckoning

Rebecca, the woman left through the door by which Rebecca had entered.

Hesitantly, she followed the woman, not knowing what to expect, her mind overflowing with questions. To compound her thoughts, the spiral stairs had vanished and in their place was a small wooden staircase. Finding it difficult to centre her attention, she headed downstairs. All the while, in the back of her mind, getting back home was nagging at her thoughts and emotions. At the bottom of the stairs, she entered a small kitchen, seemingly at the back of the summerhouse. Meredith was already sitting at a wooden table, signalling Rebecca to join her.

'Rebecca, please sit here and eat your food.'

Trying to focus on what to ask, and how to ask it, she sat at the table, and said, 'Mother.'

'Yes, Rebecca?'

'Tell me, Mother...'

'What should I tell you, Rebecca? Come along with you, what question do you have for me?'

Rebecca paused for a moment, again thinking about what she wanted to ask. 'I hope you don't mind me asking,' she paused briefly, 'how do you live with so many conditions? How do you put up with this facade, and why do you not challenge him? Most of all, how do you allow him to have that lady friend, or should I say that slapper Millicent, around all the time?' *Ooops* she thought *I shouldn't have said that*. The look on the woman's face indicated she had to improve her word choice, significantly.

'Your choice of language is quarrelsome and unladylike. Well, first of all, Rebecca, I am happy because I had a lifetime of love from your beloved father, Anthony.' Narrowing her eyes, she paused, 'I knew that once you approached marital age, such questions would follow.' She looked directly at Rebecca and shook her head. 'I also have the love of you and your brother,' her tone now gentle. 'Importantly, I am not in a position to challenge him. I have explained many times I must always consider my father's good name. Lastly, please do not call Millicent those horrid names. What was that name, or should I say term you used to describe Millicent, slap her?'

'Slapper, because that is what she is. It is a loose reference for a whore.' Out of the blue, Rebecca's thoughts returned to the spiral stairs, and she found herself again wondering if they were a doorway to this point and importantly back home. Rebecca shook herself trying to regain her focus. She could see Meredith was staring again and thought *one question this time*. 'Right, situation accepted, why is it for us to do work such as the stables, surely they have farm-hands?'

Meredith narrowed her eyes and said with a direct tone. 'Rebecca, as horrid as she is to us, she is not a...' She hesitated for a moment and continued, 'I do not understand what has gotten into you, and where this endless unceremonious choice of idioms has come from. Anyways, my situation is what it is, and we must all accept the conditions.' She looked down. After a moment, she looked up and frowned. 'I suspect one of the villagers may have told you of Millicent's past. As you suggested, she was indeed a...' Meredith stopped in her tracks as if she didn't want to talk about Millicent.

Anyways, Rebecca thought, *I can't believe she said anyways. This must be a dream.* She shook her head and thought for a moment. 'Mother, for heaven's sake, why do you put up with... I know you said it's for your father's name, but even so?'

'There you are again, another inapt word, and importantly, please refrain from blaspheming. Hush now, Rebecca.' Clearly, a little miffed, Meredith looked down at her food, and then glanced through the window. She looked again at her food, touched her cheek with the back of her hand, turned back to Rebecca, and forced a smile. She then stared through the window once more.

Sat with her mouth open, Rebecca watched as the woman gazed through the window. Her distant forlorn appearance was all too recognisable. Rebecca touched the woman on the arm and said, 'Mother, please talk to me. You cannot live like this. Your father's name is important, but not at the cost of your happiness. He will get over it. In a hundred years, no one will know, either way, this I know.' She then thought about what she's just said. 'Certainly, you shouldn't put up with living on the outside.'

'Indeed, you are right, Rebecca. I spoke with my father only four days since. He also said that if I was discontent, I should rework my arrangement.'

'He is right. You should change things to suit you. After all, it is your happiness on the line.'

'Yes, my dear,' she said appearing a little strained. 'I should challenge George for a better relationship. There may be a setback though as I believe Millicent wants to be rid of us and with George seemingly at her beck and call, well...' She glanced away for a moment. 'However, George couldn't agree to that,' she said and nodded profoundly.

'What do you mean?'

'I wasn't going to tell you this until you were older, however...' Appearing deep in thought, she said, 'the marital agreement was determined by my father. It states that George will encompass me as his spouse until either of our deaths. In return, my father pays him an annual amount. George, although wealthy, lost a significant amount of money through his shipbuilding exploits. Therefore, he is now somewhat dependent on my father's money.'

Rebecca could hardly believe what she'd just heard. 'So, if that is the case, then how did you end up becoming an outsider?'

'It is a marriage of convenience and no more. We have discussed this before, Rebecca.'

'It seems to me that the only person who benefits from this convenient relationship is George, and Millicent, huh. Your father pays him to encompass you as his wife, not to have Millicent live in the main house and subsequently treat us like galley slaves. I find the whole situation wholly unpleasant.'

The woman shook her head. 'Rebecca, you, your brother and I have a roof over our heads. We have groceries, provisions, and we are together. Importantly, my father's name is protected from disparagement, which is paramount.' She then shook her head in such a way that suggested she agreed but felt unable to acknowledge Rebecca's view.

'It wouldn't be so bad, but allowing him to have a whore living in the house. The house that we should live in, I might add, is laughable.' She thought for a moment. 'You suggested you knew of Millicent's past. What is it exactly and have you tackled her about that? I bet George doesn't know. Have you spoken to him about her? Moreover, how would your father's name appear if that news were to get out?'

The woman's changing expressions suggested she was deep in thought. A couple of moments passed before she looked up and nodded. 'Millicent was indeed a lady of the night, although it was some years past. That is all I am prepared to say on the matter. Incidentally, I have spoken with her this very day alluding to her clandestine past. She walked away cussing. No less than you would expect from a woman of her repute,' shaking her head, she huffed loudly.

'Cussing, what did she say?' Wanting to reiterate the point, Rebecca held up the palm of her hand and exclaimed, 'if your father is worried about his name, how would society react to you playing second fiddle to a former whore?'

'She said, damn you, woman. I take your point, Rebecca, a valued one.'

'Mother, damn is not cussing. However, if she called you a bloody bitch or something like... Well, what she said is immaterial. What is important is what your father would say if he found out the truth about this cowslip state of affairs?' Rebecca smiled, pleased with her terminology.

Meredith appeared startled. She widened her eyes. 'Rebecca, what has gotten into you? Your language is awful, and the like of which I have never heard you utter before. You should act like a lady at all times.' Then just like her real mother, this woman's tone pacified in the blink of an eye. 'Now where is the carbolic soap?' she said grinning.

Rebecca shook her head ever so slightly, thinking, she should hear Tommy swear. 'What's the deal with carbolic soap? You sound like my m, mum.'

'Rebecca, I sound like what or whom?'

'Nothing, it's just, not that important. I am very sorry I interrupted you, I think you were going to say something about George, please continue.' She had used this trick successfully with her real mother, and it had worked surprisingly often.

The woman appeared a little perplexed. 'I also spoke with George the last day.'

'Last day, do you mean yesterday?'

'Yes, what else could I have meant, Rebecca? The nature of your questions is of concern.' Meredith frowned, and continued, 'I advised George that this arrangement is at best, uncomfortable. Initially, he frowned although he appeared to be listening. However, once I had finished, he directly changed the subject and asked if I had arranged for the completion of the jetty in time for his boat delivery. He then paused for a moment, and without looking up from his book, suggested that if I were unhappy with the arrangements, I should speak with my father. I thought...'

Rebecca nodded and trying to keep her thoughts off the boat, shook herself. 'So, let me get this right, he said if you were unhappy. Sounds like a bit of a challenge if you ask me.'

Meredith picked up her drink and stared out of the window. She took a deep breath, looked back, and said, 'Can we please talk about something else now? I would like to talk about your real father. I was so lucky to have had such love, even if it was for such a short time. His love will live within my heart for all time, as it should yours. That keeps me happy, and that, my fair lady, is why I accept the way things are.'

Rebecca could see Meredith had become a little troubled and knew it was time to drop the subject of George. Instead, she just sat and listened while Meredith spoke about Anthony. She spoke with such fondness and contentment that Rebecca was beginning to understand why she was so accepting of her present situation. Once they finished their food, they left the summerhouse and headed along a tree-lined path towards the stables. In the distance, Rebecca noticed a slight built, dark-haired woman. As they got closer, the woman turned towards them, and distorting her pretty face, beckoned them towards her. Meredith took hold of Rebecca's hand and led her towards this woman. As they walked, she could hear Meredith muttering something under her breath.

As they drew closer, the woman took a step backwards and without making eye contact, indicated for them to stop a few feet away. She then spoke with a dialect so intense it sounded like a foreign language. 'Don't stand sa' close,' she said and again limply waved her hand before taking another step backwards. 'Jus' make sure ya' sort the 'orses proper. Vat's, if ya' able of doin' anythin' proper.'

Although Rebecca recognised this woman as Millicent, she wanted to be sure and whispered, 'Is this Millicent?'

Meredith nodded once and then forced a smile towards Millicent.

Having noticed Millicent's somewhat feeble manner, Rebecca took a step towards her and narrowed her eyes. Even in spite of what she already knew, she'd taken an instant dislike to this woman. For some bizarre reason, she felt an overwhelming need to test this woman's resolve. Using the same derisory tone often saved for her brother, she said, 'Who exactly do you think you are talking to? We are not here to serve you or anyone else, for that matter.' The way the woman flinched, Rebecca knew she'd established the upper hand and felt an insistent need to push her further. Rebecca realised English wasn't Millicent's strong point, so she decided to pitch the woman a curveball. 'I must say, your choice of vocabulary is at best, disagreeable. The adverb you should have used is properly, not proper. Indeed, a better all-around word would have been, *correctly*. As for the remainder of your comments, they could only be considered a measure of your slovenly background.' The way Millicent blinked continually and kept looking away, Rebecca knew she was there for the taking. 'So, are you prepared to talk to us as Ladies in an appropriate manner, or are you incapable?'

Having looked down for a few seconds, Millicent looked up sharply. 'I'm talking at ya' girl and ya' muvva' for vat matta'. Ya' alta watch ya' mouf.' I will 'ave the pair of ya' 'frone out. Now be off with ya', both. Be sure, I will tell Georgie of ya' nature to me, and he will cut your rations, right 'way.' She then waved her hand but took another step backwards.

Rebecca stepped close to the woman and elongating her words, snapped, 'Your threats are weak. I urge you to speak to George and I assure you that we don't care.' She shook her head and as belligerently as she could, said, 'frankly, we really don't care.' She then waved her hand flippantly in the woman's face.

Appearing startled, Millicent averted her stare towards Meredith. She then turned back to Rebecca, narrowed her eyes, and yapped. 'Are ya' challenging me, girl?'

From the corner of her eye, Rebecca glanced again at Meredith and could see she appeared uneasy but still wide-eyed with intent. She moved close enough to smell Millicent's colourless, powdery perfume. 'Yes, I am challenging you,' she said with her hand firmly planted on her hip. 'You skinny bag of bones in your fancy dress that just hides your unsavoury past.'

'How dare ya', I'll slap ya', and have ya' sent to the shed on tuvva' side of the lake, where ya' belong.'

'Is that how you deal with difficult situations, with violence, showing your true nature? Go ahead, slap me.' Rebecca stepped close enough to feel her toes touching the woman's feet and added, 'your breath smells awful.'

Millicent blinked her eyes several times and unable to maintain eye contact, turned to Meredith. Her voice flustered, she uttered, 'I suggest ya' control her. Be sure, I will sla sla sla...' Stuttering, her face red, she stepped backwards and raised her hand in the direction of Rebecca.

Meredith growled, and pulling Rebecca to one side, moved closer to Millicent. 'I urge you, desist from your unruly manner, Millicent Black,' her tone profound and forthright, 'Embark along this path again, and the consequence will be severe. Be assured, I will speak with George on the subject of your manner this very day. Now be off with you, whore.'

Millicent shuffled her feet, and with her eyes flicking from side to side, she mumbled something indecipherable.

Meredith moved close to the woman and whispered something.

Millicent stamped her foot, turned, and headed towards the main house.

Although Rebecca hadn't heard what Meredith had said, she suspected by Millicent's reaction that it was pretty damning. She gestured towards Meredith with her hand and said, 'Way to go, high five.' However, Meredith looked at her with a blank expression. So again, she gestured with her hand. 'Mum, look, hold up your hand.' Rebecca took hold of her hand and explained how it should work.

Meredith smiled. 'Oh, my word, I enjoyed that, the high, how did you refer to it? A high five, might I have another.'

Rebecca grinned, delighting in Meredith's reaction. 'I loved it when you called her a whore.'

Meredith appeared deep in thought and then said, 'well; I touched on it briefly, maybe I should explain. When she met George, she was indeed a lady of bad name and nature. By that, I mean a lady of the night. She knows that I am fully aware of her past too. Importantly, she is now aware that I know the police were at one time very interested in her and some of her dealings.'

'Does George know this?'

'Not that I am aware of.'

'So why don't you...' She stopped mid-sentence; aware something was oddly different about the main house. Trying to work out what it was, she realised Meredith was waiting for her to finish her sentence. She nodded and continued, 'Sorry, Meredith. I was distracted. That is your chance to challenge her and make this situation better for us all. Meet fire with fire as they say, especially when you have the means to start the fire and then put it out as required, which clearly you do.'

'You are using unusually emotive language today Rebecca, but I must say I am finding it enlightening and heartening.'

Still, with one eye on the main house, she asked, 'Mother, what is this shed in the woods she was talking about?'

'So many questions you have today, Rebecca. It is the old bear hunting lodge on the other side of the lake. Rebecca, surely you remember that we stayed there when we first located here. I know you were little, but you must recall.'

Rebecca was beside herself, 'bear, bear,' frowning, she continued, 'Bear hunting lodge, do they still use it as a lodge for bear hunting?'

'Rebecca, please do not be silly, there are no bears in these parts. It is just a name that relates back to the name of the forest.'

'There's none that we know about, Mother, none that we know about.'

'Oh, bless you, Rebecca. Be assured, we would have known if there were any bears thereabouts, after all, we stayed there for five long years.'

Rebecca now felt oddly comfortable calling this woman mother, especially since she'd clearly gone against her usual persona to defend her. 'Err, Mother, who is that up at the window?' Rebecca said, pointing towards the first floor.

'That is George. Who did you think it was?'

'I think he was watching us while Millicent was here, perhaps he saw our little confrontation.'

Meredith glanced back and forth between the window and the floor. Then with a stern look on her face, she gestured toward the window with the palm of her hand held up. She shook her head several times and grumbled, 'the ignominy of it. He, George, signalled us towards the stables. I am not a Lady to cuss; however, he can flipping well watch us head in the opposing direction. We shall leave the horses and instead take an agreeable amble in the crocus wood?' Meredith smiled and continued, 'It is a lovely day to walk. Then, if he is still watching over us – which I am sure he will – he should comprehend our views on the matter. Let us see how he acts in response.' She clenched her lips and nodded several times.

'Way to go.'

Meredith flicked her eyes brows and nodded. 'Way to go, indeed.'

She took Rebecca's hand and led her down the path in the direction of the woods. They had taken only a few steps when a man's voice called out.

'Meredith, may I inquire as to your route? You are to tend the horses. Keep in mind, there is the hunt in the morrow, and everything must be just so.'

With the sound of footsteps close behind, Meredith stopped dead in her tracks and took a deep breath. Slowly, she turned around. 'I have most recently communicated my concerns about the circumstances of my existence. Clearly, you failed to acknowledge or comprehend my views.'

'Nevertheless, Meredith.'

'There is no nevertheless about it, George. I find your behaviour towards my children and me tiresome and am no longer prepared to respond to your beck and call.' Clenching her hands together, she took another deep breath, and continued, 'While you are here and listening - not that you have shown any capability of doing so - I have something you should be aware of. The woman who lives with you, Millicent, has become increasingly irksome. If she ever threatens my daughter again, physically, or verbally, you should be assured that there would be consequences. Now if you have a dilemma with anything I have said, then I will be happy to take my children and leave.'

112

George appeared disturbed. Breathing deeply, he forced an odd-looking smile and spoke with a calm but nervous tone. 'Meredith, has something happened between you and Millicent?'

In a polite, yet forthright manner, Meredith explained what had happened between Millicent, Rebecca, and herself. Each time George tried to speak; Meredith appeared to become more fractious. Shaking her head, she kept talking, sticking precisely to the facts. Towards the end, her manner was aggravated and seemingly compounded when Millicent appeared at the front door and headed towards them. Frowning, Meredith, said, 'you are best keeping the whore away.'

With a look of total bemusement, George turned and waved Millicent away. Still appearing shocked, he turned back to Meredith. 'Firstly, I express regret if you feel I have failed to listen to or understand your concerns. We shall speak openly and find an agreeable resolution. Secondly, be assured, I am appalled by Millicent's threatening behaviour. It will never happen again.' George paused for a moment, and then added, 'Please, Meredith, will you explain why you referred to Millicent as a whore?'

Rebecca noticed the muscles on Meredith's cheek quiver slightly and watched as a single bead of sweat appeared on her forehead. Oddly excited by what may come next, she held her breath.

Meredith's body language suggested she'd had enough and was no longer prepared to compromise. With a consequential tone, she said, 'George, I referred to Millicent as a whore because that is what she was and still is to my mind. She has been the cause of many a failed marriage for miles about. Every individual in the village knows of her past. To make it worse, George, you are the brunt of many a yarn because you are the only one who seemingly is unaware of her past. I am here for the sake of my children and my father's reputation so I can suffer the knowing looks and finger pointing. At least with me, their thoughts are born from compassion. Importantly though, I do now consider her appointment here will only serve to lower my father's good name. So, with that in mind, a change is overdue.'

George squinted as the bright sunlight caught his dark-brown eyes. Shading his eyes, he hesitated for a moment, clearly considering Meredith's words. Seemingly, at a loss, he looked up at Meredith but said nothing.

'Come along my dear, we shall go for our walk. Evidently, George has nothing to say. He is apparently happy living with a woman of ill repute, someone who is clearly prepared to lie, and is primed to dragoon children.'

'Please wait, Meredith. I am considering everything you have said. I am not at all happy about this situation and more importantly, feel disappointed and angered by Millicent's behaviour. Why did you not inform me of her past sooner? If this is true, and indeed, I have no reason to doubt you, I must rectify this without more ado.' He shook his head, and although uncomfortable, his tone was resolute.

Meredith turned up her nose and then lifted the back of her hand dismissively. 'George, is your pronouncement to rectify the situation born from concern for us or the concept of losing the estate and my father's money? Which is your motive?'

Appearing uneasy, George held his hands up in a compliant motion. 'Meredith, my concern is for you and your children only. For me, the sad thing is that I have had to admire you from a distance.' He looked away briefly and then continued. 'Millicent's actions are of great concern to me. Indeed, her demeanour towards me of late has been, at best disagreeable. Please be assured I will have stern words with her.'

Meredith turned her back. 'Your concern is a little late, George.'

'Meredith, please go and enjoy your walk. I will get the stables checked by the gardener.'

'Yes, the one employed by my father. We will go for our walk. I anticipate, George, that upon our return you would have made a choice.'

'A choice, Meredith, what do you mean?'

'Yes George, you rid the house of that woman and make room for my two children and I. The alternative is we will leave the estate. That is your choice.'

'Meredith, for me there is not a choice to make. You are welcome to move into the main house, today if you so desire. I made ready your rooms the day we were married, and they still await you. I do not understand why you have not conveyed your concerns before this day. I was of the impression that your desire was to live in the house by the lake. I handed several letters to Millicent to pass to you, all of which invited you to the main house.' George paused for a moment. 'I am of the mind you have never received these letters. I foolishly believed that you had read them, ignored them, and chose to have no association with me.'

Appearing puzzled by this comment, Meredith spoke with an element of surprise. 'George, I have never received any letters from you, via Millicent or by any other means.' She hesitated for a moment, and then looked at George. 'I believed that the conditions of the marital agreement were that my children and I took up residence in the lake-house.'

'It was indeed a marital condition, one that was put in place by your father. He – very clearly, I might add – said that I must be aware that this marriage was a matter of convenience, no more and no less. I have waited...'

Meredith interrupted, 'George...'

George smiled and held his hand up, gesturing to speak. 'Please let me continue, Meredith. I have waited for an opportunity to discuss this with you.' He smiled again. 'Your father also stated that it was unlikely that you or your children would want, or need any friendliness from me. That is the only reason that Millicent lives here, purely as a female companion. As for children, I would love my own;

unfortunately, that is impossible. At one time, I considered adoption.' He then smiled at Rebecca. 'Overall, and without doubt, I would prefer the acquaintance of you and your children and wish for nothing more than your good company. I have long since admired your character, grace, beauty, and elegance, all sadly from afar.'

Meredith's tone softened. 'If this is true, George, I now feel rather boorish having spoken with you in such a curt manner. Perhaps my own insecurities have caused my tone and manner.' She then glanced away briefly. 'However, that does not change my view of Millicent Black.'

'Your father stated that the agreement was originated with your contentment in mind. He said that you would not want to live in the same house as me.' George shook his head, clearly showing he'd disagreed. 'I would have cherished having your company, even if it was for a short while each day. Why do you think I had the portrait of you hung in the hallway of the main house?'

Wide-eyed, Meredith turned and looked at Rebecca. 'Have you seen this painting, Rebecca?'

Rebecca nodded but didn't know what to say. She knew by Meredith's expression that she expected an answer. 'I may have seen it when it was delivered,' she offered up coyly.

'Millicent was so upset by the painting, in the end, I had to commission one of her also.' He then paused for a moment. 'Meredith, please go now and enjoy your walk. I promise you I will rectify this ugly situation. By the time you have returned, your rooms in Elm Manor will await you.'

'Bloody hell, Elm Manor,' Rebecca blurted, and then immediately placed her hand over her mouth.

Meredith and George simultaneously turned to Rebecca. Glaring at Rebecca, Meredith put her finger to her lips, then turned back to

George and shook her head. 'I suspect Rebecca has again been speaking with the lad from the village.' Glancing at Rebecca, she shook her head, 'We will go for our walk now.' With a firm grip, she took Rebecca's hand and led her down the path toward the summerhouse. Not a word passed between them until they were nearly at the lake. Meredith slowly turned to Rebecca, and said, 'How did you know about the paintings in the hallway? I know you suggested that you had seen them delivered, however...'

Rebecca shook her head.

Meredith frowned. 'I am perplexed. Not only did you know of the paintings and their whereabouts you also seemed a little too knowledgeable of Millicent's past. Those two aside, you were insistent that I challenged George, which was obviously the correct approach.' She shook her head. 'How could you know all of this? For sure, you may have seen the paintings delivered, but to know of their position within the house is open to discussion. Your view on Millicent could be conceived as no more than opinion. Speaking with George indicates wisdom beyond your years, an aptitude you have shown often. The three together added to your horrid choice of language, unusual mannerisms and your attire this very morning are something else altogether. I need time to consider all of this before we talk further on the matter.'

'I understand why you are perplexed, especially when you add it all together. However, I didn't know Millicent was an actual whore; it was just a derogatory term I used. As for speaking with George, well sadly, people don't talk to each other, certainly not about their personal concerns, and that leads to misunderstandings. Take my mu...' Rebecca shook her head and continued, 'I must have seen the paintings, perhaps when they were delivered and assumed they would go in the hallway.' She blinked her eyes and tried to focus Meredith's attention on George. 'Most importantly, you spoke to George without any help or encouragement from me.'

'It was actually you, Rebecca, the way you stood up to Millicent. That moment gave me courage. Anyways, the way she threatened you enraged me so. Whoever stood in my way would have received a forthright judgment.' Looking satisfied, she grinned. 'I think this all warrants another high five.' She then frowned. 'More than once you have indicated I remind you of someone. Whom, may I enquire?'

That was it; Rebecca had to ask. 'Meredith, when you use the word anyway, I have noticed that you always say, anyways. Is there a reason for that? You sound like...' Rebecca so wanted to tell Meredith everything, but guessed it would be too much for her to take on board, certainly for now.

'I know I say anyways incorrectly, it is just the way I have always said it since I was a child,' she said and shrugged her shoulders. 'Rebecca, you said I sound like someone, again. May I ask of whom do you speak? Many times, you have said something similar.'

'Oh, no one in particular, Meredith, occasionally you remind me of someone.'

'Is it someone I know, Rebecca?'

'I don't think so; just someone I once knew.' Somewhat spooked by what she'd just said, Rebecca quickly corrected herself. 'Actually, I should say that it is someone I know.' Feeling somewhat anxious, Rebecca looked away.

Meredith touched her gently on the arm. 'Are you all right, Rebecca?' She then narrowed her eyes and asked, 'So who is this secret person?'

Suddenly, Rebecca's thoughts were focused on how, or if she'd get back to her real mum. To compound her emotions further, she knew Meredith deserved an explanation. Not having a clue what to say, she tried to change the subject. 'You said Millicent is a dragoon, what does that mean?'

Meredith squinted and clenched her lips. 'A dragoon is someone who coerces, or intimidates people.' She then narrowed her eyes and held her hand up in an obvious questioning manner.

Rebecca could see this woman needed an answer of sorts. 'Oh, it's not a secret; it's just a woman from the village I have spoken to a couple of times.' She forced a smile, but her thoughts were with her real mother.

'Are you all right, my lovely?'

Rebecca couldn't get the thoughts of home from her head. Realising there may be no way back, she started to feel extremely restless. Averting her eyes, trying to mask her feelings, she uttered, 'Umm yeah, I am just fine.' She looked up and saw Meredith's attentive smile. Taking solace from this woman's kind nature, she held her hand out to Meredith. Feeling a little reassured, Rebecca smiled, and whispered to herself, 'She will see my way home.'

'What did you just say, Rebecca?'

'I was just mumbling to myself, again.' She smiled at Meredith, and said, 'Come on, let's walk.' She was keen to get back to the summerhouse but knew she couldn't rush things.

'I think we should go to my favourite place in the woods.' Meredith took Rebecca by the hand and headed off to the left.

They walked down a narrow path bordered on both sides with head high rhododendrons. As Rebecca lost sight of the summerhouse, her need to head home intensified. Sometime earlier, she'd made her mind up she was here for a reason and felt sure it was to help Meredith in some way. 'I wonder where this is leading me,' she muttered.

'Are you talking to yourself again, my dear?'

Focused on her mum, Rebecca hadn't heard Meredith. 'Sorry, what did you say?'

'I was only asking if you were talking to yourself, Rebecca.'

'Yeah, I guess I must have been. I was miles away.'

'I noticed that, what were you thinking about?'

'Oh, just how different the woods look today,' she said, smelling one of the large lilac flowers.

'Different, what do you mean by different, from when?'

Rebecca hesitated for a moment, and uttered, 'err; I'm not sure why it looks different, maybe it's because the flowers are in full bloom.'

'You are extremely hesitant, my dear. All this erring, are you sure there is nothing you want to say?'

'No, I am fine.' Rebecca paused for a moment knowing at some point she had to tell Meredith of her journey. She shook her head and thought now is as good a time as any. 'Meredith, I am going to tell you something. Something you will find not only bizarre, but I expect you'll doubt every word. Importantly, it needs to be our secret. Can you keep my secret?'

'Yes Rebecca, of course, I can keep your secret.'

'Well, this is difficult to explain, and I assure you it will sound absurd, but...' Rebecca paused, thinking, *no way back now.*

'Just tell me, Rebecca, I am sure it will not sound absurd. Your stories are always fascinating so nothing you say will surprise me. I gave up wondering a long time ago how you could know the things you do. Today has just compounded that further.'

Not quite ready to tell her story, Rebecca decided to give herself some thinking time. 'You said fascinating stories, Meredith. Will you explain what you meant?'

'Oh, the way you often talk of fairies and such things. You have always had a wonderful imagination, my lovely.'

Fairies, she thought. Mulling things over, she could now see a way to tell Meredith of her adventure.

'Come along with you now, Rebecca, I can see you are deep in thought. A problem shared, is a problem halved.'

Rebecca decided to go for it. 'Well, Meredith,' she hesitated and said, 'you know the spiral staircase?'

'Of which spiral staircase do you speak, Rebecca?' she said and frowned.

'The one in, oh it's not there is it?' *Damn,* she thought, not having a clue how she'd explain this.

'You are not making an awful lot of sense, my dear.'

'I know, and I am sorry, but you just need to go with me. Right, you know the small wooden stairs?'

Meredith nodded. 'Are you referring to the stairs in the lake-house?'

'Yes, I am, well the thing is...' Rebecca took a deep breath, knowing this was going to sound ridiculous. 'In a hundred or so years there will be a spiral staircase where the wooden one is now. I know this sounds outrageous, but...'

Meredith raised her eyes. 'In a hundred years indeed. Right, continue.'

121

Right, out with it, she thought. 'Meredith, just stay with me. My real life is a hundred and fifty years into the future, hence my choice of language and my clothes. I might add that I also live here in this house.' She then pointed back towards the main house. 'It has a French name in my time. We call the lake-house, the summerhouse. Importantly, there is a spiral staircase where the wooden stairs are now.' She could see Meredith frowning and knew she had to slow down a little. 'Right, I know how this must sound but for now, just think of it as a story. So, it was that spiral staircase that brought me to you.' Rebecca nodded and smiled.

Although Meredith's expression was one of bewilderment, she continued to smile. 'Story, right, carry on with your story, my dear.'

'I know, Meredith; I know how it sounds, silly at best. The thing is I will need your help because sometime soon I must try to find my way back to my real Mum.'

'Rebecca, my dear, I am your real mother, and although this is, shall I say fascinating, it does sound irregular, even by your standards.'

Although Meredith spoke clearly, Rebecca could hear the uncertainty in her voice. For Meredith to help her, she needed to prove her story. Briefly, she thought about her mobile phone, but she'd left it on her bed. She muttered, 'I know, my torch,' remembering she'd left it by the door in the bedroom.

'You mentioned a torch, Rebecca. Are you planning a fire?'

'Look, Mother, after our walk, I will show you something that might help to prove my story. I have something from the future called a torch. It is used to light your way, and I might add, without flames.'

'Will you indeed, Rebecca? Come along. Let us continue our walk and no more fanciful stories please, for now, at least.'

Rebecca followed Meredith along a path via a small brick animal shed of sorts. She knew this part of the woods well, but she hadn't seen this building before. She questioned this for a moment, but when the path took them past a tall evergreen hedgerow, she realised things were bound to appear unfamiliar. She then followed Meredith to the right, and into an area filled with red flowered Rhododendrons. Although she knew this was a weed, Rebecca still loved their sweet, subtle odour and array of colour. This was the second area dominated by these plants, and she again found herself wondering why they weren't around in her time. She paused for a moment and lost sight of Meredith. Hurrying in the direction she'd gone, she found herself in an area of tall silver birch that had a familiar feel to it. Looking around, she noticed Meredith someway in front of her, standing in a clearing. As she joined Meredith, she had an overwhelming sense of familiarity, but for the life of her couldn't work out why. It strangely looked like the place where she'd found the key, but something wasn't right about it. Then the penny dropped, the oak tree was still standing, and next to it was a small wooden seat. Memories of home again flooded her thoughts, compounded further by the shafts of sunlight filling this area just as it had in her time. She stood for a second as her emotions tussled with thoughts of home. She was aware that Meredith was watching her and trying to hide her concern, rubbed her eyes, and said, 'something must have gotten up my nose.' By the look on Meredith's face, she knew she hadn't bought into what she'd just said. In one way, she wanted Meredith to know how upset she was feeling but had always shied away from showing her true feelings. Suddenly overwhelmed with emotion, she bent to look at the foliage on some plant. Tears streamed down her cheeks as thoughts of her mum, this day with Meredith, and all she'd learnt from this woman filled her head to bursting point.

Meredith, bent beside her, and putting her hand on her back, spoke with a tone befitting of this woman's selflessness. 'Rebecca, please say that which upsets you so much.'

Avoiding eye contact, Rebecca gently touched Meredith's hand. 'I was thinking about today with Millicent and George and comparing it

123

to my real life at home. I know you doubt, and rightly so, my story, however, I ask you, stick with me.' She again touched Meredith's hand. 'Why do you think people shy away from dealing with their own difficult situations? The story is the same in your time as it is in mine. People accept their thorny existence just to avoid conflict, regardless of their own welfare. It strikes me that only in defence of a loved one are people prepared to stand up and subsequently find a previously untapped inner strength. It's a strength they held all along.' Rebecca could see Meredith was looking somewhat perplexed. 'A good example is the way you stood up to Millicent when she was aggressive towards me. Up until that point, and please don't take this the wrong way, you did what you have so often done, stood back, and just accepted the way things are. However, once you had the bit between your teeth, you then went on to tackle George. Successfully I might add, and with a commitment and verve, you were always in possession of. Today, I have realised that we must speak out not just to protect the people close to us, but also our own corner.' Rebecca nodded, satisfied with what she'd just said.

'I must say, Rebecca that your sentiment is profound and your words are beyond disputation. I too have learnt from this day.' Meredith frowned. 'I am concerned that you continue with your ideas about being a future girl, however...'

'However, what, Meredith?'

'Well, my dear Rebecca, the way you have spoken today, your clothes, many of your mannerisms have altogether made me consider, not accept, the validity of your preposterous narrative. I now find myself conceding there may be some substance to your story.' She shook her head, visibly uncertain.

Rebecca stood up digesting her thoughts.

Meredith touched her arm and pointed to the bench. 'Shall we sit?'

'Yes, lets.'

After a moment's silence, she said, 'I love it here, Rebecca. No matter what time during the day, the way the sun always finds a way through. Oddly, it is bright, even on the dreariest of days.'

'It is lovely here, I must say. Do you come and sit here often, Meredith?'

'Yes, I do come here, normally alone and talk with your beloved father. When I am feeling lonely and miss him. There is something very comforting about this place.'

'I know exactly what you mean. It has an odd, kind familiarity. When I last visited this place, I sensed the pixies were listening to me.' She hesitated, knowing it wasn't the right time to tell her about the key.

'Pixies indeed, Rebecca, what will you propose next? Here, sit close to me, you have been strong for me today. You have helped me change our state of affairs for the better.'

Looking down, Rebecca considered Meredith's words. She looked up and smiled. 'Have I? I do hope so, but I suggest it is mostly down to you. I believe my reason for being sent here was to help you in some way, Meredith.'

'Please, Rebecca, enough of these foolish ideas.'

'I know how outlandish it sounds, but I will go back to my time, and your Rebecca will return. When she does, keep your mind open, and one day, if I return, well...' Suddenly, she found herself considering Meredith's real daughter. She sat with Meredith for an hour or so often wondering about Meredith's daughter. Shivering, she looked up and noticed it had become cloudy. 'Maybe we should head back,' she said, just as it started spitting.

They hurried back to the summerhouse, and as they stepped onto the veranda, Meredith looked up. 'Goodness, Rebecca, there is going to be a storm imminently, a ferocious one too.' Just as she finished speaking, a fierce easterly wind blew across the lake.

'Wow, I have never seen the lake so rough.'

Meredith fumbled around in her pocket. 'Oh dear, I left the key on the seat in the woods. You wait here Rebecca, and I will go and fetch it.' At pace, she headed back up the path.

As Rebecca watched her hurry away, an unbearably loud clap of thunder made her jump. Her thoughts instantly filled with anguish, *what if the tree falls in this storm, what if it lands on Meredith, what if that's how the key got there.* With her thoughts in circles, she rushed after her. With Meredith disappearing into the woods, Rebecca quickened her steps. The sound of the wind howling through the trees, making a horrid whistling sound, compounded her emotions further. Panicked with fear, she ran towards the woods. Not looking where she was going, she tripped, 'ahhh.'

Chapter 8 - The Hospital

Arriving home from their day at the spa, Ruth offered to make some coffee while Liz went to check on Rebecca.

Elizabeth called out from the hallway, 'we're home, Rebecca.' There was no answer, so she headed back to the kitchen and tried phoning her. 'Strange, she's not answering. I am just going to check her room; perhaps she has her headphones on, or maybe she's nodded off.'

'Okay, Liz. Where do you keep the coffee, the beans have run out?'

Elizabeth pointed to the cupboard over the sink and headed off to Rebecca's room. Opening her bedroom door, she called out, 'Bex honey, where are you? Silly girl, are you hiding?' She checked the balcony, but there was no sign of her. Now a little concerned, she hurried back downstairs, calling as she went. 'Rebecca, if you are hiding, I suggest you come out.' She entered the kitchen, shook her head, and shrugging her shoulders, said, 'no sign of her anywhere. I hope she's not messing around.'

'Seems strange, Liz, what do you think she's up to?'

'I bet she is in that summerhouse or maybe gone to the woods. It's odd though if she goes off like this, she most often leaves a note, or lets me know.'

'Let's go and have a look outside.'

After a quick check out the back and round by the garages, they made their way towards the summerhouse, calling as they went. Elizabeth tried the door to the summerhouse only to find it locked with no sign of Rebecca. She turned to Ruth. 'I am starting to worry now. I think I might give James a call.'

'Let's not be too hasty, Liz, we haven't checked the woods yet. We do not want to worry James unnecessarily. You know what Rebecca is like. She could be anywhere. Where did she find that key of hers?'

'Well okay, but I am worried, Ruth. She may only be fifteen, but she is normally so sensible.' She looked around. 'Call it a mother's intuition, but I feel something's amiss.'

'Oh, Liz, I am sure she's okay. Perhaps you should call James if you feel that concerned, but I am sure she will be just fine, probably sitting somewhere drawing, off in one of her worlds. Let's give it a few minutes; I am sure she will turn up.'

'No, I am going to give James a call.' Just as she was about to call, she heard something. 'Did you hear that? I am sure I heard her call out.'

'I did, and it was coming from that direction,' she said, pointing towards the woods.

As they headed over, Elizabeth heard Rebecca again. 'Ruth it sounds like she's calling Meredith,' she said, frowning.

'Do we know a Meredith?'

'Meredith, hmm indeed we do,' she said, flicking her eyebrows. 'That's the name of one of those women in those paintings. You know the ones in the hallway. I'll show you later. What I don't understand is why she'd be calling her name? Come on, Ruth, hurry up.' Between panting for breath, she said, 'I heard her again, Ruth, and she is calling Meredith.' Following the sound of her voice, they found Rebecca lying on the grass, trying to untangle her legs from some bramble. Kneeling beside her, Elizabeth started to help her. 'How did you get in this mess, Rebecca? Are you okay, Sweetie?'

128

Steadying herself, Rebecca said, 'Oh, Mum... It's you.'

'Who did you expect, Rebecca? I heard you calling Meredith's name.'

'Oh, Mum, I guess I must have tripped, but I don't remember much Maybe, I knocked myself out, but...' She lifted her hand, touched her forehead, and looked at her fingers. 'Oh dear, I think I may have cut my head.'

'Careful, Honey, you are rather unsteady?'

Rebecca stretched her neck back. 'Yeah, Mum, I'm fine,' she said, thinking her time with Meredith must have been a dream. But it all seemed so real in her head. She could vaguely remember running after Meredith, but after that, it was blank. She shook her head, knowing something had happened for sure, but what exactly was now annoyingly vague.

'Rebecca dear, you seem rather distant,' her mum said, touching her cheek gently.

Ruth held her finger up in front of Rebecca's eyes, and said, 'Follow my finger, Rebecca.'

She looked at Ruth blankly for a few seconds, then shook her head, and said, 'I'm fine,' and slouched back on her elbows.

Her mum took hold of her hand and said, 'You are very unsteady. We best get you to the hospital, get you checked out. On the way, perhaps you can explain about Meredith.'

Rebecca frowned, and glanced away, unsure what to say. 'Oh, it must be the bang on my head. Maybe I had... I don't know, perhaps it was...' Not having a clue how to explain, especially as she could barely believe what had happened herself, she shook her head. Frustratingly, the more she thought about it, the more distant it

129

seemed, *just like a dream*, she thought. Trying to focus her thoughts, she was suddenly aware her mum was talking to her.

'Rebecca,' her mum said and waved her hand. 'Rebecca.'

She stared blankly at her mum for a moment, then said, 'sorry, Mum, what did you say?'

'Rebecca, you are not making a lot of sense. The sooner we get you checked out, the better.'

Helping Rebecca stand up, Ruth said, 'Yeah, I think you are right, Liz. Come on, I will drive to the hospital. I have some bottled water in the car.'

Elizabeth and Ruth helped Rebecca back to the car and headed off to the hospital.

Sitting in the back, Elizabeth gently wiped the blood from Rebecca's forehead. 'It does not actually look as bad as I first thought; even so, I think I best give your father a call.'

'Oh, Mum, you don't need to tell Dad, I am fine honest, and anyway, we'll be home before he is back.'

'Well, Rebecca, he's your father, and he loves you dearly. He would never forgive me if I did not tell him.'

Rebecca smiled, but was again thinking about Meredith and hadn't really heard what her mum had said.

After Elizabeth had finished phoning James, she said, 'Rebecca, are you listening to me?' She shook her head and said, 'Rebecca, you seem very distant.'

With her mind still on Meredith, and without thinking, she answered, 'Yeah; you are right, Mum, after all, he is my one true Dad, and he is...' She hesitated, realising what she was saying and how it must sound. She looked at her mum and smiled. 'Take no notice, Mum, I am waffling.

'Rebecca, you're beginning to worry me, this bang on your head is obviously worse than it looks.'

'Mum, sorry, take no notice.' She definitely wasn't ready to talk about her adventure just yet and knew she had to pick her words with a little more care. The problem was that she was finding it difficult to think about anything other than the events of the day.

'Take no notice, really? I find you lying in a field with blood dripping from your head, calling out for Meredith. Plus your continued vague, blank expressions and what did you say, "He is my true Dad," I am your mother, and am bound to be concerned.'

'Yeah, you're right, I'm sorry, Mother.'

'Rebecca, please stop saying sorry. We can chat about this tomorrow, but for now, I have to focus on getting you checked out.'

For the next few minutes, Rebecca's thoughts jumped between the day she'd had and how she was going to explain it to her mum. When they arrived at the hospital, her focus changed when she spotted her dad and Tom waiting outside the accident and emergency. As they got from the car, she said, 'Mum, how comes Dad is here?'

'I phoned him while we were in the car. I knew you weren't listening.'

Her Dad walked straight over, took hold of Rebecca's hand, and asked, 'Hello, Rebecca, how are you my lovely? Your mother told me you had a fall in the woods. Come along; let us go and get you checked out.'

131

'Hello, Sis. How are you feeling?' Tom asked, so nicely it caught Rebecca a little off guard.

She screwed half a smile at Tom, before turning her attention toward her father. 'Dad, I am fine, thank you, just a little bang on the head. I am sorry that you had to leave work.' She then turned back to Tom, who was looking genuinely concerned. 'Hello, Tom, I am okay thanks for asking.'

'Rebecca, don't be silly, you are my daughter, and I love you. Perhaps more than I show, but love you, I do. Work can spare me for a couple of hours. I am sure they will not grind to a complete halt without Tom and I.' He turned and patted Tom on the back.

They'd been sitting in the waiting area for around ten minutes when James stood up. 'Right, where is that Doctor. It is a head injury; they should have been here by now. I am going to fetch someone.' He kissed Rebecca on the cheek and then muttering under his breath, marched off down the corridor.

Rebecca watched her father walk along the corridor, clearly on a mission. That instant, a memory of Meredith standing up to Millicent came into her head. What with Tom's reaction, she realised that some people may need a thorny state of affairs before they show their true feelings. She was deep in thought when Tom started bouncing his tennis ball off the wall and broke her concentration.

Ruth stood up and beckoned Tom. 'Tom, come and get some crisps and a drink,' she said and nodded to Elizabeth.

As soon as Tom was out of sight, Rebecca turned to her mum. 'Mum, about Dad being so nice.'

'Yes, Bex, it's hardly surprising though. I did tell you he loves you dearly. Maybe he doesn't show it the way he should, but that's men for you. Sometimes it takes an episode of sorts before they show their true feelings.'

Talking about her Dad, made her think how George had reacted to Meredith's forcefulness. Considering this, and before she'd given herself time to think, the words just jumped out. 'Mum, maybe you should do what Meredith did and tackle Dad, because George...'

'Bex, I know who Meredith is. But who the devil is George, have you found something out?'

Rebecca hesitated. 'Err, kind of, Mum, in a roundabout way. Maybe I will tell you about it later.' She knew she had to give herself some thinking time.

Her mum pouted her lips and frowned. 'Okay, you do that, Bex,' she said, shaking her head. 'Aha, here's your father now.' She stood up, 'Hello, James, did you have any joy?'

'I did, and a Doctor will be here presently. Oh look, here he is now.'

'Hello, Rebecca, I am Dr Stevens. It looks like you have given your head a good thump. Come with me, and we can get you checked out. Would your mother and father like to come with us?' he said and glanced in their direction.

'I'll be just fine,' Rebecca said and smiled to her parents, 'I'm a big gal' now.' She then followed the Doctor.

After a clean-up, and an x-ray, the Doctor had a chat with them all, giving Rebecca the all clear. They bid their farewells to Ruth and headed off home.

When they got there, Rebecca suggested to her mother it might be best if dad didn't know about the spa. Her mum smiled and said she'd see. Heading up to her bedroom, although tired, Rebecca lay in bed for ages thinking about the day she'd had. The more she thought about it, the more details she started to recall, and now felt certain it wasn't a dream. In the end, she felt she'd learnt so much from the day's events that it didn't matter either way.

Chapter 9 - The Newspaper

Rebecca woke to a large bump on her forehead, and feeling a little groggy, made her way to the bathroom. Staring in the mirror, she found herself questioning what had really happened the day before. Dabbing her forehead, she reluctantly accepted it must have been a dream. The problem was her memories of Meredith, Millicent and all that happened were so clear. Besides, if it had been a dream, she would have forgotten most of it by now. She stood in the shower for ages trying to make her mind up one way or the other. As she got dressed, common sense started to take over suggesting it had to be a dream. When she eventually made her way downstairs, something was telling her to look at the painting of Millicent. She stared at it for a few seconds and shook her head. As she turned towards the kitchen, the name plaque caught her attention. She frowned as she read it aloud, "in memory of Millicent Black," then read it again and again. It had changed, that she knew, but no matter how hard she tried, just couldn't remember what it had said originally. Staring at the plaque, common sense said it couldn't have changed, but it had. With Millicent at the front of her thoughts, she joined her mum and Tom on the patio, her concentration briefly broken by Tom asking if she was okay. A little distant, Rebecca nodded once, smiled, and answered, 'Yeah, fine thanks.' She then smiled at her mum who was looking at her in a way only mums can.

Moments later, her dad joined them at the table and smiling, he said, 'Tom and I are off to work soon. Do you two ladies have anything planned today, especially as it's such a lovely day?' He then smiled again.

Surprised by her father's pleasantries and thinking she should bang her head more often, Rebecca laughed aloud. 'Morning, Dad,' she said and giggled.

'Glad to see you smiling, Rebecca. I hope you are feeling better, just take it easy today.'

'Good morning, James, I thought Rebecca and I might go into town and get a little retail therapy.'

James nodded. 'Perhaps you could pick up a holiday brochure?' He then patted Tom on the head.

Looking surprised, her mum sat back in her chair and said, 'Oh, okay, James.' She sipped her coffee and continued, 'I thought you normally arranged the holidays.'

'Well, Tom has been driving me wild, asking if we can go to Florida. It is not my choice, but I thought perhaps you girls might also like that. So have a look, see what you can come up with.'

Elizabeth asked tentatively, 'So, by Florida, am I right in thinking you're referring to Disney?' She winked at Tom, then raising her eyebrows a little, nodded to Rebecca.

Tom jumped from his seat and punched the air as if he had just scored the winning goal in a cup final. 'Yeah, yeah, yeah, Disney, can we go, Dad, Mum?'

'Calm down please, Tom. Yes, Elizabeth, Disney, why not, you only live once, and I do not fancy sitting on a beach for two weeks. Personally, I do not understand the attraction of Disney. However, I am sure you will all have fun.' James shook his head, appearing a little uncomfortable, but still managed a smile. 'I will add that it's not an open chequebook, woman.'

'Dad, why do you sometimes refer to Mum as woman, instead of calling her by her name? It is a little frosty, don't you think?'

He frowned appearing a little awkward. 'I see the bang on your head hasn't affected your tongue, Rebecca. Tom and I are off to work, so I do not have time to discuss it now. I am glad you are feeling better, Rebecca.' He nodded and appeared to think for a moment, then said, 'Elizabeth, please chat with me before you actually book anything as I may have important meetings. Although, what the heck, just do whatever takes your fancy.' He shook his head slightly and headed for the door, followed by Tom, who was still celebrating his imaginary goal.

As soon as the front door had closed, Rebecca turned to her mum. 'Florida,' she said frowning, 'where did that come from, Mum? Also, I picked him up on calling you woman and well... Maybe this bang on my head has done him some good.'

'Well, I am surprised too. His mood has definitely mellowed since your fall, however...' Elizabeth glanced at the floor and then smiled. 'I half expected a negative reaction when you spoke to him.' She sipped her coffee and continued, 'before you make any suggestions, I'm not sure I will find it any easier challenging him.'

'Well, you should try debating little things to build up your confidence, Mum. After all, he is just a man, not an axe murderer. You must remember that no one challenges him at work or at home, not me, well not often, and most importantly not you so he will react negatively until he gets used to it. The more you challenge him, the easier it will get for him and you. With George and Meredith, she just...' Noticing the look on her mum's face change, Rebecca hesitated. 'Err, well that's another story.'

'Another story indeed, I intended to ask you about that, Rebecca. So, who is George? I get the Meredith bit, as in the woman in the painting. So, this George, does he have some involvement with Meredith?'

Rebecca knew whatever she said was going to sound dubious, at best. She looked up and said, 'Yes and no.'

Elizabeth shook her head. 'Yes and no, what exactly does that mean?'

Rebecca scratched the side of her head, unsure how much of the story to tell, and if she should mention the spiral stairs.

'I can see you have something to say, so out with it, Rebecca. I should be used to your fanciful stories by now.'

That was it. She looked up and smiled. 'I am going to tell this like one of my stories, and you can take whatever you want from it.' She then went through the basics of her time with Meredith as if it was a story. Briefly, she touched on each character, having made a conscious decision to avoid her own involvement, although she nearly slipped up more than once.

Holding her hand up, looking puzzled, Elizabeth said, 'you hurried through that, and told it as if...' she then shook her head. 'So, Millicent is the woman in the other painting, right. Importantly, Rebecca, how do you know all this? And what was the deal with Meredith and George again?'

The way her mum was looking at her, she knew she had to be very careful what she said and crucially how she said it. 'Yes, Millicent is the woman in the other painting. And, I have something really odd to tell you about her, well that painting actually.' She paused for a moment and decided to leave that until later. 'Anyway, George married Meredith in a financial agreement. It was something to do with the family reputation and all that.'

'Right, I'm with you so far; I think. I know you said about this being a story and all, but you are telling me this as if this actually happened. Have you found a book or something on the Internet?'

'Well, Mum, it's just a story, but with a difference. I will try and explain it later.' She glanced up, and said, 'I think that was a spit of rain, Mum, shall we...'

Rebecca helped her mum clear away the breakfast stuff while trying to decide what to say and what not to say.

Elizabeth sat at the kitchen table, pointed to the other seat and said, 'sit, and continue.'

She looked at her mum and knew she needed to make things a little clearer. Deciding to explain all about the marriage clause first, she then told of the incident between the two ladies, referring to Millicent as a bloody bitch. Making a big issue about the subsequent discussion between Meredith and George, and again, she referred to the clause that had seemingly stopped them talking. She hadn't intended on using this story as a subliminal message, but it was beginning to turn out that way. She then finished it off by telling her about the storm and realised she'd talked about the storm in the first person.

Still looking a little puzzled, she asked, 'Why did Meredith become angry with Millicent? And, Rebecca, please mind your language.' Her mum then picked up the soap, waved it, and grinned. 'What storm are you talking about, because you said that as if you were in a storm, and we haven't had a storm?'

Rebecca looked at the soap and laughed. 'Okay, Millicent had a row with Meredith's daughter, also called Rebecca, I did tell you that. Anyhow, Millicent threatened her, Rebecca that is, so Meredith reacted. In fact, she became very protective; a bit like dad did last night.'

'This story is a bit all over the place, Rebecca, but I'm intrigued nevertheless. So, carry on, what happened next.'

Rebecca again went through the story right up to the storm.

'Again, you mentioned a storm, and hang on, Rebecca you said, "And I," several times this time, almost as if you were part of it all. I know you go deep into your stories, but you need to explain that please.'

Going by the look on her mum's face, Rebecca knew it was probably time to come clean and tell it as it was. She thought for a few seconds and decided to tell it straight. 'I told you about the seat under the oak tree and the key. Well, Meredith left the key on the seat, and that's how it got there. When the storm blew up, I went rushing to help Meredith. I was there, in 1850 whatever it was.' She looked at her mum's expression, shook her head, and said, 'I know, Mum, but go with me on this.' She then paused and said, 'So, I tripped and the next thing I knew you and Ruth were...' she hesitated, seeing the frown on her mother's face.

'Ruth and I were what, where do we fit into this story? And you were in the 1850s', really?'

'Right, you might struggle to accept this. Look, Mum, you know I never lie to you, ever, right?' She could see the reservation on her mum's face.

'Yes, I do, so tell me...'

'Well, when you went out with Ruth, I went to the summerhouse, and I found the small locked door was open.'

'Okay... You should not have gone there alone, but continue.'

'This is where it gets exciting, inside that door is a spiral staircase.'

'Well, Rebecca, you said there would be stairs there somewhere,' she said and narrowed her eyes.

'Okay, so these stairs lead up to a door, there may be more, but the first one opened, so...' She hesitated for a moment, 'I've kinda deduced that Meredith unlocked the door to let me in, I think.'

'Right, Meredith, who has been dead, for I don't know how long, opened a door, just for you?'

Rebecca maintained eye contact, reckoning her mum would dismiss her out of hand if she didn't. 'Well it opened, and I went through the door, and it slammed shut behind me. Now, this is weird, the next thing I knew I had become Meredith's daughter.' Her mum went to speak, but Rebecca held her hand up and continued, 'I know this sounds silly, Mum, but it really happened. There I was back in the eighteen hundred's and still me. I know how bizarre it must sound, Mum, but honestly, it really happened.'

'Rebecca...'

She wanted her mum to believe her, but the way she was looking at her, she knew what was coming next. 'Mum, I have questioned it myself so many times. Obviously, it had to be a dream, but I know just too many details and Millicent's painting has changed. What is that all about?'

'This is all very interesting, but it does sound like another of your wonderful stories, outlandishly told with more verve than normal, but a story, nonetheless.'

She puffed out her cheeks. 'No, Mum, honestly. Just listen to me and try to believe it, please. So, there I sat, waiting for Meredith to return with the key, and then this storm blew up. I panicked and ran after her, and that is when I fell and knocked myself out. The next thing I knew, you and Ruth were standing over me.' Although her mum was nodding, Rebecca could see the look of disbelief on her face. She still wasn't one-hundred per cent sure it had actually happened herself, so how could she expect her mum to believe it.

'Well, Rebecca, it sounds somewhat farfetched to me. Perhaps you had a dream while you were unconscious. However, I must say it is a fascinating and enthralling story.' She then clenched her lips together and frowned. 'You are not making this up because you want me to challenge Dad, are you?'

'No, Mum, it's all true. Let's go and check the door now, come on the shopping can wait for a bit.'

'Well, we can't be too long because I agreed to meet up with Amanda for lunch. We do have an hour or so, so come on then, let's go and look.'

Elizabeth finished her coffee and followed Rebecca down to the summerhouse. On the way, she handed Rebecca her torch.

'Where did you get this Mum?' She asked, believing she'd left it by the door on the stairs in the summerhouse.

'Oh, I found it on the kitchen table.'

'What the kitchen table indoors?' Rebecca said and suddenly realised she hadn't shown her mum the name plaque on Millicent's painting. For a moment, she considered going back and then as quickly decided to leave it for later.

'Well, that's the only one I know of unless of course, you are going to tell me...'

Rebecca took the torch, totally befuddled how it ended up back indoors. As they arrived at the summerhouse, she headed for the door at the end of the corridor. Taking a deep breath, she gripped the handle, and muttered, 'Meredith, are you going to let my Mum see?' She glanced over her shoulder. 'I asked her yesterday if she would let me in, and she did. I know how it sounds, Mum, but try to stay with me on this.'

Her mum just nodded and pointed to the handle.

She turned the handle and nothing. Again, she turned it, and still nothing. She'd half expected to find the door locked, but was nonetheless peeved. Feeling flummoxed, she knew her mum would now dismiss her story out of hand. She banged the door and muttered, 'Come on, let me in.'

Her mum touched Rebecca gently on the arm. 'Come on, Bex honey, perhaps you dreamt it while you were unconscious.' She then smiled the way only a mum can smile.

'No, Mum, I didn't dream it.' She paused, feeling somewhat upset. 'It really happened.' She banged again on the door, and as she did, heard a noise in the other room. She looked at her mum and said, 'what the hell was that? It sounded like a drawer slamming in Meredith's room,' she said, heading down the corridor and into the room.

Standing in the doorway, her mum said, 'Everything looks the same, Honey, must have been the wind.'

She stood in the middle of the room certain she'd heard something. 'Mum, I am going to check the tallboy.' Unsure what she was expecting to see, she was working her way through the drawers when her mum suggested it was time to head back. 'Just one more drawer, Mum,' she said, and as she opened it, shrieked, 'look Mum; Meredith has left us an old newspaper.' She turned to her mum and said, 'it definitely wasn't here when we looked before.'

Leaning on Rebecca's shoulder, her mum peered at the paper.

Rebecca carefully laid the paper on the floor and knelt beside it. 'This looks very old, Mum.'

Her mum sat next to her on the floor. 'Oh, this bit is very weird,' she pouted, 'it's as if it's been purposefully folded open on this page.' She pointed to the paper and read, "Millicent in Hunting Accident." 'Oh, my word, Rebecca, how strange.'

'Read it, read it all Mum.'

Her mum put on her glasses and peered down. 'It's very small type.'

'Curiosity, the cat, and all that, Mum, read it.'

Slowly, she read aloud, "On the seventeenth day of April, in the year, eighteen-fifty-eight." She turned and frowned, then continued, "At three in the afternoon, Millicent Black, aged twenty-nine, a native of Scotland, and resident for the past seven years at Elm Manor, in Cumbria, died in a tragic hunting accident." She looked again at Rebecca, and said, 'well that's the original house name sorted.'

In a flash, Rebecca thought about the name plaque and knew she should have shown it to her mum earlier, guessing she might now say it had always been like that. 'Mum, read it all, I need to know... And when we get back, remember I told you about Millicent's name plaque changing.'

'Did you?' Her mum frowned. 'Right, where was I? "Millicent, pronounced dead at the scene, was shot to death by a miss-aimed shotgun. She will be missed," said her friend and confidant, George Miller. Her other acquaintance, and wife of George, she turned and looked deep into Rebecca's eyes, 'Meredith Miller refused to comment." It then says the funeral was on the eighteenth of April eighteen-fifty-eight at St Andrews Church. Isn't that the church at the top of the hill?'

Busy searching the words for something more, Rebecca turned to her mum and said, 'Church, err yeah.' She opened her eyes wide and gasped, 'Hang on; that church has been closed for years. I'm sure there was a leaflet that was delivered, something about raising money to re-open it.'

'Crumbs, this is all a bit bloody spooky Rebecca.' She sat back, shivered, and then turned to Rebecca. 'I'm not sure if I can get my head around this. How did you know, how could you? Oh, this is more than a little weird. Really, did you... No, you must have read it somewhere?'

Aware her mum was thrown and trying to see it from her point of view, she said, 'Mum, I know how bizarre it all sounds. It must be hard for you to understand or accept it all. Even I'm struggling with it. But how could I have dreamt all this, although I didn't know about the hunting accident?' She shook her head. 'If it was an accident, I wonder...' she paused for a moment. 'Mum, I mentioned this earlier and should have shown you. This morning, I noticed that the name plaque had changed on Millicent's painting.'

'You keep mentioning that, tell me more.'

'Well, here's the thing, it now reads, "in memory of Millicent Black." I can't remember what it said before, but it has definitely changed since yesterday.'

'What did you mean, if it was an accident? And Rebecca, sorry, but brass plaques don't, or can't change on their own.'

'Well, it's changed, from what I don't know, but changed it has. As for Meredith, she was very cross with Millicent so I wouldn't be surprised if Meredith was involved someway and perhaps...' Suddenly an odd idea popped into her head. She thought for a moment, and uttered, 'what if Meredith's spirit brought me back, or should I say, took me back?'

'I am really finding it hard to get my head around all this, Rebecca. So, let's say you did somehow go back in time. And perhaps her spirit or something like that opened...' Her mum shivered and then continued. 'Brrrr, it's all a bit spooky for me. I wish I hadn't said that.' She shivered again. 'I don't believe in things like this. This is sounding ridiculous.' She stared at Rebecca, and said, 'really?'

Unsure what to say, Rebecca looked at her mum and shrugged her shoulders.

She raised her eyebrows. 'I just don't believe in spirits and certainly not ones who unlock doors. And as for time travelling, well it's all a bit extreme.'

Although Rebecca had questioned the whole episode earlier, there was now too much evidence. 'Mum, just try to keep your mind open. If it was a dream, where did the newspaper, coincidently opened on that page, come from? It is not as if it is a local paper either, we know there wasn't one. I mean, how did that happen? And then there's the name plaque. You must admit that it is starting to add up.'

'Maybe we missed the paper the other day. And, perhaps you found it yesterday, read it, fell and banged your head, then dreamt it all, blanking out you'd read the paper.'

'Yeah right, missed it, read it without knowing, now that does sound daft, Mum.'

Her mum smiled and, all of a sudden, her whole persona seemed to change. 'Hey, Bex, I was just thinking, and this is a maybe, I am not saying I buy into this, but perhaps there is more for you to uncover.'

She narrowed her eyes and held her hand up in a questioning motion.

'Okay, let's say it happened. Perhaps other doors on the stairs lead to other events.' She shook her head. 'No, that's a silly idea. I am obviously getting carried away with your story,' she said and shook her head again. 'You did say there were other doors, didn't you?'

'Not silly, Mum, that is exactly what I was thinking. And that is more like it, open up your mind and see it for what it is, strange and amazing. And yes, it was hard to see, but the stairs went up past the door I went in, so...'

'I don't think we should tell your father; he will think we have gone completely bonkers. Actually, I don't think we should tell anyone, not

146

even Ruth and Amanda. It's all a bit too bizarre.' She lifted her head once. 'I know I do, but I trust you, and it's hard to ignore your conviction.'

'Yeah, let's just keep it as our secret, for now at least. Hey, let's try the door once more before we go and meet Amanda.'

'No, Bex, save it for another day. Say the door opens, and then we will end up being a hundred and odd years late for Amanda,' she said, giggling. 'Plus, I think it has spooked me a little, what with talks of her spirit and all. I'll need some time to get my head around all this.'

The two went back to the main house and after a quick clean up, made their way into town to meet up with Amanda. On their way, her mum was noticeably quiet. Rebecca was desperate to say something but knew she'd have to give her mum time, so decided not to mention it until her mum did.

They entered the car park just as Amanda was getting out of her car. 'Hi, Amanda, it is a lovely day. I thought we could sit outside at the cafe by the river and have some lunch, fancy that?' asked Elizabeth.

'Yeah that will be nice, Liz, I could do with a coffee. Rebecca, are you okay, Sweetie, I heard about your fall, how's your head?'

'Thanks, A, I am just fine. It probably knocked a bit of sense into me. It didn't do Dad any harm either. Mum and I have been having some fun. Hey, get your head around this; Dad said we could get a brochure for our holiday. And, he said we could go to Florida, not just Florida, but Disney. How brilliant is that?'

'Crikey, what brought that on?'

'To be honest, Amanda, I am still a little surprised. There we were last night sitting at the dinner table, and he said...'

'Mum, it was this morning. Let me tell her.' She grinned and turned to Amanda. 'It's her age A; she can't think straight, she makes it up as she goes along.'

'Oh, look who is talking, make it up as I go, do I? And of course, you don't.' She chuckled and gently patted Rebecca on the head. 'Whoops, sorry, forgot about your head.'

'Mum, my head is okay, but I'm not Tom, patting my head.' She said, flicking her eyebrows and grinning. 'Well, there we were, sitting having breakfast, and he said, in the most pleasant of tones, "Nice day ladies." That got my attention, I can tell you. Anyway, then he asked if we had anything planned, and when we said shopping. He then just came out with it.'

'What, going to Florida?'

'Yeah, he just came out with it,' Elizabeth added.

They finished their coffee and headed down to a new department store. After trying on a dress or two and a light lunch, they headed for the travel agents.

Laden with brochures, and heading back to the car, Rebecca asked, 'Mum, can we go back and buy that pink dress. It really suited you, and it fitted perfectly.'

'She's right, Liz. You looked fabulous, and I am sure James will love it. To be honest, it would turn anyone's head, but I suspect you won't want that.'

'Maybe next time we come shopping; I am not really in the mood to buy a dress today.'

'Mum, you're never are in the mood.'

She gave Rebecca one of her annoying looks, and said, 'oh, come on then.' She took Rebecca by the hand, and giggling, suggested, 'you're so pushy.'

After trying the dress on again, Elizabeth finally agreed it looked nice. To Rebecca's surprise, she also purchased a matching handbag and shoes. They headed back to the car park, said their good-byes, and headed home. In the car, Rebecca was tempted to mention Meredith but decided it was probably best not to, especially as she was now again having doubts about the whole episode herself. A clear run home meant they were home well before James and Tom.

When her dad walked in, Rebecca was wholly absorbed in a Disney brochure.

'Don't we even get a hello then, Rebecca?' he said, smiling to Elizabeth.

Elizabeth, who was preparing potatoes, said, 'Rebecca, your father and Tom are home.'

Rebecca looked up and smiled. 'Hello, Dad, Tom. Sorry, miles away' she said and waved her Disney brochure, which resulted in Tom jumping up and down.

'Thomas, calm down a little please.'

'Sorry, Dad,' he said, stood next to Rebecca, and leant over her shoulder.

James shook his head, and then turned to Elizabeth, and asked, 'so, how was your day, Elizabeth?'

'It was lovely, thank you, James. The girls twisted my arm into buying a new dress. It is your favourite colour too.'

Rebecca, who was now trying to stop Tom from turning pages, looked up and said, 'Dad, you wait; she looks a million dollars, very appropriate for the US of A,' she said, grinning at Tom.

'Okay, you must show me after supper.'

Later, that evening while Rebecca was getting ready for bed, her mum sat with her chatting. 'I am still getting my head around your story, honey. Although it's very intriguing, it has spooked the hell out of me.'

'Yeah, I understand. Even I am struggling to get my head around it in spite of it initially all feeling so real.'

'What do you mean, Honey?'

'What you said about it being a dream while I was unconscious and all, well, I just don't know what to think now. I keep wondering if I had read the newspaper, then dreamt about it and somehow forgot everything, what with a mild concussion, and all. The thing is I know so much. What I don't get is the name plaque that has changed.'

'I really don't know what to think. I was looking at the painting when we got back, and I can't honestly say it has changed. I didn't take a lot of notice in the first place. Although, I also know that if anyone knew if it had changed, it would be you.'

'I kind of feel the same, Mum. The one thing I am certain of is it has changed, but it can't of, can it?'

The next couple of days passed quickly for Rebecca, having endlessly *googled* Elm Manor all to no avail. Between planning the holiday, they chatted at length about the summerhouse. Clearly intrigued, her mum even agreed to go and check the door a couple of times. Each time they went though, Rebecca's memories of her journey seemed to fade a little more. This just compounded her doubt to the point where she told her mum that as fantastic as it was, it couldn't possibly have happened.

Up early, she was again searching on her computer for Elm Manor. Deep in thought, her mum walked in and reminded her it was back to school today. Her memories were becoming fuzzy at best and troubled by this she sat staring at the screen, hoping for a sign of sorts. 'I need that door to open again,' she mumbled and started getting dressed for school. Hearing her mum call her for breakfast, she headed downstairs. As she entered the kitchen, her thoughts were preoccupied with Meredith. Then she spotted her mum making a packed lunch bringing her back to reality with a crash. She slumped herself down at the table. 'Good morning, Mother. School today, yippee, and I have all my exams this term,' she grumbled, 'I don't mind really but have had such a great time with you over the last couple of weeks, and I don't want it to end. Then, of course, there's Meredith, ha-ha.'

'Well, I hope you focus, Honey. Perhaps put the summerhouse to the back of your thoughts for a while and just think about your exams. It will make so much difference to your life if you do well, especially if you decide you want to go on to university. If I had my time again, I would love to do it differently.' She glanced through the window briefly, sighed, and then smiled. 'I have had the best of times with you, although the Meredith thing still has me spooked,' she said and smiled. 'You are my best friend as well as my daughter. I am blessed to have you.'

'You're my best friend too, Mum. I love you so much that it hurts sometimes. I will do well at school, I promise. Remember that I actually like school. And before you say, it is okay, I will not tell anyone about my little adventure.'

Chapter 10 - Final Exam, then Florida

Rebecca's exam laden term was made even worse by one of the worst Junes on record. Although miffed by it raining every day, she found it easier to focus on schoolwork and put the summerhouse to the back of her thoughts.

With just one exam to go, she'd decided to have a break from studying and sat in the kitchen chatting to her mum. After discussing her school work, the subject turned to Meredith. Much to Rebecca's frustration, her recollection was now an array of jumbled, blurred memories. Trying to put the pieces back together, she rambled back and forth. Although her mum showed interest, she could sense her reservations. Deciding to go back to her bedroom, she stared through the window for a few moments. Begrudgingly, she turned to her math's course work, and even though she didn't mind a bit of algebra, she just couldn't focus.

Stepping out onto the balcony, she stared down towards the lake. Fallen cherry blossom covered the grass, and her mind turned to summer. 'Soon be the holidays,' she sighed, impatient to escape the drudgery of her revision. Knowing she had to concentrate, she groaned and went back inside. Slumping down at the computer, she twiddled her fingers through her hair. That very morning, her mum had said that she loved it long, 'But not halfway down my back,' she mumbled.

Still unable to focus, she returned to the balcony and watched the grass swaying in the gentle breeze. Eventually, she puffed out her cheeks, lumbered back to her work, and spent an ineffective hour studying. Sighing, she'd had enough and needed a proper break, so made her way downstairs to re-join her mum in the kitchen. She intended to avoid the subject of her journey, and instead chat about their holiday.   In passing, her mum innocently mentioned the summerhouse, and in a flash, her thoughts were back with Meredith.

'What I don't get, Mum is the door opening that once.'

'I really want to believe it happened, Bex.   I know about the newspaper and all, but I can't escape the dream notion.   The door being locked just compounds my thoughts further.'   Her mum frowned.   'I don't doubt you believe this really happened, and I can only suggest that the dream was so vibrant it has left you believing it to be a reality.'

Rebecca knew if she was going to prove it to her mum, the only option was to open the door again.   'Well, Mum, I stand by what I said, although I do occasionally wonder myself, more so of late.   Hey, did I tell you about my history teacher?'

'No, Honey, what was that then?'

'Right out of the blue he started talking to me about our house and said he had struggled to find any history.   No surprise there, but he did mention the Second World War.   Evidently, our house was an orphanage for children who had lost their families.   How cool is that?'

'Oh right, Ruth said something along those lines.   I am sure we talked about it.   It just compounds the matter, what with your teacher being into history, and unable to find anything.   So not much hope for us, I guess.'

'I spoke to him at lunch, and he said that it was all a bit odd, especially having the original and present name.   He suggested there might have been a cover-up after some sort of incident.   I must say, I thought it was bloody weird when he said, "in the nineteenth century."   But when I asked him, he implied that it was just a period when affluent people had a habit of covering up controversial incidents.' she smiled.   'Not much changed then.'

'Well, Ruth's contact at the council office suggested a cover-up, and we have definitely talked about that before, she said and laughed. 'You didn't tell your teacher about your little trip, did you?'

'No, Mum, don't be daft.'

'To be honest, I didn't think you would,' she said and raised her eyebrows. 'It crossed my mind to get a psychic to have a look around?'

Wide-eyed, Rebecca exclaimed, 'Nooo, Mum. Honestly, that will end it forever. Then we will never know.'

Taken aback, she asked, 'how much more is there to know about Meredith and co, and end what forever?'

'Mum, the other history, Meredith played one small part. There are also all the other people who have lived here. This house goes back many years, and I want to know everything. First thing, I have to find out what really happened to Millicent.' She shook her head, 'a psychic will end it there and then.'

With a fickle tone, her mum said, 'If your history teacher wasn't able to research the house, then...'

Rebecca lifted the palm of her hand. 'Mum, I am fed up trying to find something on the Internet and want to find out for myself. There are parts of this house that date back four-hundred years. That leaves us a whole lot of history to uncover.'

'I understand, but how are we going to find anything, because at the moment it is two rooms and a locked door.'

'Mum, we had the books, the photos, and then the newspaper turning up. What will we find next? Everything we've discovered so far has carried a message of sorts, a message from the past. We just need to jig them all together. It's a puzzle.'

154

'I like the puzzle idea, but everything has a rational explanation. Even the newspaper, which I have no doubts was there all along, as we said before.'

'No, don't think so, Mum, it was right at the top and what about the drawer slamming and all, remember that? And, you were the one who said there may be more doors on the stairs.'

'Perhaps.' she smiled, 'I hear what you are saying and want nothing more than to believe it's true.'

Although Rebecca could understand her mum's indifference, she still found it a little frustrating. She nodded and said, 'Perhaps nothing, Mum. It's a bit like the fairies, and the pixies, and for that matter, the bears too. You need to open your mind, not just your eyes. The problem is, as people become older, they lose their ability to see things for what they are, and there you have it. What was it Nan said, "Stay young, be happy?" She was right. Bless her. I bet she knew where the fairies lived.' She shook her head. 'Actually, the fairies are a fanciful ideal, but Meredith is real. Well, she is for me.'

'Lose it when we are old, do we?' she said and grinned. 'So, Rebecca, when do you finish school, soon I think?'

'Oh, let's change the subject, shall we? Two more days actually, Mother, I told you last week and the week before.'

'Sorry, you did say, I was just thinking about our holiday. I am so excited.'

Inwardly shaking her head, Rebecca knew the Meredith conversation was over. She smiled, leant over, and touched her mum's hand. 'Not as excited as Tom, playing Mickey Mouse video games, and when he's not, he's bouncing that flipping Mickey Mouse football off every wall. Mind you, I'm rather excited too.' After chatting about their holiday, Rebecca told her mum she needed to get on with her maths. Inside, it was the last thing she fancied but knew that once finished, that would be it, and she'd be free to do what she wanted.

Over the next couple of days, Rebecca got her head down and worked hard. It was worth it in the end as her final exam left her feeling very confident. With school now finished, the first opportunity, she went straight down to the summerhouse. Infuriatingly, the door was again locked. She stood there for a few minutes and reckoned she wasn't feeling it, whatever it was. Deciding to leave the summerhouse for a while, she spent a couple of days in the woods sketching. On a particularly lovely day, her mum joined her, writing and catching up on Rebecca's stories. Rebecca had made a conscious decision not to talk about her trip, not at least until she had some hard evidence. Indeed, when her mum had asked if they should write about her journey, Rebecca said she wanted to get it straight in her own head first.

Bleary-eyed, after a restless night caused by their new resident *hooting owl*, Rebecca peered at her watch. She groaned, seeing how early it was, but suddenly remembered they will be off on holiday tomorrow. Yawning, she laid there for a few minutes and then decided to get up and have a shower. Just as she got in the shower, her mum walked in. 'Mum, you made me jump,' she called out.

'Morning, Rebecca. Have you got everything packed?'

'Mum, it is Florida, and it is ninety degrees, and it is Disney. How much stuff do I need?'

'Well, I'm just checking, Honey.'

'Tom is the one you need to check on. I think you'll find he has packed his computer and no clothes,' she laughed, 'pass me that towel, please.'

'He had better not, I told him, little monster.' She handed Rebecca the towel. 'I'm going to check on the little so-and-so,' she said and chuckled.

Rebecca decided to spend some time on the balcony drawing. She was miles away when Tom's bellowing voice made her jump. For some reason, he was running up and down the hallway screaming at the top of his voice. Feeling a little irritated, her mood soon changed when he walked in with a daft Mickey Mouse mask on making her laugh aloud. The rest of her day passed off with relative calm other than Tom's odd interruption, which in the scheme of things didn't actually bother her too much. That evening her dad sat at the dining table for around ten minutes without saying anything other than hello. Noticing this, Rebecca asked, 'Dad, you're quiet, are you okay, perhaps looking forward to our holiday tomorrow?'

'Well, I cannot believe we are actually going, and I am certainly not buying any Mickey Mouse tee shirts.' He then sort of grinned and frowned at the same time.

In her best smiley tone, Rebecca said, 'Dad, don't be like that, after all, it was your idea.'

'Well, it may have been my idea, and right now it seems like a bad one. We should have gone to New York, the financial capital of the world, much more interesting.'

The way her dad flicked his eyebrows, Rebecca suspected he was secretly looking forward to it. 'Oh yeah, yippee, that would have been fun unless there's a *Disney Finance* theme park.'

'Oh, I don't know, Rebecca. I actually find the New York idea rather appealing. You have all those stage shows, so many fabulous shops, and then there are some of the best restaurants on the planet,' her mum said.

'Well okay, Mum, maybe next time we can go to New York. However, if we go, I don't want to visit a bank, other than to get some money for the shows and such-like. Anyway, I am sure we are all going to have a whale of a time in Florida.'

'I'm not sure that a whale of a time is the right description. However, I am mildly interested in visiting the NASA space-centre.'

'See, there you go, Dad.'

'Yeah, Dad, can we go to NASA because I want to be an astronaut when I grow up.'

'If you grow up, Tom,' Rebecca said, pulled a face, and giggled.

'Dad, tell her.'

'Rebecca, I have told you before, you should always speak to people in a way you would expect to be spoken to.'

'Yes, Dad, you're right on that one.' Rebecca thought, *practice-preach*. She then turned to Tom. 'So, is there any particular planet you fancy going to, Tom? I was thinking Uranus.' She looked at Tom waiting for a response, but he didn't even blink an eye, and she guessed he was either too excited or didn't get the joke or didn't care. However, she did notice both her mum and dad frowning. The rest of the evening passed off peacefully, well as quiet as it could with a younger brother bouncing off the ceiling.

'So, Rebecca, are you packed?'

'Yes, Mum. Twenty times you've asked. I hope you didn't pack that heavy coat you were trying on yesterday, Mum. It's ninety degrees in the shade.'

'Yeah, yeah, whatever,' her mum said and made her fingers into the shape of a "W".

158

'Mum, what are you like? I'm guessing you picked that up from Tom?' she said, laughing aloud.

'I might have done. Whatever.'

This tickled Rebecca, and giggling, she said, 'somehow, Mother, I think you are a little over excited, maybe you should join Tom on the ceiling.'

'I might just do that to get away from you, miss prim and proper.' She then did the W sign again.

After Rebecca had helped tidy the kitchen, she decided to have an early night. She was just dozing off when her mother popped in.

'Goodnight, Rebecca, I love you, Honey.'

'I love you too, Mum. I'm looking forward to our holiday so much. I do hope Dad lets his hair down while we are away.'

'Yes, me too 'coz that's all he needs you know.'

'Yeah, I know, Mum. Hey, I was thinking about Meredith.'

'What, Bex, if she ever went to Florida?'

'Don't be daft, Mum, just how things turned out with George, and how her daughter is, err was.'

'I have to say, I occasionally think, or wonder, or both. Hmm.'

'Think or wonder what, Mum?'

'Oh, I don't really know, just what it was like in those days. Women did not work in most parts, certainly not in those high-society circles. As a result, I guess they became very dependent on the men. Perhaps that is why the suffragist movement started. Anyways, I

159

suppose they must have felt trapped if they were in a loveless relationship. At least now-days women are independent and do not have to put up with such situations. That is why it is so important to have a good education, Honey.'

'And you're telling me. Finally, she's getting it, hello Earth to Mum.' Rebecca elbowed herself up, kissed her mum and said, 'Don't worry, Mother; I intend on being a career girl, well at least until Mr Right comes along, if he does.'

'You are a beautiful woman and have such a lovely soul. I am sure your Mr Right will come along. Any man would feel blessed with you by his side,' her mum said, kissed Rebecca on the forehead and said goodnight.

The following morning was dark and gloomy, having a permanent threat of rain in the air. Everyone was up early and taking a light breakfast before the cab arrived at 6 am. Just as Tom was getting himself in trouble, the doorbell chimed. After a couple of moments frantically checking their passports and tickets, they set off for the airport. Other than Tom becoming a little fidgety, the flight was stress-free, and they were landing in Florida in what seemed like a blink of the eye. The fact that James had secretly upgraded them to business class not only went down well but undoubtedly helped with the long journey.

In spite of the odd torrential downpour, which seemed to catch them out every time, they had a fantastic holiday. The only minor debate was about where they should eat each day. Rebecca and Tom always fancied the all-you-can-eat options, while mum and dad preferred the posh restaurants. Over the two weeks, they found a good compromise. It wasn't until the last day that Rebecca and Tom finally hoodwinked dad onto one of the rides. Even then, he'd maintained his stiff upper lip, although Rebecca saw him grinning on more than one occasion. The fact that he went on two more rides was the icing on the cake. The two weeks flew by, and they were soon landing at Manchester Airport.

They walked into the arrival's lounge and spotted Ruth waiting for them, complete with a Mickey-shaped sign with all their names on.

'Hello, Ruth. I didn't expect to see you here,' Elizabeth exclaimed.

'Come on guys, this short stay car park is costing me a fortune,' she said and laughed. 'It is about thirty quid a minute.' Ruth kissed Elizabeth on the cheek. She then took her case, placed it on the trolley, and indicated for James's case.

He frowned and in a somewhat brusque tone, he said, 'Ruth, you didn't have to...'

Elizabeth nudged James, glared at him, and mouthed, 'don't you dare.'

He glanced once at her, then smiled at Ruth, and politely said, 'Thank you for coming, Ruth. I will be more than happy to pay for the car park. It's the least I can do. And please let me push the trolley.'

On the journey home, Tom talked incessantly about their adventures in the greatest of detail. Indeed, every time Rebecca, Elizabeth, or James tried to say something, Tom went off on another story. In the end, Elizabeth put her hand over Tom's mouth and said, 'Tom, let someone else speak please.'

'So, James, you liked the Tower of Terror?'

'Well, it was okay. I must say I did not expect it; perhaps it was the best way. We live and learn, as they say, Ruth.' He glanced at Rebecca and grinned. 'This child tricked me onto the ride.' He then paused for a moment, and said, 'a pity she didn't do it sooner. Now, we might have to go back again, and that will never do.' He grinned, and with a fake cough, muttered, 'but not before Christmas.'

Rebecca sat up in her seat, nudging her mum, and then noticed Tom was sitting there with his mouth open. Not wanting to miss this opportunity, she screwed up a piece of paper and stuffed it into his mouth. He tossed the paper at her and started on another story. Rebecca sat and wondered how long it would be before he ran out of things to say, *if ever*, she thought. Hmm, maybe not before we go back, she thought and smiled.

Chapter 11 - Bear Forest

Following a week of cloudy days, summer finally kicked in, bringing those long warm evenings Rebecca loved so much. Although desperate to get outside to do some exploring, she'd offered to help her mum organise a garden party and knew the woods had to wait. In an attempt to get the idea past James, her mum had suggested that the party could tie-in with Tom's birthday. He surprised everyone by agreeing without hesitation, although he'd insisted on an alcohol-free affair.

While loading the dishwasher after breakfast, Rebecca had an idea. 'Mum, I've been thinking, how about you go out one evening with Ruth and Amanda. Then you can wear your new pink dress, the one you chose to forget about. I'd be interested to see what Dad's reaction would be if you went out looking fabulous.'

'I really do not think I would feel comfortable wearing that pink dress, not without your father. Besides, in reality, I don't think he would agree.'

'Mum, if you don't ask him, you don't know what he will say.'

'Well, for a start, what would he and Tom do about supper?'

Unable to believe her mum's mind-numbingly passive excuse, Rebecca sat with her mouth open. 'Mum, tell me you're not serious.' She puffed. 'For heaven's sake, I can cook you know. It might be fun me cooking for him and the twit. Have you ever been out without him?' She shook her head, 'besides, surely Dad can cook.'

'Of course, I have, but that was way back when we were younger. I just don't think he would agree nowadays. By the way, don't call Tom a twit, there's a good girl.'

'Well if Tom keeps copying Dad, he will end up a real twit.' By her mum's reaction, Rebecca knew she'd touched a nerve.

Her mum stared down at the floor briefly, and then looked up. 'Yes, Rebecca, I have noticed, especially since Ruth and Amanda pointed it out. However, you calling him a twit won't help.'

Surprised by her mum's answer, she knew there was no need to emphasise the point and so decided to get back on track. 'Hey, Mum, how about you go out for Ruth's birthday, which is Wednesday, right?'

'Funny you should say that, Ruth said it would be nice if we went out. Amanda turned around and said I would say no. Am I that predictable?'

'Yep, in a word, Mum. I believe in you, but even I knew you'd say no.'

'But it is only a few days before the garden party, so I couldn't possibly put him in that position.'

'What position, Mum, having to think about something other than work?'

'Well, he... I don't know. Besides, I have things to arrange for the party, and so on. And, I haven't been out on my own for years so it would be unreasonable to drop it on him like this.'

Rebecca looked to the ceiling. 'Mum, you're putting barriers in the way to avoid him saying no. Just ask him and see what he says. Don't expect him to say no, and if he does, have a pretty good reason why he should agree. Have you ever tried that? You certainly do it with Tom and me, so... You asked him about the party.'

Her mum nodded a couple of times and changed the subject back to the party arrangements. Although Rebecca felt frustrated, she knew her mum had acknowledged what she'd said. She spent the remainder of the day creating a party tick-list with her mum. She mentioned Ruth's birthday a couple of times but each time got the same; *I get the message,* okay.

The following morning, Rebecca was up early and out on the balcony. Watching the mist over the lake, it started to drift in the warmth from the sun, and her mind instantly went back to the woman in the boat. She shook her head, realising it could well have been Meredith. *Why didn't I think of this before?* Her recollection of the journey had greyed considerably, but this thought brought colour back to her memories. She knew she had to get behind that locked door and soon. Just as she was trying to come up with a plan, her mum opened the balcony door and broke her concentration.

'Come on, Honey let's have breakfast on the patio. It is a lovely day.' And almost as if her mum had tuned into Rebecca's thoughts, she looked down toward the lake and said, 'I love that mist, the way it hovers over the lake in the morning. It creates a mystical feel.'

'Absolutely, Mum, I was just thinking about that, makes your imagination run away with you. Anything could happen on a day like this. This is a day for the fairies, the pixies, and Meredith.'

'Oh, back on Meredith are we, so what makes you mention her?'

'You remember that woman I saw on the boat?'

Her mum squinted. 'Thought you saw, you're not going to tell me it was Meredith, are you?'

'Just a thought, but...' She could tell from the look on her mums face she was wasting her breath. She got up and followed her mum downstairs. Seconds after they had sat down on the patio, James came out.

'Elizabeth, I will take my breakfast inside, thank you.'

165

'But Dad, it is lovely out here.'

'I have some work to prepare, but thank you,' he said and went inside.

Rebecca followed her father inside. Although he'd come across as a little stiff, he'd thanked her nicely, and she decided to seize the moment and mention Ruth's birthday. 'Dad, did Mum tell you about Ruth's birthday on Wednesday?'

James looked directly at Elizabeth, and asked, 'Who is Ruth?'

It was all Rebecca could do to stop herself from huffing. 'Dad, you know who Ruth is. Mum's mate, she picked us up from the airport and took me to the hospital when I had my accident. You do know who she is, and I know you do.'

He frowned at Rebecca, but she could see he didn't have an answer. He then turned to Elizabeth and said, 'Okay, what about your friend's birthday?'

'Well it's next Wednesday, and she has invited Amanda and me to a restaurant for the evening.'

He appeared unmoved, and before he had a chance to say no, Rebecca jumped in. 'Dad, I was hoping to take the opportunity to cook for you and Tom. I am all grown up now. I have to learn to cook somehow, and there's no one better to test out my culinary skills than my father, the most important man in my life.' Rebecca noticed his eyes soften, and realised she might actually be making some headway.

'Well, Rebecca, as you put it like that, I will think about it while I am at work. Your Machiavellian approach young lady is,' he shook his head, 'perhaps best suited to the financial world. I shouldn't, but I admire your stealth.'

'Dad, Mum needs to let Ruth know this morning, so they can book somewhere. And, importantly, if I am to cook supper for my two favourite men, I need time to prepare. You've always said, prepare to fail, or prepare to succeed.'

He squinted at Rebecca, and then looked directly at Elizabeth. 'I am sure your mother is capable of speaking for herself. I hope you are not trying to gang up on me, Rebecca.'

'Tut-tut, Dad, I wouldn't do that, even I am not that Machiavellian,' she said and giggled.

He sipped the last of his coffee, stood up, and through squinted eyes, said, 'well I am off to work.' He called Tom, and as he was leaving, he turned to Rebecca. 'Beef will be nice, Young Lady.' He then turned to Elizabeth and nodded once.

After he'd left, Rebecca and her mum went back outside and sat for a few moments without talking.

'Machiavellian indeed, I would call it conniving. You should have let me ask him; however, I suspect you think... Hmmm, you will have to help me to sort out what I am going to wear.'

After going over a few suggestions, her mum surprised her by agreeing to wear the new pink dress. While she was helping tidy away from breakfast, Rebecca suggested they went and had a go in the boat. She'd noticed the lake was like a millpond earlier and thought it might be a good day to try to make it to the forest. Her mum was a little hesitant, suggesting they still had things to do for the party. Rebecca showed her the completed list, which she looked at for several minutes until finally nodding. After preparing some lunch, they headed down to the lake. Within minutes of climbing aboard, Rebecca suggested their rowing skills had improved so much that they could easily reach the forest. Her mum thought for a moment, shrugged her shoulders, and agreed.

With minimal effort, they soon found themselves in the middle of the lake. 'It's spooky, Mum.' Rebecca said, noticing how far they were from either shore.

'What is, Honey?'

'Being in the middle of the lake like this, I think it being so calm just adds to it.' She then peered over the side. 'Mum, have you seen how clear this water is?'

'Crumbs, you can see right to the bottom.'

'Yeah, exactly and they can see right to the top.'

'Rebecca, what or who can see right to the top?' she said shaking her head. 'You are not going to tell me pixies are living in the depths, are you?' her mum said, and then leant over the side again, rocking the boat.

'Mum, stop rocking the bloody boat,' Rebecca said, grabbing the side. 'And don't ask silly questions. I've told you before that pixies loathe open water.'

Her mum put her hand to her chin in that irritating way. She then said, 'Oh do they, you learn something new every day.'

'Now, Mum, don't be sarcastic, it doesn't suit you.'

'Okay, so who might be watching us? And, stop swearing or else it's...'

'I'm not sure yet, Mum. It could just be a big old pike, but there might just be something else watching us, who knows.'

'I see, Rebecca, and what makes you think some big old pike are living in this lake?'

'Actually, Amanda's boyfriend told me, well not me exactly. Do you remember the guy in the removal lorry? He said something about wanting to go fishing for pike. I overheard him asking Amanda.'

Rebecca kept peering over the side, but as they got close to the shore, her focus changed. The huge pine trees cast diluted shadows along the silvery shingle beach, creating a slightly eerie feeling. These had to be the largest pines she'd ever seen, and while contemplating their age, her mum's voice broke her attention.

'I have to say I find it a bit creepy, Bex. It's somewhat daunting, especially these huge trees. No wonder we can smell them back home.'

'Mum, perfect for bears,' she said and giggled.

'Bex, I told you, Honey, there are no bears here. To be frank, I'm not sure there has ever been any around here.'

'Is that right, so why did they build a bear hunting lodge, Frank?'

Her mum looked puzzled. 'A bear hunting lodge, what are you talking about?'

'I told you, Mum, when we were at the hospital. It was where Meredith lived before she moved into the summerhouse.' Rebecca thought for a moment and said, 'I did tell you, didn't I?'

'You may have done, but to be honest, you were doing a lot of talking and, well... I was more concerned with your head, so I only half listened. I thought we decided it was a dream.'

'Not a dream, Mum. An increasingly vague memory, but not a dream.'

'Hmm, so tell me about the bear hunting lodge.'

'Well, it's where she lived, and I think we should go and search for it. Look, there is an old landing stage just up there, and I suspect the lodge won't be far away. When we find it, then perhaps you will... Well, I don't need to say anymore.'

'Well I guess we can try to dock there; I emphasise try,' she said and laughed. 'And you won't say any more, really.'

Much to Rebecca's surprise, they successfully navigated their way alongside the old wooden landing stage, only to find it was on its last legs, with half of it hanging in the water. She was just thinking about how they could climb out when her mum started prodding the remains with her oar.

'I think we may have to land on the shore, Bex. And this is not one of your oak pieces, is it?' she said and then screamed as part of the jetty collapsed into the water.

'Well, with all these pine trees, I guess... I wonder if Meredith was the last person to use it.' Rebecca shivered. 'Crumbs, what a spooky thought that is, we're the first people here since Meredith.'

'Oh, I am sure someone must have used it since, but thanks,' her mum said and shivered.

'How exciting, we could be the first people here for over a hundred and fifty years.' Hearing her own words intensified Rebecca's mood. Staring aimlessly, the sound of her mum's voice broke her thought process.

'You okay, Bex?'

Rebecca smiled. 'Miles away, sorry, Mum. I was just thinking about Meredith. I would love to know if she ever found happiness. I so wish I could speak to her again.'

'Hmmm,' her mum said and raised her eyebrows. 'Shall we start rowing towards the shore?'

A few seconds later, the boat made a horrid scraping sound as it juddered to a halt a few feet from the bank. Unable to get any closer, Rebecca removed her socks and shoes, jumped out the boat, and started wading. 'We got no choice, Mum. Once we're both out, we can pull the boat ashore.' She gritted her teeth as the coarse gravel bit into her feet. Stepping onto dry land, she turned and watched her mum tiptoe ashore. With every step, she shrieked a muddle of laughter and pain. 'I love seeing you so happy, Mum.'

'I am happy all the time, Honey. Perhaps I don't always show it, but I have you and Tom to make me smile. Your father always made me laugh, especially when we were...' She hesitated, staring into the distance.

Guessing what her mum was going to say, she asked, 'Mum, what was your relationship like with Dad when you first met him?'

Her mum stared at Rebecca for only a few seconds, but it was as if a whole lifetime of thoughts showed in her eyes. She briefly looked away, and then said, 'Oh we had so much fun. Your father had a red sports car, and I was as mad as a March-Hair, well...' Rebecca could see that pensive look again. 'Often, we would stay out all night, and we even slept in the car a few times. We never had a plan or route, just used to let the car go wherever it wanted.' She grinned. 'We ended up in London once, in some dodgy hotel. We laughed so much when we went down for breakfast in the morning. The place was full of low-lives and drop-outs.'

'So, what happened, Mum, when did things change, when did you and Dad stop laughing?'

The way her Mum shrugged her shoulders and glanced away, Rebecca knew she shouldn't push her on this and let her speak in her own time. As they wandered along the beach, she was suddenly aware her mum wasn't with her. She turned and could see her standing still, staring across the lake. Rebecca walked back and held her mum's hand. 'What are you thinking about, Mum?'

Still staring across the water, her mum said, 'I really don't know. I often look back and ask myself what happened to the fun. Soon after we got married, I gave up work and became entirely dependent on your father. I guess when I lost my own income, with it went my independence. He was the only person I knew. I'd lost contact with all my friends and ultimately left myself alone. I didn't have Amanda in those days, just relied on his company. Insanely, I had lost touch with Ruth, which made me sad.' She scratched her head and gave a sideways glance to Rebecca. 'I guess I just lost my ability to contest anything with him. I was so happy when he got in from work, I accepted everything he said. He'd become central to my whole life, and it didn't help I'd chosen to not have an opinion on anything. We lost our way, and with it, lost the fun.'

On the one hand, Rebecca was pleased her mum was opening up to her but somewhat saddened by her story. 'Mum, what a sad tale, but at least you know that Dad is fun, not just a financier. Have you ever tried to get things back to where they were?' Rebecca suddenly remembered something. Pouting, she said, 'Hey, when we were in Florida, Dad described our Mustang as just a red car. I might have a word with him about that.' Seeing her mum frown, she grinned and said, 'in a nice way of course.'

'Oh don't, Honey, I would prefer it if you didn't. Hmm. Actually, I wouldn't mind mentioning it myself.'

'Yeah, and that is what's wrong, Mum, anything for a peaceful life. You need to challenge him on things like that, in a slightly passive way, but still make him answer. I am going to say at dinner, hey dad, I heard you had a red sports car when you were young. Just see what his reaction is, do it nicely, but with a hidden agenda.'

'I so wish I had your resolve, Bex. I often want to say something, but I get tongue-tied and somehow lose my ability to speak. Let alone put a challenging sentence together. So, as always, I say nothing.'

'You know things were fun, Mum, so take it back, a bit at a time. When we are having dinner tonight, why don't you tell him you mentioned his old red sports car to me, and see how he reacts? I bet he changes the subject, but it will still make him think. And you are never lost for words with Tom and me, so you can't use that excuse.'

'Yeah, or he could get irritated and start calling me woman again. I hate that.'

Rebecca groaned loudly, 'well, Mum, tell him how much you dislike it. I hate it too.'

The way her mum shrugged her shoulders without saying anything Rebecca knew the subject was becoming uncomfortable. She squeezed her mum's hand. 'Come on; let's see if we can find this elusive lodge.'

'Yeah, let's.'

Moments later, Rebecca spotted an old worn path leading through the woods. 'This looks like it might lead somewhere,' she said, taking her mum by the hand.

The path soon became so overgrown that Rebecca found herself wondering if it was actually leading anywhere. To compound her hesitation further the light beneath the huge conifers had become diluted to the point where she could barely see. Feeling a tad uneasy but nonetheless, determined, she gripped her mum's hand and tentatively led her a little further. Arriving at a fork in the path, she decided to go with a hunch and follow it to the right. After a couple of minutes, their progress was blocked by a mass of bramble, ivy, and fallen branches. At her feet were huge buttery coloured toadstools and in the dimmed light, she knelt down for a closer look. 'These have got

173

to be poisonous,' she said, turning to her mum. She stood up and looked around. As she was about to turn back, she noticed a shaft of sunlight someway off to the left. Pointing, she turned and glanced at her mum. 'I think we should have taken the left fork, although that clearing doesn't look too far away.'

'I think we should turn back, Rebecca. How do you know it's a clearing, you can't possibly see from here?'

'I know, but this path must lead somewhere,' she said, carefully treading the bramble down with her foot. After a few tentative steps, she could again see a way forward. On the other side, a thick spongy moss covered the path and combined with the strange muted light, intensified her mood.

'Crumbs, Rebecca, this is very weird. Now, I could imagine pixies and such-like living here.'

'You don't know anything, do you, Mum? Not the type of place you would expect to see a pixie or fairy, they don't like it this gloomy. They would only be here if they were lost. No, it's much more likely to be elves. Then, of course, you've got the bears too,' she said and giggled.

'Okay, now you have to explain that.'

'Explain what, Mum?'

'The difference between them all, 'coz I'm lost, I am sure you said elves like elm trees, and as there's no elm, well...'

'Yep, they do like elms, but it's only by choice, not a must. You obviously listened to some of what I said, Mum. So, to the difference, I will explain and sketch some pictures as we walk along, if I can see to draw, that is, ha!' She pulled a small pad from her rucksack and started doodling. After a couple of moments, she held up a sketch. 'Let me explain, fairies are gentle, soft creatures that love the sun,

174

especially when it filters through the leaves, but they definitely don't like direct sunlight. Hey, Tinker Bell, she's a fairy and whoever created her must have seen a real one.' She then flipped the page over, scribbled for a few seconds, and handed her mum the pad. 'Although pixies are also friendly by nature, they are very shy when humans are around. Generally, you will only see the males, and that would be from a distance. Usually, the females stay underground, although they occasionally come out in the evening so their young can play among the crocuses. If you are lucky enough to see them, you can't mistake them, they are tiny little critter type creatures, pointed ears, and wear really long pointed hats they make from dried crocus leaves. If you were to see a male, it would probably be near a fallen tree, rummaging for mushrooms. Like the fairies, they don't like direct sunlight; it hurts their sensitive likkle eyes.'

Her mum flicked between the two drawings. 'Hmmm, similar but obvious differences.'

Rebecca started doodling again but couldn't get it right. Puffing, she kept rubbing out her sketch and starting again. Finally, she was satisfied and handing over the pad, said, 'Okay, now we have elves. They are not spiteful or mean in any way, but let's say, if you dropped your pencil, they would keep it, whereas the fairies and pixies would eventually give it back.' She paused for a moment and puffed out her cheeks. 'Elves are definitely not interested in human interaction. They are not even remotely inquisitive about us. It's very unlikely that you'd ever get close to one, let alone see one. If you were to see one by chance, they could be mistaken for a fairy or even a pixie. However, their wings – if they have any because they don't all have them – are more pointed, jagged, perhaps like a hawthorn. Hmmm, thorny is a fitting word. In fact, all their features are pointed, including their nails, which they use to scrub around in the undergrowth. If they were flowers, a fairy would be a pink rose, a pixie would be a crocus, obviously, and elves, well, probably an unripe blackberry, disagreeable and watch out for the thorns. Then you have the bears...'

Her mum squeezed Rebecca's hand. 'It's okay, Bex, no need to explain; I know what a bear looks like.' She grinned, and continued, 'I must say, I love your tales, but how do you know all this?'

'If I sense they are about, then I just watch carefully and listen. You have to keep your ears, eyes and mind open.' She paused for a moment. 'When I was a little girl, I saw them all the time, although I rarely saw elves. As I have gotten older, I find it difficult to focus. I become distracted by other thoughts and...'

'Oh dear, Bex, that is rather sad.'

'It's okay; I will never lose them completely because I will always know they are there. Sometimes, I just have to look harder that's all, and most importantly, want to see them. The only chance of seeing an elf would be as the sun fades. And as I have no intention of staying here at night, what with the bears, well...' She said and laughed nervously.

'Bless you, Honey, come on, and let's see if we can find this elusive lodge.'

'I think we should keep to this path; it must lead somewhere, Mum.' She stared down at the path. 'I wonder how old this path is because even with it overgrown, it was obviously well used at some point. Kind of makes you think.' She paused briefly staring again into the distance. 'I know there was that bramble and such-like back there, but it's still reasonably clear, dark bits aside, makes you wonder if it's been used recently.'

'Yeah well, I guess it could be a bear path,' her mum said, and then giggled. 'Realistically, it's probably just a deer path, which is boring, but I'd rather meet up with *Bambi*. That's a point actually if this is one of their paths, I doubt it will lead to the lodge.'

'Well, there is only one way to find out. Shall we?' Rebecca said pointing further into the forest.

She led her mum down the path to an area where the trees thinned allowing just enough sunlight to see another fork in the trail. She stood briefly, suggesting she was picking up the vibes. Although her mum frowned, she sensed she was happy to go along with her. After a couple of moments, she decided on the left-hand fork just because it felt right. She slowed a little when this route became particularly dark and dingy Now unsure if she'd chosen the right path, she turned to her mum.

'Do you think we should put some markers down, Rebecca? We don't want to get lost, do we?'

'Bit cliché, but it's actually a good idea, Mum. I will use some of my tissues and wedge them in the branches as we go.'

They continued until they entered an area where the tall pines had knitted together, virtually blanking out all light. Hesitantly, Rebecca continued a little further but could barely see the path, let alone where she was going. She dithered for a moment. On the one hand, she wanted to carry on, but at the same time was starting to think this might be the wrong way. She turned and shrugged her shoulders.

'Honey, perhaps we should have taken the other path back towards the lake.'

'Yeah, I was thinking that.' She glanced at her watch. 'How about we continue just a little further, and if we haven't found anything by twelve o'clock, then we turn back? It's ten to now; I will set my alarm, okay?'

'Okay, that sounds like a plan.'

She continued down the path, what she could see of it, towards another shard of light in the distance. Just as the alarm rang, they entered an open grassy area with a derelict wood cabin on the far side. 'I knew it,' she said, heading toward the building. There was bramble covering both windows and most of the front door. She prodded the bramble, not having a clue how they'd get inside.

'It looks very old and rickety. I really don't think we should even try to get inside, Bex. It doesn't look like oak, probably pine again, as the jetty was.'

Rebecca knew the minute she spotted the broken front door that her mum would say something like that. Although she realised, she was probably wasting her breath, she had to try to twist her mum's arm. 'Oh, Mum, come on, how bad can it be? If nothing else, let's look through the door and see what's inside. After all, it's taken us an eternity to get here, be rude not to try.'

Next to the door, hidden beneath some twisted bramble, Rebecca spotted something interesting. She pulled at the thorny undergrowth and could just make out a rectangular piece of wood. She yanked a few more branches and revealed a sign. It read, *The Hunting Lodge*. The similarities with the Nadine sign; even down to the green letters made her wonder if she was again on the Meredith trail.

'We are in the right place, Mum.'

'Well, it looks like it is ready to fall down, right place or not.'

Rebecca ignored her mum's indifference and peered through a small window in the door. She widened the beam on her torch and could see rooms to the left and to the right, there was also another door further down the narrow corridor. Rebecca's curiosity took hold, and before her mum could stop her, she pushed the broken door open and stepped inside. Ignoring her mum saying no, she trod her foot down heavy a couple of times. It felt spongy but reasonably stable. Feeling optimistic, she turned. 'It seems okay, Mum, let's have a quick look, hey?' Without waiting for a response, Rebecca stepped inside and opened the door on the right.

'Rebecca.'

'Too late, Mum, I'm in, and it's safe, and the floor is oak. Come on, don't be a lightweight.' Although her mum groaned, Rebecca heard her step inside the front door. On the far side of the room, she could just make out an old chest of drawers and a bed of sorts. As she made her way over, a picture frame standing on top of the chest grabbed her attention. She turned to call her mum and was surprised to find her standing behind her peering over her shoulder. 'Mum, you made me jump,' she said picking up the frame.

'Be careful, Bex.'

Rebecca wiped the glass with a tissue and gradually began to reveal the photo. Dampening her tissue, she rubbed a little harder and narrowed the beam on her torch. 'Mum, it is a picture of Meredith. She is with a young girl, perhaps her daughter. It needs a good clean, but I am sure it is Meredith. Oooh, I am all goosy.'

Her mum put her glasses on and peered at the picture. 'Crumbs, Bex, I think your right. It certainly looks like the woman in the hallway, but the girl looks...'

'What, Mum, what about the girl?'

Somehow, her mum managed to shake her head and nod at the same time. 'This is odd. She looks like she's wearing...' she paused and breathed heavily through her nose. 'She's wearing a cardigan that looks like the one you lost around the time you banged your head.' She shook her head again. 'It can't be, can it? Odd, it certainly well looks like it, and I don't suppose that style of crop top cardigan was exactly common in those days.' Again, she breathed heavily. 'Now this is becoming rather too spooky for my liking. Hmmm, and just to make it worse, the girl looks a little like you. Oh, I so wish I hadn't said that.'

'Hey, Mum, maybe I left it with Meredith, and her real daughter found it, and just happened to wear it when this photo was taken. But that doesn't make sense because they would have had to come back

179

here after I left. The thing is they actually lived in this Lodge way before I ever met Meredith. And they did not intend on coming back. It's all a bit jumbled.' She paused, and looked at the photo, 'you're right, she does look a little like me. Hmm, spooky as you would say.'

Her mum was again shaking her head and nodding simultaneously. 'I can't get my brain around this. We need to clean the picture up and then think about this. Have another look and see if there is anything else.'

Rebecca checked all the drawers, but they were empty. Her mum double-checked, and after finding nothing, suggested it was probably time to head back home. Even though they managed to find their way back to the boat with relative ease and the rowing went well, it was gone three when they arrived home. First thing, they went to the kitchen and tried to clean the glass, eventually deciding they were better off removing the photo. The two stared at the photograph, and although it was a little faded, it was unquestionably Meredith. The girl, however, was difficult to make out, although there were obvious similarities to Rebecca.

With a magnifying glass, Rebecca scrutinised the picture. 'It is hard to see, Mum, but the girl looks very similar to Meredith, more so than me, and it sure looks like my cardigan.'

'Thinking about it, Bex, it can't possibly be. I know what I said earlier, but it's just a similar shape. That's all it is, and you're right, she is more like Meredith than you. That said you are not that dissimilar to Meredith, certainly the same bone structure.'

Aware of her mum's uneasy tone, she said, 'perhaps you're right. It's a shame the picture has faded, because if we could see if the top button was missing, then we would know for sure.'

'Well, buttons fell off in those days too, when did you say it was?' She said, appearing increasingly hesitant.

'It was the eighteen-fifties and buttons always fall off. Even so, it would be a spooky coincidence.' Rebecca shook her head, knowing that even if it said *Rebecca's jumper*, her mum would be doubtful.

'Rebecca that is all it would be, a coincidence. Sorry, but that is all it is. It is a captivating idea, and all, but...'

'Mum, you said but, but what?'

'Just but, that's all.' Her mum then glanced at her watch. 'Right, I need to get on with supper, so you go and get yourself cleaned up please.'

The following evening Elizabeth went out for Ruth's birthday. As promised, Rebecca did cook a beef supper. Her father complimented her on her cooking several times, often nudging Tom to do the same. The following morning, Rebecca was surprised how interested her father was in where her mum had gone and what she'd had to eat. Rebecca was hoping her mum would take advantage of this and do something similar soon. Three days later, they had the party, which was a huge success, although, by the end of the evening, Rebecca had had enough of Tom's friends. On one occasion, she lost the plot completely, when she heard Tom suggest they use her as a target for football. She grabbed his ear, and a pulled it as hard as she dared, blurting, '*do, and I'll pull your ear off.*' Clearly embarrassed in front of his friends, and waving his arms about, he made a growling sound, but still managed to mouth *sorry* under his breath. Taken aback by his passive response, Rebecca decided to leave it there, although she couldn't help waving her fist at one of his mates, who was a little too cute for her liking.

Reflecting on the evening, including Tom and his silly friends, and thinking about how many times she'd heard her father laughing, she knew they had to do this type of thing more often. To cap it off, she'd heard her father mention to her mum how well the party was organised.

Chapter 12 - The Door Back

It was now mid-July. Rebecca and her mum had splashed around in the boat a few times but never got as far as the hunting lodge. She had suggested it many times, but her mum always found a reason not to go. Although frustrated, Rebecca suspected her mum had felt a little spooked by their previous venture. This was evident by her mum's reaction when she'd mentioned the photo a couple of times.

It was a Tuesday morning, and her mum mentioned that Amanda and Ruth were coming over at lunchtime. Immediately, Rebecca started working on a plan to get them all in the boat and maybe back to the lodge. Tentatively, she suggested the idea, but her mum just turned her nose up and said, 'Not today, Bex.'

Never to be one to take no for an answer, she said, 'Come on, Mum, don't be boring, the four of us always have such a laugh on the boat. Besides, it's a nice day for it.'

'Look, I will ask Amanda and Ruth, and see if they fancy the idea. In the meantime, help me tidy up until they get here. And, in case you've got any ideas, we're not going anywhere near that bear lodge.'

'Ok,' Rebecca grumbled and grabbed the tea towel.

Her mum touched her on the shoulder. 'I know I keep putting you off, Bex, and I promise we will go back, one day soon. I need some time to get my head around the whole thing, the photo, the lodge, and you knowing it would be there, your tale of Meredith and well...'

'I know, Mum. Hard for me too you know and I guess that's what makes me so anxious to get back. I need answers.'

Her mum just looked at her and smiled only the way her mum could.

Rebecca was just finishing tidying up when the doorbell rang. She jumped up and headed to the door. 'Hi-ya, gals, come on through, mum is in the kitchen getting the coffee on,' she said, smiling. 'Nice day, how do you fancy going for a row and have a look at the old hunting lodge? It's well spooky.'

Amanda smiled while applying her lipstick and although she nodded, it was clear she wasn't really listening.

Ruth, however, narrowed her eyes inquisitively.

'You should see the photo we found.'

'Hi, Liz,' Ruth said, as they entered the kitchen, and held her hand up in a questioning way, 'what's this about a photo Rebecca mentioned?'

'Hi, girls. I thought I heard her mention that,' she said, glancing in Rebecca's direction. 'It was something we found in an old lodge on the other side of the lake. Rebecca has been pestering me for ages to go back for a look. It's a long way, and, well...'

'She did suggest going for a row in the boat, and it's a lovely day.' She then gave Rebecca a sideways glance. 'So, it might be a nice idea. Although, I am not sure Amanda is dressed for it,' Ruth said, pointing at Amanda, who was again doing her lipstick. She then turned to Rebecca. 'I so knew you were up to something, Young Lady, blurting out about the boat before we were through the front door.'

'She can borrow a pair of my jeans.' Rebecca jumped up. 'Come on, Amanda, you are about the same size as me.'

Amanda stood up, still appearing distant.

183

Elizabeth nodded. 'Up to you two really, I don't mind, nice day for it, I guess.'

'Up to us for what, may I ask?' Amanda said, holding her palm up.

'Well I am happy to go, so why not, might be a laugh,' Ruth said, turning to Amanda, who was now doing something to her eyelashes. 'Amanda, we are going for a splash in the boat, be a dear, go with Bex, and get some appropriate clothing on.'

Amanda glanced towards Ruth, and then followed Rebecca without saying anything. While she was trying on a pair of jeans, she asked, 'why am I trying your jeans on, Bex?'

'I knew you weren't listening. We are going for a row in the boat. You're rather distant, A, any reason?'

'Oh, nothing important, just thinking how to get shot of the latest bf. He's a bit of a twit, to be honest.'

'Ah, that's why you're so vague,' Rebecca responded. 'Isn't it cool to text "see ya later" or something like that nowadays?'

'Hmm, I did think about it, but he is too much of a twit to get it. He'll think I am saying goodnight or something. I shouldn't say this, but...' she then sniggered, 'his name is Tom.'

'Err, not surprised. Good luck with that one, A.'

They made their way downstairs only to find Ruth and Elizabeth waiting outside.

'Sorry we took so long, we got chatting about Rebecca's boyfriend.' Amanda blurted and chuckled.

Rebecca's mum instantly held her hand up in a questioning fashion, but before she could get the words out, Rebecca stated, 'As if. Right now, boyfriends are... Well, just don't have the time.'

On the way down to the lake, her mum told Rebecca to get any ideas of the lodge out of her head. Although she nodded, she was still hopeful of hijacking the trip.

As they arrived, a north-easterly breeze gently rippled over the water easing the warmth of the mid-day sun. Amanda looked out from the jetty and then turned to the others. 'I hope that breeze doesn't become any stronger, or it will put more than a ripple on the water, and we won't get very far.'

'Oh, with us now are you, Amanda?' Ruth said, and giggled.

Remembering she didn't have her torch, Rebecca turned to the others. 'Would you mind waiting for a moment? I need to go fetch my torch,' she said, pointing towards the summerhouse. 'It's on the veranda.'

'Quickly please, Rebecca, and be a good girl, don't go snooping. More importantly, why, may I ask, is your torch on the veranda?' she said, wagging her finger.

Rebecca had often asked her mum not to use such a condescending manner, especially in front of the girls. Embarrassed, she glared. 'I will, Mum, and I will be right back. I left my torch ages ago when you were with me,' she said and shook her head, 'and finger-wagging isn't going to make me find it any quicker.'

Arriving at the summerhouse, she spotted her torch exactly where she'd left it. Before picking it up, she dithered. She knew her mum, and the girls were waiting, but just had to have a quick nose around. Heading straight for the locked door, she turned the handle and heard it click. 'Typical,' she mumbled. Hesitating briefly, she decided a quick look around wouldn't hurt. Stepping through the door, she

185

stared up into the darkness and unable to resist the temptation, made her way up to the first door. She gripped the handle, and like the one downstairs, it turned easily. *Now what,* she thought. She contemplated going back for the others, but just knew it would be locked by the time she got back. Knowing time wasn't on her side, and that she'd waited months for the door to open, she decided to go for it, quickly.

She stood there gripping the handle, and with the dream debate regurgitating, she pushed at the door. She felt it move slightly, and memories of Meredith flooded her thoughts. Then in a flash, her attention turned to the others, all waiting down by the jetty. She knew she shouldn't be doing this but just couldn't help herself and so pushed the door open.

Now stood just inside the door, she peered into the darkness, and again memories of her previous journey flooded her head to bursting point. Panting, she took a couple of deep breaths in an attempt to calm her nerves. Although she'd been here before, it was as if it was happening for the first time. Unable to see more than a couple of feet in front of her, she tentatively took two steps forward. As uncertainty took hold of her nerves, she searched in her pocket for her torch. 'Downstairs,' she mumbled. Breathing deeply, trying to steady herself, she waited for her eyes to adjust to the darkness. *Been here before*, she thought. On the far-left side of the room, she could just make out what looked like another door. Without moving her feet, and still holding the entrance door open, she leant forward, trying to see a little better. As she did, the door pulled from her hand, slammed shut, and instantly the room filled with the smell of baking bread. Although hesitant and apprehensive, she had this overwhelming need to know more. She took a couple of steps forward and banged her knee hard, instantly bringing her back to reality. Knowing she had to return to her mum, she reluctantly turned towards the door and tried the handle. It didn't move, so she tried it again, and still nothing. Now feeling anxious, she banged her hand on the door, and muttered, 'Come on, door, open.' Simultaneously, the room filled with bright sunlight, flooding her consciousness with thoughts of her previous jaunt. Still gripping the door handle, she heard a woman's voice.

'Come along, Missy, we have jobs to do in the field. I can't believe how long you've slept. You didn't sleep this much when we lived in London, even after we'd been awake all night with the incessant bombing. It must be all the fresh air, I guess.'

She could hear someone moving behind her and turned slowly not knowing what to expect. Adjusting the curtains was a tall blonde female, dressed in a smart but slightly worn brown uniform. Between questioning who this was, where she was, and if this was really happening again were overriding concerns for her mum waiting by the jetty. With tangled emotions and struggling to focus, Rebecca took a deep breath as the woman turned.

With an austere, yet gentle tone, and looking directly at Rebecca, she said, 'Why do you appear ill at ease, Rebecca? Were you daydreaming, again, with your head in the clouds, chatting to yourself? It is indeed a wonder we complete an entire task. Come along, we have work to do in the wheat field, and that includes giving those goddamn orphan girls lucid directions.' She raised her eyes and continued, 'The Major has given explicit instructions, and if we fail there will be no rations for anyone, and that includes us.'

Rebecca rubbed her forehead, as this woman's words took over from thoughts of her waiting mother. From what she'd said about orphans, bombing and rations, she reckoned she was in a period sometime during the Second World War. She looked at the woman and wondered if she was a relation. From the way she spoke, she was clearly close to her. As memories of her relationship with Meredith came flooding back, she found herself thinking she may again be the daughter of this woman and the house.

'Come along, Missy, you're looking so uneasy. I really haven't seen you like this for some time.'

'Umm, err,' she muttered, at a loss what to say.

'Umming and erring again, are we? Spit it out, Rebecca.'

This woman referring to her as Rebecca, again, sharpened her attention. Focused, she muttered, 'Well what you said about no food. It reminds me of...'

With her palm up, the woman looked at her.

Knowing any mention of her previous journey would be wholly inappropriate, and trying to avoid the mistakes she made with Meredith, she uttered, 'Oh, it's really not important.'

'Come along, Rebecca, get ready, and join me downstairs.' She then headed through a small wooden door in the far-left corner.

Rebecca sat on the side of the bed for a moment gathering her thoughts. She hesitated for a second and then decided to try the door she'd entered by once more. Although, she hoped it would be unlocked, half suspected it wouldn't be and was right. *Blast it,* she thought, knowing her mum would probably have her knickers in a proper twist by now. At a loss what to do, she decided a note under the door was her only option, even though she didn't know how her mum would find it. She took a piece of paper from her pocket, and scribbled, "*Sorry, Mum; I went through this door and can't get back, for now at least. I am okay. I will see you soon. Love Bex, kissy, kissy. PS, I seem to be somewhere in the 1940s.*" She then slipped it under the door, shrugged her shoulders, and headed towards the other door. Making her way down a narrow, creaky flight of stairs, she dithered halfway. Although concerns for her mother were niggling away in the back of her mind, strangely she felt okay now she'd left a note. Curiosity now had a grip on her thoughts, and she continued downstairs to the sound of the woman calling.

'Rebecca, come along, what is taking you so long?'

'I am just coming,' she said, as she pushed at a small door that opened into an oddly familiar kitchen, but it wasn't Meredith's kitchen. *So why do I know this room,* she thought? Before she'd time to consider these thoughts any further, the woman handed her a plate of warm bread, and a chunk of odd coloured, horrid smelling cheese.

'Now sit, Missy, and eat all your food, you will need the sustenance. If we don't finish our work today, you know only too well what the penalties are.'

Rebecca sat, staring at the plate, wondering how this could be so similar to the last time, yet so different. She then looked up at the woman and asked, 'Do I know what the penalties are?'

'Rebecca, you know how the Major has been since the death of your dear mother, combined with his injuries during the war, and moving up here, well...'

Still peering at the plate, Rebecca considered what this woman had just said. She nibbled at the dry bread, and turning her nose up, muttered, 'injuries.'

'Are you talking to yourself again, Rebecca, and to make it worse, again with your mouth full?'

'Err, yeah.' Rebecca hesitated, having so many questions running through her head. And still, concerns for her waiting mother chipped away in the back of her thoughts.

'Whatever is wrong with you, Missy? All morning you have been in a world of your own, and unusually you have failed to address me by my name. Your father says we should all address everyone by their correct title. You know he prefers you to call me Judith as opposed to Mother. I am not sure how he would react to this, err yeah, response of yours.'

Although the woman smiled, Rebecca was aware of the seriousness of her tone. She pushed her plate to one side, and asked, 'Judith, have you wondered why my father dislikes me referring to you as Mother? And what happened to my real mother.' She grimaced, knowing how absurd that question must sound. However, the way in which Judith's eyes softened, she guessed it might have fallen on good ears.

Judith narrowed her eyes, but there was an obvious empathy in her appearance. 'It does concern me how many times you ask me this. However, I understand why you have blocked that episode from your mind.' The woman averted her eyes, appearing thoughtful. 'If that has been on your mind all morning, I suppose that is why you have appeared so distant. Okay. Your real mother died in London, four years since, amidst exceptionally sad circumstances. During an air raid, she evacuated your house with your little brother. Believing you were still inside, she went back. Seconds later, your house took a direct hit. Sadly, there was no escape for your dear mother.' She again hesitated for a moment. 'Right, you are a grown woman now. In the past, I have avoided some details, and there are things you should know. The moment your father received news of your mother's death, he hurried home from the battlefields of France. Sadly, while returning from the front line, he sustained horrid injuries from a land mine. The combination of those two incidents has changed him unrecognisably, especially according to his friends and close family members. When you consider this, his change of disposition is to be expected. It would change anyone.' Judith paused.

'Continue please, Judith.' Rebecca knew her tone was pressing but had to know more.

'It is perhaps not my place to say this; however, we get on so well I feel I can confide in you.' She then paused, nodded once, and continued. 'It occurred to me that your father blames everyone else for all that has happened.' Judith hesitated again.

'Judith, you mentioned that my mum died when she went back for me. Can you tell me a little more detail? Also, can you explain why you believe the Major blames everyone else?'

'Rebecca, you ask me that, as if you know absolutely nothing of your mother's death.' She smiled calmly, and continued, 'You have clearly blocked it from your consciousness.'

'Perhaps I was in shock when I was first told, and maybe it didn't register. I probably didn't want it to register. Tell me a little more please.' Rebecca was quickly warming to Judith's sensitive and gentle smile. Leaning forward, she touched her hand, and said, 'I am sorry that you have had to tell me this before. For some reason, today I feel ready to know everything.'

Sitting upright, Judith said, 'Okay, the house next to yours in London was hit by a bomb known as a doodlebug. Prior to the bomb hitting – during an air raid – your mother left through the front door with your Brother in tow. They went to the Anderson shelter at the end of the road. Aware that you were not in the shelter, she panicked and went back to the house for you. She'd obviously forgotten that you were staying with your aunt. As soon as she entered the house, the bomb hit and everything collapsed around her. The family doctor suggested her death would have been instant, and that she would have felt no pain. The doctor also said that you were in a serious state of shock, and as a result, may have little or no recollection. He suggested that you may ask about this event often.' The woman then nodded, clearly receptive to the emotional quandary. 'You may ask me as many questions, whenever you wish, dear Rebecca. I am sorry for the way I initially reacted when you asked, only we spoke just yesterday about this.' She smiled and squeezed Rebecca's hand.

Considering this woman's words, Rebecca's emotions were becoming cloudy as thoughts of her real mother returned. She breathed deeply, turned toward the woman, and forced a smile. 'So why does the Major believe it is everyone else's fault?' She paused, wondering if he blames her. 'Something I still don't understand is why I can't call you mother. Presumably, you took his name when you married him, and as such became our step-mother.' Rebecca took a deep breath, realising she had made a big assumption. However, Judith's lack of reaction suggested she had indeed married the Major.

Judith touched Rebecca on the arm and smiled affectionately. 'Well, that's easy to answer. He loved your mother dearly. As such, he believes she should be the only one you refer to as mother. I am content with that.' She nodded, but Rebecca detected an element of melancholy in her eyes. 'When I met your father in the hospital, I was his nurse, and he said he had no family. I guess initially, I felt sorry for him, if that makes sense. Nevertheless, he was charming too, especially considering he was so poorly. Well, they call it something when a nurse falls in love with their patient. I can't think what it is right now. It is surprisingly common, anyways.'

Hearing that word, Rebecca muttered, 'That word again.'

'Rebecca, what do you mean by that word again?'

'Judith, sorry I was just mumbling, please carry on.' Rebecca looked at her, smiled, and although she was still worried about her mum, felt oddly relaxed. She was feeling comfortable around this woman, with her kind eyes, endearing smile, and genuine empathy.

'Well, during his rehabilitation, which took many months, I fell in love with him. So, when he explained that he had a lovely big house in Cumbria, and asked if I would go with him as his nurse, I agreed. The day after the move, I met you and your brother, which came as a surprise. Even so, I was in love, and it didn't bother me he hadn't mentioned you two. I just put it down to shock or something. When I eventually asked him about it, he shrugged his shoulders and changed the subject. I knew he didn't have an answer, and I didn't want to push for one. Besides, I found you and your brother so easy to love, and...' She then touched Rebecca's hand gently.

Rebecca responded by squeezing her hand. 'I know that shrugging of shoulders,' she said.

'Well, you should do. He is your father, and he does it often enough.'

'No, I meant I know what it implies. I think it's a kind of passive aggression.'

'Oh, do you indeed, passive aggression. I presume you to mean a hard done by smokescreen, something employed purely to make you feel bad.' The woman nodded agreeably. 'Anyways, over the next few months he started to change, a little initially, but his unhappiness became alarming.' Judith then looked away.

'What do you mean, alarming?' Rebecca could see Judith was uneasy and asked, 'Are you okay talking about this?'

She nodded a couple of times and forced a smile. 'I guess at first he started to become distant and then came his moods. Soon after, he became dismissive, of everyone, not just me. Some days, he wouldn't even answer me when I talked to him. I tried many times, but he either ignored me or just cut me short. He would say, "Not now, Judith." I guess I have become accustomed to it and somewhat conditioned by it, although...' She then turned away and averted her eyes.

Rebecca not only recognised this woman's acceptance of her situation but also felt disturbed by it and was determined to learn more. She smiled gently, and enquired, 'although what, Judith?'

'I want to understand what makes him feel the way he does, and then perhaps I can help him deal with his anger.'

A little alarmed, she asked, 'When you say anger, what do you mean? Is he aggressive, or violent?'

'Oh no, he just seems angry inside. Whenever things go wrong, he tries to blame someone or something else.'

She was beginning to think all the women in this house seemed forever destined to a passive existence. She looked back to Judith and asked, 'Do you talk to him about this, the way you are talking to me? Perhaps express your views on how things have changed and how things should be.'

'In the beginning, it was okay, but as time passed, he became distant and difficult to talk to. I can't recall the last normal conversation we had. Whenever I do try to engage him – which is increasingly rare - he seems disengaged, although I wouldn't say he was dismissive, just indifferent.'

Watching the wilted expression on this woman's face, Rebecca was determined to help her in some way. 'Well, perhaps deep inside he actually believes it is his own fault. My understanding is that when people become cantankerous, it is because they have issues, they are hiding, from themselves sometimes. In the deep recesses of their brain, they believe they are responsible for the situation, and because they can't face or deal with their own demons, they put the blame elsewhere.'

'This, Rebecca, is a lot of worldly knowledge for one so young? You've always amazed me with your tales, but this is, well...' She paused, 'I remember your Grandmother saying you are a second-timer. I understand what she meant now. As nurses, we were trained to deal with victims of injury, their stresses, and anxiety. However, you have a depth of understanding that no one could teach.'

'We touched on it at school, and I wanted to understand people, so I researched it a little, well a lot actually. To be honest, much of it is gut instinct, for me anyhow. I read somewhere that some suggest we are on a spiritual path. By that, my understanding is that if you are open to it, then you learn during your life. The more you learn helps you empathise and consider others, sometimes ahead of yourself.

194

Evidently, many suggest that individuals, who are seemingly a long way down that spiritual path, have been here before. Maybe that is where the second-timer expression comes from, hmm.' Rebecca raised her eyebrows, contemplating how often she'd heard this.

'I wish I understood people, well men in particular. Maybe, a man should write a book, on men, from a woman's point of view. Talking of education, I did not know they did things like that at your school.' She shook her head and continued. 'In any case, you seem to think inside he blames himself. That does make sense, I never thought of it that way.' Judith smiled, and said, 'I asked your Grandmother what she meant by a second-timer, and she just said, "been here before." I rather knew what she meant. I did quiz her further, and she suggested that you knew too much about this world for one so young. It adds weight to what you said and have read. Have you been here before,' she asked and chuckled?

'Hey, maybe I have,' she said and giggled. She smiled but found herself beginning to wonder if she could actually be on some kind of bizarre loop, one that was just repeating itself. Feeling a little uneasy with these thoughts, she suddenly realised Judith was looking at her. Inwardly shaking her head and dismissing her previous thoughts, she decided she needed to return her attention to the Major. 'So, back to my father, I think we need to talk to him, both of us together. Perhaps if we can get him to face up to his feelings, head on, that might be all it needs. When and if we do challenge him, we will have to be prepared for him to try to brush us off. If we go together, and then we can be strong for each other.'

'Carry on,' Judith said and sipped from an empty glass.

Rebecca was aware of how deep this conversation had gone and seeing Judith staring at her empty glass emphasised this. She knew she had to help this woman. Recalling Meredith situation, she now found herself wondering if she'd travelled back to help Judith in a similar way. As much as she didn't want to consider it, she was also aware that this wasn't a million miles from her own world.

'Rebecca, have you drifted away, perhaps thinking about your mother?'

'Umm, well kind of.'

Judith smiled, 'kind of, okay, dear Rebecca.'

Refocusing, she smiled. 'It strikes me that women often allow their men to behave the way they do. We treat them as if we are replacement mothers, and they in return treat us with contempt. Men are like children and need to be reminded that we are not there at their beck and call. If they take us for granted, and we accept it, we only have ourselves to blame. For centuries, women had to accept their relationships, because they didn't have a voice, a choice, or a way out. It is not like that any longer. We need to toughen up and make sure we are heard. Relationships are two way now and rightly so.'

'But he is so distant all the time, and I feel intimidated by his remoteness. As silly as that may sound, I can't help the way I feel. Although what you said is totally right and makes me question my own weaknesses.' She nodded several times. 'And, importantly, young lady, I suspect you didn't learn this at school.'

'Are you intimidated by his remoteness or the distance you've allowed to come between you? Because, Judith, if it is the distance you've had a hand in creating unwittingly or not, then you are as much to blame as he is. We need to go and talk to him. If he doesn't answer, we just carry on talking. In the end, he will talk. What is the worst that can happen? He shouts at us, so what if he does, might get some anger out, and perhaps open him up. In fact, why don't we go now and talk to him?'

'Oh, I don't know what to think. I agree with all you've said, but...' she said, and shook her head appearing uneasy.

This scenario was all too familiar, and Rebecca realised this one needed a head-on approach. 'But nothing, Judith...'

Shaking her head, she said, 'But, we do have our work to complete.'

'The work can wait a while.' Rebecca could see this woman was going down the, 'let's do it tomorrow,' road, a road Rebecca knew very well. 'No Judith, we have talked long enough.'

As if a light bulb had come on, and looking straight at Rebecca, Judith nodded her head. 'Enough is enough; the work can be done between the land-army women and the orphans. Let's go and see Christopher, or should I say the Major,' she said, groaning her words. She then took a deep breath. 'I must say, I am still a little uneasy, however.'

'Things can't get any worse, can they? Come on, no time like the present, as they say.'

'Okay, let's go and see the land-women first.'

'Let's do just that, I am not hungry, so I will take this bread with me, perhaps one of the orphans could do with it more than me,' she said, really unsure why she had, because she had no reason to suspect they were ill-nourished.

As the two headed for the door, Rebecca noticed a newspaper on the side. She grabbed it and searched for the date – October 22, 1943. 'Is this today's paper?' she asked.

'No, it is yesterdays or the day before, I'm not sure. We have to wait until your father has finished before we get to read the papers.'

Widening her eyes, Rebecca muttered, 'have to wait for him to finish first. That's reasonable, I think not.'

'What did you say, Rebecca?'

'I said... Oh, just mumbling.'

'For the umpteenth time today.'

As Rebecca followed the woman outside, she was taken aback by the warmth of the mid-day sun. A few yards away, she could see a ramshackle cart with a horse tethered to one side. Just beyond were half a dozen young children sorting vegetables into wooden boxes. Placing boxes on the cart were three older girls whom Rebecca guessed were about her age. As she glanced in their direction, they all stopped what they were doing. Staring, and pointing in her direction while whispering, she assumed they were talking about her. One of them - a dark-haired girl - seemed to be sneering, in what she considered a deliberately hostile manner. It reminded her of a couple of the girls back when she started her new school. Shaking her head, she noticed Judith was deep in conversation with four women who were dressed in brown uniforms. Returning her attention to the girls by the cart, she made her way over, half-expecting an unfriendly reception. 'Morning girls,' she said and smiled. One girl half nodded, while the other two didn't even look in her direction. She flicked her eyebrows, decided to go and talk to one of the small girls, and made her way over. Kneeling down beside a dishevelled, skinny faced, blonde girl, she offered her the bread she'd kept back from lunch.

The girl, who Rebecca guessed was aged about five, grabbed the bread. Then without making eye contact, she mumbled in an odd accent, 'Fanks missies.' She took a bite, glanced briefly at Rebecca and nodded.

The girl's pinched dirty cheeks, uncombed hair and sad eyes had an instant impact on Rebecca. It was a stark contrast to what she was used to, and their obvious predicament was all too plain to see. With this in mind, she turned back towards the older girls and with a measured tone, asked, 'How are you girls doing today?'

Two girls didn't flinch, acting as if she wasn't there. The third one, a redheaded girl, screwed her face up. She then shook her head very slightly and in a similar accent to the little girl, grumbled, 'All right, I suppose.' The hostile mood made Rebecca wonder what had gone before to create such a terrible relationship.

Still mindful of the quandary these girls were in, Rebecca smiled again. 'Can I ask, where do you ladies come from originally?'

'Wot' again', we told ya, London, all of us,' the redhead, snarled without making eye contact. She then looked up, and if anyone could turn up their nose further, Rebecca hadn't met them.

Rather than be put off by this, it actually tickled her. The way one of the other girls glanced at Rebecca from the corner of her eye, without turning her head, reminded her of Tom when he was up to no good. Although she tried to stifle her laughter, she couldn't help grinning, and to hide this, put her hand to her mouth faking a cough. 'Oh, I didn't know you were all from London.' She smiled, but once more, it was met with disdain. Again, thinking about what may have gone before, and realising this probably wasn't her battle to fight, she made her way over to Judith.

'Morning, Rebecca. Are those girls again being thorny?' one of the women asked in an agreeable, considered tone. 'I thought after the kerfuffle the other day we had come to an agreeable resolution between you all.'

Rebecca smiled. 'Good morning, ladies. No, the girls are okay, just a little cheerless. To be fair, these girls find themselves in an extremely complex circumstance. Torn from their families and expected to work in an alien environment, with little food. Well, the best of us would find it disagreeable, even on a good day.'

Judith smiled. 'I applaud your empathy towards the girls, which is a complete change from yesterday and far more agreeable. So, what is different?'

'I just imagined myself in their position and well...'

Judith smiled. 'Good for you, Rebecca.'

With her focus back, Rebecca asked, 'So, what's happening Judith, are we going to see the Major?'

'I must arrange for certain jobs to be done by the ladies first, Rebecca.'

While waiting, Rebecca sat on an old wooden seat near the smaller girls. She had just thought of her mum when the little blonde girl came over and sat next to her.

'Fanks for the bread.'

'You are very welcome, Missy. So, tell me, do you like being here?'

Before the young girl had a chance to answer one of the older girls came over, took the little girl by the hand, and said, 'Come on, don't wanna talk to 'er, stuck up cow.' She then waved her fist at Rebecca.

Although she empathised with these girls and knew it probably wasn't her battle, she wasn't going to allow them to bully her. Rebecca stood bolt upright and in a resolute tone, responded, 'Hey, Madam, she can talk to me if she wants. More importantly, who are you calling a stuck-up cow?'

The older girl pointed at Rebecca, and said, 'You're the stuck-up cow, always looking down ya nose at all us.'

Just as Rebecca was about to respond, Judith came over and stopped her in her tracks.

'Come along now, Rebecca.' She took Rebecca by the hand, then pointed at the other girl, and said, 'I will speak to you later, Madam.'

'That's it, let ya' ma' fight ya' battles.'

Rebecca pulled her hand from Judith. She marched back to the girl, stepped a breath's distance away, and snarled, 'Listen, I can fight my own bloody battles, especially with a bag of bones like you.'

With a look of surprise, and clearly taken aback, the girl averted her gaze.

In a forthright tone, Judith said, 'Rebecca, hush your mouth this minute.' She then turned to the girl and waved her away. Holding Rebecca's hand tightly, and without saying anything, Judith led her toward the main house. She seemed to wait until they were out of earshot, and said, 'Rebecca, what has gotten into you?'

'I do not take that sort of treatment from anyone.'

'Right, that is enough of the bad language, Rebecca. I tolerated it for a moment while you were angered by that girl, but please stop it now.'

The woman's forthright tone, yet gentle manner had an immediate impact on Rebecca. 'Sorry Judith, I will watch what I say in the future.' Feeling compelled to say something, she continued, 'I must say, even though I was furious, your tone and purpose instantly defused my anger. If you'd been bolshie with me, I would have argued and sworn for the sake of it, but because you were polite yet direct, I listened. My question to you is if you can handle situations like this so well, why do you feel unable to deal with the Major?'

With her hand on her chin and narrowed eyes, she said, 'I really do not know where all these philosophical views are coming from, Rebecca. Your focus is normally fairies, pixies, or drawing. However, I take your point.' She then narrowed her eyes even further. 'In fact, you have been acting strange all day.'

Suddenly aware that she had to be a little more considered about what she said, and how she said it, she thought for a moment. 'Recently a few things have occurred to me, and it has changed the

201

way I think.' She glanced back towards the girls. 'Once you realise that you're not made of glass, it becomes easy to stand up to others, even if you are frightened.' Rebecca let out a heavy sigh and said, 'I shouldn't have spoken to that girl like that though. It made me just as bad as her, but I was furious and well... I am not going to be bullied anymore, by anyone.'

'I shouldn't say, but after the way they treated you yesterday, I admire the way you stood up to her, even if you were a tad aggressive.' The woman put her hand to her chin, again. 'You shouldn't have called her a bag of bones. She's not always been like that, but none of them has had a decent meal for months. The Major is rather tight with the food, especially for the land girls. You did shock her though, the way you challenged her. I rather suspect she's not used to anyone standing up to her.'

'Really, they've not had a decent meal for months just because the Major is stingy with food. That has to stop?' Annoyed with herself for being so thoughtless, she immediately turned back toward the girls.

'Rebecca, leave it now.'

'Judith, I need to apologise. What's that girl's name?'

'Millicent, I believe.'

Rebecca looked up to the sky and thought, *well it would be*. She glanced at Judith, and said, 'I must apologise, and I need to do it now.' She then headed over towards the girls. As she arrived, they stopped talking, got down from the cart, and faced Rebecca, almost as if they were expecting trouble.

'Millicent, is it?' Rebecca said, smiling.

The girl nodded uneasily and said, 'Millie, and yeah, what about it?'

'I am so very sorry that I called you skinny.'

'Yeah, of course you are,' she said, then turned to the other girls, and mumbled something.

'No, really I am sorry. Judith just told me that you don't get enough to eat. I intend to make sure you have more food from today onwards. In fact, Judith and I are going to see the Major now. I am really peed off with his behaviour. Father or not, I am not having this. This is a bloody farm, food shortage, I think not.' She then offered a handshake.

Millie had a strained look as she turned to the other girls. She then turned back to Rebecca, and half-heartedly shook her hand. This time though, the girl did smile, and although slight, it seemed genuine. Rebecca noticed the girl had an odd look and suspected she wanted to say something. 'Millie, are you okay?'

Appearing uncomfortable, the girl shook her head. 'But, I askt' for more food in da past, I was told that there ain't no food. Oh, and summit 'bout a damn war and rations, as if I need reminding, living in London and being bombed every bloody day.'

Rebecca shook her head. 'Rations, hey, is that what they said? I will see about that, after all, as I just said, this is a farm. Derrr hello, we grow our own bloody food. Right, leave it with me, Millie. I will be back shortly with some food, that I promise.' She then nodded several times, turned back to Judith, and as she did, the girl tapped her on the arm.

'Derrr, 'ello, I like that and must remember it. Me finks afta' our little miss-hap that you might be alright.'

Rebecca smiled and turned back to Judith. She wasn't at all sure what Millie had just said, but got the feel of the gesture.

'I am so proud of you, Rebecca, although I have to question the language.'

Rebecca shrugged her shoulders. 'Sometimes you have to use a language they will respond to. Right, now let us sort things out with the Major. Did you know that Millie asked for more food and was told there's rationing because there's a war on? As if, she needs reminding. This is a farm, no food for us, no food for them. Does he think this is a prisoner of war camp? I am going to speak to him because I am not putting up with this.' She then huffed loudly.

'Well, we may need to come back later if he is busy, perhaps make an appointment.'

Rebecca opened her mouth but was so shocked no words came out. Shaking her head several times, she lifted both palms. 'Are you serious, Judith, an appointment to see my father. Major or not, this isn't the flipping army.' She huffed again, so hard it made her cough. 'I want to get some grub for the girls, as soon as we can, ideally.'

'Grub, Rebecca?'

'Don't worry about it, Judith; it's just another word for food.'

'Well, you are making me smile by your choice of words today, not the swear words though, Rebecca.'

'Yeah, but you should be smiling all the time, Judith. Your sadness shows, even when you smile. And that is why we need to change things.'

'Does it really? I haven't always been sad you know. When we were first married, well, I even smiled in my sleep.'

'Yeah, and you let him change, which in turn, changed you. It's not your fault as such, but you allowed it to happen. You stood by his every word, even though you knew it was wrong. So, you are responsible to some degree, mainly to yourself for allowing it to continue.'

Judith was staring at the floor. She looked up slowly and said, 'I guess so, can't say I have thought about it, but it does make sense. I just don't know what to do now. How do I change him back?'

'It will be difficult at first, but if you continue to talk to him, he will open up in the end. It is a long road, but you are older and wiser than I am, so trust your life experiences for the answers. You need to find inner strength, maintain a conviction in your words, and importantly stay resolute. You love him, so the conviction's there. The road back won't be as long as the road here. The way you were with me and the way you are with the girls, well that resolve will see you through.'

'Please explain a little more, Rebecca.'

'Well, you know that he was nice when you first met him, so you know that side of him exists, correct?'

'Yes, I do, and your point is that if I want him back to how he was, then I need to drag him back, even if he kicks and screams?'

'Well, there you go; you know what is required, so just do it.'

'Thank you, Rebecca. I feel all energised now, ready for any challenge.'

'It will be a challenge for sure, and it may take some time, but it will be worth it. Say it takes six months to get back to where you were. Compare that with a lifetime of unhappiness. It is your happiness, your marriage, and importantly, your dignity that's on the line here.'

Judith nodded several times. 'I need something to help me stay focused. If I think about when he was in the hospital, and it was my job to make him well, maybe that will help my resolve.'

205

'That's good, but your aim is to make your relationship better, not him.' In the back of her mind, Rebecca wished she could talk to her mother like this. She then stared down, wondering when, or if, she'd get back home. Feeling a little upset, she quickly reassured herself, certain Meredith, wherever she was, would see her way back.

With Judith still nodding, the two headed up towards the main house. As they arrived, Rebecca was just about to knock at the door, when Judith grabbed her hand, and said, 'No, Rebecca, it is our house too, no knocking on doors, not today. He will be in the drawing room, I would guess. So, I am going in, cover me,' she said and giggled.

As the two entered through the front door, Rebecca's attention was instantly drawn to the paintings of Meredith and Millicent. Although startled, she thought about it for a moment and realised they would be there. 'I love these paintings. Did you know that there is a story behind them, a somewhat out of the ordinary story too?' She then shivered, thinking how very bizarre this was becoming.

'Is there, how do you know this, Rebecca?'

'Oh, I looked it up on the net, um; err, in a book I mean, err, sorry.' Rebecca took a deep breath, realising just how stupid that was.

'Uming and erring again, are we? You have been doing a lot of that today. Well, you will have to tell me all about the paintings, later perhaps.' She nodded once, turned the handle to the study, and glanced again at Rebecca. She then seemed to brace herself before walking in.

Following Judith in, Rebecca was instantly spooked by the familiarity of the room. Just to compound her emotions further, the Major was sitting in the same chair that her father uses.

The Major instantly looked up, and said, 'Judith, Rebecca, I was told you two were working in the wheat field, managing those displaced girls.'

'The WLA ladies are doing the work on their own. They are more than capable. We need to talk, Christopher.'

'Not now, I am busy, Judith,' he grumbled and turned back to a photo album of sorts.

Judith turned away, hesitated, and turned back. 'No, Christopher, I need to speak to you now. We need to sort some issues out, issues that cannot wait.'

'By your tone, I suspect you consider your issues salient enough to interrupt me, Judith,' he said, without looking up.

'It is vital enough for you to look up when you address me, at the very least,' she said, clenching her hands together so tightly, it turned her knuckle's white. She glanced around, and Rebecca could see a look of determination.

Rebecca watched as he slowly closed the album, and lowered it to the floor, allowing it to drop the last couple of inches. He glanced briefly in Rebecca's direction and offered a shallow smile. The black rings around his cold blue eyes just exaggerated his pale fatigued appearance, and the way he flickered his eye contact, had the mark of someone who was heavy of the heart rather than angry. He slowly turned to Judith, lifted his palm, and in a weary, but still with a slightly fractious tone, said, 'Okay, you have my attention. It is clearly imperative you speak now.'

She took a deep breath, glanced away, and then looked directly at him. 'Perhaps not having me here as your wife is vital enough. Because it has occurred to me, I am only looked upon as your farm worker, stable hand and orphanage manager, Christopher.'

Appearing startled, he asked, 'What do you mean, Judith, not having you as a wife?'

'Look, Christopher, we were very happy when we met, you must remember that. Things changed when we moved up here from London, as well you know. The final straw has been this threat of no food unless we complete our work.' Judith looked away briefly, and Rebecca could see she was still angry in spite of his somewhat passive tone.

He frowned, appearing puzzled. 'Who told you that, Judith? The food rationing is to keep those petulant teenage land girls in check, not for you.'

Although Judith had seemed uneasy when they first arrived, Rebecca detected a distinct air of resolve. With her body language assured and uncompromising, she lifted her hand in a way that would leave no one doubting her intentions. 'That half-wit maid you hired told me about the food, Christopher. She came down this very morning, in her usual prissy way, and syphoned off half of our milk. She followed this by informing me we must complete all our jobs, or we will not be fed.' Judith then lifted her palm, clearly awaiting an immediate answer.

He looked up with a resolute expression. 'Judith, the food rationing was not meant for you and Rebecca. I assure you I will have words with the maid on this subject. The conflict of the last few days was brought to my attention. I considered the food restraints purely as a tool for you to maintain some authority over those girls.' He looked down briefly and continued, 'I gave the maid explicit instructions, and that did not include syphoning your milk. I have been considering her position for some time and have become increasingly aware that her intentions are at best, devious. In fact, I will summon her now. She has to be dealt with at once.' Appearing impatient, he made his way over to the door and rang a small bell attached to the wall.

Judith put her hand gently on his shoulder. 'Christopher, please do not act in haste, conceivably she made a mistake, or perchance she misunderstood her directives.'

Shaking his head defiantly, he said, 'No, no mistake, no misunderstanding. I know this because I gave her clear and lucid instructions, and a note to clarify my points. So, she knew.' He rang the bell. Then he turned to Rebecca, smiled, and asked, 'how are you dear, Rebecca?'

Having listened intently for a few minutes, she wasn't quite ready for this question. Nodding, she smiled, and uttered, 'Oh, I am okay thank you, err, Father.' She smiled again. 'Can I just say that I am worried about the girls from London? Did you know they have not eaten properly for months? They were sent here, having been through the bombing, and are now without their families. I believe this may be the reason for their hard-boiled exterior and quarrelsome inclination. They arrived here alone, are expected to work god-knows how many hours, in jobs they are ill suited to, only to discover little food for them. I appreciate your idea of rationing their food, but this may have been the catalyst in the first place. After all, this is a farm, and it generates food plenty enough for everyone, and that should include those who actually help produce it. I have found that when you get under their harsh exterior, they are rather pleasant. I find their dialogue hard to follow, and it reminds me of my friend Roxy. The first time I met her, I also thought she was hard-boiled.'

'That is a fascinating and noble viewpoint, Rebecca. My maid informed me they were aggressive, hostile and stole food at any opportunity. She never said the girls were undernourished, and she certainly didn't show any consideration for their emotional scars. Living through the London blitz would have had a dreadful impact on them all, something we know very well. I really should have been more thoughtful, especially when we reflect upon our past. My understanding was that they showed total disregard for everyone and everything. That is why I suggested rationing the food, to keep a small element of control, however, that was only two days ago, after the fractions started to manifest themselves.'

'Christopher, it has been like this since the day they arrived. That woman, your maid, was very clear about the food rationing. She instructed us, via a list supposedly written by you, that there was to be a limited amount of food. Barely enough to feed five people, let alone the fifteen of us. The older women go into the village often and with their own money, buy back the food we have sent just, so there is a little more to go around. I was informed a shopkeeper had said he bought extra supplies from someone who lives here. I think we can now guess who that might be.'

Shaking his head, he growled loudly. 'I see. The food control was her idea, and that indicates that she intended to plunder it for her own personal gain. What is taking that woman so long?' He then rang the bell again, almost pulling it from the bracket.

Moments later a woman dressed in a cream maid's uniform walked in. 'You rang, Chrissie?'

'Yes, twice. Do not address me as Chris, Chrissie, or indeed Christopher. You are the maid, and as such you will always refer to me as the Major.'

The woman wriggled her hips. 'Oh sorry, I am sure.' She sneered at Rebecca and Judith. 'What are you two doing here? You should be working, like the rest of us.'

Christopher banged his hand down on the table. 'Actually, you are incorrect. Judith and Rebecca are my wife and daughter and as such are the ladies of the house. Therefore, they will not be called upon to work anywhere, not by you or indeed anyone.'

'Well, I hope you do not expect me to work for them.' The woman said and flicked her hand in the direction of Judith and Rebecca.

'With the attitude you show, and increased familiarity, you have made my decision easy. I as a result of this dismiss you from the position as a maid. Indeed, I would like you to leave forthwith. Go and get your belongings together, and only that which is yours. I expect you to be out of this house within the hour.'

The woman stepped back, waved her arms, and blurted, 'You can't dismiss me, jus' like that.'

'I just have and do not ask for a reference, unless you would like me to explain exactly what you have done and how deceitful you have been. I know all about the food rationing you alone instigated. Indeed, I now firmly suspect you have been syphoning food and selling it in the village. Pack your bags as quickly as you can, and be gone with you.'

As the woman headed for the door, she made an aggressive hand gesture towards them all.

'More of that and you will not get this week's wages. Now be gone with you.'

She glared at them all, before leaving and slamming the door on her way out.

Christopher turned and smiled. 'Judith, would you please go with her to make sure she takes only that which belongs to her. I am sorry that I have to place such an imposition on you, but your good self and Rebecca are the only people whom I can trust.' He then glanced down, looked up and said, 'I am so sorry we have lost our way. My ghastly moods and fractious emotions have bothered me to a point where I consulted my doctor. I know the distance that has grown between us is for me to redress. I have a long way to go, and I am working hard to dismiss my demons. I assure you that our family happiness is paramount.'

'Thank you, dear Christopher. However, I must share the responsibility for I accepted the way things were and did nothing. Your daughter, dear Rebecca has helped me enormously. Indeed, she suggested that I talk with you today.' She smiled and nodded. 'I will go with the maid now.'

To allow herself some thinking time, Rebecca waited until Judith had closed the door. She then sat opposite the Major and smiled. 'Well done Major, you made short work of the maid,' she said, feeling uncomfortable calling him Major.

'Thank you, Rebecca, but please call me Father. May I ask, earlier you referred to someone called Roxy, I do not recall that name?'

Thinking quickly, she uttered, 'Oh, she's just someone I knew, umm when we lived in London.' Trying to change the subject, she asked, 'Were you looking at photographs earlier?'

He picked up the book and started thumbing through the pages. Pointing to a photo of a woman cradling a baby, he said, 'this photo is of you and your dear mother. I have been adding photos since you were born.' He then turned to the back of the album and pointed at a wedding photo. 'All day, I have been looking through this album. I kept coming back to Judith and my wedding photos, and it made me realise how far we have drifted apart. So, our meeting today was timely, favourable, and poignant. I loved your real mother dearly, and will always carry her memory close to my heart. I also thank her for blessing me with you and your brother. However...'

'You said, however, Father. Please tell me what you were going to say.'

'Well, I loved your mother, and you must never doubt that.' He looked away and then continued, 'I met her when we were both very young. Shortly after we met, the war started and sadly interrupted our relationship. We were rarely together, and when we were, it was a couple of stolen days here and there. Therefore, we never had a chance to cement our love.' He looked down, staring at the album.

Rebecca smiled and waited for him to continue in his own time. After a few seconds, he looked up and breathed out a heavy sigh. Although he smiled, she could see the uneasiness in his eyes.

Staring at the album, he took another deep breath, and then briefly made eye contact. 'When I met Judith, she was my nurse and only that. Over the coming weeks, she showed me a great amount of compassion and understanding. Far more than you would expect from a nurse. I found myself looking forward to her visits, and began to depend on her kindness, care and smile. We would talk for hours, even when she was off duty. I began to feel she was a soul mate, although, I never saw her as anything more than a beloved friend. Over time, I couldn't help but fall deeply in love with her.' He let out a gentle breath, nodded, and smiled. 'I have hidden that love from you, out of consideration for your dear mother. Consequently, and unwittingly, I have suppressed my feelings to the point where I've pushed Judith away.'

'So, you believe we would object to Judith? Also, do you think Mum would want you to be this sad, and importantly, her children to be unhappy too? Your happiness is important to me, and if that means you being with Judith, then so be it. She is beautiful, honest, intelligent, loves you dearly, and I am sure mother would have approved. Father, if you leave it too long, it will just create bitterness and a void between you two, one you may not be able to cross.' Hearing a noise in the hallway, and suspecting it was Judith, Rebecca hurriedly said, 'Father, talk to Judith and tell her how you feel.'

'I will, Rebecca, I will. Thank you, I love you.'

'I know you do, Dad, and I also know you love Judith, which is cool.'

'Cool?'

'Yes, Father, it means good, fine, excellent, all of those words.' She then glanced towards the door as Judith entered.

'Okay, cool it is, Rebecca.'

'Judith, err, Mother. I would like to go and see the girls in the field. Perhaps take them some food, is that okay?'

'Yes, that is fine, Rebecca. Is that okay, Christopher?'

He nodded several times, and said, 'Yes that's fine. I will send for the matron, and she will get some food ready.' He then rang the bell and moments later, an elderly woman appeared at the door. The Major politely asked her to arrange some food. He then turned to Rebecca, and once again thanked her.

'You have thanked Rebecca a couple of times; may I inquire why? Perhaps I missed something,' Judith asked with an enquiring look on her face.

'Dear Rebecca and I were discussing these beautiful photos of our wedding, Judith.' He nodded gently and smiled openly. 'I have made some serious misjudgements that have damaged our relationship and must explain my reasoning and behaviour. I have acted like a fool and now realise the errors of my ways, dear Judith.'

'We do, Chris, and I must say I am also somewhat to blame.'

Satisfied there was nothing more she could do here and feeling desperate to get back to her real mum Rebecca bid her farewells. Halfway along the hall, the matron greeted her with a basket of food. 'This is what the Major ordered, Miss. There is some bread, and some cheeses, and some milk, and some fruit, all for the girls in the field. If they need more food, tell them to come and see me. The Major has said that I should give them all they need.'

Rebecca thanked her and took the basket. As she left the house, she stood there for a moment trying to take it all in, then spotting the girls working in the field, broke her attention. She followed a narrow path through a wheat field. As she drew closer, she noticed the girls were watching her with a distinct air of suspicion. Rebecca smiled. 'Hi, Millie, hello girls, as I promised, I have some food for you.'

'I did'n 'fink you would do it at all, let alone sa quickly, fanks.' She grabbed the basket and placed it carefully on the floor, beckoning the other girls to join her.

Rebecca sat on a bale of hay and watched Millie smiling as she handed the food out. Her disposition had changed entirely to the point where she glanced up at Rebecca a couple of times and smiled meaningfully. 'There's plenty more food for you. You just need to go to see the Matron and ask. And that has come from the Major. I might add that this food rationing had nothing to do with Judith or the Major. It was the housemaid, who, I might add, has been dismissed.'

Millicent, now with the little red-haired girl sitting on her lap, asked, 'one o' the ladies said you is from London too. So 'ow come you don't talk like us?'

'I don't know, to be honest. I think my mother spoke the way I do, so I guess I copied her. Sadly, she is dead now, and as sad as it is, I can't really remember much about her.'

'Oh sorry, my Muvva' died too, ya' know. There's just little Hayley and me left now to fend for ourselves,' Millicent said and blinked her eyes several times.

'Umm, what about...,' Rebecca said but could see how upset the girl was, so stopped.

Millie looked up, and asked, 'what was ya' gonna say, Becky?'

Rebecca nodded to the girl, and in a gentle tone, asked, 'Millie, where is your father, if you don't mind me asking?'

'He snuffed it in the bloody war, barely nu' him tho', and Hayley's never seen him. He was gonna take us back to America with him when the war ended.'

'Oh, that is so very sad for you and Hayley.'

215

'Well tis' the same for all us. All the little-uns, and us olda' gals are all in the same boat. We big 'uns gotta be the mum's now, although I worry about Tabitha coz, she's all on her own and doesn't 'ave any kin.'

'Rebecca's emotions were going in circles. She felt a deep sadness, but having never been through such turmoil, wasn't sure what to say. 'Oh, I am so sorry. Which one is Tabitha, may I ask?'

'She's the one you gave the bread too. And no need to be sorry, ya' almost in the same boat ya-self.'

They chatted for a little while longer, but a sudden need to get back to her real mum came over Rebecca. 'Right, I must go. I have been here far too long, got places to go, people to see. It's been a joy talking to you all, especially after our little quarrel this morning?'

'Yeah it has, seeya, Becky,' Millie said and smiled.

Rebecca said her good-byes, and as she started towards the summerhouse, Tabitha came over. She pulled at Rebecca's sleeve. 'Missies, will you give me a cuddle. I miss me Mum, and you is like her.'

Without saying anything, Rebecca picked the little girl up and held her tightly for a few moments. She then lowered her carefully and ruffled her hair. As much as she wanted to say something, she just couldn't find any words. She bent over, kissed the girl on the cheek, and with tears streaming down her face, hurried back toward the summerhouse. After a few steps, she turned to wave, but the girl had gone back to the others. Without turning again, Rebecca quickened her steps. On the way towards the summerhouse, she thought about her journey and was sure Meredith had somehow instigated the whole thing. She didn't know why, because it didn't make any sense, but it just felt right in her head. She hurried through the kitchen, up the stairs, and back into the room where it all started. Pausing, she looked around for anything she could show her mum. Remembering the newspaper downstairs, she nipped down and grabbed a couple of pages from the middle. On the way back up, she wondered if the sole purpose of this journey was to help Judith. She then thought about the girls in the field and wondered if that was part of Meredith's plan. She pondered everything for a moment and smiled, knowing there was no more for her to do here, and Meredith would see her home safely.

Gripping the handle, she held her breath until she heard it click. She opened the door, and a gust of warm air blew the newspaper from her hand. Holding the door open, she turned, but the newspaper was just out of reach. Stretching her fingers, she could feel the door pulling from her grip, almost as if it was trying to close on its own. Suspecting the paper blew from her hand for a reason, and not prepared to take a chance and go back for it, she begrudgingly stepped through the door. With the door now firmly shut behind her, and waiting for her eyes to adjust to the sudden darkness, Rebecca stood on the landing for a moment, wondering what she was going to tell her mum. Going over everything in her mind, she made her way downstairs, knowing the paper was probably her only chance of proving her story to her mother. Standing by the door at the bottom of the stairs, she stared back into the darkness and wondered if she'd ever be here again. She stepped through the doorway, and within a second of shutting the door behind her, her mum's voice called from outside.

'Bex, I so knew you were messing around with that door again. We have been sitting on the jetty waiting for you. You said you'd be two minutes, not ten,' her mum said and narrowed her eyes but still had a grin on her face as she stood by the front door.

Rebecca stood with her back to the door thinking about what her mum had just said. Looking at her mum, she was thinking, *more like three hours.* 'Sorry, Mum. Umm, what's the time then?'

'Just coming up to 12, why?'

'Just curious,' she said, wondering *how that was even possible.* 'Mum, I love you,' she said and cuddled her.

Frowning, her mum said, 'I love you too Rebecca. Tell me, why such a big cuddle? You're not trying to get around me, are you? What have you been up to?'

'Err, Mum.' she shook her head, 'I feel like I've been gone ages,' she said, knowing she'd been gone for more than ten minutes.

'Hmm, well you said two minutes, so I guess ten minutes is a long time.' She laughed, gave Rebecca another cuddle, 'not that either of us needs an excuse for a cuddle.'

As Rebecca followed her mum back to the jetty, her thoughts were going in circles. On the one hand, she desperately wanted to tell her mum all about her journey but knew what reaction she'd get. *If only I had the newspaper,* she thought. 'Mum, I really do feel like I have been gone for ages, I mean ages.'

'Well, I would hardly call ten minutes a long time, Honey. Why do you feel like that?'

'Oh, I don't know, Mother. I just...' Rebecca knew this was no dream, not this time, but how could she convince her mum, and how come it's only ten minutes. As they made their way along the jetty, she was still thinking about the newspaper, and then decided to hide something next time. 'Hmmm, if there's another time,' she muttered loudly.

'Another time, Bex?'

'Oh nothing, Mum,' she said and gasped as she spotted the boat half submerged with a gaping hole in the side. 'What happened to the boat?'

'Rebecca, we are going to have to give our trip a miss.'

'Yeah, Mum, I was just looking at that hole in the side, how do we think that happened?'

'I suspect it occurred during that storm the other night. And, it didn't help in that I didn't tie it up properly.'

Rebecca shook her head and said, 'Oh that's a shame, but I doubt it had anything to do with the way you tied it up.' After her journey, she'd actually gone off the idea of a trip across the lake, even though she desperately wanted to get back to the lodge. She then decided to suggest a shopping trip, which would give her time to get her story right in her head before telling her mum. 'So, how about we go shopping instead, and if we are late, Dad and Tom can get their own supper. That's providing, they have done their work.' Rebecca didn't know why she'd just said that.

'Rebecca, "done their work," what are you talking about? And, "they can get their own supper?"'

'Oh nothing, Mother, I will tell you later. I'm just being silly.'

'Tell me what later, Rebecca?' her mum asked with a look of suspicion.

Wondering how her mum always knew when she'd been up to no good, she said, 'Mum, it is nothing important. I just need to, well, never mind.' The way her mum shook her head and then nodded; Rebecca knew there'd be questions later. Trying to deflect the attention, she asked again, 'So, how about we go shopping and go to that restaurant for supper, Mum.'

Her mum narrowed her eyes at Rebecca, then shrugged her shoulders to the girls, and said, 'What do you think, girls, shopping?'

Amanda smiled, nodded agreeably, and said, 'new beauty salon in town.'

Ruth glanced at Amanda and grinned. 'I really don't mind. Clearly, we're not going in the boat. And, I'd like to know why

219

Rebecca thinks she's been gone for ages,' she said and squinted in her direction. 'Maybe she can explain on the way to town.'

'Hmmm, my thoughts exactly,' Elizabeth said, narrowing her eyes in Rebecca's direction.

Chapter 13 - Supper

They parked in the new multi-storey car park and headed into town. Miles away and dawdling along, Rebecca was thinking about her journey. One thing she knew for sure, this hadn't been a dream. Her only debate is whether she tells her mother. Guessing how she would react, she decided to say nothing, for now at least.

'What are you thinking about, Rebecca?'

'Oh, nothing really, Mum.'

'Well you seem miles away, so I don't suppose it was nothing,' she said and frowned.

She knew that look on her mum's face and guessing she wouldn't leave it, uttered, 'just about the boat and what a shame it's damaged.' She flicked her eyes, 'Dad will be miffed, but it's nobody's fault so he can get as miffed as he likes. Storms happen.'

'Not as miffed as he will be when he finds out he has to cook his own supper.' She laughed but had that uneasy look that Rebecca had seen so often before.

'Mum, if you've never asked him to cook, how do you know how he'll react?'

'And when he finds out I didn't tie the boat up properly, there's bound to be another storm.'

'Mum, the only person Dad will get cross with is the weatherman for once again not predicting the storm.' she said wide-eyed and puffing loudly.

'She's right, Liz,' Ruth said and blinked her eyelids as if she didn't want to have this conversation. 'Anyway, it's a nice day, so why don't we have a look around town and then have our picnic down by the river? And, I like the idea of going out this evening for supper.'

Amanda nodded. 'Good idea, Ruth, I hope you mean that nice spot behind the cafe that makes a divine coffee, almost as nice as yours, Liz. And, don't forget we're going to the salon too.'

'Liz, are you listening?' Ruth asked.

'Just wondering how James will react when he gets my voice mail. I told him we were going out and not to expect us til' late. I do worry though about him having to cook.'

'You're just like the Major's wife, too considerate and nice.' *Why did I say that me and my big mouth*, she thought?

'Rebecca, are you going to enlighten us? Who is the Major?' Ruth asked and glanced at Elizabeth.

'I suspect it's another of her stories, Ruth.' Elizabeth smiled, and added, 'I am sure it's a wonderful story, they always are.' She then placed her arm around Rebecca's shoulder. 'I love your tales, Rebecca. You must tell me all about the Major.'

'It's nothing really, just something I read on the internet about a marriage between Judith who was a nurse and a former army Major.'

'Rebecca told me a story about the ladies in the hallway paintings, convinced she actually went back to their time and met them. Hmm, I said it was probably something she'd dreamt when she banged her head,' Elizabeth said.

'Wow, sounds fab, you must tell us more, Rebecca,' Ruth said, clearly curious.

She told Amanda and Ruth all about Meredith, explaining about the door in the summerhouse. Trying to avoid mentioning her latest trip, she focused on the details, still wanting to convince her mum it really happened.

'Bex, I love your stories, but I still find it hard to believe that it was anything other than a dream,' her mum said, shaking her head slightly.

'What a great story,' Ruth said, 'even if it was a dream.'

'The way you described it, Rebecca, it sounded real to me,' Amanda said, 'but surely it was no more than a dream.'

She'd had enough of the dream debate and couldn't help herself. 'Not a dream, I know because...' she hesitated, and thought *just out with it*. 'Because it has all happened again, just in a different time period.'

Turning around, Elizabeth asked, 'What do you mean it happened again? It doesn't have anything to do with the Major and that Judy you mentioned earlier, does it?' she said and shook her head in a way that always vexes Rebecca.

'Well, this is going to sound bizarre, but you need to trust me on this.' She glanced at her mum and continued, 'This morning, while you were all waiting by the boat, I went back to 1943. That's where I met Judith and the Major. And it is Judith, not Judy,' she said. 'I know it sounds ridiculous, but try putting yourself in my shoes.'

'Oh, Rebecca, really, 1943 indeed,' her mum said and narrowed her eyes. 'You kept saying you'd been gone for...' she shook her head, 'no; I'm not having that.'

'Mum, don't give me that look. It's hard enough with everyone suggesting it's just a dream, without you, well...' Over the next few minutes, Rebecca explained about Judith, Christopher and the land girls.

'See girls, I told you her stories are fabulously imaginative.'

She pulled her mum's arm, and groaned, 'Mum. It is not a story, trust me.'

Her mum turned and glared at her. 'Rebecca, please do not say trust me, unless you mean it. You were gone for about ten minutes at the most. So how do you expect me to take you seriously?'

'Mum, trust me,' she said wide-eyed.

Elizabeth looked down, clearly deep in thought.

'Are you okay, Liz?' Amanda asked.

'When we were by the jetty, Rebecca kept going on about how long she'd been gone.' She then turned to Rebecca and looked her in the eyes.

Amanda shook her head. 'She does sound convincing, Liz.'

'For months, I've wondered if Meredith was a dream. Mum, you need to trust me on this one. I even had a page from a newspaper with the date on it. Sods-law, when I opened the door, it blew from my hand.' She shook her head and added, 'It was as if something was stopping me bringing any proof back. I am confused enough, without everyone compounding my thoughts by referring to my trips as dreams or stories, or even worse, that I am lying, which I never do, Mum.'

Elizabeth turned and whispered, 'your two stories have obvious similarities. I am starting to think you're trying to tell me something.'

'No, I'm not, Mum. For sure, each time the women were having difficulties with their men, however, that was because they stopped talking to them. That's the only similarity. It did make me wonder about the house though.'

'The house?'

'Yeah, as daft as it sounds, I was beginning to think our house only attracts a certain type of man and well...'

Her mum narrowed her eyes and shook her head. 'Maybe your trips are the same as the fairies and elves. What do you always say? They are there because you want them to be?'

Speaking a little louder, she said, 'Mother, I know how hard this is to believe. I had even decided not to mention the latest trip because I knew how you'd react, and I don't blame you. I planned to say nothing, and then on the next journey hide something noteworthy, something I could show you when I got back. That way, I'd have proof.'

'Rebecca, I am not happy that you're going to the summerhouse on your own, you know that. I need to be with you next time. I do not want to take the key from you, but I will, so you must give me your word.'

'But Mum, nothing would have happened if you were with me.' She looked straight at her mum and said, 'I shouldn't have to give you my word because you know you can trust me.'

'Can I say something please, Liz?'

'Yeah, fire away, Ruth,' Elizabeth said, while still looking directly at Rebecca.

'Well, Bex, your mother is right when she says you shouldn't go alone. Look what happened when you banged your head. However

225

wonderful your tales are - and they are truly splendid - it is still unsafe for you to go to the summerhouse on your own. Let us say - for the sake of the argument - you did go back to, when was it, 1940 something? Anyway, just suppose you went during a period of excessive bombing.' She glanced at Elizabeth and shrugged her shoulders. 'Or you couldn't get back home.'

'I do understand what you are both saying about the summerhouse. By all accounts, Liverpool took a real pounding during World War 2. However, this area was seen as safe, and that is why our house was used to evacuate young orphaned people.'

Ruth looked around. 'So, what are you saying? Is it always your house, just in a different period?'

'Yep, and to compound it, I am always Rebecca. I think I have said this before, Meredith treated me like her daughter, and so did Judith. And both called me Rebecca. I know that it sounds ridiculous, but it was the same both times. The weirdest aspect is that they actually see me as their daughter, and make me feel like I am at home. I know that sounds odd, but I very quickly felt comfortable around these people, almost as if I was at home. Now, you see why I need you to believe me, my emotions and thoughts are like a tin of worms, going in all directions.'

Amanda, who had been quiet for ages, spoke. 'What about your clothes, Bex, you may have gotten away with those jeans in the forties, but certainly not in the eighteen, whenever it was.'

'Yeah, I know, Amanda, and I have thought about that so many times. Meredith and Judith mentioned my choice of words, and Meredith made the occasional comment about my clothes, but that was it really. Actually, thinking about it now, there were a couple of very bizarre things.' She thought for a second, and realising this would probably make it sound even more like a dream, said it anyway. 'As odd as it sounds, both women used a word that mum uses, and

Meredith waved a bar of carbolic soap in my face when I swore, which mum also does, often. Hmm, very weird, I think.'

'You can say that again,' Amanda said, shook her head several times, and asked, 'what word, Rebecca?'

'The word is anyway, but they say it the same as Mum does with an s on the end, anyways. I've never heard anyone say it like that before, how weird is that? Which I know makes it sound more like a dream,' she said and puffed. 'Mum, tell them about my lost cardigan in the photo.'

'Rebecca, it just looked similar, and that's all it was, nothing more than a coincidence.'

Amanda, who had been clearly intrigued, said in an animated tone, 'oh, Liz, you have to tell us about this cardigan.'

'Well, Bex and I found a photo of Meredith with a young girl. It was in a hunting lodge over in the forest. That's where we were heading this morning in the boat. Meredith is one of the women in the paintings, you know, in the hallway.'

'Yeah, yeah, go on.'

'Well, the young girl standing next to Meredith in the photo appeared, I will say it again, appeared to be wearing a jumper, not unlike the one Rebecca lost the day she banged her head.' She tightened her lips, and mumbled, 'I have to admit the girl was similar to Rebecca. However, the photo was very faded.'

'Don't you think that is all a little strange, Liz?' Ruth asked, wide-eyed.

'Yep, but how can you explain it away, other than a coincidence. It is just like some kind of fantasy story, and we know how delightfully amazing Rebecca's imagination can be.' Elizabeth then shook her

227

head in a flippant way that Rebecca was beginning to find annoyingly regular.

Just as Rebecca was about to say something her mum's phone rang.

'Hello, James,' Elizabeth said and smiled, 'Are you?' She paused again, 'Oh okay, well that will be nice so we will see you later, have a nice time the pair of you, byeee.'

Ruth held her hand up in a questioning manner. 'Well, curiosity, the cat, and all that. So, are you going to spill the beans Elizabeth? Then we can get back to Rebecca's story.'

'Evidently, James is taking Tom to watch a football match.' She shook her head a couple of times. 'Someone at work offered him a couple of spare tickets for a Liverpool pre-season friendly this evening. James said they are going to grab something to eat on the way. And then said we have the day to ourselves, and he will see us, whenever we get home.' She shook her head again, and mumbled, 'maybe we should do this more often,' and glanced at Rebecca.

Knowing she didn't need to say anything, Rebecca touched her mum's arm gently and smiled.

'Well, Liz there you go. Hey, I was just thinking, perhaps you might now reconsider our walking trip to Wales. In for a penny, as they say,' Ruth said.

'What walking trip, Mum? You never mentioned it to me.'

'The girls are going for a few days to North Wales on a walking holiday. Wait for it, near an area called Fairy Glen.'

The way her mum grinned, Rebecca knew she was in with a chance of going too. 'That sounds cool. So, are we going white-water rafting too?'

'Not sure about that, might mess up Amanda's hair,' Ruth said and laughed aloud. 'And, young lady, we haven't said we are going, and I am not sure we invited you,' she said and sniggered.

Amanda giggled, held Rebecca's hand, and said, 'I'm glad you said we, I was hoping you'd come too, Bex? I'll go white-water rafting with you, rather than these two and their wet hair dramas.'

'Mum, can I go, please?' Rebecca said, pulling a face, she knew her mum couldn't resist.

'Well, Bex, I haven't said I am going yet. If, and I mean if, Dad says it is okay, yeah, of course, you can come. Thinking about it, it would be lovely, and then you and Amanda can go and get your hair messed up together, while Ruth and I do something a whole lot more civilised. G&T, Ruth?'

'Mum, why not just say to Dad you're going, in a pleasant way. Hey, I know, how about we say it is part of my Edinburgh award program. After all, it was his idea I get involved with that, although it is a kind of white lie.' Rebecca nodded, but it was half-hearted, knowing fibbing wasn't the right way to go.

'It's an interesting idea, but... No, Bex. We will have to think up a different plan. We can't lie to him, even if it's a white lie. I know that much and so do you. However, I am rather fancying the idea of this holiday now. I could do with a few girlie days, as it goes.'

'It might do Dad and Tom good to be on their own because they are bound to miss us. We will have such a laugh too, rafting, climbing mountains, going to see the waterfalls, maybe a few fairies, if you lot can keep quiet long enough. And actually, it will help with my Edinburgh Award thingy.'

Ruth nodded several times. 'You could do worse than listen to your daughter because she is right again, Liz. A *second-timer* you are, Rebecca.'

229

'Well that's weird, Ruth, you calling me a *second-timer* because my Nan and someone at school called me that. Then that woman this morning, Judith, she said it too. How funny is that, hearing it twice in one day, 60 years apart?'

'She did, did she? Well, I must say you have wisdom beyond your years,' Ruth said and glanced at Rebecca and then at Elizabeth.

'She does, Ruth,' Elizabeth said. 'I have always wondered where all these profound thoughts come from because she doesn't get it from me. She puts me to shame the way she thinks. It doesn't come from James either, although he has always been super intelligent and rather sharp-witted, especially when he was younger. He used to twist my parents around his little finger. However, he has never shown this inner wisdom that Rebecca has.'

'Mum, I do get it from you, and a little from Dad. You always seem to know what I am up to, almost as if you are reading my thoughts. Shame Tom didn't inherit any. Read my mind, Tom, sod off.' She then giggled but could see her mum wasn't at all impressed.

'Rebecca, you were nearly as petulant as Tom when you were his age.'

'Mummm, how very dare you, I have never been like twit-face.'

'Rebecca, don't keep calling him a twit, please. You know I don't like it. He is silly sometimes and maybe a tad more than you was at that age. He is eleven, so give him a chance, hey, and he is a boy.' Elizabeth laughed aloud.

'Sorry, Mum,' she muttered, 'Tom's a twit, end of subject.'

As timely as ever Ruth changed the subject. 'So, what's the plan?'

'Well, far be it for me to remind you, especially as you seem to be leading the way, Ruth. I thought we were going to town for some

230

retail therapy, then a picnic, then the new salon, and then an Italian meal,' Amanda said and giggled. 'If we have time that is.'

'Very funny, Amanda. I meant what's the plan for the holiday. And we've passed half the shops while we've been chatting.'

'Ruth, we all knew what you meant, darling. We were just giving you a taste of your own medicine. I think Elizabeth should just tell James that we are all planning to go away for a few days on a walking holiday. See what he says and how he responds. Keep it simple. Why lie, you only get found out in the end.'

'Yeah, right, Amanda. I have just managed to swim a metaphorical width and you want me going for the Olympics,' Elizabeth said and chuckled.

'Mum, what are you talking about?'

Elizabeth raised her eyebrows and replied, 'what I mean is...'

'Mum, I know what you mean, I was kidding.'

'Hey, how about Amanda and I come over one night for supper. Then, while we are eating, we can idly mention the trip. Ask if you two would like to come with us. Maybe even be a little ironic, nicely, of course, something like, err...'

Amanda added, 'yeah cool, Ruth, you could ask if Elizabeth and Rebecca can come out to play.'

'Why am I asking him, Amanda?' Ruth said and giggled.

'Girlies, actually that is such a good idea, wish I'd thought of that. Besides, Mum, think how easy he was when you asked him about tonight, and remember Ruth's birthday party. Every time you ask him, he is fine about it, so I don't really know why you make such a fuss. Come on let's do it. They can come over on Friday, and I can say, without lying, of course, it will help me with my Edinburgh Award project, which it will.'

'Umm, well I guess so. What day is it, Wednesday? Maybe, I will mention it at breakfast tomorrow and see how he responds.'

'Mum, just say you've invited Amanda and Ruth for a curry on Friday, and we know he loves your curries. The point is, Mum if you sometimes choose the terms, he will become used to you making decisions, and having an opinion. Think of it as a game, think about the things you did when you were young, how you kept him on his toes.' Rebecca thought for a moment. 'You did keep him on his toes, Mum, tell me you did.'

'That's a great point, and very true, Liz. You did keep him on his toes, and you were very good at doing so. I remember that time you intentionally arrived at the restaurant an hour after you'd agreed, just to make him wait. You told us – laughing, I might add – that he waited and never once mentioned your timekeeping, and paid the bill – in a ludicrously expensive restaurant, that you'd picked simply because it was pricey. By the way, the curry is a great idea, Bex, and a good compromise.'

'I can't believe that you can remember that far back, Ruth.'

'I remember you sat in my house as we watched the clock, giggling.'

Amanda smiled and said, 'I wish I had known you two when I was younger. It sounds like you had such a laugh.'

'Oh, we did have a laugh, Amanda. Liz had a queue of boys, and she was so good at keeping them all on their toes. She never said yes, never said no. I was just the ugly mate.'

'Ruth, you never have been my ugly mate, and never will be. I am cross you said as much.'

232

'Mummm, a queue of boys, what are you like?'

Elizabeth flicked her hair back. 'Well, even if I say so myself, I was rather dishy. And Ruth was equally eye-catching, and the boys were always after her, she just chose to ignore them.'

Ruth turned to Rebecca and said, 'she was such a looker that when we walked along the road every man – and some of the women – would just stare with their mouths open.'

They continued chatting on their way around the shops eventually arriving at the new salon. Unfortunately, it wasn't due to open for another week, so they headed down to the river. Rebecca and her mum set up their picnic, while the girls went to get coffee.

As they were unpacking, Elizabeth said, 'tell me about Judy, Judith?'

Rebecca then explained all about Judith, Christopher and the farm girls just finishing up as Ruth and Amanda were heading back. 'Mum, I don't much feel like talking to Ruth and A about my story, not just yet. Is that okay?'

'Yes, of course, Bex, need you ask,' she said, narrowing her eyes? 'We need to have a long chat about this because I have never known you this serious about anything.'

After the picnic, the girls spent the rest of the afternoon shopping. In a buoyant mood, they headed for the restaurant, their laughter causing a few looks from the other customers, much to Ruth's dismay. This, in turn, made them laugh even more. Around ten, they headed back, and as Ruth pulled into the drive, Elizabeth suggested a coffee.

The girls entered the kitchen just as James and Tom were tucking into some fast food. Tom, with half a burger in one hand, stood up and proudly displayed his new Liverpool shirt.

233

Elizabeth smiled at James indicating to Tom with her thumb. 'Hello, Tom, nice shirt, did you have a good time?'

Dancing around and with a croaky throat, he yelped, 'Yeah, it was brill, Mum, and they won too, and Dad got me this shirt, and it's got me name on the back, and we are gonna go again. And we got me favourite burger on the way 'ome.'

James rolled his eyes, and with a wry grin, said, 'Tom,' he shook his head, and continued, 'Oh forget it.'

'James, I thought you detested this type of food.'

'Well, I do, but it is so long since I've cooked anything, and well, I couldn't let the blighter starve.' He shook his head and laughed. He then smiled at Elizabeth and asked, 'So, ladies, did you have a nice time?'

'Yeah, Dad, we had the most excellent time, and you will have to come next time. The restaurant is Italian, wonderful food, no burgers there, but maybe they will make you one if you ask.' Rebecca laughed, and wanting to take advantage of her father's good mood, asked, 'Hey, Dad, on the subject of food, you like a curry, don't you?'

'Yes, Rebecca, why may I ask, as if I don't know something is coming? So, go on, what have you planned?'

Elizabeth and Rebecca went to speak at the same time. 'You go, Mum.'

'Well, James, we thought it would be nice this Friday to invite Ruth and Amanda over for a curry. They are planning a hiking holiday, and we fancied chatting about it over some food.'

'Walking, rather than hiking, Liz,' Ruth added and smiled.

'So why did you not talk about it today? Why do you need to wait until Friday, unless of course, you are planning...?'

'Unless, James, what did you mean unless we are planning?' Elizabeth said, grinned, and glanced in Rebecca's direction.

'Elizabeth, I have known you long enough, and know when you are cooking something up, and I do not mean a curry, either. And that grin is a dead giveaway.' A little sarcastically, James smiled, still appearing pretty relaxed. 'So, do I have to wait until Friday, or is one of you ladies going to enlighten me now? Curiosity, cat, and all that,' he said turning to Ruth and Amanda.

Elizabeth glanced at the girls, and before she had a chance to answer, Rebecca stepped in. 'Dad, the girls are going for a walking holiday for a couple of days in North Wales. I said I would love to go as it may help me with my Edinburgh award. Mum said I can't go without her.'

Although James still had half a smile, his tone was ironic. 'So, let me get this right. All four of you want to go away for a couple, although I rather suspect it is a few days, on some trek in Wales. And the best excuse you could think of is your Edinburgh award?'

Rebecca glanced at her mum who, tight-lipped, frowned back.

'Yes, James, basically that's it, and we were thinking of five days. That's right, Ruth, isn't it?' Elizabeth said as she glanced at Ruth.

Ruth just nodded and smiled.

James raised his eyes, shook his head a little, and asked, 'Okay, when exactly?'

'Monday after next, Dad,' Rebecca said in an excited tone. 'That's right isn't it, Ruth?'

'Well, that's what we had in mind, although nothing is booked as yet. And by the way, I am not a travel agent, don't have to keep checking every detail with me,' she said and grinned.

'Oh, give me some notice, why not? Actually, that may fit in well with Tom and me. The Liverpool team is going on a pre-season trip to Belgium that week. Perhaps, Tom and I could combine that, with a trip to Brussels, from an educational point of view, of course.' Again, James laughed.

Tom, with a handful of fries, was jumping around the room, punching the air. Rebecca, trying to ignore him, asked, 'Oh, so are you two into Liverpool now? And you accuse me of a flimsy excuse to go somewhere, an educational trip to Brussels, indeed.'

'I have to say, I did enjoy tonight. I never thought I would, but as they say, live and learn.' He pointed at Tom, indicating for him to sit down. He then turned back to Elizabeth. 'So, Elizabeth, are we still having a curry on Friday, or do you no longer see the need for that scam?'

'No, James, it will be lovely to have the girls over for a curry.'

They sat and chatted about the restaurant and football for ages. Eventually, James told Tom it was time for bed after seeing him nodding off in the corner. He then turned to the girls and bid his farewells suggesting he was turning in as he had an early start the following day.

Over another coffee, the girls set about planning their trip. Suddenly, Amanda jumped up, exclaiming it was two in the morning and that she had to be up at seven for a meeting.

As Rebecca and her mum headed up to bed, her mum asked, 'Rebecca can I ask you a question?'

'Mum, just ask away, you need not ask if you can ask,' she said and touched her mum gently on the arm.

'You said something about it being easy to form a relationship with the women you met. What exactly do you mean, because I felt you were trying to say something more?'

'It's hard to explain really, but in essence, I felt comfortable around them, as if I had known them forever. It is weird, I want to say, I instantly felt affection for them.' She shook her head, unsure of how to explain. 'It is as if there is a natural bond there, the likes of which I have only ever felt towards you, Dad, and Tommy. I know that sounds daft, but it really is like I know them and have known them forever.'

'Hmm, it's all a bit strange. I can see why you struggle with the whole thing, explaining it, and having us lot suggesting it's a dream.' She hesitated for a moment, and then continued, 'Don't get me wrong, I am not saying I am ready to accept it really happened, but I am increasingly open to the idea. Right, I think it's time for bed.'

Chapter 14 - The Next Article

The week leading up to their holiday passed quickly for Rebecca, and it was just a couple of days away now. Although Judith was still in her thoughts, her focus was towards the upcoming adventure with the girls. This was the first time she'd been away without her dad and Tom, and she was beside herself with expectation. Her dad and Tom had left for Belgium the day before, and this just served to magnify her excitement. She was helping her mum pack the last essentials while they waited for Amanda and Ruth to come back with a Chinese meal they'd agreed on earlier.

'Mum, where have you hidden my black socks this time?' she called out to her mum in the kitchen.

'In the drawer at the bottom of that old cupboard in the corner of your bedroom, the brown one that was here when we moved in.'

'The bottom drawer doesn't open, never has? Anyway, I thought we were going to throw it away, so why are you still hiding my clothes in it?'

'Yes, I know, but I tried it randomly last Thursday, and it opened. I will come and show you. Your father said it's an antique, and suggested it goes back about two hundred years, so I thought I would have a look at it, and it opened. By the way, I don't hide your clothes; you just need to try looking.'

'I tried it two weeks ago, and it didn't open, so you'll have to show me,' she called out, now standing at the bottom of the stairs.

'Quickly then, before the girls get back.'

Rebecca followed her mum upstairs to her room; certain it wasn't going to open. She stood there somewhat surprised as her mum bent down and pulled the bottom drawer open.

'There you go, look, there are your socks. All four draws open, so maybe we didn't try properly. The top three are empty, and I expect them to stay that way, as they are not another store for art materials.' As she turned to the door, she said, 'I will be next door as I think that's where my heavy coat is. And on that subject, make sure your room is tidy, and shout if you can't find anything else. Ten minutes, Rebecca.' She then opened her eyes wide and said again, 'Ten minutes.'

Rebecca rolled her eyes and bent down to the drawer. She had tried it umpteen times in the past but had never been able to open it. Miffed, she tried the top draws first and as her mum had suggested they were empty. She then opened and shut the bottom drawer a couple of times and puffed as she picked out her socks. As she turned, something caught her eye and instantly claimed her attention. Turning back, she lifted the corner of her clothes and could see what looked like an old newspaper lining the draw. Removing her clothes, she carefully lifted out the newspaper. 'Mum,' she screamed.

Seconds later, her mum appeared at the door, and asked, 'Whatever is the matter, Rebecca, why did you scream?'

Barely able to get her words out, Rebecca handed her mum the newspaper, and panted, 'Mum, Mum, look. Do you remember the newspaper I told you about, the one I tried to bring back? Well, this is the same newspaper. It was in that drawer as lining paper. This is so spooky. How did it get to be in my drawer, the one that has never opened?'

'Rebecca, calm down, Honey. What newspaper are you talking about?'

'The one I tried to bring home from 1943, you know, when I was with Judith. I told you it blew from my hand as I was coming back,

239

look.' She then pointed at the paper. 'I don't understand this because I lost it in the summerhouse, so how did it end up here?' At a total loss for words, she just sat staring at the paper. She kept going over in her head, *how can this be?* Then pointed to the date, and uttered, 'October 22, 1943, just as I told you.'

Her mum shook her head. 'It's just a coincidence Rebecca, a spooky one admittedly, but still a coincidence. Hey, probably you saw it in your drawer, and somehow it registered in your brain, which caused you to dream about it.'

As loud as she could, she puffed, knowing her mum would say something like that. 'Mum, the drawer has never opened until you opened it. I've tried it so many times, don't you think I'd know if I opened it before. Look, I told you about the newspaper, the exact same date, and all.'

'Well, I vaguely recall you mentioned 1943, but even so.'

'Oh, Mum, it happened just as I said, I promise you. What I don't get is how the paper ended up here.' Rebecca sort of understood her mum's point of view, but annoyingly knew by the look on her face that no amount of words would change her mind. 'For what it's worth, I reckon it was brought from the summerhouse in 1943 and used to line this drawer. That's the only possible way, I think. And it is not just another bizarre coincidence. You can't call everything a coincidence, Mum.'

'Rebecca, as much as I delight in your tales, you have to agree that the latest ones are rather farfetched. I mean, time-travel, a spiral staircase I have never seen, and you were gone for how long. Your tale about Meredith, and what was the other woman called, Judy. Yes, for sure, we found the photograph of the woman and a young girl in the lodge, and now this. Really, Honey, you must see it from my point of view. Ruth would say, "circumstantial evidence," and that's all it is.'

Frustrated, but also understanding her mum's point, Rebecca said, 'I do appreciate why you think it's a dream, Mum, but you must see that my stories have a little substance. I oddly wish it was a dream, at least then I would have a handle on everything.'

'Well, that's as maybes, but can we drop the subject now, we must finish our packing before the girls get back.' Elizabeth said as she turned towards the door.

'Mum, we have all weekend to pack.' She shook her head, but knew by her mum's tone and knew there was little if any leeway.

As her mum walked to the door, she turned and said, 'I will have a look at the newspaper later. I must say, either way, it is rather cool, finding a newspaper from the war. If nothing else it will make an interesting read.'

'You will see one day, Mum, like I said, I will hide something next time, and then you will see. Anyway, I reckon Meredith put it here because she knows how difficult it is for you adults to open up your mind and see the blatantly obvious,' she said and pointed again at the paper. 'By the way, it is Judith, not Judy.'

'Well, I rather hope there won't be a next time, certainly not without me. Anyways, explain what Meredith was doing in 1943.'

'Mum, Meredith is unlikely to let you in because you're not a believer. And I don't know, maybe it was her spirit. Brrr, wish I hadn't thought that.'

'What do you mean by that, Rebecca? Moreover, Meredith's spirit, really, whatever next.'

'Well, I've said before that adults lose their ability to see with an open mind. Once common sense influences your opinion, you stop looking with the eyes of innocence, eyes that see anything as possible. As I said about the fairies, Mum, open your mind and then your eyes,

241

maybe you will see them. You don't believe because you've forgotten how.'

Elizabeth rolled her eyes. 'Right, I am going to finish off packing, I suggest you do the same, Honey.'

Ruth and Amanda returned a little later with the Chinese supper. They sat in the kitchen chatting about the holiday, and although Rebecca joined in, her mind was elsewhere. In the end, she felt she had to mention the newspaper. 'Mum, tell them about the old newspaper, the one that magically appeared in my drawer that has magically started opening.'

Amanda was the first to respond. 'Magical newspaper, tell us more, Bex? Does it fly by any chance?' she said and giggled while holding Rebecca's hand.

'Do we get to see it, Rebecca?' Ruth asked.

Rebecca dashed upstairs and returned holding it like it was a work of art. She then explained again about the chest of draws and mentioned the exact date several times.

Clearly intrigued, Amanda was again the first to respond. 'This is all a bit weird, Liz, don't you agree?'

Elizabeth shrugged her shoulders, clearly a little uncomfortable. She sipped her coffee and glanced at Rebecca with that, I'm still not buying it look. 'I know it is all very intriguing, but it is also a little farfetched. It is a lovely story; Rebecca's tales always are intriguing, charming, but...' She then frowned for a moment as if she was thinking. 'I don't know what to think, part of me wants to believe it, but a time-travelling staircase? And the latest addition is Meredith's spirit, who can also time jump.'

Ruth looked up from the paper and said, 'circumstantial at best, Bex, sorry, but that's all it is.'

Rebecca could feel her mum looking at her, so turned and smiled sarcastically.

Amanda smiled at Rebecca in a way that suggested she could see her frustration. She then turned back to Elizabeth, and said, 'It's a little surreal, but nonetheless, I find it all very interesting. Rebecca seems to know an awful lot of detail, even down to the date on this paper being the date she mentioned the other day. When you add everything together it kind of stacks up if something like this can stack up.' She glanced at Elizabeth. 'And Rebecca saying the drawer has never opened before, really. I mean really. So, Bex, tell me about Meredith's spirit.'

Wide-eyed, Rebecca looked at her mum. 'Amanda is right, Mum you must see all the evidence, the photos, two newspapers, both coincidently from the exact time I visited, it more than adds up. How do you suppose Meredith moved the newspaper in 19 flipping 43 unless it was her spirit?' Rebecca paused and thought for a moment. 'Right now, I'm not sure I want to think about that, coz if I do, I will need to know why her spirit was floating about in 1943.'

Elizabeth smiled at Rebecca the way only a mum does. 'Believe me, Rebecca; I would so love this to be true, if for nothing else but your peace of mind. It's the same as the fairies, the pixies, and the elves, which I am desperate to see, but the harder I look, the less I see. So, like the fairies, I only have your word for it. If it's because I am an adult, and I've lost my ability to see such things, I can't do much about that. For now, though, they are just lovely tales. I am sorry, Honey, but that is all it is.'

'Liz, you know me, boring, and a little frumpy, but I have to say, this whole idea has me, well, let's say fascinated, a little circumstantial or not.' Ruth then smiled at Rebecca. 'So, tell me, Bex, what happens? You told us about the stairs, and the different doors, but what happens when you actually go through the door?'

Rebecca beamed, delighted by Ruth's interest. 'I climb the spiral stairs and open the first door I come to. Inside, the room is pitch black, to the point where I can barely see. But as soon as I step into the room, it fills with light. Although that's only after the door slams behind me, which it did both times. And there I am, still Rebecca, just in a different time. The bit I struggle to get my head around is Meredith and Judith treating me like their daughter. I know I mentioned this before, but for me, that's the weirdest bit. I know this sounds silly, but it really is as if they know me personally, even my odd bits, including my maverick imagination.'

With her chin in her hand, Ruth asked, 'So, do you always end up back in the main house?'

'No, Ruth, I stay in the summerhouse, although both times, I ended up visiting the main house. Although, the summerhouse is not as run down as it is now. I find it odd though the way I just seem to fit into their lives. I must say, it's brilliant seeing it from their point of view. I find it remarkable how things are so different, yet so similar. Like the men being... Well, let's just say they pushed their women away, or the women retreated, or both. Hmmm.'

'It's all very interesting. If I am honest, this type of stuff has always fascinated me. Maybe, Rebecca, it happened in some sort of dream, and because you have focused so heavily on the past, it makes it all seem real.' The way she frowned suggested Ruth wasn't at all sure about what she'd just said.

'Ruth, I understand what you're saying, and realise how strange the whole thing must seem, it is to me, but...' She shook her head and took a deep breath. 'If you all think it's weird, how do you think I feel? You must realise that I question it myself, repeatedly. I go through the whole bizarre experience for real and then go through it in my head over and over again, and no one believes me.' She looked down and then glanced up at her mum.

Ruth suddenly gasped. 'Have you read this paper, Liz, Bex? I think this is an article about your house.'

'Really,' Rebecca said, leaning on Ruth's shoulder, peering at the paper.

'It may be easier if I read the article to you. It says the old house up by Serinpool Lake, that's your lake, right?'

'Yeah, yeah, carry on, Ruth,'

'Okay, it reads; the old house, blah-blah, was at the centre of a murder mystery, and the county police record office has re-opened the case. It rambles a bit and then says there was a murder sometime around the 1850s', which the local police initially thought was an accident following an annual hunt. It goes on to say that soon after the police charged the resident woman of the house with the murder. It also suggests that shortly after the affair, the police apprehended an unnamed individual who destroyed all records that related to the incident and all historical records pertaining to the house, known as Elm Manor. It says that the paper has no names available at this time and will profile the events further if details are forthcoming.' Ruth took a deep breath. 'Rebecca isn't that the...' She then looked back at the paper. 'Hmmm, this is interesting; it says that the murdered individual was a local former courtesan. Doesn't that mean prostitute?'

'Yes,' Rebecca blurted, still getting her head around what she was hearing. She was certain Meredith hadn't murdered Millicent, *but what else could it mean* she thought. 'That was around the time I was there. Mum, I told you Millicent was a whore, and I told you Meredith was continually exasperated by her. I couldn't have dreamt all that, could I? And if Meredith was accused unfairly, that's why her spirit is still hanging around. Flip, maybe she's waiting for me to sort it all out. I feel rather anxious now.'

Shaking her head, Liz said, 'Now, now, Bex honey, it's only an old newspaper article, and there are no names. It's just another coincidence. That's all it is, so can we please drop the subject for now,' Elizabeth said, rubbing her arms, clearly ill at ease.

Rebecca knew her mother's tone and suspected the article had made her uncomfortable. Even though she was at bursting point and so wanted to discuss it further, she reluctantly decided to drop the subject. 'Ok, Mum, sorry. Maybe we should think about our holiday,' she said and smiled. She then glanced at Ruth, who smiled and held one finger to her lips, presumably having recognised how edgy Liz was.

The rest of the evening passed with a lot of laughter, with the focus on their holiday. Occasionally, Ruth discreetly asked a little more about Rebecca's adventures, but mostly they talked about white-water rafting, hiking and *Fairy Glen*.

Sunday passed quickly, with no mention of Meredith, even though Rebecca couldn't get the thoughts from her head. She spent a little while trying to find something on her computer, but it was soon evident she was wasting her time. Monday, she woke from a dream about fairies. With it still hanging around in her head, she tried to recall the details, while taking a shower. Drying herself off, she realised what the time was and so quickly got ready. Walking into an empty kitchen caught her by surprise. While pouring herself some orange, she spotted her mum, Ruth and Amanda sitting outside.

Sipping a coffee, Ruth said, 'It seems we are in for another Indian summer, September tomorrow, and it's still so warm. Hey, it's your birthday in a couple of days, sixteen and all, Rebecca. Do you have any ideas what you want?'

'Yeah, Ruth, I'd like to give school a miss until October and not have to go back so soon after my birthday. Give me some time to get my head around being a grown up.' she said and glanced at her mum.

'I thought your Mum said that you were going back on the 17th. Isn't that enough time, Bex?' Ruth turned toward Elizabeth. 'Liz, why is Rebecca's school going back so late, I think all the other schools are due back next week?'

'Something to do with it being A-level year. I'm sure that's what the letter said.'

'I enjoy school and all, but well, I've just had such fun this summer; I don't want it to end. And yeah, Mum, A-levels, yippee. And yes, Ruth, the 17th, which in my mind is too soon.'

So, Bex, your last summer as a girl, all grown up this time next week,' she said a laughed. 'I wish I was your age again.' Ruth touched Rebecca affectionately on the arm.

'Don't we all, Ruth, don't we all.' Liz smiled, also touching Rebecca gently on the arm. 'You will always be my little girl, Honey.'

'Well, I think I might just give the growing up a miss, especially if it means I have to say goodbye to my friends.'

'What do you mean, say goodbye to your friends, Honey?'

'Mum, getting older might mean me having to say goodbye to the fairies, pixies, even the bears, but mostly Meredith and Judith. Anyway, can we change the subject?' She picked up her drink and went over to look at a rose bush.

'Is she okay, Liz?' Ruth asked, raising her eyebrow.

'Yeah, I think so, leave her be a while, she will be okay. I think she is struggling to come to terms with being sixteen.'

'Well, maybe you should tell her it only has to be on the outside and that on the inside, she can stay as young as she wants.'

'No need for me to tell her, Ruth, she is always telling me to see it from a youthful point of view.' Elizabeth glanced over and said, 'Perhaps I will have a chat with her while we are on holiday.'

'No need to, I can hear you, being over here doesn't mean I'm deaf.' Rebecca said, laughed, walked back over, and sat at the table. 'I'm all right you know, just... Anyway, what time are we leaving?'

'As soon as we've all finished breakfast,' her mum said, glancing at the others.

Although the journey to North Wales felt like it took forever for Rebecca, it seemed no sooner they'd arrived, she was packing to leave. She sat for a few minutes staring at her suitcase, reflecting on the brilliant time they'd had, in particular, one special day by an amazing waterfall called *Fairy Glen*. Most importantly, she'd seen a positive change in her mum's outlook. She was aware this was the first time her mum had been away from her dad and had wondered a few times if this had allowed her to let her hair down. But on reflection, there had also been a couple of times when her mum had been really quiet, and when Rebecca had asked if she was okay, she'd suggested she was missing Tommy, which Rebecca took as she was missing her dad too. Thinking about this and all they had done, and still gazing at her empty suitcase, she was miles away when her room door burst open and in walked her mum, Amanda and Ruth carrying a birthday cake, singing happy birthday. She was a little taken aback having completely forgotten it was her 16th birthday; well, she was just ignoring it. Just as her mum handed over some presents from dad and Tom, her dad phoned. The way her mum grinned and handed her the phone, she guessed the call was planned and besides the timing was just too perfect. Her dad chatted to her for ages, saying he was sorry he was not there, but thought it was great for her to celebrate with her mum and the ladies, especially now she was a *lady*. He wished her happy birthday again, said he had missed her and mum and then handed the phone over to Tommy. After the call, she was a little surprised just how nice they had been on the phone and was now actually looking forward to seeing them in a couple of days. She was also delighted to hear her dad say he had missed both her and mum. *A perfect end to a brilliant holiday*, she thought.

The journey home was so dull for Rebecca, intensified by two lots of stop-start traffic around roadworks. She tried to focus on something else, but every time she drifted off, her mum kept mentioning the traffic. Arriving home at gone midnight, and after thanking her mum for a fabulous time, Rebecca headed straight to bed.

Chapter 15 - Amanda's Birthday

Amanda and Ruth had stayed the night and were still there at lunchtime the following day. Rebecca was enjoying their company – that was until her mum reminded her, they had to pick up Tommy and dad from the airport. Ruth had offered to fetch James and Tom from the airport the night before, but her mum had insisted on going even though she hated driving into Liverpool. Rebecca had noticed a gradual change in her mum's outlook over the last few weeks and in particular since they returned from holiday. But her mother's conviction still came as a surprise to Rebecca.

As they pulled from the drive, she noticed it was four o'clock. 'What time are we picking them up, Mum?'

'Six they land.'

'Mum, aren't we leaving it a bit fine.'

'Well, it won't hurt them to wait a while. Besides, they could have ordered a cab,' she said, laughing, but was clearly serious.

On the way there, Rebecca found herself grinning at every red light, hoping they'd be late just so she could see how her mum handled the situation. So, when they arrived with plenty of time to spare, she was somewhat disappointed. As soon as she saw her dad and Tom, it was apparent they'd had a good time, particularly Tom, who had one of those annoying grins on his face. She was actually pleased to see them both, which surprised her a little. As they were heading to the car park, her dad mentioned that they would like to go again, what with Liverpool's important European matches coming up. Tommy immediately started jumping about in his usual way, causing a lot of attention from other people in the airport, which amused Rebecca. She looked at him, thinking once a twit, always a twit. Clearly, though, her mum didn't find it funny at all, pulling on his ear, while referring to him as a possessed child.

While James was putting the cases in the boot, Elizabeth winked at Rebecca and whispered, 'Looks like another jaunt for us girlies.' She put the key in the ignition, and before starting the car, turned to James. 'We were home late last night, and I've not had time to get any food. Sorry to be blunt, but I really don't feel like cooking either. So, if you two are hungry, let me know, and I'll stop off on the way home for a takeaway.'

Still shocked by her mum's tone, Rebecca had to take a deep breath when her dad responded with, "another burger wouldn't go amiss, I guess," and then laughed. On the way home, Rebecca chatted to Tommy about both their holidays but kept an eye on her mum and dad. She found herself wondering if her mum was finally taking back a little control. At one point, she nearly laughed aloud when she heard her mum say, "James, I am talking, please let me finish." She tried to stifle her laughter unsuccessfully, and then blamed Tommy, whose face was priceless, not having a clue what she was going on about. In fact, Tommy looked at her as if she was from another planet. *So, no change there,* she thought.

A half-hour or so into their journey they came to a complete stop, stuck in a traffic jam. Elizabeth puffed her cheeks out and said, 'Blast. I forgot about this blinking roadworks. I intended to go a different bloody way too.'

James turned to Elizabeth with a look that made Rebecca wish she had a camera. Just as he was about to say something, her mum stopped him dead. 'Don't give me that look, James. Do not tell me you didn't hear a lifetime's worth of swearing at your flipping football matches.' She then turned, looked at him the same way she often looked at Tom.

Rebecca knew she was once again wishing her life away, but couldn't wait to see how long her mum would keep this up. She kept asking herself if this had started that day when they went to the park and planned their holiday or was there something that happened while they were on holiday. Either way, she wasn't going to knock it, just wished she could see into the future, which made her laugh aloud, wondering if Meredith could arrange something.

After they'd stopped off and had some food, they eventually arrived home at ten in the evening. Her mum kissed Tom on the cheek and pointed to his bedroom. He glanced at her with his mouth open, went to say something, and for some reason, shrugged his shoulders and headed to his bedroom without so much as a mumble. She then turned to James, also kissed him on the cheek, and said, 'I'm going to bed because I'm completely bushwhacked. Bex, you must be tired,' she said and indicated for her to follow.

On the way upstairs, Rebecca said, 'Mum, when did...' Before she had a chance to finish, her mum stopped her.

'It was that moment at Fairy Glen when we talked about the silence behind the sound of the waterfall. The penny dropped, if that makes sense, I don't know when and why I got it, I just did. I just saw things for what they are and how I had allowed myself to lose sight of where I am and where I should be. You always said *talk to Dad,* and when I did, he was fine. To be honest, as odd as it may sound, I can't even remember how I felt before.' She paused and appearing a little tearful, kissed Rebecca on the cheek. 'Thank you, Rebecca, I love you.'

Rebecca gave her a big hug, and said, 'I love you, Mum, and I love the new you. But the waterfall, explain.'

'I wish I could, Rebecca. When you said to me to listen for the silence, all I could hear was the sound of crashing water.' She stared at the floor for a moment. 'Something happened. I looked at you and could almost hear your thoughts. Then I heard it, nothing, the silence as you called it. Strangely, it gave me a focal point. I saw you, and in you, I saw me as I was,' she said as a tear rolled down her cheek, 'that was it, Rebecca.' She then kissed Rebecca on the cheek and wished her sweet dreams.

Rebecca lay in bed thinking about what her mum had said, but being so tired soon dropped off. The following morning when she arrived down for breakfast, she was shocked to see her mum, dad and Tommy, all sitting outside. 'How a family should be,' she muttered while pouring a glass of orange.

'Morning, Rebecca, I am so sorry we were away for your birthday, sixteen too, a woman now, hey?' her dad said with a smiley tone.

'Thanks, Dad, and thanks for my lovely present, perfect, just what I needed, a notebook, mine's been on the way out for months.' She then kissed him on the cheek but was surprised when he stood up and cuddled her. As if that wasn't enough, Tommy also stood up, and half cuddled her with one arm. *What you'd expect from an eleven-year-old boy,* she thought. She then thanked Tommy for the football card and Liverpool poster.

After her dad and Tommy had gone to work, Rebecca helped her mum tidy up. 'Mum, I can't believe Tommy; he was nearly nice to me. And to make it worse, I was pleased to see him yesterday.'

Her mum grinned. 'Well, I don't know how many times I've told you, these men, well you just have to take a stand with them, put them in their place. Let this be a lesson to you, Young Girl.' She then beamed a smile, and said, 'Or should I say, young woman.'

'Hmm, I'm not too sure about being a woman just yet. Inside I don't feel any different.'

'Well, you are a woman now, sixteen and all. Nevertheless, you know better than most that age is just a number, and inside you can be whatever age you want. On the subject of age, we should talk about sex.'

'Mum, don't even go there. Things in school are different nowadays. I have been educated to the nth degree, thanks all the same.'

The rest of the morning passed quietly as the two pottered about tidying up. Around mid-day, the phone rang, and it was Ruth. After chatting for a few moments, Rebecca handed the phone to her mum and carried on tidying up the kitchen.

When her mum had finished on the phone, she turned to Rebecca. 'Ruth has asked if we want to go and get Amanda's birthday present.'

Instantly, Rebecca's brain was hatching a plan to get back to the summerhouse. 'Oh, Mum, I'd love to, but I must do my homework. I'm back to school next week, and am miles behind.' She was a little behind but knew this may be her last chance to try the stairs before going back to school. She looked at her mum, nodded, and said, 'you two go, Mum. I am a woman now remember,' she laughed and flicked her head. 'I am capable of looking after myself.' She was sure her mum wouldn't agree, but with the idea fixed in her thoughts, had to push it. 'I know what happened last time, what with the fall and all, and I've learnt from that.' All the time, she had her fingers crossed hoping her mum wouldn't ask her to promise.

'Well, I'm not sure, Honey. If your father finds out I left you on your own again, he will be cross.'

She could see her mum was considering the idea, so pushed a little more.

'I am just not sure it is right, whatever your father thinks. It is me it is down to.'

'Mum, I learnt from the last experience, banging my head and all.' After a lot of persuasions, her mum finally relented. In an attempt to reassure her, she grabbed her new notebook and busied herself doing her homework. When her mum leant over her shoulder, Rebecca was ready and responded by showing her something geography related. 'I've been putting this off all summer; it's to do with people building houses on the water tables.'

'Well, make sure you stay here, Rebecca. I'll be back by four.' She then kissed her goodbye and again told her to stay doing her homework and be good.

As soon as she heard her mum's car pull away, Rebecca grabbed her torch and a sturdy plastic bag. She'd had this idea for ages that she would get something from the past, bury it, and then dig it up when she got back. She knew it was a long shot, but reckoned that if it worked, it would finally prove her trips were real, if nothing else, to her. *That's if there's another trip for me,* she thought. She nodded, sure there was more, pulled on her cardigan, and marched down to the summerhouse.

As she approached, memories of the last trip flooded her thoughts. Having gone over it so many times, she was still adamant her trip had taken hours, even though her mum had said otherwise. She had thought several times that her journeys were some kind of time-lapse thing and that even if she stayed for a day or more, it could possibly only be minutes in her time. She stood there for ages, again trying to fathom out what could have happened regarding the murder, and if it involved Meredith and Millicent. With it still playing on her mind, she stepped on to the veranda and stared at the key wondering what lay in store this time. After a few seconds, she decided the only way she would find out was to get back inside. She opened the front door, and without even glancing in the direction of the other rooms, headed straight down the hallway. Feeling oddly calm, she gripped the handle and turned it. It was stuck fast, and it wouldn't budge, not even slightly. She tried a few more times, but like the first time she was here, it was as if the door had never been opened. She'd always had a notion that the door wouldn't open if she had her mobile phone with her, and was now thinking the plastic bag might be a problem. She nodded, and placed it, along with her torch, by the front door. She went back and tried again, but there wasn't even the tiniest movement.

255

Suddenly, an idea came to her that made her laugh aloud but frustrated she reckoned anything was worth a try. Shaking her head and still thinking it was a bizarre thought, even by her standards, she whispered, 'Meredith, I promise I won't hide anything.' She meant it, somehow knowing that if she didn't, it wouldn't work. She didn't know why she knew this, just did. She braced herself and tried again. This time the handle turned freely. She took a deep breath, eased the door open, and with purpose, moved over to the staircase. Without hesitation, she climbed to the first door but found the door locked, and for some reason, wasn't that surprised. She moved up to the second floor, only to find that locked too. Looking up into the darkness, she hesitated for a moment and wondered if there could possibly be another door further up. *This is daft* she thought, knowing there was only the ground floor and the first floor, and she was preparing to go up to a mysterious third floor. She had briefly looked up into the darkness the last time she was here, but it was so dark it had left her feeling edgy. Besides, there'd been no need to venture any further. She turned back and tried the door she had gone through last time, but it was definitely locked. Having no choice, she cautiously edged her way up. Somehow, these stairs felt steeper and narrow by comparison to her previous trips. She knew this was unlikely, but the sensation still left her feeling jittery. She stepped on to the landing and paused a moment while her eyes adjusted to the darkness. Even though it was dark downstairs, peering back, it seemed light in contrast. Barely able to see and stretching out with her hands, she could just make out another door. She scrabbled around until her hand settled on a peculiar shape. Unsure if it was a handle, she suddenly felt a cold sensation, almost as if someone was holding her hand. Although this made her tingle, she felt strangely calm. The instant it happened, something in the back of her thoughts told her it was Meredith leading her way. Assured, she turned the handle and gulped as she felt it click. Feeling a shiver of uncertainty, but nevertheless, unruffled, she pushed her shoulders back and eased the door open.

'Here we go,' she muttered.

The room had a muted light, and unlike her previous trips, she could see reasonably well. Looking around, she spotted a tiny shard of light coming from what appeared to be a window. *No change there,* she thought, *other than it's on the third floor.*

Suspecting the door would slam behind her, she braced herself and let go, but it barely moved. *That's odd,* she thought as she made her way to the light. She went to pull at what looked like curtain material but was somewhat surprised when it felt like wood. Reckoning it was probably a shutter of sorts, she tried sliding it, but it wouldn't budge. Standing there for a few seconds, she didn't know what to think and then decided to try closing the door behind her. She hadn't a clue if this would make a difference, but it seemed like a good idea. She shut the door, went back, and took hold of the shutter, but inexplicably it was now material. Baffled, she stood there for a moment gathering her thoughts. She then shrugged her shoulders and pulled the fabric. Initially, it barely moved, but after a couple of firm tugs, it slid open easily, filling the room with bright sunlight.

She eased the second curtain back, and going by the warmth from the sun, reckoned it was probably late summer, again. Just about to turn away, her attention was drawn to a small boy in the garden, standing on a stool, stretching for an apple, which was clearly out of reach. The strain on his face brought a smile to her face, and she decided to go and find her way outside and help him. Just as she turned away, she turned back, realising she wasn't on the mysterious third floor at all, just the first. 'How odd is this,' she muttered.

She tried the door she'd entered by, but as per usual, it was locked. Making her way over to the other door, she suddenly realised how dusty the room was. She stood there for a moment and reckoned it was unlikely this room had been used for a long time. She went to the other door, which opened easily, and with assured familiarity made her way downstairs. As she entered what had previously been a kitchen, she was a little taken aback to find the room covered in dust and in a state of total disrepair. She opened the back door, and stepping outside, was greeted by the sound of the boy grumbling and groaning.

As she approached him, she guessed from his appearance and gestures he was perhaps a similar age to Tommy, although tiny by comparison. The way he was dressed in dark-green corduroy shorts, a scruffy cream Hessian shirt, and bare feet, left Rebecca wondering what year it was this time. Briefly, she considered asking him but knew she'd sound silly, guessing she'd find out soon enough.

She made her way over, smiled, and asked, 'Can I help you with that apple?'

He jumped off the stool and exclaimed, 'are you offering to help me, Rebecca? Well, that will make a pleasant change.' He frowned and added, 'I suspect you want that big red apple for yourself. That will be it.' He then nodded several times.

The combination of his bedraggled appearance, yet polite, eloquent response instantly triggered Rebecca's curiosity. Eager to know more, she climbed up on the stool, wondering what to ask him. She reached up and picked three apples. 'There you are, three of the reddest,' she said, offering them to him.

Appearing startled, he looked at her, and then the apples. After a few seconds, he grabbed all three, and without a glance in her direction, walked off, quietly singing to himself.

'Hang on a mo,' she called out.

He turned back, pulled an odd face, and asked, 'what, may I ask, is a mo, Rebecca?'

'It is short for a minute.' On the outside, he was scruffy, but there was something about this boy. Wondering if he had perhaps recently fallen on bad times, she gave herself a little thinking time. She pointed up, and asked, 'would you like any more apples?'

He nodded, holding out his jumper.

Unsure what to say, an idea came to her, something her teacher had taught her about indirect questions. 'So, tell me, where's mother?'

Frowning, the boy asked, 'You know that I don't have a mother, so what are you asking me?' He then glanced up at the tree and shook his head.

Well, that answers that she thought. 'I was asking about my mother, sorry for the confusion,' she said and decided on a quick change of direction. 'May I ask, do you know of Queen Victoria?' she said, not having a clue where that came from, but thought it might give her some idea as to the era. The way he looked at her and frowned made her feel a little uncomfortable. She shook her head inwardly, knowing she really had to think instead of saying the first thing that came into her head.

Having already turned away, he looked back and said, 'why would I not know of our Queen.' He shook his head, took two steps, and glanced back again. 'Your mother is at the back of the main house with Christopher. She is getting him ready before he goes off with the army.'

Victoria, war, she thought, *must be early nineteen hundred.* She then came over all funny, suddenly realising it could be a young Christopher, Judith's husband. She looked up to say something, but the boy had vanished. She glanced around and could just see him, in the distance, disappearing into the woods.

She made her way up to the main house, still thinking about the little boy. She walked around to the back of the house, and spotted an elegant middle-aged woman, standing by a white table and chairs, exactly where she has breakfast with her mum. The woman was dressed in a pale green lacy blouse with a long fawn skirt. She appeared to be packing a rucksack of sorts while chatting with a young man. She watched them for a few moments and decided to head over. As she drew close, she guessed the man was probably in his late teens, instantly Christopher returned to her thoughts. The way he was

259

moving, gave his dark-brown uniform the appearance of cardboard, which brought a smile to her face. As she tried to work out what Christopher may have looked like when he was young, the woman looked up and waved.

'There you are, Rebecca. Now, come and help Christopher, there's a good girl.'

Rebecca joined the two and nodded. Still wondering if this was Judith's Christopher, she really didn't know what to say. Just as she was about to say hello, the woman started speaking.

'Can you not even manage to say hello, Rebecca?' The woman looked her up and down and said, 'Why are you all covered in dust? I hope you have not been inside the old servant's quarters again. You know that nobody has been in there for fifty years, not since that horrid shooting incident. It is dangerous, as well you know, especially after the last time when you banged your head.'

She acknowledged the woman with a nod, but her thoughts were focussed on what she'd just heard. As her consciousness jumped between the hunting accident, Christopher, and banging her head, she suddenly realised the woman was staring at her. 'I am sorry. I was thinking about something else. I only went in there for a minute to look for something to help me reach the apples.'

'Has that child from the village been pestering you again for apples?' she said and raised her eyebrows. 'Oh, well, I guess we won't eat them all. You must stay out of there,' the woman said and started brushing Rebecca's legs. 'I see you are once again wearing your brother's old trousers.'

Rebecca's focus was still on what the woman had said. 'You mentioned a shooting incident. Remind me what happened please.' The instant she said it, she knew she shouldn't have.

The woman shook her head, and said, 'I really do not understand why you bother yourself with such things. I heard you asking Christopher only two days since.' The woman packed something into the rucksack, glanced up, and said, 'It was a tragic incident. A woman named...' She turned to Christopher and asked, 'Was it, Meredith or Millicent?'

He smiled and said, 'Millicent.'

'Yes, that is it, Millicent, so we understand from an article in an old newspaper we found in the servant's quarters. It suggested she was shot in a theoretical incident. It was all a bit too vague for my attention.'

'Please tell me more. You said that it suggested she was supposedly shot in an incident. May I ask, is that what the paper said, or are you saying that?' She shook her head, unable to believe how many things seemed to be focussing on this shooting.

'Rebecca, we do not really have time now. However, in essence, the newspaper indicated that they'd discovered Millicent's body inside the servant's quarters, shot to death. It then goes on to say that a certain Meredith - I can never recall her full name - who was the lady of this house,' she said and indicated with her thumb. 'Anyhow, Meredith was indicted for murder sometime later. I said supposedly, because why would a woman of such statue murder a maid, or whatever Millicent was. That too is unclear, as is the rest of the story.' She then turned back to the rucksack. 'Hold this string, Rebecca, while I tie a knot.'

Holding the string, Rebecca looked up and asked, 'do we know any more about either of them, perhaps what the outcome was and so on? Do we know if the summerhouse was closed because of that incident?'

'Summerhouse...' the woman said, appearing puzzled, 'what summerhouse?'

261

'Err, I meant the servant's quarters.'

Appearing perplexed, the woman asked, 'why did you refer to it as a summerhouse?'

The woman was now appearing a little miffed, and Rebecca knew she had to be careful of what she said, and how she said it. 'No reason, it just seemed like a nice name, being by the lake and all. Maybe one day it will be used as a summerhouse.'

The woman raised her eyebrows and sighed. 'You and your imagination, Rebecca, summerhouse indeed, I guess I should know what to expect by now.' The woman shook her head. 'I do not know any more about Millicent or Meredith. After reading the old newspaper article, we tried to find out more and even contacted the local registry office, but they said there were no records of either woman or the incident. All we have is an old newspaper we found in a bureau in the servant's quarters, and that says little.' The woman then handed the young man a pair of brown shoes, similar to the ones Rebecca's father wears. 'There are of course the paintings of Millicent and Meredith that your father found while working in the basement.' She shook her head. 'That was one of the rare times when he wasn't skiving,' she said in a forthright tone. Again, she shook her head, clearly irritated. She then turned back to the young man, pointed to a wooden box, and using the same tone, said, 'Christopher, your shirts are in the box, be careful with them. They have been neatly ironed.' She then turned to Rebecca and said, 'these men need constant direction, or nothing ever gets done.'

While the woman was talking, Rebecca was thinking about how strong and forthright this woman was, completely changing any ideas of this house being male-dominated. Oddly, though, in spite of her demeanour, there was a kindness that made Rebecca feel comfortable, just the same as with Judith and Meredith. It was once again as if she'd known this woman all her life. Mixed up in her thoughts was the idea there might be a basement, one she knew nothing about. She was staring aimlessly at the rucksack when the woman started talking again.

'He will mess those shirts up; you watch,' she said, and shook her head. 'The little information we gathered indicated they closed the servant's quarters shortly after the accident. In recent years, no one has had either the inclination or indeed, the money to fix it up. Not as if your father would be capable, is it? It is hard enough getting him to do his daily chores.'

Rebecca had a million questions, but this woman's unyielding manner had her attention. Intrigued by her relationship, she asked, 'What do you mean by daily chores?'

'Oh, Rebecca. How many times are we going to have this conversation? If you paid more attention to me instead of your blessed fairies, you'd hear me the first time. Even the second time wouldn't go amiss.' She sighed and pointed to her ear. 'Listen this time please, I don't want to go through this again with you. Unfortunately, hard work and your father do not go hand in hand. Indeed, work in general is not your father's strong point. That is why I give him a list of chores. Besides, completing what little he does do is some way towards paying for his mistakes, as well you know.'

'Mistakes, what mistakes?'

'Oh, Rebecca, to my mind your fanciful stories occupy too much of your time and thoughts.' The woman shook her head slightly and continued, 'you must know that your father lost all of his money gambling,' she said, holding her palms up. 'I guess you were very young when it all happened and perhaps didn't understand the concept, but even so. This is neither the time nor the place to be discussing this. However, I will explain it quickly, and we can go over it in more detail sometime later. Your father's bad gambling habits sadly became regular, and he ultimately lost everything. It is not his fault; his father introduced him to it, and he has a compulsive nature, so he finds it hard to control his habits. Had it not been for my family's money, we would have lost this house. My father gave explicit instructions that your father should desist from gambling, and focus his attention on his family commitments.' she grumbled, 'focus and your father do not go hand in hand, and that is why I must point him in the right direction.' The woman then indicated towards the rucksack and said, 'We must now help your Brother to get ready before he joins up with his army colleagues.'

Reckoning time wasn't on her side, and feeling the need to know more, Rebecca asked, 'I know we are busy and must get on, but can I ask you a couple more questions while we help Chris?'

'You are normally far too busy wrapped up in your own thoughts, so I should be grateful for your interest. So yes, ask away.'

'So, do we still have the newspaper, the one that relates to Meredith?'

'It is somewhere in the house. Perhaps we can look for it another day, Rebecca. And there was me thinking you were going to continue asking about your father. The way your brain works, Rebecca, is beyond me.'

'You said you found it in an old bureau in the...' she hesitated, '...the servant's quarters, is that right?'

'Yes indeed, and it was in rather peculiar circumstances. When I first looked through the drawers, they were empty. The next time I looked, I found the newspaper. I don't know how I missed it the first time.' The woman then pursed her lips and pulled a face, showing a somewhat different side to her forthright persona.

Seeing this, Rebecca suspected this incident had made her feel somewhat uneasy. 'That really is rather strange, don't you think?'

Chris handed the woman the neatly folded shirts and turned to Rebecca. 'I said that, but you know mother, dismisses anything that is

264

remotely out of the ordinary.' He then paused and appeared deep in thought. 'It is like the woman we saw in the boat. She was standing up, wearing a long graceful white dress that billowed around her legs. She was just standing there, seemingly oblivious to us. Inexplicably, she appeared to have a scarf around her neck. I say a scarf, but it looked more like a rope to me. When I pointed her out to mother and mentioned the rope, she said there was nothing there, and suggested it was just mist. She then said; besides it is a scarf.' Wide-eyed, he looked directly at Rebecca. 'So, what am I to make of that? She obviously saw her because she thought it was a scarf. Oh well, we never saw her again. Maybe she came from the village, although heaven only knows why she'd be standing in the boat, with a rope or a scarf - knotted at the back I might add - around her neck.'

Taking deep breaths, Rebecca's heart felt like it was pounding through her chest. She knew she'd seen someone in a boat that day. Adding everything together, she was beginning to believe it was Meredith, and for years, she'd been in limbo, trying to draw attention to her situation. Although she was struggling to take everything on board, her thoughts were dominated by a certainty that Meredith wasn't capable of harming anyone. She shivered and took a gulp of air, breathing out slowly, trying to regain her composure.

'Why are you so out of breath, Rebecca, you've hardly done anything?' She then glared at her and asked, 'Have you heard a single word I have said?'

Rebecca shook her head and smiled, acknowledging the woman. She knew the woman had said something, but it hadn't registered. With so many thoughts filling her mind, she was beginning to feel somewhat overwhelmed. 'Umm, the paintings, have we put them up in the hallway?' She didn't know why she asked that it just came out.

'Well, there's a question,' the woman said, groaning her words, 'Your father should have hung them months ago, but they are still on the floor in the study. Importantly, Rebecca, you know all this; you are acting as if you have been away, probably with those fairies.' She

265

shook her head. 'Right, go and make sure the Servants' quarters are locked up, because if that lad returns and goes inside...' She closed her eyes and shook her head. 'Come straight back, with the key, it's the only one, and I don't want you to mislay it again. Hopefully, you will have a little more focus when you return, because your brother will be leaving soon.'

Rebecca suspected she wasn't going to get much more out of this woman for now. Besides, something was nagging at her to get back to the summerhouse and it wasn't just this woman's words. She took one more look at Christopher, still unsure if it could be Judith's Chris. She noticed he was smiling, so smiled back, and headed towards the summerhouse. On the way, her thoughts returned to Meredith. She knew she was innocent, but how was she supposed to do anything about that. It wasn't as if she could return to Meredith's time. Thinking about her appearing in the boat again, she knew she had to do something, but what. The more she thought about it, the more convinced she was that Meredith had brought her here for a reason. Then an idea popped into her head that Meredith - what with her appearing in the boat and all - had opened a door in this time zone and nobody had used it. *Perhaps there's a way back to Meredith from here*, she thought.

She stepped up on to the veranda and wondered if approaching the stairs from the front would take her back to Meredith. Opening the door, a sweet odour filled her nostrils, somehow reassuring her with its familiarity. She made her mind up to check the bureau first, but as she entered the room, had a gut feeling it would be empty, and she was right. As she turned, she remembered the tiny doors at the top. She stretched but couldn't reach properly. Now on a mission, having a feeling there was something there, she thought about it for a moment. Then she recalled the stool by the apple tree. Returning with it, she placed it in front of the bureau. Although still on tiptoes, she opened the door and with her hand, could just make out something right at the back. She stretched, and after nearly falling from the stool a couple of times, eventually removed a dust-covered envelope. Staring at it, she felt a tingle of expectation. She broke the seal, opened it carefully,

266

and started reading. The handwriting was pale and scribbled, but legible enough to read even in the muted light. She breathed in deep, reading each word slowly. *"This is to anyone who reads this who might actually care. I expect there are few if any at all. My name is Millicent Black, and I have become an outcast in this household, my household. I cannot return to my old ways or my penniless-life, and therefore, I will end my life here, on this day, the 17th April 1858."*

Rebecca took a deep breath and read the letter twice more. Realising what she had in her hands, she breathed heavily. She knew this would finally put Meredith's spirit to rest, 'but what do I do with this letter,' she muttered. Sitting back outside on the veranda - thumbing the letter - her thoughts were awash with Meredith. Trying to put some logic to it all, she was becoming increasingly certain that Meredith, in her desperation, had also opened the door in this time to the girl who lived here. She suspected from the way that Christopher had described the boat scene he might have been capable of picking up on Meredith's offer.

Moreover, from the way this woman had spoken to her, she was sure that the Rebecca of this time was also open-minded enough. *So why no takers*, she wondered. She sat there - aware of what she had in her hands - entirely at a loss what to do next. The one thing she was hoping was that going through the front door in this time would probably take her back to Meredith.

Chapter 16 - Which Way Now?

With the envelope carefully placed in her pocket, Rebecca re-entered the summerhouse. Feeling positive, she walked up to the door, but the moment the lock clicked, she felt a tinge of anxiety. With the handle firmly gripped, she wondered if this was the wrong way, and if so, would she be able to find her way back? She took the letter from her pocket, reread it, and reassured herself that Meredith would see her right.

Slowly, she started climbing the stairs, trying each door she passed. Standing at the top, on what appeared to be bizarrely the third floor, and with every door locked, again she started to question her decision-making. Feeling a little confused, she went back down and again tried each door. With no success, she hesitated at the bottom of the stairs, not having a clue what to do. She wondered if she was missing something, or this was just the wrong way.

After a moment or two, she headed around to the back door, only to find that also locked. She took a deep breath and tried again, but still nothing. She stood there for a few seconds gathering her thoughts. Feeling tired, confused, and unsure what to do next, she slumped down and leant her back against the door. She closed her eyes, and muttered, 'help me, Meredith.' She then stood up, and before she had put her hand anywhere near the door, it clicked open. With a mixture of excitement and apprehension, she assured herself she was doing the right thing. She entered the kitchen, and instantly a whoosh of cold air hit her face.

Shivering, she went back outside, and although the sun was high in the sky, it was bitterly cold. As she stood there trying to work out what was going on, she noticed a blue flashing light coming from the direction of the main house. Breathing deeply, she tried to calm herself and transfixed by the blue light, suddenly realised it was an ambulance. Hurrying up towards the house, she could see her father – her real father - with Tommy and Ruth, all standing by the ambulance. Unable to see her mother, and thinking the worst, she blurted, 'Where's my mum?'

She ran towards them calling, but no one even glanced in her direction. She waved her arms in front of Ruth, but there was no reaction, not even a flinch. Spooked, she went over to her father and to see him crying just intensified her anxiety. Frightened, she turned slowly towards the ambulance and could see a body covered by a blanket. Then she spotted her mother's shoe beside the wheel. She screamed, but it was as if she wasn't there, no one so much as glanced in her direction. She tried to grab Tommy's arm, but her hand passed through him as if she had missed him. Sobbing, she screamed again, and still, no one heard her cry. Stricken with grief, she tried to steady herself, and as she did, heard her father speaking to Ruth. Appearing almost inconsolable, he stumbled through his words, "If only I'd fixed that boiler. Trust Liz to try to fix it on her own. She's been going on about it ever since it turned chilly back in October. Oh, why didn't I take a few moments from my wretched schedule and get it sorted? I've let everyone down, but most of all, my children."

'It was an accident, James,' Ruth said and touched him on the arm. 'I must try and phone Amanda.'

Rebecca watched her flip open her mobile and couldn't believe what she was looking at. The date on Ruth's phone was showing November, three months into the future of her real time.

"Oh, dear Elizabeth, what have I done," her father cried, "If only I'd listened, then maybe you'd still be here."

In a flash, she realised Meredith had taken her into the future, and knew nothing could be changed here and now. Although still shredded with anguish, she had to focus her thoughts and find her way home. She stood there for a moment trying to get her head straight. She had to get back to her father and tell him but knew he would

269

dismiss her story out of hand. She couldn't even convince her mum, so she had to come up with a very good plan. After a few moments, she decided to go back to her original plan and hide something that would still be there in her time, which would be the proof she needed. The problem was she was in the future and needed to try to find her way back to Chris, Meredith, or even Judith, just as long as it was in the past.

As focused as she could be, she ran back to the summerhouse trying to control her emotions, and at the same time thinking about what to hide. Panting for breath, she stared at the front door feeling uncertain but realised she had to trust her instincts. *Go through the door and see what happens,* she thought. She reassured herself, knowing she had the proof that would finally allow Meredith's spirit to rest, and in return, this woman would show her the way.

She opened the door, and climbed the stairs confidently, feeling assured she was doing the right thing. Her apprehension returned as each door she tried remained locked. Once again, she was standing there, uncertain of what to do next. She decided to go back outside, only to be greeted by a warm sunny day, and the sound of that woman's stern voice calling her. The woman was heading towards her, waving her arms, with Christopher a few steps behind. She instantly knew she had somehow ended up back in the early 1900s, *but why.*

'Rebecca, I told you not to enter this building,' she grumbled and shook her head. 'Lock the door, go to the study, and fetch your brother's army papers. They are in the tallboy in the corner of the room. Here is the key and don't lose it again. Hurry and then meet us at the back of the house, Christopher is leaving presently.'

She thought for a second and realised that this might be her opportunity to hide something inside the main house. Suddenly, the penny dropped. The woman had said tallboy, and she wondered if there was a remote chance it was the same as the one in her father's study. She knew that one was Victorian and recalled him saying

270

something about missing keys and never been used. As her plan came together, she muttered, 'That's it.'

'Are you talking to yourself again, Rebecca,' the woman asked in a stern voice, 'now, go,' she said, shook her head and pointed towards the main house. 'Don't stand there daydreaming, go now.'

'Sorry,' Rebecca said, and started up the slope, quickening her steps, she hurried, aware her emotions were all over the place.

She pushed open the front door, and before entering the study, noticed Meredith's painting propped up at the side. She patted her pocket, and muttered, 'I have what you need.' Opening the study door, the room was laid out almost identical to her time. Spotting her father's tallboy in the corner churned her stomach, reminding her of her mother's plight. She breathed deeply, trying to focus on what she needed to do. She knew she had to get this right and had one chance, and this was it. Standing there for a few seconds, she mulled over a few ideas. Eventually, she decided to try the skinny drawer, reckoning it would be an excellent place to hide something. She turned the tiny key, and after a couple of attempts, it finally clicked. As she opened the drawer, an idea popped into her head to lock it after and take the key. That way, no one could use it until she opened it in her time. The more she thought about it, the more convinced she became that this might actually work. Thinking, she suspected she would need more than a key to convince her dad. She now wasn't feeling so certain and glanced across the room hoping something would grab her attention. Then she had the idea to leave a note but knew there had to be something more.

She knew a note was her best option and made her way over to a writing table. She picked up a quill pen affair and after a few fumbled attempts, started writing. From the corner of her eye, she spotted a penknife and decided to use it to cut a section from the inside of one of her dungaree pockets. That way, she could put it with the note, and show her dad it matched up exactly to the missing section.

Carefully, she cut a small section from the inside of her pocket, folded it inside the ink-covered note, and placed it in the drawer. She locked the drawer and slipped the key into the same pocket as Meredith's envelope. Now standing there, she wondered if she'd done enough, and then heard the woman's voice calling her. *Blast it,* she thought, grabbed what she believed to be Chris's paperwork, and hurried out the front.

'You took your time, Miss. I suspect you were wool-gathering again,' the woman said and held out her hand for the papers.

'Yes, sorry, I got a little side-tracked,' she said and nodded as she handed over the papers. She then thought, *wool-gathering, what does that even mean.* She shrugged her shoulders and turned back to the woman. 'I just need to nip back to the summer... servant's quarters. I left something there but will be straight back.'

'Rebecca, no going inside that building and what is so important that you have to go now. Surely, it can wait until your brother has left?'

'Err, oh, I guess so,' she said as she spotted Chris walking up towards them.

'I should think so too, young lady. Anyways, here he is now and right on schedule, so is the army vehicle.'

Desperate to get going, Rebecca breathed in through her nose, knowing she had to wait at least until Chris had left. For some reason, she felt an overwhelming need to say goodbye and reckoned this could be because she still thought he might be Judith's Chris. This reassured her, knowing he would return safely to fight in the second war. Just as quick, her reassurance turned to anguish as she realised that he was injured in the next campaign. Now she had a dilemma, because if she told him, it may change the future and besides, how would she explain it all? She shuddered and tried to rid the thought from her mind, knowing she couldn't tell him. Time seemed to stand still for her as she watched him say goodbye to the woman. Although the woman maintained a firm exterior, she could see the intense emotions in her eyes. Chris turned to her. Although she wasn't his real sister, he thought she was, and so Rebecca cuddled him with every ounce of feeling she could muster.

Chris turned once more and kissed his mother. He then turned to Rebecca, touched her cheek, and gently said, 'Be a good girl, sis.'

Right away, Rebecca thought of Tommy, and once again, her pulse raced. She pushed her shoulders back, looked at Chris, and said, 'come back safe. I will be waiting for you.'

He climbed aboard, and as the vehicle rumbled out of sight, he waved one last time.

The woman turned to Rebecca and in a stern tone, said, 'okay, Rebecca, you can go and do what you need to do now.'

Rebecca could see the anguish etched on the woman's face. She so wanted to cuddle her, but this woman seemed so unapproachable. Then she thought, *to hell with it,* and held her arms out.

Instantly, the woman started sobbing, then as quick she stood upright, nodded, and said, 'well. It is just you, me and that excuse for a man now, so I must be strong.'

Although Rebecca wanted to stay and reassure this woman, her focus was on her own family and her need to get home was beginning to feel desperate. She knew she had to try to come back and help this woman, soon. She touched the woman gently on the arm, smiled and headed towards the summerhouse. As she made her way along the path, she again found herself wondering why her emotions towards all the women she'd met were so profoundly intense.

As she arrived, she could see the little boy once again reaching for an apple. She hesitated for a moment and decided a few seconds wouldn't hurt. As she walked over, he smiled and pointed up.

'Would you pick that one for my sister, Rebecca?'

She went and fetched the stool, climbed up, picked two apples, and handed them to the boy. As she moved to climb off, she spotted a big shiny red one hidden by leaves. She reached, but just couldn't grab it, so stretched, and as she did, the stool wobbled. Steadying herself, she reached again, and although she could feel the stool moving, the apple was almost in reach. Just as she thought about moving the stool, it slipped from under her legs. Instinctively, she closed her eyes and braced herself.

Chapter 17 - Where am I

Rebecca sat up and rubbed a small bump on her head. A little disorientated, she wondered if she had perhaps been dreaming again, which annoyed her. Then she remembered the little boy, but there was no sign of him and she guessed he'd probably taken the apples and ran off. She sat there for a few seconds, regaining her composure, again considering the dream notion, which irritated her a little more. Glancing up to see if she'd managed to reach the big red apple, she muttered, 'where's the tree.' She now knew something very odd was going on. While rummaging in her pocket for Millicent's letter, her thoughts returned to Chris and the note she'd left for her dad. Taking the letter out carefully, she stared at it, and nodded, knowing she hadn't been dreaming. She then checked for the key and breathed a sigh of relief feeling it in the corner of her pocket.

Still feeling a little uneasy, she stood up aware something was different. Other than the missing tree, she couldn't put her finger on anything specific. She looked around trying to get her bearings and noticed that the summerhouse had a new look about it. Just then, she heard a woman's voice, very faint, but strangely familiar. *Is that Meredith,* she thought? Tentatively, she called, 'Meredith, is that you?' There was no answer, so she called again, louder this time. Following the voice, she turned the corner and immediately spotted Meredith. So pleased to see her, she couldn't stop herself running over and giving her a hug. Holding her, she knew instantly something was wrong. Although Meredith cuddled her, it seemed half-hearted. She stepped back and could see a disturbed look in her eyes.

'Whatever is wrong, Meredith?' she asked.

Meredith shook her head. 'I have been searching everywhere for you. You need to come with me as a matter of urgency.' She then

275

took hold of Rebecca's hand and led her in the direction of the main house.

'Meredith, where are we going?' Meredith's anxiety fuelled Rebecca's imagination, and she was now wondering if this was when the Millicent incident happened.

'We are going to see father, and we must hurry. The Police are with him, and they will not wait.' Although her words seemed assured, the grief in her voice was palpable.

With her brain at bursting point, she knew she had to stay focused. 'The police will not wait for whom, Meredith, and why do we need to see father so urgently? Whatever has happened?' Rebecca couldn't fail to notice the intensity of Meredith's drained appearance and was now certain this was something to do with Millicent's death. On the back of this notion, she felt in her pocket and breathed a sigh of relief. Just as she was about to tell her about the letter, Meredith started speaking.

'They found Millicent dead after some kind of hunting accident. Inexplicably, the police believe I had something to do with it. Now hurry, they will not wait.'

'Meredith, it's okay because I found a letter from Millicent, a suicide letter. I have it in my pocket.' As she lifted the letter from her pocket, she felt the tiny key fall. Panicked, she groped around in the nettles by her feet. Pushing them flat, she spotted the key and held it firmly in her hand.

'Careful, Rebecca,' Meredith said but seemed preoccupied with the letter.

Rebecca watched the tension lift from Meredith's face as she read the letter. Ever since she'd found the letter, she'd been sure this was the reason for her journeys. Thinking about her mother's accident, she was now beginning to speculate. She found herself wondering if she

276

and Meredith had been brought together to help each other. Somewhere in the back of her thoughts, she even considered there might be an overriding power at work.

Meredith looked up from the letter and wide-eyed, said, 'Oh my word, this letter certainly alters the aspects of my predicament.' She then shook her head and asked, 'Rebecca, why did you stick your hand in the nettles?'

Rebecca held up the tiny key. 'I need this key like you wouldn't believe. It could be the most important key in my world.' She thought for a second. 'Actually, it's the second most important key in my world, but that's another story.'

'Why is this key so important,' Meredith asked, 'and which key is the most important, young lady?'

'I will explain later, Meredith. We really should go and show this letter to the coppers.'

'Rebecca, coppers indeed, your choice of language is once again, well, shall we say, uncharacteristic.'

As they headed towards the main house, they could see George talking with two policemen. All three turned simultaneously and watched Meredith and Rebecca approach.

'There you are, Meredith, we must go with the Policemen now,' George said. 'Rebecca, young lady, you need to go with the housekeeper, and she will look after you while I go with your mother to the Police station.'

'But, Father...'

'No buts, young lady, the Police have waited long enough and have graciously allowed your mother the time to locate you.'

'No, Father, we have something significant for you. Show him, Mother.'

Meredith handed George the letter. He read it, and appearing animated handed it to the policemen.

After a few seconds, one of the officers said, 'It seems we have a resolution to this dreadful situation. You must accept our apologies for this awful inconvenience. You are free to go about your business, Madam. I will take this to our chief inspector, and I am sure that will be the end to the matter. Madam, Young Lady, Sir, I bid you farewell.'

'Rebecca, I presume you discovered this letter while on one of your adventures. How lucky we are to have such an inquisitive daughter. You may well have saved your dear mother from a potentially horrid state of affairs.'

Although Rebecca desperately wanted to spend more time with Meredith, she knew time wasn't on her side. She now had to try to find her way back to her real parents, and ideally, as soon as possible. She smiled at both. 'Mother, Father, you must excuse me for a few moments as I have something I must do.'

'Before you go, Rebecca, please tell me where you found this letter and explain why the key is of such importance,' Meredith asked.

She seemed so animated that Rebecca felt compelled to explain. Something was telling her she needed to do this to complete her journey, and although eager to get home, it just seemed right. Besides, as odd as it sat with Rebecca, she felt Meredith was asking her, almost as if she somehow knew it would be her last chance to do so. Also, she realised she was in the past, and her mum's predicament was a long way off.

Right on cue, George said, 'I will leave you two ladies to speak alone. I will see you both later for a splendid supper.' He then kissed both on the cheek, beamed a smile and went inside.

She walked with Meredith for a while and explained about the letter, and the key. She also tried to describe how she got here, without sounding ridiculous. Although Meredith smiled and often nodded, whenever Rebecca mentioned travelling from another time, it was referred to as one more quirky Rebecca fantasy. Unlike the first time she told her of her journey, oddly, Meredith's dismissal wasn't quite so indifferent, and there was a tiny element of acceptance within her questions and response. That aside, it was blatantly obvious that a living Meredith had played no part in any of her journeys. She now felt confident that the woman in the boat was actually Meredith's wretched spirit, and that spirit had opened the door back. She carried on chatting briefly, but her emotions were telling her it was time to head home. 'Oh, I just remembered that I need to go to the summerhouse as I left something there.' As soon as she'd said the last word, her thoughts focused on how she was going to get home. Just as she was trying to console herself in the belief that she'd always found her way home, the woman touched her on the shoulder.

'Well, young lady, your tone suggests that you need to visit the lake-house and complete that which occupies your thoughts. I suspect it may be another of your keys,' she said and grinned. 'Please be back in time for...' glancing down, she paused, 'supper.' She smiled in a comforting, knowing way, the likes of which Rebecca had only ever seen from her real mother.

Rebecca held her arms open. 'Can I have a hug before I go?' She suspected this would be the last time she would see this woman and needed to cuddle her. Although Meredith had only been in her life for a short time, she felt an overwhelming affinity with this woman.

Meredith held her so tight it once again made Rebecca wonder if this woman knew more than she was letting on. With her emotions all over the place, she gave her hand one more squeeze and bid her farewells. Walking down the path, a tearful Rebecca turned for one final wave, certain she'd accomplished all she could.

Right from the first day, she'd always felt there was a reason for her journeys. Knowing she had nothing left to do here, and focused on her mother and the passage back, she quickened her steps. Although feeling a little anxious, she had underlying confidence that Meredith, or indeed Meredith's spirit, would lead her home. She didn't have a clue how this was all working but had decided a long while ago that it didn't really matter. The one thing she knew for certain was that she had to get back and convince her dad that this wasn't a dream.

She stood by the summerhouse, a little concerned where she might end up, but at the same time, felt strangely reassured. Emotionally drained, desperate to see her real parents, she stepped inside the front door and stared at the handle. Thinking about Meredith and realising the importance of what she'd achieved, she was sure she'd finally helped this woman's tormented spirit to rest. She also understood that if that was the case, then it could mean an end to her journeys.

She took a deep breath and turned the handle, but once again, it failed to open. *Blast*, she thought. While considering her options, an idea came to her. She nodded, deciding to retrace her steps, go back through the room and down the spiral stairs. 'Yep, that's it,' she muttered and headed outside. The back door was open, and without hesitation, she passed through the kitchen, climbed the stairs, and entered the room where it had all started. She took a deep breath when she noticed the dandy green dress, on the bed, exactly as it was the first time she was here. Standing by the door, she glanced around and again wondered if this would be her final visit.

Now on her last legs, and desperate to get home, she quickly made her way downstairs. She had one final glance up into the darkness, before turning the handle. Although the lock clicked, the door wouldn't open. She tried it several more times to no avail. Breathing deeply and feeling anxious, she slumped down on the floor with her back to the door, wondering if she'd missed something. Her emotions were running on empty and feeling both tired and hungry wasn't helping one bit. She sat there in the darkness, yawning. Trying to focus her thoughts, she closed her eyes.

Chapter 18 - How Did that Happen

Rebecca opened her eyes and shook her head. 'Where am I?' she mumbled, aware she was still sitting with her back to the door, but bizarrely instead of on the inside, was now on the outside. *What's going on*, she thought, climbing to her feet. She gripped the door handle and tried it, but it was stuck fast, just like the first time she laid eyes on it. Exhausted, and with her emotions in tatters, she made her way to the front door. As soon as she stepped outside it felt like she was home, she didn't know why, it just did. Taking a deep breath, having wondered how she ended up on the outside of the door, she decided it didn't really matter. She smiled, knowing Meredith had played some part, and right now, the only thing that mattered was her mother. She took another deep breath and tried to focus on what she needed to do. With a resurgence of energy, she hurried up the slope. Halfway, she looked back and whispered, 'thank you, Meredith.' Standing by the front door to the main house, she paused for a second and checked for the key. *Blast it*, she thought, and then breathed a sigh of relief finding it once again tucked right in the corner of her pocket.

Opening the front door, she shouted, 'Mum, where are you. Is Dad home yet?'

'Ah, there you are, Rebecca. I was about to come to look for you and show you Amanda's present,' she said and handed Rebecca a necklace she'd bought. 'Your father won't be home for another hour or so. Why do you ask?'

'Oh, nothing, Mum, I just wanted to show him another key I'd found.'

'Well, young lady, I hope you have not been snooping around in that summerhouse again. Have you?'

'No, Mum, I found it in the study.'

'Hmm, did you indeed, young lady?' she said, narrowing her eyes. 'Well, I hope you have left his room exactly how you found it.'

'Kind of, mum.'

Her mother rolled her eyes in a delightfully familiar way that made Rebecca feel warm inside. She chatted with her mum about Amanda's present and although tempted to tell her all about her latest adventure, knew this wasn't the right time. While they sat chatting, Rebecca kept glancing at the kitchen clock, willing the hands to move faster, but it seemed the more she looked, the slower it seemed to go.

Her mum stood up and took her gin and tonic glass from the cupboard. Rebecca jumped up and said, 'Mum, let me make you a lovely cup of coffee. You are always making one for the girls, about time someone made one for you.'

Her mother again narrowed her eyes and said, 'well, as you put it like that, how can I refuse?'

As she tried to fill the coffee machine with water, the tap vibrated loudly. She turned it off and on again. This time there was a hissing sound, followed by a horrid clunk coming from somewhere. She turned to her mum, and asked, 'Mum, what is going on with the tap?' Then there was another clunking sound and water spluttered from the tap, going everywhere.

'Oh, it's that infuriating boiler playing up again. It's been like it for a couple of days. I need to go and have a look at it at some point and see if I can see what is wrong,' she said and puffed loudly. 'I might just nip down and have a look now.'

Unable to believe what she'd just heard, Rebecca jumped up and grabbed her mum's arm. 'No, Mum, not now, have your coffee. Dad will be home soon, and he can have a look. Actually, he can call the gas board out, best get an expert, don't want to be messing about with boilers, do we? After all, it sounds awful, and who knows.'

Her mum looked at Rebecca questioningly. 'I have told your father, he did say he was going to call today, but I've not heard back yet.' She then shook her head. 'If you want something done, it's best sometimes doing it yourself. That said, I take your point about an expert.'

'Yes, Mum, it is vitally important that we get someone in. Besides, the gas engineers are probably busy and need to allocate us a slot. However long it takes, so be it. I don't think any of us should be messing around with gas. Besides, what did Dad say about the Summerhouse, *no going inside until we get an expert to look at it*? Enough said I think.' She smiled, pleased with her idea.

Just as the coffee machine had run its sequence, Rebecca heard the front door and guessing it was her dad, quickly placed the coffee down in front of her mum. Before she had a chance to go and greet her dad, her mum held her hand up and stopped her.

'Rebecca, dear, I know you're in a hurry to show your father the key, but at least let him get through the door, there's a love.'

Rebecca nodded, slumped down in the chair, and started gazing aimlessly at a magazine. Moments later, her father walked in and said, 'Good evening. Please call me when supper is ready. I will be in the study. If I don't go and have some peace and quiet, I will end up strangling that boy of yours, Elizabeth.' He grinned, but his tension was evident.

'That boiler has been playing up again, James; we need to get someone to fix it.'

'Yes, Dad, we do, urgently.'

He nodded to Elizabeth and then turned to Rebecca. 'I didn't know you took an interest in such things. May I inquire as to the urgency, Rebecca?'

'Dad, I know you've had a long and busy day, but can I come and talk to you for a few minutes? I promise you it is of the utmost importance.'

'I don't think you should be bothering your father with your key, there's a good girl, Rebecca.'

'No, it is fine, Elizabeth. I haven't had a proper chat with Rebecca since our holiday.'

Rebecca followed her father to the study, with her mind jumping from one thought to the next. She couldn't make up her mind if she should start right at the beginning or cut to the chase. She glanced over, spotted the tallboy, and breathed a sigh of relief seeing it was the same one. Feeling a little easier, and deciding to go with the flow, she sat next to her dad and smiled.

He smiled back and asked, 'So, Rebecca, what is it that is so important that it can't wait?'

Rebecca shook her head, still feeling a little uncertain. 'Err, well, Father, it's like this,' she said and handed him the key.

'It is a key, a tiny one at that. I suspect there's a story coming, Rebecca.'

'Hold the key tightly for a moment while I explain, Dad.' She then went through her story starting right at the beginning, including the first time she'd met Meredith. As tactfully as she could, she then explained about her mother's accident with the boiler. The way he was staring at her, she knew to get on with it. 'While I was with Meredith, I hid something in the old tallboy. I then locked the drawer, and you are holding the key.'

He continued to stare, and although he still looked bemused, his eyes had narrowed suggesting he was prepared to give her a chance to explain.

She stood by the tallboy and pointing towards the key, said, 'that opens this drawer.'

Narrowing his eyes, he said, 'okay, Rebecca, get on with it,' and handed her the key.

Clasping the key in her palm, she took a sharp intake of breath, and muttered, 'Key, you need to work.'

'It's no good talking to the key, Rebecca, you best hope it works,' he said and shook his head. 'This is some fanciful tale you have just laid at my feet and a horrid one at that.'

She went to slide the key into the slot, turned to her father, and said, 'the keyhole has been painted over. Do you have your penknife, Dad?'

Shaking his head again, he huffed and picked up his briefcase. 'Here you are, but be careful with that tallboy, it is...'

'Dad, I know it's a hundred years old. I saw it when it was new,' she said, and grimaced, wondering what his reaction would be.

'That I doubt very much, Rebecca,' he said and looked away.

She smiled, trying to appear calm, but inside her heart was pounding. Carefully, she cleared the keyhole, took another deep breath, inserted the key, and turned. 'See, Dad, I told you,' she said, hearing the drawer unlock. She glanced around to see her father sitting on the edge of his seat. She pulled the handle, and although it creaked, it didn't move. Realising she had no choice, took the knife and ran it around the edge of the drawer. She then wriggled the drawer, and after a few seconds, it started to move. She was so focused she hadn't noticed her father come and stand next to her. She looked him in the eyes and said, 'Dad before I open this drawer, you must promise me you will respond to the letter that is in here. I know this all sounds ridiculous. It does to me too, but, Dad you must trust me.'

He nodded once without saying anything.

She faced the drawer and for a moment again wondered if it had all been one big dream. Slowly, she eased the drawer fully open and peered inside. There were her dust-covered note and the cutting from her dungarees sitting exactly where she'd placed them. She breathed deeply and took the cutting from the drawer, making sure her father was watching. She then showed him the missing section inside her pocket.

Appearing stunned, he nodded, and without saying anything, pointed at the drawer.

Rebecca reached for the note and carefully dusted it off, not wanting to disturb the seal she'd made from candle wax. She handed it to her father, and said, 'you must promise me you will take my note seriously and act accordingly.'

He took a deep breath, nodded, and said, 'we have come this far so I will promise you.' Appearing apprehensive, he took the envelope and staring at it, slowly returned to his seat. He sat there continuing to stare at it until he eventually looked up and said, 'Rebecca...' He then returned his eyes to the note and stared at it again.

Rebecca was now feeling restless and was willing him to open the note but realised he had a lot to take in. All along, she knew how he would react and was surprised that they had come this far without too much indifference towards her story.

After a few moments he looked up again, nodded, and said, 'Okay, I best open this. Before I do, Rebecca, you must understand how difficult this is for me, what with your outlandish tale of time-travel, however...' Gradually, he broke the seal and started reading the note.

With her emotions jumbled, Rebecca stood shuffling from one foot to the other.

After a couple of minutes, he folded the note and looked up appearing uneasy. 'Rebecca, I am at a loss for words.' He then twiddled the note several times, before reading it again. He took a deep breath and looked directly at Rebecca. 'I do not for one minute understand how your story could be true. However...' He puffed his cheeks out and fiddled with the note again. He sat bolt upright, and said, 'Well, there does seem an element of truth to your tale, as outlandish as it is, and as I promised to take action, I will do exactly that.' He then glanced up, 'odd one this. I had an expert look at that,' he said pointing to the tallboy, 'and he said we would have to dismantle it to open any of the drawers without a key. Hmmm.'

Having held her breath through her father's every word, she let out a sigh. 'I know how difficult this is, Father. Imagine how I felt, stuck in the 1850s', knowing all this was going to happen and there I was, unable to do anything about it.' She glanced at the floor, and then tearfully looked directly at her father. 'I am scared, Dad. I was frightened you wouldn't...' She'd tried hard to stay focused all through this, but the moment her father stood up and cuddled her broke her resolve. She continued to cuddle her father, and the combination of exhaustion and relief made her sob almost uncontrollably.

He gave her a squeeze and handed her his hanky. Holding her hand tightly, he said, 'well, my beloved daughter, we need to act upon this now. It will take me a while to understand and comprehend your story, and at some point, soon, you will need to go through everything in detail. I've not talked about this type of thing since I was your age, but like you, when I was younger, I saw things the way you do. I guess the drudgery of my work has closed my eyes a little, so I thank you, Rebecca.' He then gave her another cuddle. 'I know this directly

288

concerns Mum, but for now, I think it might be a good idea to keep this story to ourselves.' Grabbing his phone, he took her by the hand, heading for the kitchen.

As they entered, Elizabeth turned, smiled, and said, 'Supper will be a while yet, the water has been playing up again, and I've not started yet.' As she finished speaking the boiler made a horrid rumbling sound.

Her father walked over to Elizabeth and touching her gently on the arm, said, 'I am so very sorry you have had to put up with this boiler for so long. I am going to call an emergency engineer out as soon as possible before it breaks down completely.' He squeezed her hand, then went to the door and called Tommy.

Elizabeth glanced at Rebecca and narrowed her eyes, and just as Rebecca was going to say something, her father started speaking.

He called Tom again, and said, 'I want Thomas here because I have a surprise for you all.'

Seconds later, he came bundling through the door, and said, 'you rang me, Lord?' He glanced at James who was frowning, and sheepishly sat down.

'It's okay, Tom, don't look so worried,' he said and smiled. 'Okay, I thought it might be nice if we went away for Christmas this year. Don't want you slaving over the cooker, Elizabeth. It should be a holiday for us all.'

'Where, Dad?'

Glancing at Rebecca, Elizabeth nodded several times, and asked, 'yes, James, where indeed. Not New York I hope, although...'

'Well, as we all enjoyed Florida, even though it took me a little while to get on board, I was thinking a week in Disney. And perhaps

289

follow it up with Christmas and the New Year on the Disney cruise ship. This time, I promise to go on all the rides.' He then winked at Rebecca.

'What about your work, James? I thought Christmas was an important time for you,' Elizabeth said, frowning.

Rebecca turned to her mother and frowned, unable to believe what she'd just said.

'If they cannot manage for a few weeks without me, there's no point in employing them.' He nodded and added, 'In fact, I am thinking maybe four weeks, for the whole duration of the school holidays. How's that sound?'

'Yeah, yeah,' Tommy said, waving a fake football scarf over his head. 'Do they have a football pitch on the Disney ship?'

James glanced at Tom and shook his head. He then turned to Rebecca and smiling, shook his head.

She smiled back and put a fake phone to her ear.

'Right, I need to call for a gas engineer.' He picked up the phone and went into his study.

As he left, Elizabeth held her hand up to Rebecca. 'What is going on, Young Lady, what did you talk about, your blinking key, of that I am sure?'

'I will tell you tomorrow, Mum,' she said as her father returned.

'Don't worry about supper, Liz. The gas engineer will be here in twenty minutes, and we can go out to eat. That's if everyone fancies?'

'James, how did you get someone that quickly?'

'It is my employee's brother, and he agreed because I explained, well...'

On the way out to the car, James placed the key under a flowerpot by the front door, and said, 'I have told him where to find the key. So, let's go, I was thinking that Italian, Liz, the one, you and your friends went to.'

Winking at Rebecca, she nodded and said, 'sounds perfect to me, James.'

Chapter 19 - Realisation

Rebecca sat in the restaurant, staring into oblivion. Her mum touched her on the arm, bringing her back to reality with a jolt.

'Are you okay, honey? You haven't touched your food.'

With her head crammed with all number of possible outcomes to her day, she just stared at her mum. Sensing her father looking at her, she turned towards him. The way he smiled and gently shook his head at her was as if he had read her mind. She smiled and turned back to her mum. 'I'm just a bit tired, Mum.'

'Rebecca, dear, if you're not enjoying that risotto, you can leave it or have something else.'

'It is fine, Mum. I'm just not that hungry.' She glanced at her dad and suddenly realised his head must also be at bursting point. Thinking how brilliantly he was dealing with all this, she smiled at him and nodded, guessing they will talk about it soon enough. Just as she was about to say something to him, his phone rang and stopped her in her tracks.

He looked at his phone and standing up, said, 'Excuse me please, I best take this. It's the gas engineer.' After the call, he returned to his chair, apologised to everyone, and explained that the engineer had said the boiler needs replacing as soon as possible. Looking directly at Rebecca, he said, 'he also suggested it was a good job he came out tonight because the earth lead had shaken loose, making the boiler a potential death-trap.'

With her emotions all over the place, Rebecca opened her mouth, but no words came out.

Her dad leaned across the table and squeezed her hand. 'Thanks for reminding me about the boiler. It seems we got it just in time, before it...'

She smiled at her dad, and mouthed, 'Thank you, Meredith.'

'What did you say, Rebecca dear? Or was you mumbling to yourself again,' Elizabeth said and smiled.

'Nothing really, Mum, I was just muttering about the boiler. I guess all that rumbling and rattling caused the earth to... Hmm, well, just in time, hey, Dad?' Realising that she needed to be a little more sociable, she spent the rest of the evening focusing her thoughts, even asking Tommy how his football was going. She soon regretted that, having to listen to him tell her ten different ways how he'd scored the winning goal.

As soon as they got home, and on her last legs, Rebecca stood on the bottom stair and said she was off to bed. She thanked her dad for a nice meal, and as she turned, he asked her to wait a moment.

As soon as Elizabeth and Tommy were in the kitchen, he turned and looked Rebecca in the eyes. Holding both her hands, he said, 'I don't think my brain will ever comprehend or understand how or if you travelled through time. For all that, it would seem you did, so there we are. Soon, we need to sit down and go through it bit by bit.' He then squeezed her hand. 'One thing I do know for sure is that I thank you for being strong enough to tell me. I know I can be a cantankerous old so-and-so sometimes, most of the time,' he said and lifted his head a little, 'so it must have taken an exceptional inner strength and self-belief, things that will serve you well. Your road through this world will be smooth, and I suspect, an exciting one, my beloved daughter.'

Over the next couple of days, Rebecca witnessed a remarkable change in her father. The terse huffy persona had vanished, and in its place was a considerate, thoughtful manner. Occasionally, she

293

wondered if he would slip back into his usual ways, but a week had passed, and if anything, his behaviour had improved. That evening after supper, he asked Rebecca to join him in his study. Over the next couple of hours, she answered all of her father's questions in the greatest of detail. A couple of times, she said something that even sounded farfetched to her, but not once did her father show anything other than keen interest. The couple of times he did raise his eyes, Rebecca could see this was more by way of surprise.

When her mum popped her head in for the third time and asked if they were okay, it made Rebecca smile, knowing she was being nosey. After she'd gone, she asked her dad if they should tell her about the story. They chatted about it for a while and eventually agreed it might not be the right time. Although a little frustrated by this, Rebecca understood her dad's point, guessing in time, perhaps... Before she left, he thanked her for everything, even though he'd already thanked her several times. She smiled and said she was just pleased to see him and mum getting along so well.

The next couple of months passed in the blink of an eye, with Rebecca focused on her exams. On the run-up to Christmas, she was going through her mock exams, and even though she had the family holiday in her thoughts, knew how important it was to stay on track. Whenever Meredith came to mind, which was often, she'd been far too busy to go near the summerhouse and instead focused her thoughts on school. The couple of times she had tentatively considered venturing down, the idea had felt oddly uncomfortable. She'd questioned this emotion, but in the past had trusted her gut feeling, and at the moment, it was saying no. She didn't know if this was because of her exams or there was something else, whichever, she pushed the thought to the back of her head.

Having just come in from her last day at school before Christmas, she sat in the kitchen and chatted with her mum about her exams and their imminent holiday. As she helped her mum prepare the evening meal, the subject changed to her father.

'Rebecca, I can't imagine what you said to your father that evening. I am not sure I want to know, but whatever conversation you had certainly changed him. For that, I thank you.'

'I just chatted to Dad about our trip to Wales and told him how often you laughed. All of a sudden, it was as if the penny dropped and his whole demeanour changed.' Focussing her thoughts, Rebecca paused for a moment. She smiled at her mum, held her hand tightly, and said, 'I am so pleased you two are getting along so well. Just make sure it stays that way. That's how you can thank me, Mum. Oh, and by the way, I am so pleased you have a coffee.' Wide-eyed, she nodded her head towards the wine-rack.

Her mum grinned, and said, 'Well, yes indeed.'

'Right, Mum, I have to go and email Roxy. We have been chatting about spiritualism and such-like. I know it's an odd subject, but we got chatting one day, and she thinks her Nan, who died when Roxy was seven, has followed her around ever since. Incidentally, she said it's a good thing.' She glanced at her mum and could see an expression that suggested she was wondering where this was leading. 'It may sound farfetched, but it is fascinating when you read up on people's experiences.'

Her mum raised her eyebrows, and said, 'a bit like Meredith, hey?'

'Yeah, I guess so,' Rebecca said and chuckled. Inside she was desperate to tell her mum everything but knew this wasn't the time. 'Right, I am going to email Roxy, give me a shout when supper is ready.'

The following morning was a mad rush getting ready for a lunchtime flight. Much to the surprise of Rebecca, her Mum insisted on driving to the airport. Her dad had agreed, and even said it would be nice. During the holiday, the family mood was entirely stress-free with more laughter than Rebecca had ever known. To add to her delight, Tommy had mostly avoided winding her up, although there

295

had been a couple of times, she'd chosen to bite her lip, reassuring herself that he was still a twit. Her dad staying true to his word and going on as many rides as Tom pleased her most of all. Often, Rebecca and her mum had to drag them away for some food. The cruise was fun too, although, by the end of it, Rebecca had started to have enough of a particular cartoon character, who wouldn't leave her alone. She had wondered if she was getting too old for such things but quickly dismissed the idea after meeting Tinker Bell at breakfast.

Once they were home, it was back to school for Rebecca and the long run-up to her exams. Although it seemed like an eternity, she sailed through and actually enjoyed it, mostly. There were exceptions like the history exam where she'd wanted to put a different slant on a question that related to nineteenth-century women. She erred, realising that debating the recognised views might be harmful to her result and so chose the expected answer. On the last day, she sat back in her chair and smiled, feeling content she'd done her best.

It was early summer, and she could not believe where the last year had gone. It seemed she had only just had her sixteenth birthday and now was staring her seventeenth squarely in the face. She was sitting on her balcony, thinking about the warm summer days ahead, and wondering what she'd do with herself. Fortunately, Roxy was coming over today, and Rebecca reckoned that weather permitting, a paddle on the lake would be fun. Thinking about the lake, the summerhouse returned to her thoughts for the first time in ages. Briefly, she contemplated telling Roxy all about her journeys but decided she'd save that for another time. She still wasn't ready to talk about her experiences and suspected this was because she knew it was real and wasn't prepared for any kind of debate on the subject. Besides, she was content her dad knew, and for now, that was enough.

Over the coming weeks, Roxy and Rebecca took it in turns staying at each other's homes. It was now mid-July, and Roxy's mum had invited Rebecca down to London for a few days. After Elizabeth had had a lengthy conversation with Roxy's mother, it was all agreed.

Rebecca was so excited that she'd driven her mum mad asking questions, to the point where her mum had suggested it was just a city.

'But Mum, it's London, for heaven's sake. You spent enough time there with Dad, so you should know, there are all the shows, galleries, fancy restaurants, and I can't wait.'

'Yes, Rebecca you're right, and I'm sorry.' Smiling, she said, 'you're kind of reminding me of Tommy at Christmas,' and laughed. 'On the subject of Tommy, did your father tell you that Tom is going for a week-long football trial with Preston North End?'

'No, when did that happen, Mum?'

'Evidently, they have had their eye on him since we lived in Chester and have followed him to the new school. Anyway, his trial is next week while you're in London.'

Rebecca jumped up and said, 'Bloody hell, Mum, why didn't you say earlier? How brilliant, I have got to go and tell him well done.' She dashed off, calling at the top of her voice. 'Tommy, where are you, you bloody twit?' After checking his room, she spotted him out front kicking his ball about, once again, *like some kind of circus act.* She headed down, and when she finally got his attention, albeit interrupted by his kick-ups, she told him how proud she was. 'You're so going to nail it and do brilliantly.'

While in London, she rang Tommy every day to find out how things were going. On the last day of her trip, Tommy rang her. Out of breath with excitement, he told her they had offered him a place in their academy team, with his first match the following week. Once off the phone, she went in search of a present. She'd flirted with a training top, but guessed he would probably get all he needed from the club. In the end, she settled on a huge card and a football game for his computer.

When she arrived home, it turned out that Tommy was playing in his first game that evening in a pre-season warm-up match. Her dad suggested that even though Rebecca was obviously tired, she might like to come along and watch, especially as they were playing at home. Rebecca smiled to herself several times while her dad was speaking, his obvious excitement showing in his every word.

Alternating her smile between Tommy and her dad, she said, 'I wouldn't miss it for anything.'

During the game, Rebecca grinned to herself, wondering how she could be so proud of such a twit. Just as she was thinking about the way things had changed over the last year, Tommy got the ball near the goal. He swerved his body in a familiar way that Rebecca had seen so many times in the garden and took a shot that cannoned in off the post. Instinctively, Rebecca jumped up and shouted, 'go on the twit.' Then she realised her Mum, Dad, and most of the surrounding people were laughing. Grimacing, she sat back down, smiling at her reaction. Many times during the game, she shouted Tommy's name but chose to leave the twit bit out.

There were many games over the coming weeks, and the summer seemed to fly by. It was now September, and Rebecca was facing her last year at school and the second year of her A-levels. She had woken early today, even though the family had had a long trip back from one of Tommy's games. She went downstairs, made herself a mild coffee, and wandered outside. Just then, the summerhouse came into her thoughts, and she decided she was ready to have a look.

'Right,' she mumbled, 'let's go. A familiar but strangely distant emotion went through her body as she walked up to the door. For some reason, she wasn't getting that vibe that had nagged at her inner thoughts so often in the past. 'Hmm,' she muttered, as she opened the door, 'no whoosh of air.' *That's odd* she thought, glancing in either room, which just looked like dusty old rooms. Something had changed, but she couldn't put her finger on it. It just didn't feel the same. She paused by the third door, as she always did, but this time she wasn't getting any sensations, gone was the feeling of anticipation. The emotions were there for sure, but she wondered if they were just because of her memories. She thought about this as she gripped the handle and turned it slowly. To her surprise, it moved freely. She tightened her lips, opened the door, and gasped. Rubbing her eyes, the spiral stairs had vanished, and instead, she was standing in a room that looked like an old kitchen. There was a wooden flight of stairs in the far corner and a door leading outside. It was just how she remembered Meredith's kitchen, but she'd never gotten into the kitchen this way. With her thoughts going in circles, she took a deep breath, wondering what was going on. She made her way over the stairs, having decided to have a nose around upstairs. She wasn't that surprised to find that instead of her bedroom, with the dandy green dress and all, there was just an old room.

Gradually, she made her way outside and sat on the veranda. Her thoughts were all over the place, and she again wondered if it had been one long series of dreams. Briefly, she questioned if she'd really met Meredith. Even though there was the Tallboy and the note, she was now considering she might have set the whole thing up in some kind of dream state. *But what about the boiler,* she thought? The minutes turned into an hour, and she was miles away when she heard her mum calling from the house. She got up and made her way back. Once indoors, she went straight to her father's room to check the tallboy. It was there okay, complete with the tiny key. Sitting in her father's chair, she stared aimlessly for a few moments and then had this bizarre idea that perhaps the stairs were only there so she could help Meredith, and ultimately, Meredith could help her. With this thought firmly in her head, she made her way to the kitchen. As she walked in, her mum waved a letter.

'Is that what I think it is, Mum?'

'I think so, probably best if you open it, Rebecca,' she said and handed her the envelope. 'Let me call your Father. He is outside with Tommy, and I am sure he would like to be here when you read it.'

Seconds later, her father and Tommy joined them.

She took a deep breath and opened the envelope slowly. She glanced around and started reading, *"Dear Rebecca. We have carefully considered your application and interview. In line with our point's process, if your results are as expected, we would be delighted to offer you a place at Warwick University studying English literature. Your expected starting date will be September 2010."*

Chapter 20 - Return from Uni

The opening year at University went well for Rebecca. On the first day back for the summer holidays, she sat with her mum in the kitchen. They'd talked for hours about this and that when unexpectedly, her mum mentioned the Summerhouse.

'Dad finally got someone in to rebuild the summerhouse, and you won't recognise the place. It has had a complete overhaul and is now like new. I wasn't sure how you'd react to this, but you wait until you see what I have for you.'

'Well, he has been threatening to sort it forever. So, cat and curiosity and all that, Mum.'

'Hmm, he's a changed man, certainly since the boiler episode. You will have to tell me again what happened between you two, not that it really matters now.' She narrowed her eyes a little, shook her head. 'Anyways, summerhouse, so, here's the thing. There was no sign of a spiral staircase, I might add. We found, well the builder did, a whole bundle of stuff. I've left four boxes in your room. Two are wooden, and two are metal, one of which needs a key of sorts. As much as everyone else wanted to look inside, including me, I insisted you had to be the first to look. Besides, we didn't have a key for the one that interested me, and well, you and keys go hand in hand.' She then smiled in a way that made Rebecca feel good inside. 'I am so excited because there is one that appears considerably older than the others. And it is labelled Meredith's box, and that is the one in need of a key. There is one dated 1943, another 1911 and one with no markings. Hmm, not saying I believe your stories, but... Well, you go look for yourself.' She then looked away; I really am not sure if I should tell you this, but there was a green dress lying on an old bed in the loft. Although it was delicate, I managed to save it.

With her mouth open, Rebecca wasn't sure what to say, and uttered, 'why didn't you phone me and tell me?'

'I didn't want to interrupt your focus, Bex. And you know it would have,' she said and smiled.

'Oh, my goodness, Mother. Shall we go and look together?'

'I would love to, but I also recognise that it might be best if you looked first. It's your thing, Meredith and all.'

Rebecca made her way up to her room, unsure of what to expect. She sat on her bed, staring at the four boxes uncertain which to open first. Breathing deeply, she wasn't sure if she was ready for what might be inside.

While she was at university, her focus was principally on work. Occasionally though, something would remind her of the summerhouse. She'd then invariably annoy herself, as the dream notion reared its ugly head. Every so often, generally at night, vivid memories flooded her thoughts taking her back once again to Meredith. As these reflective memories pulled at her senses, the realisation that she wouldn't see Meredith again made her both sad and happy.

After staring at the boxes for ages, curiosity took over, and she chose to open the one marked 1943. Meredith's box was going to be opened last because it didn't have a key. The truth was she needed a little thinking time.

Staring at a stencilled 1943, Rebecca's thoughts were going in circles. She wanted to do this on her own, but at the same time wanted her mum to be with her. She also thought she'd like her father with her. She'd only talked to him regarding the boiler, but he had shown an evident empathy to her way of thinking, and importantly had never suggested the dream notion.

302

She then sat there wondering why she was even considering involving anyone else. After all, she'd never needed anyone in the past, *other than Meredith*, she thought, which made her smile. Now realising this had to be done on her own, she was once more alone with only her inner thoughts and Meredith for company.

'Right,' she muttered, lifted the wooden lid, and peered inside. At the top was a Daily Telegram newspaper declaring <u>World War Is Over</u>. Beneath this were some papers that related to the orphan girls. After carefully sorting through, she came across one labelled Tabitha Renaulds. With excitement, Rebecca started reading, discovering that Tabitha had been adopted by Judith and Christopher. It stated that Tabitha had settled into the family well, enjoying life with her new siblings Rebecca, and Jeremy. *That's why Judith called me Rebecca,* she thought.

Towards the bottom of the box were many family photos. Rebecca sat staring at the first one, unable to believe what she was looking at. It was a family beach scene, and although dusty, it was surprisingly clear. There they were, Judith and Christopher, just as she remembered them. Sitting alongside was little Tabitha and a boy probably aged around 10, and... She blinked her eyes several times, but no matter how close she looked, the other girl in the photo appeared to be her. She held her breath so long that her chest started pounding. She then let out a sigh and muttered 'how can that be?'

She sat there staring at the photo, totally perplexed. On the one hand, she wanted to go and show her mother, while her need to know more was too strong. She carefully lifted out the other photos, dusted them off, and stared at all ten lined up in front of her. So startled by what she was looking at, she got up and walked around the room. In every photo, she was there. Not a look alike, not even close, it was her okay. The fanciful Rebecca's thoughts were going in circles, while her common sense side was trying to find a rational answer. It was one thing that she was able to recognise Judith and Chris, but the fact she was in every photo was a little too much.

Sitting there for an hour or so, she looked around the room, staring through the window, glancing at the other boxes, but her eyes always settled back on the photos. One photo, in particular, was of her and Tabitha up close, leaving her in no doubts she was in the picture. She even compared a photo of herself from her phone, which made her laugh, but also confirmed it was her okay. She glanced at her watch and knew her father would be home shortly. Right, she thought and decided both her mother and father needed to be with her before she went any further. This was a whole lot more than time-travel, a fanciful dream notion, or child-like imagination - something she was still capable of – it was seriously bizarre, and she needed her parents around.

This is real, isn't it, she thought? She had no choice, mum, and dad needed to be here. She went downstairs and joined her mother in the kitchen.

'Well, Rebecca, anything of interest in the boxes. As you often say, cat and curiosity.'

'Mum, we need to wait for Dad. You both need to come and look at what I have found before I open the other boxes.'

'You have been all this time, and not looked in all the boxes. I expected you to have them all open at once. Whatever have you found.'

'I only looked in the 1943 box and well...'

'Well, what, Rebecca?'

'Mum, trust me on this one, you and Dad need to see the contents of the first box before I go any further. I am desperate to tell you, but you must both be with me. By the way, Dad knows about Meredith and so on.'

'Does he now, and how did he react to that?'

'Surprisingly well actually. We can talk about that after, but I told him about Meredith when the boiler was playing up.'

Right on cue, she heard her dad's car pull up in the drive.

With him standing in the doorway, she bellowed, 'Hello, Dad. How was your day?'

'All the better for knowing I was coming home to see my baby girl,' he said and smiled. 'You're a woman now, but you will always be my baby girl.'

'Thanks, Dad, I have been missing you, Mum. And, Tommy a little bit,' she said and laughed.

'How has Uni been? I know we chatted last week on the phone, but...'

'Absolutely brilliant, and my classmates and main tutor love my fairy tales,' she said grinning. 'Dad, I want to talk to you about Uni, but can I ask you and mum to come and look at what I have found in the first box.'

He squinted, said, 'yes of course,' and glanced at Elizabeth.

'She's been telling me it is so important that we both need to be with her to see what she's found. It got my curiosity, I can tell you,' she said and shivered.

Rebecca led them up to her room, and before entering, said, 'You need to prepare yourself for this. If you think my stories are bizarre, well...' She nodded, and continued, 'this is mad, even by my standards.'

As she opened her door, memories of her first visit to the summerhouse came flooding back. She took a deep breath, sat down, and picked up the papers relating to Tabitha. Handing them to her

305

mum, she said, 'Mum, do you recall me telling you about the little girl who was all on her own in the orphanage? It was in 1943, and I said how much she pulled on my heart-strings, and you said what a lovely name.'

'I do actually,' she said and nodded.

'Dad, I will explain later. Well read this Mum, and try to remember all the names I mentioned. Do you recall a Judith or Judy as you annoyingly called her?'

After reading for a few moments, she handed the papers to James. She then looked at Rebecca and said, 'Well it is a lovely story in that she ended up happy with them.' She narrowed her eyes, 'curious their daughter had the same name as you.'

'Is that it, Mum? A lovely story, and curious about the name?'

'Well, yes I guess so.'

'But, Mum, I knew all their names, how could that be?' she said and frowned. 'Okay, here is something you can't explain away. Both of you need to look at these photos and tell me what you see.' She handed six photos to her mother and six to her father.

There was silence for a few minutes, and then her mother was the first to speak. 'My word, the Rebecca in these photos looks a little like you,' she said while staring the whole time at James. 'You haven't photoshopped them, have you? No, ignore that, I know you wouldn't, and I can see they are old,' her eyes never leaving James.

'Dad?'

He breathed out slowly, 'Crumbs, Rebecca. I don't understand, and I actually can't think of anything else to say other than that.'

'How do you think I feel?' she said, wide-eyed. 'What, may I ask am I doing in a photo in 19-blinking-40-whatever?'

Her dad reached over and held her hand. 'Rebecca, we need to look in the other boxes. Before we do, we also need to keep everything in its exact order.'

'I am with you on that one Dad, even the sequence of the photos. I have written down the order of everything. I've not even looked at everything yet. As much as I want to open the other boxes, we need to go through this one first.'

'I suspect there may be an order to this, which may answer some of the many questions that your mother, I, and importantly you have.'

'James, are you saying you believe this time-travel thing?'

'Elizabeth, I am not saying anything. I will say though that Rebecca did show me some outstanding evidence the night of the boiler. However...'

Over the next two hours, they systematically went through every item carefully, eventually ending back with the photos.

'Right, I need to get supper on as it is getting late.'

'Liz, I don't want you cooking this time of night. Let's go and grab something out, maybe that Italian, again. That was a good find.' He smiled and nodded, 'we need some thinking time.'

They headed downstairs and got into the car without a word passing between them. While at the restaurant, her father's conversation was obviously deliberate, focussing on Rebecca's time at university. Occasionally, the box subject came up, but just as quick, Elizabeth changed the subject. It was clear to Rebecca that her mum knew only too well it was her in the photos and just wasn't ready to think about it, let alone talk about it. If nothing else, this distraction was what they

307

all needed, including Rebecca, whose senses had been tangled by the photos.

It was late by the time they got home, and it was agreed - as it was the weekend - they would go through everything tomorrow.

'Rebecca, I think we need a strategy, and some clear thinking, so no peeking tonight. Get a good night's sleep and you'll feel more focused in the morning. See you bright and early,' he said and gave Rebecca a cuddle. He then turned and said, 'see you upstairs, Liz.'

Rebecca had one more glance at the photos, and although her mind was racing, fell straight asleep. The next thing, she was being woken by her mother with breakfast.

'Thanks, Mum. That is something I've missed, I can tell you,' she said and gave her mum a cuddle.

Her mum sat on the bed next to Rebecca and asked how Roxy – at the same university - was getting on. After chatting for a while, they heard James moving about.

Her mum stood up and said, 'I'll go and sort his breakfast while you get showered and whatnot.'

While in the shower, Rebecca realised her mum hadn't looked at or mentioned the photos once. She knew it always took her mum a while to get to grips with anything out of the ordinary. Even so, by the next day, she'd generally be ok. Clearly, this wasn't the case, but then Rebecca still felt a little odd about everything, so knew it would take her mum longer to come to terms with this information overload. *Even with such undeniable evidence*, she thought. On the way downstairs, she decided to wait until her mum, and dad brought the subject up. She'd learnt at university, that if you let the topic be someone else's idea, then their focus would be that much stronger. She needed her mum and dad on board with this, so reckoned this was the right strategy.

Sitting outside with her mum and dad brought back thoughts of the summerhouse. Just as Rebecca was becoming restless, her dad started speaking.

'Right, I guess it's time to go and have a good look at your boxes, Rebecca.'

Although her mum nodded, Rebecca could see how uncomfortable she was. 'I will tidy up and join you two shortly if that's okay with you guys?'

'Mum,' Rebecca said. Her dad immediately intervened.

'That's fine Liz,' he said, nodding to Rebecca. On the way upstairs, he explained that it would take Elizabeth a little while to come to terms with this, to which Rebecca nodded in agreement.

'I know that, Dad. It is hard for me, because whichever way I look at it, it is definitely me in those photos, as mad as that sounds. How comes you are so cool with the whole thing? Even back with the boiler, you took it in your stride, how comes?'

'Well, as I said at the time, I can remember being your age and seeing the world the way you do. Believe me; it was much more difficult for a boy to be like that, especially in my day.'

They sat in the room again going through the papers and photos.

'Well, time to move onto another box, I think, Rebecca,' he said and nodded. 'Whichever way we look at it, the photos seem to have you in them. I think we need a photo expert and maybe a historian of sorts.'

Pondering for a few minutes, Rebecca said, 'I think I will open the 1911 box next. Not sure I am ready for the Meredith box yet, and I'm certainly not ready for the unmarked one.'

'I understand that, not sure I am either,' he said, and although he frowned, he had an animated expression.

Having gone through the papers in the 1911 box carefully, all Rebecca established was that Chris had returned home from war safely. She explained to her dad all about her experience with Chris, and the story behind his household.

'Oh, that's her name,' Rebecca said while reading some papers.

'The name of whom, Rebecca?'

'Oh, sorry Dad, I knew what I meant. I was talking about Chris's mother.'

'And it was?'

'Sorry,' she said, and laughed, 'Veronica. I never ever established her name.'

Just then, her dad frowned and handed Rebecca a photo.

'Oh, my goodness, it is Chris's wedding photo, and...'

'Yep, whichever way you look at it, it is you again in the photo. And look on the back, it has your name, along with Chris and Veronica,' he said while staring directly at Rebecca. 'This is becoming increasingly atypical, even by our standards.'

Feeling a constant tingle of anticipation in the back of her thoughts, Rebecca asked, 'Are there any more photos, Dad?'

'No, it is the only one. Interesting, it refers to Chris as your brother and Veronica as your mother. Bizarre. Not sure how your mother will handle this, on that subject, where is she?' He smiled and said, 'Well, we both know why she isn't here.'

Rebecca sat there staring at the photo, occasionally glancing at the other two boxes. 'I've just realised something, Dad. In all the photos, I am wearing clothes more appropriate for that period. Maybe it is just a coincidence that the girls who have lived in this house are called Rebecca and look similar to me.'

'That is exactly what your mother would say. Now I am not saying you or your mother's opinions are wrong. However, the way I see it, the girl in every photo is you.' He then looked directly at Rebecca and nodded.

'Well, we need to look at the other boxes. The question is Meredith's, or the unmarked one. I think Meredith's as I am guessing the other one may hold some questionable answers that may confuse matters. Perhaps Meredith's may help us piece it all together, not that I know why I think that, I just do.'

'Going by what you have told me about Meredith, I reckon she has put the fourth box together, with some answers, just for you.'

She shook her head. 'That is exactly the sort of thing I would think and say. At least now, I know where all my fanciful thinking comes from,' she said and held her dad's hand.

As Rebecca moved over towards Meredith's box, her father handed her the small key from the tallboy.

'That's strange; I thought that the key would fit too.'

He flicked his eyebrows, 'obvious really, well it is for the likes of you and I. Besides, if Meredith played such a significant role in all your journeys, which I have never doubted, then it would be fitting it would fit.' He laughed in a way that showed his uncertainty.

Chapter 21 - Meredith's Box

Rebecca inserted the key into the hole, glanced at her father, and took a deep breath. As she turned the key, memories of her time with Meredith flooded her thoughts. Another deep breath, as she heard a gentle click. She opened the lid, and instantly the room filled with the smell of Christmas.

'That happened the first time I opened the summerhouse door.'

'What did, Rebecca?'

'The smell of Christmas, well, the smell of almonds actually,' she said and nodded, feeling oddly reassured.

Aside from a few old decrepit newspapers, one of which referred to Millicent's suicide, there was nothing of significance. Disappointed, Rebecca was just about to close the lid, when her father spoke.

'Let's not rush, Rebecca. That box is deeper, maybe there is a panel or a secret compartment. Besides, it is a metal box and has a wooden floor. Let me look,' he said, producing a penknife from his pocket. 'I came prepared.' After carefully removing the top papers, he rummaged around a bit. He then opened his penknife, fiddled about briefly, and lifted out the wooden base. 'I knew it, sounds like the kind of thing your Meredith would do from what you've said.'

'Dad, you're so clever. Let's look.'

They lifted out the contents, and again there was a handful of decaying papers. Right at the bottom was a card envelope, labelled in italics, *Rebecca open carefully*. Rebecca could feel her father watching her as she sat staring at the envelope.

'As you always say Rebecca, curiosity and the cat.'

'I know Dad. I have this odd feeling that there is something in here that is likely to...' she said while looking directly at her father. With care, she then opened the envelope. Inside was a hand-written letter, which she started reading to her father.

Dear Rebecca, I hope that when you find this letter, in the future, you are well. By future, I refer to a life beyond the 1800s. The first time I met you in 1853, I knew immediately you were from another time. Although you were my daughter, in essence, I was aware I had two of you in my time. I must add that we were fortunate that my daughter was staying with an aunt, which kept you separate. I need to explain further, as I am certain that the coming words will bamboozle your conscious mind. Although the sub-conscious, I suspect, will be more open.

Your soul, spirit, and being have always lived in this house as Rebecca. Your first journey started in 1635, soon after the house was built. As hard as that is for you to understand, you must remain unprejudiced and flexible in your thinking. Something I know you are capable of with ease. I recall how I felt the first time I learnt the truth of your immortal existence.

Wide-eyed, Rebecca looked at her father, and then continued to read.

You will find two photos in this envelope, of which one is my beloved Rebecca and me in a boat. It is the same boat, which you saw me in when I was trying to establish contact with you. I suspect the Rebecca from the twenty-first century is reading this, as you were the only one who found your way back to me. I am sure you concluded the boat lady in the mist was my tormented spirit, hanging in limbo awaiting your intervention. You were correct. The other photo is of you with me by the oak tree, before it fell in that horrid storm. Under that tree, you found the key, the key that brought you back to me. You have already uncovered - I suspect - the third photo that I placed for

313

you in the bureau. That photo was my Rebecca - the one from my time - wearing the cardigan you left behind. I hoped you would see its relevance and the message would be sufficient for you to continue your quest. In my other unmarked box, I hope the mothers from the future have been as objective as I have and have added to my papers. You will find evidence showing a trail of your existence and lives in this house. Some of the older papers are sketchy and lack proof. I hope you find some answers to your many questions. I also hope that your journey to me was one of many your life brings you. Either way, you have in your deepest mind, evidence that you have been here before, and I hope and believe, will continue to remain happy in this house for always.

You will see at the top of the fourth box, Millicent's suicide letter, and a newspaper stating such. You brought this letter to me. I cannot find words deep enough to express my gratitude.

Of interest, my own spirit engaged me to write this letter to you, long before your first visit. This is my understanding of this bizarre and beautiful series of events. I am unable to find any other reasoning.

Finally, I have your marriage certificate from 1858 to a gentleman named Joshua Elm. You may recall the house was once named Elm Manor. You had a happy life with 3 beloved children. Your children loved your drawings and writings of fairies. I suspect you, my dear Rebecca, still have that within you. I would love to have met you when you knew of all this. However, I am certain the powers-at-be would deem that too consequential. Be safe, be well, be happy, and continue to remain true to your farsightedness.

My love,

Meredith

Rebecca stared at her father, unable to find any words, she did, however, realise this was probably just the beginning, rather than the end of her journeys.

Made in the USA
Las Vegas, NV
22 February 2021